DAY OF WRATH

IS LARRY BON...

"DAY OF WRATH may be his best novel yet.... Larry Bond stands out as the writer most able to forge an exciting, post-Glasnost story ... a feel for the deadly forces of our brave new world that many other authors can only envy."

—James Grady, author of Six Days of the Condor and River of Darkness

"Nail-biting ... pretty darn cool ... If you're like me, you've continued to enjoy Larry Bond's thrillers....The resourceful Thorn and the sturdy Gray will do nicely."

—Bookpage

"Fortunately Larry Bond has a new book out and it may be his best yet.... In fact, he's giving Tom Clancy a real run for his money.... Bond really delivers here.... It is fair to say he's getting better with each new book.... Terrorism, politics, violence, romance, who could ask for more?"

—Houston Public News

"Considerable pleasure ... exciting, page-turning prose."
—Baton Rouge Sunday Advocate

more ...

DAY OF WRATH

Other books by Larry Bond

RED PHOENIX
VORTEX
CAULDRON
THE ENEMY WITHIN

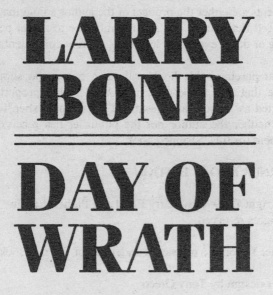

LARRY BOND

DAY OF WRATH

WARNER
VISION
BOOKS

A Time Warner Company

WARNER BOOKS EDITION

Copyright © 1998 by Larry Bond and Patrick Larkin
All rights reserved.

Warner Vision is a registered trademark of Warner Books, Inc.

Cover design by Tony Greco

Warner Books, Inc.
1271 Avenue of the Americas
New York, NY 10020

Visit our Web site at
www.warnerbooks.com

W A Time Warner Company

Printed in the United States of America

Originally published in hardcover by Warner Books.
First International Paperback Printing: December 1998
First United States Paperback Printing: September 1999

10 9 8 7 6 5 4 3 2 1

To Katie and Julie Bond and Olivia Larkin

ACKNOWLEDGMENTS

We would like to thank Mennette Masser Larkin for all the hard work, skill, and sound, shrewd advice she put into this book.

Thanks also go to Matt Caffrey, Dwin Craig, Steve Hall, Dave Hood, Don and Marilyn Larkin, Colin Larkin, Duncan Larkin, Greg Lyle, Eleanore Neal Masser, Bill Paley, Tim Peckinpaugh and Pam McKinney-Peckinpaugh, Jeff Pluhar, Jeff Richelson, and Thomas T. Thomas for all their help, advice, and support.

Thanks also to the Defense Weapons Agency Special Operations for the reality check.

AUTHOR'S NOTE

After five books, high-school English teachers now ask me to come into their classes and lecture on how to collaborate. It's supposed to be the hardest way to write, but I can't imagine doing it any other way.

It's not perfect, of course. When creative ideas are blended, there are always points where they don't mesh smoothly. The conflicts can be the result of different viewpoints, different visualizations of the story or characters, or even basic philosophies.

Resolving these conflicts is a day-to-day part of any collaboration, and the vital thing to understand is that nobody has a monopoly on good ideas, and that almost any idea can be improved. If you keep the focus on the story as a whole, and making it as good as it can possibly be, then you're willing to change or even abandon an idea when a better one comes along. Professionals don't become emotionally attached to a plot twist.

There's also an old saying that collaborations succeed only if each partner does 60 percent of the work. It's funny and a little true, but even if it's entirely true, it's still a lot better than doing 100 percent of the work.

And imagine doing all that work alone—without anyone to bounce ideas off of, receive encouragement from, or commiserate with when problems arise.

If I can teach others how to make a partnership work, it's because I've collaborated with Pat Larkin for ten years now. It's interesting that even as our styles and skills have grown, the rules for working together haven't. And we're still doing it all on the basis of a handshake.

As a partner and friend, Pat Larkin has both created and molded our stories. Sharing an intimate creative vision, crafting the books chapter by chapter, sometimes word by word, his contribution is the best 60 percent of this story.

DAY OF WRATH

PROLOGUE

MAY 20

OSIA Inspection Team, 125th Air Division Base, Kandalaksha, Northern Russia

The twin-engined Antonov-32 turboprop roared off the runway and climbed sharply before banking right. Within minutes, Kandalaksha's barbed-wire fences, watchtowers, camouflaged aircraft shelters, and SAM sites dwindled and then vanished astern.

John Avery waited until the Russian military airfield was completely out of sight before allowing himself to relax even to the slightest degree. He shivered, still chilled by what he had seen. He checked his watch. They had a little over three hours left in the air. Three hours to safety. Three hours before he could make his report to the proper authorities in the U.S. Embassy at Moscow.

Until then, he and his team members were at risk.

Avery glanced out the window again. They were flying southeast over the White Sea at ten thousand feet. Red-tinged light from the setting sun reflected off the cold gray water below.

He turned in his seat, surreptitiously checking out the other people aboard the plane. The An-32 transport plane's passenger compartment was almost empty. Fewer than half the aircraft's thirty-nine seats were occupied—eight of them by his joint Russian-American weapons inspection team. The other passengers were a few Russian Air Force officers flying home to Moscow on leave.

Avery's eyes narrowed. The Russian officers were a bedraggled bunch—unshaven and poorly dressed. Some of them were plainly fighting massive hangovers after a day spent knocking back vodka in the mess. All in all, the assembled Russians were a far cry from the proud, square-jawed pilots portrayed on old Soviet propaganda posters.

It was like that all across the fragments of the old Soviet empire.

Like the U.S. military, Russia's armed forces were being cut back. But where the American downsizing was deliberate, the Russian reductions were chaotic and uncontrolled—the result of not enough money and not enough support from Moscow. Utility companies had cut the electric power supply to bases because of unpaid bills. Other units were left without regular food deliveries. Tens of thousands of soldiers, sailors, and airmen had not been paid in months.

Kandalaksha had proved no exception.

Seen up close, much of the Russian air base had resembled a ghost town. Trees killed by the harsh arctic weather had fallen across the rusting perimeter fence—tearing gaps that were left unrepaired. Few of the guard towers were manned. Fewer than half of the 125th Air Division's one hundred and twenty Su-24 Fencer fighter-bombers were combat-ready. Many of the aircraft shelters, maintenance hangars, headquarters buildings, and barracks were boarded up, or stood abandoned, with doors and windows gaping open and empty. Grass grew wild through cracked sidewalks and concrete runways.

It was an environment that invited corruption.

Avery grimaced.

After spending three years in Russia as the leader of a treaty compliance team for the U.S. government's On-Site Inspection Agency, the OSIA, he'd thought he'd run across every form of graft and crime imaginable. He'd met officers who stole their men's paychecks and others who sold their units' arms and equipment. He'd found bordellos, gambling clubs, and bars being run out of barracks, armories, and headquarters buildings.

But Avery had never stumbled into anything remotely as dangerous as what he feared was going on at Kandalaksha. And he'd seen a lot of danger in his time.

Before joining OSIA four years before, he'd served in the U.S. Army's Special Forces, first as a demolitions man and then as a "special weapons" expert. Very few people meeting him for the first time would have believed that.

The tall, lanky ex-soldier knew his open, round face, thinning brown hair, and thick glasses made him look more like a mild-mannered professor than a former Green Beret. Others were often surprised at the intensity that lurked behind the soft cadences that were all that was left of his boyhood Alabama drawl.

Avery loosened his seat belt and leaned back, pondering his next move. Should he brief the rest of his team now? He dismissed that notion as quickly as it arose. There was no

way he could inform the other Americans without telling
their Russian counterparts—and they were still on a Russian
plane over Russian territory. There were still too many
unanswered questions to take that chance.

He risked a quick look across the aisle at his own opposite number, Colonel Anatoly Gasparov. The squat, jowly
Russian had his head back and his eyes closed—to all appearances dead to the world.

Every American arms inspector had an assigned Russian
counterpart who accompanied him from Moscow. Gasparov
had evidently finagled the assignment because it let him
travel frequently. Rumor said the Russian colonel had shady
contacts on bases all across the former Soviet Union. There
were stories that he made tidy profits as a deal-maker in the
black market—buying and selling everything from Western
cigarettes to Russian-made small arms and air-to-air missiles. Some said he had contacts inside the *Mafiya*, the loose
slang term covering Russia's powerful organized crime syndicates.

Avery believed those rumors. Especially now.

He'd noticed Gasparov's apparent chumminess with the
commander of the 125th Air Division, Colonel General
Feodor Serov, during both the welcoming dinner the night
before and the inspection today. That could just be part and
parcel of his counterpart's usual brownnosing. Or it might
be an indication that the two men were deeply involved in
some shady business together.

Either way it made no sense to alert Gasparov to his findings.

Avery turned again to the window, trying to trace their
course southward across the sunlit sea. Every kilometer the
An-32 flew put them that much further out of any enemy's
reach.

He felt suddenly weary, wrapped in a haze of utter mental and physical exhaustion. The stresses and strains of the long day were finally taking their toll. Lulled by the unvarying roar of the plane's engines, he felt himself starting to drift off. His eyes closed . . .

Avery sat bolt upright. Something was wrong. He rubbed the sleep out of his eyes and checked his watch. He'd been asleep for less than half an hour. But what had startled him awake?

The sound came again. The steady, comforting drone of the An-32's starboard engine faltered, roared back to full power for a split second, and then died. The plane sagged to the right, drifting downward.

"Christ." Avery yanked his safety belt tighter.

Seconds later, the portside engine revved higher and the An-32 leveled out again, then banked gently to the left.

A calm voice crackled over the passenger compartment PA system. "This is Major Kirichenko, your pilot. I regret to inform you that we have a slight problem. Our starboard engine has failed. But there is no danger. I repeat, there is no danger. We can easily maintain flying speed with the remaining engine at full power."

Kirichenko paused, muttered something inaudible to his co-pilot, and then continued. "However, as a precaution, we are diverting to an emergency field at Medvezhyegorsk. We should be on the ground in approximately fifteen or twenty minutes."

Chilled again, Avery looked out the window and down at the terrain below. They were "feet dry" now—well inland after the relatively short hop across the narrow White Sea. According to the maps he'd studied, they were over a wilderness of pine forest and marshland that stretched for hundreds of miles in every direction. But he couldn't make out anything definite. This close to nightfall, it was dark down there—pitch-black. There were no lights. No signs of any civilization.

He pulled his eyes away from the blackness below and found himself staring across the aisle at Anatoly Gasparov.

The Russian colonel stared back, white-faced. He licked his lips, muttering, "My God . . . my God . . ."

The smooth roar of the port engine changed abruptly—running ragged for an instant before surging back. Then it, too, sputtered, once, twice . . . and stopped.

The An-32's nose tilted forward—angling downward toward the ground.

Avery's chest tightened at the silence. Air rushing past the fuselage showed they were still flying—but for how much longer?

The sound of pumps cycling broke the silence, and the plane shuddered. He craned his head and saw a dark mass streaming away below the port wing—a spray of droplets glistening in the fading light. Their pilots were dumping fuel—desperately lightening the An-32 to stretch its glide path as far as humanly possible.

As the transport plane descended, falling at an ever-steeper angle, the plane's crew chief, a frightened young Russian sergeant, struggled through the passenger compartment—stowing loose gear and double-checking safety belts. The buffeting worsened as low-altitude winds and roiling updrafts tore at the powerless aircraft.

Avery's inspection logbook slipped off the seat beside him and slid out of his reach before he could grab it. The An-32's nose dropped further.

The PA system squawked again. This time the pilot's voice sounded strained. "We're going in! We're trying for a clearing or a river. Brace for impact! Brace for impact!"

Avery couldn't tear his eyes away from the window, desperate to know how high they were. He could see the trees now, pointing upward like a bed of nails, their tops needle-sharp. His heart froze.

Still moving at more than one hundred miles an hour, the An-32 slammed into the forest. Avery was thrown forward against his seat belt with agonizing force. Horrified, he saw the fuselage rip open in front of him. Too late, he opened his mouth to scream. A tidal wave of flame and shredded metal swallowed him whole.

CHAPTER ONE

THE SHADOWED WOODS

MAY 24

U.S. Special Investigative Team, Over Northern Russia

The shadow cast by the giant Mi-26 helicopter rippled over mile after mile of evergreen forest—brushing across vast stands of northern pine, spruce, and fir trees. Many of the trees were dead or dying, choked by acid rains and smog-laden winds from Russian mines, smelters, and industrial plants. Wherever the forest thinned, pools of standing water glistened in the pale sunlight. Much of northern Russia was a tangled mix of woodland and swamp.

A lean, tough-looking man sat next to one of the helicopter's fuselage windows, staring down at the ground. From a distance, his taut, sun-darkened face looked boyish.

The illusion disappeared up close. Years spent in the field and in command had put lines around his steady green eyes. And the same stresses and strains had turned some of his light brown hair gray.

Colonel Peter Thorn frowned.

They were more than one hundred miles out from the Arkhangelsk airport, and nothing in the view below had changed. Except for a thin strip of settled land around the fringes of the White Sea, this stretch of Russia six hundred miles north of Moscow was empty. There were no roads. No buildings. No signs of human life. A few villages had sprung up over the centuries and then vanished. Even Stalin's prison camps, the gulags, had been abandoned—left to rot and molder and sink back into the swampy wilderness.

Thorn looked away, shifting around in his fold-down seat to face the helicopter's cavernous interior.

"Hell of a country, isn't it?" the tall, gaunt man seated next to him said into his ear, pitching his voice just high enough to be heard over the clattering roar of the Mi-26's engines and rotor. "Probably hasn't changed much since the last Ice Age."

Thorn nodded. The tall man, Robert Nielsen, was a pilot and aeronautical engineer by training, not a geologist, but he had a good eye for terrain. Stone Age hunters following the retreating glaciers north would have moved through the same dark, wet woods.

Thorn grimaced. "Bad place for a crash."

"There's no good spot, Colonel," Nielsen said tersely. The head of the National Transportation Safety Board's investigative team tapped the open map on his lap. "But I'll admit our access to this site stinks. It's more than fifty miles to the nearest road or railhead. The Russians are going to have to ferry everything in by air. Tents. Food and water. Floodlights. Generators. Everything."

Thorn glanced back at the large cargo crates piled high across the Mi-26's rear clamshell doors. Besides the eight Americans and their assigned Russian interpreter, this heavy-lift helicopter held nearly twenty tons of equipment and supplies. He fought down the urge to tell the other man he had an excellent grasp of the obvious. Their situation was awkward enough without crossing swords so early.

Anyway, he understood why the NTSB's chief investigator was so clearly off balance. When an aircraft went down in the U.S., Nielsen and his six-man "go-team" were in complete command from the moment they touched down at the crash site. Here they were only consultants—and unwanted consultants at that.

Russia's Federal Aviation Authority was touchy about its prerogatives. Moscow had only agreed to accept an NTSB observer team because American nuclear experts were among those killed in the An-32 crash. The Americans could ask questions, provide technical assistance, and offer opinions. Final authority, though, would remain firmly in Russian hands.

The Russian argument was simple: It was their aircraft. Flying in their airspace. And it had crashed in their sovereign territory.

All of which put Nielsen in a grade-A bind. Thorn had seen his type before. Like any investigator worth his salt, he was a control freak. When the cause of any given accident could lie in something as small as a pinhead-sized piece of twisted metal, somebody—one man—had to be in charge. And Nielsen was used to being in charge.

Thorn grinned wryly to himself. Perceptive diagnosis, Colonel, he thought. But where exactly does that leave you?

The honest answer was—even further removed from the real action than the NTSB investigator.

If mechanical failure or pilot error had brought down the inspection team's An-32 transport, Nielsen, his team, and their Russian counterparts would all have roles to play. If terrorism or sabotage were involved, the Russian Ministry of the Interior, the MVD, and the FBI would take over the investigation. In contrast, as a liaison officer from the U.S.'s On-Site Inspection Agency, Thorn had precisely zero real authority. He was an observer—a consultant to consultants.

And that was not a position he found comfortable.

Counting the time he'd spent as a West Point cadet, Thorn had been in the U.S. Army for twenty-two years. He'd commanded troops for most of those years—first an airborne infantry platoon, then a company, then elite Delta Force commandos, and finally a full Delta Force squadron. He'd viewed his various staff postings as necessary evils—as the hoops the Army made you jump through before you got to do the fun stuff like leading soldiers in the field.

But now he was stuck riding a desk inside the OSIA's Dulles Airport headquarters. So stuck that he'd never get another chance to command an Army combat unit. Officially, he was there to add his counterterrorist expertise to the OSIA staff. Terrorists with nuclear, chemical, or biological weapons were one of Washington's biggest nightmares. Unofficially, he knew the powers-that-be viewed his assignment to the inspection agency as a way to keep him quiet until they could edge him out of the Army altogether.

After all, Thorn thought grimly, you couldn't tell the President of the United States to go to hell without paying the piper.

Irritated with himself for dwelling unprofitably on the past, he pushed away his regrets. He'd known what he was doing, and he'd known the price he was likely to pay for disobeying a White House order. What mattered now was the job at hand.

Even if Nielsen and the others couldn't see what he was doing aboard this helicopter, Thorn was determined to make himself useful. If an accident had downed the An-32, he could at least help out with the grunt work—searching for wreckage, bodies, and personal effects. If they turned up evidence that sabotage had brought down the Russian plane, he would move hell and high water to help the FBI and the MVD find the bastards who were responsible. He owed John Avery and the others on the OSIA inspection team that much.

The Mi-26 banked suddenly, spiraling tightly to the right and losing altitude in the turn.

Thorn looked down. They were orbiting a patch of forest that at first looked no different than any other for hundreds of miles around. Even this far from any industrial city, dead pine trees stood out among the survivors—stark brown, branching skeletons against a dark green backdrop.

"There it is!" Nielsen said urgently.

Thorn followed the other man's nod and saw the An-32 crash site for the first time. When it slammed into the forest canopy, the turboprop had torn a long, jagged scar across the countryside—splintering trees, gouging the earth, and flattening the undergrowth for several hundred yards. Blackened scorch marks showed where aviation fuel spraying from the mangled wreckage had ignited.

The Mi-26 continued its orbit, slowing further to hover over an area several hundred meters east of the crash site.

Orange panels laid across the muddy ground in a ragged clearing marked a makeshift landing pad. A Russian-made Mi-8 helicopter sat off to one side of the clearing. Mechanics and other ground crewmen swarmed over the smaller bird, refueling it and attaching a cargo-carrying sling.

Thorn mentally crossed his fingers. He hoped the Mi-26 pilot had perfect depth perception. With its rotor turning, the giant heavy-lift helicopter was more than a hundred and thirty feet long. From this high up, trying to set it down in the space available looked akin to threading a sewing needle with a garden hose. If they came down too far in one direction, they'd hit the trees. Too far in the other, and they'd slam into the parked Mi-8 and half a dozen fuel drums. Neither alternative seemed particularly appealing.

Almost without thinking, he fingered the thin, almost invisible scar running across his nose and down under his right eye. That scar and a couple of small metal pins in his right cheekbone were souvenirs of a helicopter crash he'd survived as a young captain. Walking away from one whirlybird crack-up was enough for a lifetime, he decided.

Turbines howling, the Mi-26 slipped lower, slid right, then back left, and settled in to land with a heavy, jarring thump. Almost immediately, the engine noise changed pitch, sliding down the scale as the pilots throttled back. The helicopter's massive rotors spun slower and slower and then stopped.

They were down.

Thorn breathed out softly, unbuckled his seat belt, snagged his travel kit from under the seat, and stood up—grateful for the chance to stretch his legs. To stay fit at forty, he relied on a rigorous daily exercise regime, and too much sitting left him stiff. Unfortunately, except for a five-minute stop at Arkhangelsk to board this helo, they had been in the air since leaving Andrews Air Force Base the day before. And the aisles aboard Air Force passenger jets were too narrow for running or vigorous calisthenics.

He controlled his mounting impatience while Nielsen and the others carefully gathered their own gear and assembled at the forward left side door. For now, this was the NTSB's show. They were entitled to set the pace. Air accident investigations always put a premium on slow, methodical, and absolutely painstaking work. No matter how tough it might be, he would have to rein in his own innate impulse to push for rapid, decisive action.

At least he couldn't fault their working clothes. All of the civilians wore plain jeans, long-sleeve shirts, waterproof jackets, and hiking boots. His woodland camouflage-pattern battle dress and combat boots were equally practical. Suits and neckties and dress uniforms had no place this far out in the wilderness.

A Russian helicopter crewman emerged from the flight deck, pushed his way through the waiting Americans, and unlatched the side door. It fell open, becoming a set of steps down to the ground.

Thorn followed Nielsen, his team, and their interpreter outside, pausing briefly at the top of the stairs to scan the surrounding area.

Stumps and sheared-off branches poked through the mud in places, showing where engineers had blown down trees to make this crude landing pad. Several large drab canvas tents were clustered at the far end of the clearing. Urged on by shouting NCOs and junior officers, teams of young Russian conscripts in mud-smeared uniforms were busy erecting more tents along the treeline. Other soldiers were hard at work stringing floodlights through the nearby woods. Chainsaws whined off in the distance. The dull, pulsing roar of diesel-powered electrical generators throbbed in counterpoint.

Some of the Russian troops had stripped down to sweat-stained T-shirts. Spring came late this far north, but it was cool—not cold. He guessed the temperature was somewhere in the high fifties. Smells lingered in the still air—an acrid, sickly-sweet mix of spilled aviation gas and raw sewage from hastily dug latrines.

Two men—one older and balding, the other younger and fair-haired—stood just beyond the arc of the Mi-26's now motionless rotor blades. A reception committee. His heartbeat quickened when he saw the familiar face of the tall, dark-haired woman waiting with them. Thorn lengthened his stride to catch up with Nielsen and the rest of the NTSB team.

The older man stepped forward to meet them. He growled something in terse, guttural Russian to their interpreter, folded his arms, and stood waiting—silent and apparently utterly uninterested in any response.

"This is First Deputy Director Leonid Mamontov of the Federal Aviation Authority," the interpreter said hurriedly. He hesitated and then went on. "The Deputy Director welcomes you to Russia and looks forward to close cooperation in this important investigation. He has prepared a preliminary briefing in the headquarters tent."

While Nielsen made his own introductions, Thorn carefully eyed the short, stocky, unsmiling man in front of them, sure that the interpreter had massively shaded his translation. Mamontov looked more likely to welcome close-quarters combat with his American counterparts than cooperation.

The Russian official raised a single bushy eyebrow when Nielsen introduced him. Then he simply grunted, shook his head in disgust, and swung away, stomping toward the largest tent across the clearing.

Nielsen shrugged apologetically to Thorn and hurried after the Russian—followed closely by the interpreter and the rest of his team.

Terrific, Thorn thought grimly. This mission was off to a bang-up start. If others at the accident scene shared this bureaucrat's evident disdain, they were all in for a very rough ride.

A polite cough broke his bleak train of thought. Embarrassed at being caught off guard, he quickly turned back to face the man and woman who had accompanied Mamontov to meet the helicopter. They were still standing close by, waiting to be noticed.

"I apologize for Director Mamontov's behavior, Colonel," the man said quietly in almost flawless English. Then he grinned, showing white, perfect teeth. "But I assure you it is nothing personal. The minister does not like soldiers or policemen of any sort. Whether they are American or Russian is immaterial."

Still smiling, the younger Russian held out his hand. "I am Major Alexei Koniev of the Ministry of the Interior, by the way. So I, too, am one of Mamontov's untouchables."

Careful to hide his surprise, Thorn shook hands with the slender, fair-haired man. "Glad to meet you, Major."

He wouldn't have suspected Koniev was a plainclothes policeman—especially not one with such a high rank. He looked too young and his clothes seemed wrong somehow. The Russian's jacket, shirt, and jeans, though clearly rugged and durable, were also immaculately tailored and expensive-looking.

Faint warning bells rang in Thorn's mind. MVD officers were charged with protecting Russia against everything from outright rebellion to organized crime—a sort of National Guard and FBI all rolled up into one. But they were also notoriously poorly paid. So how could this Koniev character afford the latest Western outdoor wear?

He knew one of the possible answers to that question. The need to pad their skinflint salaries led a lot of MVD officers down the road to corruption. Russia's powerful criminal syndicates were only too willing to distribute generous bribes to bury their hooks deep inside the government and its law enforcement agencies.

He made a mental note to keep a close eye on Koniev. His first impressions of the MVD officer were favorable. But first impressions could get you killed. And even old friends could betray you. He'd learned that lesson the hard way in Iran two years before.

"Permit me to introduce you to my American colleague, Special Agent Helen Gray of your FBI," Koniev continued.

Thorn turned to the slim, pretty, dark-haired woman at the Russian major's side, noting the faint smile she was trying unsuccessfully to conceal. Her eyes seemed even bluer than he remembered.

"Thank you, Major," he said gravely. "But Special Agent Gray and I already know each other fairly well."

She nodded calmly. "I thought you might try to poke your nose under this tent, Colonel Thorn. But I didn't see your name on the flight manifest. How exactly did you manage to swing an invitation from the NTSB?"

"Held my breath. Refused to eat my lunch. Threatened to wire their office coffeepots with C-4. All the usual stuff," Thorn said flatly. He shrugged. "They finally caved in."

Helen laughed softly. "I see you're still as smooth and charming as ever, Peter."

"C-4?" Koniev had been swinging his head from one to the other in growing puzzlement. Now he snapped his fingers. "Ah! Now I understand. You are old friends, yes?"

Without taking his eyes off Helen Gray, Thorn answered quietly, "Yes, Major, that's right. We're old friends. Very old friends."

An-32 Crash Site, Near the Ileksa River, Northern Russia

Colonel Peter Thorn wearily pushed back the hood of the rubberized chemical protection suit he'd been given. He wiped the sweat and dirt off his brow. After spending two hours tramping across the crash site with Major Koniev, he needed a breather.

He and the MVD officer were alone on this trek. True to form, Helen Gray had surveyed the debris field on her own as soon as she'd arrived on the scene. Right now she was busy setting up the joint FBI/MVD investigative team's communications and coordinating their plans with Mamontov and Nielsen.

His thoughts strayed to Helen. The female FBI agent was the only woman who had ever really gotten under his skin.

Thorn shook his head ruefully. Why use the past tense? His heart still skipped a beat whenever he saw her. Or talked to her. Or even thought about her.

Certainly, when he'd argued his way onto this mission, he'd hoped their paths might cross. After all, even this long after the end of the Cold War, the official American community in Moscow was still a small, close-knit world. And they hadn't seen each other for six long months—not since the FBI had sent her to Moscow as a legal attaché.

A couple of eagerly anticipated visits had been short-circuited by work emergencies—both on her end. As a legal attaché, Helen was the FBI's eyes and ears inside Russian law enforcement. With drug trafficking, smuggling, and contract killing all on the rise, her workload kept piling up.

Other attempts to meet had also fallen by the wayside. Even their weekly phone calls had begun to sound impersonal somehow—cold and unsatisfying, however warm the words.

Thorn sighed. Seeing Helen in the flesh brought all his memories of her, his longing for her, to the surface. Somehow he would have to find time to be alone with her—to see if he still held her heart the way she gripped his. If nothing else, that would at least offer a small measure of relief from the grim task at hand.

Reluctantly, he forced himself back into the ugly present.

Back in D.C. he had believed the doomed An-32 had come down in rough, trackless country. Now he was sure that it had crashed in hell—probably somewhere near the marshy banks of the River Styx.

The impact had scattered pieces of the aircraft and its passengers across a nightmarish landscape of dense, dark forest and brush-choked pools of stagnant water. The stench of rotting vegetation, charred wood, and burnt human flesh hung in the sluggish, unmoving air—separate odors that blended in an invisible, sickening fog. Midges and other biting insects swarmed in thick black clouds beneath the trees and above the marshy ground.

"Christ!" Thorn slapped at a stinging fly, smearing blood across his cheek. He glanced at Koniev. "I can think of better places to spend a few days, Major."

"This region will never appear in our new tourist brochures, that is true," the Russian officer agreed tiredly. He sighed. "We are in the midst of what some call the Devil's Eden. Personally, I do not believe even the devil would want this country for his own." The younger man mopped his own forehead and then quickly wiped his hand off on the gray, rubber-coated fabric of his protective suit.

With so much wreckage still strewn through the woods and the swamp, Thorn realized that the suits were a necessary safeguard. They were also hot, confining, and horribly uncomfortable. Even in the cool weather of the northern Russian spring, wearing them while engaged in heavy labor meant risking dehydration and heat stroke.

The sound of splashing and weary, repeated commands drew his attention back to the work crews they were observing.

Barely visible through the trees, a line of Russian soldiers moved slowly through the tangled undergrowth. Their baggy protective suits made them look like gray, wrinkled ghosts in the gathering evening gloom. Hunched over to see more clearly, they poked and probed through every thicket and scum-coated pond—searching for debris from the crash.

Technical experts from the Federal Aviation Authority followed close behind the search line. They charted the precise position of smaller pieces of wreckage or human remains before crews came in to haul them away. Larger chunks of torn metal were tagged and left in place for later removal by winch-equipped helicopters.

Koniev frowned. "The work proceeds at a glacial pace, I am afraid." He sounded embarrassed. "This plane came down four days ago. Four days ago! And only now does the recovery effort truly begin!"

Thorn shook his head. "From what I've seen so far, Major, your people have worked miracles just getting this much done so fast."

He meant that. Seeing what the Russians were up against at first hand revealed the true magnitude of their task. Search planes had finally found the An-32 crash site two days after the aircraft disappeared off air traffic control radar. From then on, the search, rescue, and investigative teams had been in a race against time and miserable conditions. Considering the logistical strain involved in setting up and supplying a sizable base camp by air, their progress really was nothing short of remarkable.

Thorn spotted movement off to one end of the search line. Two Russian soldiers paced into view, moving carefully and scanning the woods all around them. Each carried an AK-74 assault rifle at the ready.

He nodded toward the sentries. "You expecting trouble, Major?"

"Perhaps." The MVD officer hesitated and then went on. "There are many predators in these woods, Colonel. Bears. Foxes. Even wolves."

True enough, Thorn thought. But not all wolves ran on four legs. He noticed that the armed guards spent at least as much time watching the search team as they did the surrounding forest. He suspected the Russians were trying to make sure their poorly paid rescue workers didn't loot any of the crash victims' personal effects.

He and Koniev stepped aside, clearing the narrow path for two panting conscripts carrying a large black plastic bag back toward the camp. Part of the bag snagged a low-hanging branch and ripped open, revealing a blackened lump of flesh that was barely identifiable as a human torso. One of the soldiers muttered a tired apology and hastily shifted his grip to close the gash in the body bag.

Thorn's eyes narrowed. He'd seen death in almost every form on the battlefield or in the aftermath of terrorist atrocities. But no one could ever be fully prepared for the havoc a high-speed impact could wreak on the human body.

He heard Koniev gag and then quickly take a deep, shuddering breath. He turned to look at the young MVD officer. "Are you all right, Major?"

"Yes." The other man looked pale, but otherwise in control. He straightened his shoulders. "Have you seen enough, Colonel? It will be dark soon."

Thorn nodded sharply, pushing the image of that blistered corpse out of his mind. "Yeah. I've seen enough. For now. But I'll be back here at first light."

They turned and silently made their way back up the shadowed trail toward the camp.

Investigation Base Camp, Near the Ileksa River

Colonel Peter Thorn stopped near a small tent set up beneath a tall pine tree and buttoned his uniform jacket. His breath steamed in the chilly night air. The temperature had dropped rapidly after dark—dipping close to the freezing mark.

He stood still for a moment longer, gathering his thoughts while making sure he wasn't being observed. Private quarters were the sole concession Helen Gray had accepted as lone woman on the investigative team. She had worked damned hard to be accepted on her merits in the male-dominated precincts of the FBI. And, for all their Soviet-era propaganda boasts about building a truly equal society, the Russians remained an even more intensely conservative lot. Getting caught visiting her tent alone after sundown could easily put her professional reputation at risk. He was determined to avoid that if possible.

Floodlights lit the compound and surrounding forest with a cold, harsh, sharp-edged glare that made the blackness outside the light absolute. The smell of cheap tobacco and cooked beets wafted from the crowded tents used to house Russian enlisted men. But there were no signs of movement among the trees. After a long, hard, backbreaking day at the crash site, the search effort had shut down for the night. Moscow would have to ferry in more men, equipment, and supplies before they could accelerate the recovery operation onto a twenty-four-hour cycle.

Thorn turned back toward Helen's tent and then stopped dead in his tracks. Maybe he should wait and see her the next morning. Maybe he was pushing too fast.

He shook his head, angry at himself for wavering. He'd been awarded medals for bravery under fire. Right now, though, none of them meant a damned thing. What the hell was his problem? If she still loved him, everything would be fine. And if she didn't love him anymore? Well, better to find that out now—to force a clean, crisp break before their screwed-up emotions started interfering with their work. This investigation had to come first. It was time to start acting like a man and a soldier instead of a scared teenager.

He took a quick, deep breath, squared his shoulders, and tapped softly on the canvas tent flap. "Helen? Can I come in?"

"Peter?" The tent flap opened, spilling a warmer light onto the dark and muddy ground. Helen stood in the opening, framed against the glow from a lantern. She eyed him calmly for a second and then motioned him inside, closing the flap behind him.

Her tent contained little beyond a cot made up with rough wool Russian Army blankets, a couple of battered wooden folding chairs, her travel bag and laptop PC, and an empty supply crate that apparently served as a desk. And, of course, Helen herself.

Thorn tried to ignore the pulse pounding in his ears. Even in travel-worn jeans and a heavy green fisherman's sweater, she was lovely. Her wavy black hair silhouetted a heart-shaped face and stunning blue eyes.

He wanted to kiss her, but he held back. They'd been apart for too long. He couldn't read her mood with any certainty. It seemed best to play it safe.

"How have you been, Helen?"

She arched an eyebrow. "I've been fine."

After an uncomfortable pause that seemed to last an eternity, she nodded toward one of the chairs. "Why don't you take a seat, Peter? You look so formal standing at attention in that uniform. I keep having this urge to salute you."

"Yes, ma'am." Thorn obeyed gladly, relieved to hear the

bantering tone in her voice. That was a lot more like the Helen Gray he'd come to know and love over the past two years.

She sat down gracefully on the cot facing him and said more seriously, "I really was surprised to see you pop out of that helicopter, you know."

"I know," he answered simply. "I almost didn't."

"Oh?"

Thorn shrugged. "I wasn't exaggerating much when I said I had to hold my breath and throw a tantrum to win a spot on the team. Even then my boss practically told me that he'd yank me back to D.C. the second he heard any complaints from the NTSB . . . or from the Russians, for that matter. I'm the inspection agency's liaison here on sufferance."

Since a team from the On-Site Inspection Agency had been aboard the downed Russian plane, both Washington and Moscow were willing to allow an observer from the agency at the crash site—somebody who could help identify the victims, round up their personal and professional effects, and funnel reports back to OSIA's Washington headquarters. But none of the top officials involved in either capital were likely to have much patience with him if he pissed off the experts tasked with the real work of investigating the crash.

Helen leaned forward and asked softly, "Is OSIA really that bad, Peter?"

"It's Siberia without the perks." Thorn tried smiling and failed. "Seriously, I have a nice carpeted office, a nice new computer, and a nice clean desk . . . but nothing important or interesting ever comes across that desk. I write reports analyzing terrorist threats that go straight into a circular file somewhere. And the rest of the time I sit around waiting to answer questions that are never asked."

He snorted in disgust. "I'm forty years old, Helen, and I'm stuck behind a desk when I should be out leading troops.

But I wouldn't mind that so much if they'd at least let me do the job they hired me for."

"Then why not resign?" Helen asked bluntly. "Why stay in the Army if they won't let you do what you're best at?"

Resign? Leave the Army? Thorn pondered that for a split second and then shook his head decisively. "Can't do that. They can fire me if they want to, but I won't quit."

She frowned.

"Jesus, Helen. I know that sounds stubborn, even mule-headed. But I'm a soldier. That's all I've ever been. That's all I've ever wanted to be since I was just a kid." Thorn paused, remembering the pride he'd felt as a little boy watching his soldier father march past with that green beret sitting proudly on his head. "I took an oath to serve my country. I'll honor that oath however I'm allowed. Whether it's behind some goddamned desk . . . or out here in these damned woods."

Helen's frown faded. "Now that's the Peter Thorn I'm used to hearing." Her lips curved upward into a slight smile. "Pig-headed, yes. Opinionated, yes. But not a whiner . . . or a quitter."

Thorn winced. "I guess I did sound pretty damned bitter, didn't I?"

"Yep." She reached out and put a hand gently on his knee. "And not a bit like the same man who told me to stay in the FBI whenever I wanted to give up. Who pushed me back into the ring every time I got knocked down."

She looked down at her lap for a moment. "I haven't forgotten the months you spent getting me back on my feet, Peter. Not a second of them."

Thorn nodded slowly. While leading an FBI Hostage Rescue Team raid on a terrorist safe house in northern Virginia, Helen had been badly wounded. Her doctors had warned her that her injuries might be permanent. That she might never walk unaided or without a severe limp. Well, she'd proved them wrong. It had taken months of rigorous physical therapy—months of constant pain and hard work—but she'd regained the full use of her legs.

He'd encouraged her to fight for her health and her career every step of the way. Some members of the FBI's old-boy network would have been very happy to see her accept a presidential commendation for heroism and retire on disability. But she'd surprised them all. She'd reported back for active duty with a clean bill of health from every doctor she could corral.

Thorn smiled to himself. Helen had more courage in one of her little toes than all the bureaucrats at the FBI's Hoover Building headquarters put together.

Her sigh startled him. He looked up and found her studying him intently.

"Peter . . ." She hesitated, then fell silent. She tried again. "Peter, I think we need to talk—"

"Yeah. We do," Thorn cut in hurriedly. Those were not words he wanted to hear right now. He took his hand off hers and quickly tried to change the subject. "You've had more time on the ground here. What's your first take on this plane crash? Do you buy the accident theory? Or do you think we're looking at some kind of sabotage?"

Christ, I'm babbling like an idiot, he thought.

Helen rolled her eyes. "Peter Thorn, you are the most irritating man I've ever met." She sounded exasperated beyond endurance.

Bingo.

Thorn grinned slowly. "Does that mean you still like me?"

Almost against her will, Helen matched his grin. "Probably." She shrugged. "Maybe I even still love you."

Aware again of the pulse pounding in his ears, Thorn lifted the hand she had on his knee, enclosed it in his own, and pulled her slowly toward him. Her lips parted, met his gently, and then pressed back even harder.

Suddenly he felt her stiffen.

Slowly, reluctantly, Helen pulled her lips away from his. She whispered, "Someone's outside, Peter. I just heard a twig snap."

He sat up and faced the tent flap—watching her hand slip toward the shoulder holster hanging from a peg over her cot. Her combat reflexes were obviously still good.

Someone rapped on the canvas. "Special Agent Gray? You are still awake, I hope?"

Helen visibly relaxed. "It's Alexei Koniev." She sat back on the cot and smoothed her sweater into shape. "I'm awake, Major. Colonel Thorn and I were just talking. Come on in."

Koniev slipped through the tent flap and stood looking down at them. His eyes twinkled. "I hope I am not interrupting anything of importance."

"Nothing much, Major," Thorn heard himself say stiffly.

"Ah, that is good." Koniev tossed his officer's cap onto Helen's improvised desk and sat down in the empty folding chair. He crossed his legs casually and leaned forward. "Perhaps we can discuss our strategy for tomorrow, then. Our game plan, I believe you Americans say?"

Thorn bit down hard on his irritation. Koniev had as much right to visit Helen's tent as he did—maybe even more. And he couldn't fault the Russian major for wanting to get a head start on the next day's work. He just wished the younger man didn't look so much at home in her company. His love life and this investigation were already complicated enough.

CHAPTER TWO

EARLY WARNING

MAY 25

Headquarters, 125th Air Division, Kandalaksha

(D MINUS 27)

Colonel General Feodor Serov slid the pile of brochures and bank transfers into a special file folder and nodded to himself. Cuba would serve as the ideal shelter for his family and his newfound wealth.

His lips thinned into a mocking smile. Some of his old comrades-in-arms might attribute his decision to a liking for one of the world's few remaining communist states. Despite his professed fondness for "the U.S.S.R.'s good old days," they would be wrong.

Ideology was a younger man's luxury, he thought. Socialism was dead or dying. The mighty Soviet state he had served all his life was gone—leaving only a pale, shrinking ghost in its place. His lopsided smile turned into a sneer. Yeltsin's Russia could not even maintain its grip on Chechnya—a piss-poor region inhabited only by ignorant Muslim bandits. Four centuries of Russian and then Soviet imperial conquest were being thrown away by the quarreling fools in Moscow.

No, Serov had far better reasons for settling in Cuba. Hard currency was king in Castro's island nation. Land was cheap. Wages were low. And Fidel's hard-pressed government didn't ask inconvenient questions when wealthy expatriates brought their resources to its aid. He and his family could blend in with the growing colony of other newly rich Russians who had already moved there—drawn by the sunny, warm climate, and by the chance to spend ill-gotten gains safely outside the reach of their own country's law enforcement agencies.

His watch beeped. It was time to attend to more routine matters. He grabbed the folder off his desk and jammed it into a leather valise as he headed for the door. His military aide looked up as he hurried through the outer office. "I'll be on the flight line for the next hour, Captain, and then I'll be at Maintenance."

Serov clattered down the steps, still mentally organizing his afternoon. With his relief due in two weeks and his retirement slated for the week after that, his days were crowded. Kandalaksha was a large, complex base, and he wanted—no, needed—the turnover to go smoothly. Especially with the secret venture he knew only as "the Operation" so close to completion. The ongoing An-32 air crash investigation was bad enough. He couldn't afford any more slipups that might draw even closer official scrutiny.

His staff car and driver were waiting, with the engine running. Serov yanked the back door open and slid inside. He snapped out a brusque order: "Let's get to the flight line, Sergeant."

Only then did the Russian general realize he wasn't alone.

The other man in the back seat was slightly smaller than Serov and thinner. He wore a perfectly tailored olive-green Italian suit, and his stylishly cut hair was more gray than black. His face was commonplace, much like that of any anonymous bureaucrat or businessman. Only his steel-gray eyes betrayed his intensity and ruthlessness.

Rolf Ulrich Reichardt waited for the car door to close behind Serov, then nodded at the driver. "Go."

Serov scowled. "What the devil are you . . . ?" His voice faded when he realized the sergeant sitting behind the wheel was not his regular driver.

They accelerated away from the curb in response to Reichardt's order. At the end of the headquarters building, the driver turned left instead of right. Serov's blood turned to ice.

He licked his lips nervously and glanced at Reichardt. This man had been his primary contact throughout the Operation. Some of the other man's subordinates had made the necessary transportation arrangements; still others had handled payment and security concerns outside Kandalaksha. But Reichardt had supervised every step. He sometimes referred to "his employer," but Serov had never asked who that employer might be. The enormous sums of money he was being paid made such information unnecessary.

Now Reichardt sat impassively, with his eyes fixed on Serov as they drove past the base administration buildings. The Russian didn't bother asking him what was going on. He knew the other man would only ignore him.

Serov knew little about Reichardt's background, but he could make several educated guesses. From his appearance, Reichardt was probably in his late forties. Since he spoke fluent Russian with a German accent, Serov also guessed he had grown up in the DDR, East Germany.

Reichardt's behavior, his mannerisms, also marked him as a former member of the Stasi, the DDR's feared secret police agency. Members of the Stasi were cut from the same arrogant, thuggish cloth as the old Soviet KGB. The Russian general hid his distaste. The Stasi had been a necessary evil under the old system. Now they were shadows—dangerous shadows, but shadows nonetheless. Most had gone underground—assuming new identities to avoid arrest after German reunification.

Serov knew more about Reichardt's methods. The German was a meticulous organizer. He paid almost obsessive attention to every detail. He was also utterly ruthless. One of Serov's junior officers, officially listed as a deserter from Kandalaksha's engine maintenance facility, actually lay buried in a swamp a hundred kilometers outside the base. Reichardt had "removed" the young man simply because he was a potential threat to the Operation's cover story.

They'd driven for almost five minutes before Reichardt broke the increasingly uncomfortable silence. He nodded toward the driver. "This is Sergeant Kurgin, Feodor Mikhailovich. He's just been assigned to Kandalaksha. He will be your driver and orderly until you retire and leave Russia. Do you understand?"

Irked, Serov nodded. So this Kurgin was one of Reichardt's spies. Given the German's predilection for holding all the reins of power, it wasn't surprising that he would keep Serov under close surveillance for as long as possible. Not surprising, perhaps, but insulting. And worrying, too. Exactly how far did Reichardt's arm reach?

"And where are we going now?" Serov asked quietly.

"For a private discussion," the German replied flatly. "A very private discussion."

They drove in silence for several more minutes before coming to a large, two-story building. Serov recognized it immediately. Big enough to be a factory, it had housed a jet engine rework facility before being abandoned a few years ago. Other deserted buildings and equipment yards surrounded the building—making it the perfect spot for a covert enterprise. He and a few carefully selected subordinates had used the site for just such a purpose in recent weeks before stripping it again.

The car paused only long enough for Kurgin to hop out and open a heavy metal sliding door before getting back in and pulling the car inside.

Serov and Reichardt stepped out of the car into the abandoned building's chilly, damp interior. Rusted metal fittings jutted up from the stained and spotted concrete floor, marking where machinery had once been mounted. Dirty windows lined the galvanized metal and bare concrete walls. They admitted just enough light to let them pick their way across the debris-littered floor.

Sergeant Kurgin left the car, walked outside, and pulled the door shut behind him. The sound of the door closing echoed through the building's cavernous interior.

Serov and Reichardt were left alone inside.

Reichardt dropped any pretense of civility, his face suddenly clouded with cold fury. "Very well, Serov. I have a number of questions for you. And you will give me the right answers to those questions . . . if you want to leave this place alive."

Shaken by the explicit threat, the Russian general fought hard not to show his fear. He knew the German well enough to know that he never made idle threats. "You cannot afford to have me disappear, Herr Reichardt. That would only draw more unwanted attention to this base."

Reichardt laughed derisively. "More attention? How could we possibly get any more publicity? 'Arms Inspection Team Crashes After Visiting Russian Bomber Base,'" he quoted. "Your blunder is now front-page news!"

Serov hesitated for a moment, marshaling his arguments carefully now. "We had no choice in the matter. We could not let them return to Moscow—not with what the American had discovered."

"You mean, after the American had detected your foolish mistake!" Reichardt's voice was low and menacing—like the growl of a lion closing in on its prey. "So now the Americans or the MVD will send more people to probe your activities here. And this time they will sweep Kandalaksha from one end to the other!"

Serov nodded stiffly. "Yes, that is a possibility." With an effort, Serov tried to regain his composure and put himself back on an equal footing with the German. "But I have taken additional steps to ensure that any official investigation will find nothing of interest. After all, the American, Avery, only stumbled across our operation by chance. We can withstand additional scrutiny."

"So you hope," Reichardt replied icily. He paused a moment, considering. "But if you are right, then this crash investigation is our biggest remaining problem."

Serov felt himself starting to relax. The phrase "our problem" reinforced his growing belief that the other man had decided against liquidating him—at least for the time being. He leaned forward. "They should find nothing incriminating in the wreckage. Captain Grushtin is an efficient officer. He does not make mistakes."

Reichardt frowned. "A purely Russian investigation of this air crash would not trouble me, Serov. Such an investigation could be controlled." He scowled, thinking aloud now. "But I find the American presence worrying. Managing them will require activating special assets I had hoped to preserve for another day."

Serov kept quiet. The German had already made it very clear that security arrangements beyond Kandalaksha were not Serov's concern.

Reichardt shrugged. "That is another matter." His voice sharpened. "You are quite sure there are no more 'mistakes' waiting to be found at your end of the Operation?"

Increasingly confident, Serov nodded. "My officers and I have taken every possible precaution, Herr Reichardt."

He froze, suddenly aware of Reichardt's cold gray stare boring into him.

"Do not try my patience, Serov. You promised me perfection once before. You failed. And your failure placed this entire operation in jeopardy."

Reichardt paused, then took two steps closer to the Russian, bringing them only an arm's length apart. He lowered his voice to a harsh whisper. "Let me be very, very clear, Feodor Mikhailovich. One more error. One more accident. Anything. Anything at all. If this transaction is compromised in any way by your actions or those of your men, you will die."

The German smiled cruelly. "And I promise you that your death will be painful, as will be the deaths of your wife and daughters." He let that sink in, watching the horror spread across Serov's face with satisfaction. "Sergeant Kurgin is not my only agent on this base. I will be watching you, Feodor Mikhailovich. Remember that."

Reichardt turned abruptly and strode toward the door. Serov followed him, moving slowly on legs that felt shaky.

At the door, the German issued one final warning. "Your only chance of survival is to keep this operation secure and secret. And you had better hope to God the investigators find nothing incriminating at that crash site."

He rapped on the door twice, and it slid open. Kurgin came in and walked over to the staff car. Another car was waiting outside.

Without another word, Reichardt turned his back on Serov and climbed into the second car. Moments later it sped off, leaving the Russian general and his new orderly alone.

Stunned, Serov shuddered.

Then, aware that Sergeant Kurgin was watching him, he fought for control over his expression. You knew what you were undertaking, he told himself sternly. He was not a child who could run home crying because the game had suddenly turned sour.

As a fighter pilot, Serov had developed a reputation as a skilled gambler—as a man always willing to push his aircraft to its limits in pursuit of victory. Nothing in his personality had changed with increasing age and rank. And, despite Reichardt's threats, the Operation still appealed to him. The risks, even now, were manageable, and the rewards—he allowed himself to visualize a vast estate perched above sunlit Caribbean waters—the rewards were dazzling.

No, Serov told himself again, nothing had changed. Not really. Nothing except that he now knew with absolute certainty that Reichardt would kill his entire family without remorse—should he fail. Well, he should have anticipated that. The stakes were high, very high, both for winning and for losing.

MAY 26

Near Taif, Saudi Arabia

(D MINUS 26)

Prince Ibrahim al Saud's country estate covered several hundred acres of rolling hillside south of Taif. Located in the foothills of the Asir mountain range paralleling the Red Sea, the town was a popular summer getaway for many Saudis. It provided a restful contrast to the bustling cities of Jedda and Riyadh. The higher elevation made it marginally cooler, and irrigation held the sun-baked brown rock of the surrounding landscape at bay.

Entirely surrounded by a low rock wall, Ibrahim's estate was almost a small town in its own right. Marble from Italy, wood from Turkey, and coral from the Red Sea merged in a series of buildings that were more than a mansion but less than a palace. Outbuildings for the servants and security staff, a garage for a small fleet of luxury automobiles, a helicopter pad and hangar, and a private mosque all surrounded the central residence.

Ibrahim al Saud knelt in the mosque now, facing northwest, toward Mecca. His entire staff, save only the security guards actually on duty, knelt and prayed beside and behind him. By Islamic law, only the noon prayers on Friday required attendance at a mosque, but Ibrahim carefully cultivated his public image as a man of deep religious faith. As a member of the vast Saudi royal family, he felt it important to maintain the proper appearances in this intensely conservative Islamic land. His various business and other enter-

prises ran smoother without attracting the unwelcome attention of the Kingdom's fanatical religious monitors.

He finished the *rakat*—the cycle of prayer—and stood.
Tall and slim, Ibrahim's dark hair and complexion framed a
pair of even darker, penetrating eyes. None of his staff liked
to attract his attention, because that meant being pierced by
those eyes, searched for flaws, and studied as an object to be
used—or discarded.

Barefoot like the rest of the worshippers, the prince
turned and watched his staff quickly disperse. He moved
toward the door outside, retrieved his own sandals, and
walked the fifty meters to the south wing of his residence.

The mansion's white marble walls reflected the fierce
sun, but stepping into the shady portico that surrounded the
single-story building brought instant relief from the glare
and the noonday heat. Ibrahim sat down at a small table facing an immaculately landscaped garden—a fantastic mix of
flowers and shade trees that would never have survived the
Arabian peninsula's harsh climate without massive irrigation and constant care.

He had never asked how much maintaining this garden
cost. Whether a hundred thousand or a million dollars, the
figure was immaterial—a tiny droplet from the boundless
sea of his personal fortune.

Like all the Saudi princes, Ibrahim had been born to
wealth. And like them, he had been well educated—
schooled first in Cairo, then in Oxford, and finally at Harvard. Unlike most of his royal peers, however, he had
demonstrated an uncommon flair for organization and finance.

Over the past thirty years, he had painstakingly built an
international business empire that now ranked second to
none in Saudi Arabia—Caraco. Most of the corrupt and
foolish members of the Saudi royal family had only par-

layed their vast oil wealth into still vaster debts—mortgaging their kingdom to the West for fancy automobiles, aircraft, showcase cities, and other baubles. But Ibrahim and his allies had carefully diversified their own holdings before the worldwide slump in oil prices. Now Caraco's yellow-and-black corporate logo flew over banks, engineering firms, transportation companies, and import-export enterprises around the globe.

By blood, he was merely one of several thousand princes—a minor member of Saudi Arabia's sprawling elite. But when money and personal power were thrown into the equation, Ibrahim al Saud could walk as proudly as any of the great kings of antiquity.

A servant appeared with lunch—followed by Hashemi, his personal secretary, bearing the usual thick sheaf of faxes and phone messages. Ibrahim studied the first and most important:

"Mr. Lahoud of the Persian Gulf Environmental Trust will arrive in Taif at one o'clock this afternoon. He requests the honor of an appointment with Prince Ibrahim al Saud—at the prince's convenience."

Ibrahim looked up at Hashemi. "Arrange for Mr. Lahoud to be brought to the estate as soon as he arrives in Taif. I will meet with him as soon as he has refreshed himself."

"You have appointments at two and three this afternoon, Highness," the other man gently reminded him.

"Reschedule them," Ibrahim said.

Hashemi nodded silently and glided away to obey his orders.

Ibrahim was still at work an hour later when Hashemi reappeared.

"Mr. Massif Lahoud," the secretary announced.

The prince rose to greet his visitor, a shorter, darker-skinned, and older man. He noted the armed guards hovering in the background and dismissed them with a wave of his hand. Their presence was customary when he met men who were not members of his personal household, but he would dispense with custom whenever it interfered with operational security.

Ibrahim smiled thinly. He trusted no one absolutely, but he considered Lahoud levelheaded and discreet.

An Egyptian by birth, Lahoud had been handpicked to head the Persian Gulf Environmental Trust by Ibrahim himself—as had all the trust's personnel. It was a separate company, privately held by Ibrahim. Its public charter proclaimed a determination to counter the rampant pollution in the Gulf by funneling a fixed percentage of Caraco's corporate profits into worthy environmental efforts.

"You found your trip a pleasant one, Mr. Lahoud?" Ibrahim asked, signaling Hashemi for coffee.

Lahoud nodded. "Both pleasant and speedy—thanks to your generous assistance, Highness."

A Caraco helicopter had been waiting at Taif when Lahoud's plane landed—bringing him directly to the estate.

"And your family? They prosper?" the prince continued.

"They do, by the grace of God," Lahoud answered.

Ibrahim let the conversation drift through the pleasantries that always preceded any meeting in the Middle East for several more minutes before turning to more serious matters. "I assume the trust has been approached to fund another special endeavor, Mr. Lahoud?"

"Indeed, Highness." The Egyptian handed him a slim manila folder. "A most worthy venture in my judgment."

Ibrahim flipped it open. A single cover sheet moved straight to the heart of the matter.

Project Summary

The Radical Islamic Front has learned that Anson P. Carleton, the American Undersecretary of State for Arab Affairs, will visit Riyadh from June 6 to June 8. Carleton's mission is to press the Saudi government for a renewed rapprochement with the State of Israel. Among other incentives, he intends to offer an extensive military aid package conditioned only on an agreement by Saudi ministers to meet directly and covertly with representatives of Israel—either in Washington itself or in an undisclosed neutral capital.

The Front has developed a plan to assassinate Carleton as soon as he arrives on Saudi soil. They seek the funds necessary to carry out this action.

Ibrahim turned to the detailed proposal attached to the cover sheet. He studied it intently in silence and then nodded. The Radical Islamic Front was a small group—a breakaway faction of the much larger and more loosely organized Hizballah. They were known to have good intelligence sources, and it looked as though they'd scored quite a coup this time.

The Front's plan was a clever one—simple, direct, and with only a minimal chance of detection by the Saudi security services. And he agreed wholeheartedly with their choice of target. He'd followed this American's activities closely now for a number of months. Carleton had apparently dedicated himself to restarting the perennially stalled Middle East peace process once again.

The thought of instigating Carleton's assassination intrigued Ibrahim. The man was one of the U.S. State Department's rising stars, and his official visit would naturally be made under tight security. Killing such a high-ranking diplomat would not only embarrass the Americans and the Saudi security services, it would also make them afraid—unsure of where the next terrorist blow would land. It was also guaranteed to paralyze American policy-making in the region for weeks or months—at least until a new undersecretary was appointed to fill the dead man's shoes.

All of which would dovetail rather nicely with his own larger plans, Ibrahim decided.

He smiled thinly, imagining again the horror that environmental scientists with Persian Gulf Trust grants would feel if they ever learned they shared funding with some of the world's most ruthless terrorist organizations. Not that they ever would. He had spent most of a lifetime living and working in two very separate worlds—one the world of international business and finance, and the other the armed struggle against Israel and its allies in the West.

Only a handful of men still living—all of them his most trusted servants—knew that Prince Ibrahim al Saud, the chairman of Caraco, was also the hidden financier of international terrorism. For year after year, he had funneled money into carefully selected terrorist operations—always laundering his contributions through a labyrinthine maze of front organizations and other cutouts. And, as other sources of funding for terrorism had dried up, the prince had gathered more and more of the reins of power into his own carefully concealed hands. His word was fast becoming law for terrorist groups as diverse as Hizballah, Hammas, the Radical Islamic Front, Japan's Red Army, and Colombia's M-19 guerrillas.

Month in and month out, year in and year out, the cycle continued. Proposals for major terror actions percolated their way upward through his networks until they reached his desk. And then orders issuing the necessary funds filtered back down to the men carrying the guns or bombs.

Sometimes Ibrahim felt as though he had been fighting his covert war with America, Europe, and Israel forever—that the long, weary struggle stretched from the moment of his birth and would last until his death.

But he knew that was not so.

Ibrahim could pinpoint the instant, the very second almost, that his hatred for the West had first flared to life.

His eyes closed briefly. Even now the memories were painful.

He had been just seven years old. His father, a far-thinking man in many ways, had seen the outside world fast encroaching on Saudi Arabia's isolation—drawn by the oceans of oil beneath the Kingdom's desert sands. Oilmen from Texas, Great Britain, and other Western countries were pouring money into the once-impoverished land at a fantastic clip—altering age-old patterns of life in the span of just a few years. To prepare his oldest son to meet the challenges of this new age, Ibrahim's father had arranged for him to be taught English and schooled in the ways of the modern world.

But his father, so wise in many things, had been so weak and so foolish in others.

The memory stabbed at Ibrahim yet again.

It had been early in the evening. He had come into the room his father used to entertain his prized Western guests—eager to show off the top marks he'd just received from his tutor. Two American executives were there. Americans who worked for one of the major oil companies. Both of them stood looking down at his father with expressions of utter contempt on their faces.

And his father? His once-loved father lay in a drunken stupor on a divan, still clutching the bottle of forbidden whiskey his "guests" had plied him with.

Ibrahim's stomach churned. It was almost as if he could smell the smoky reek of liquor still hanging in midair.

He remembered one of the Americans glancing quickly toward him, then swinging back to his companion with a harsh, muttered laugh. "No problem. It's only the sand nigger's boy."

From that moment, Ibrahim's path—his duty—had been clear to him.

His formal education gave shape, form, and purpose to his hatred. During his years at university in Cairo and Oxford, he gravitated toward fellow students and teachers who preached the need for radical change—first by words and then by violence. Their creed was simple, strident, and seductive. Israel, its American and European backers, and those Arabs and Muslims corrupted by Western money were the source of all that was wrong in the Arab world. Only by armed struggle could the peoples of the Middle East throw off the shackles of their Western exploiters and regain their true place in the world order.

Determined to play a leading role in this new war, Ibrahim had even spent a summer training at one of the new terrorist camps springing up across the Middle East. The men masterminding the resurgence of Arab radicalism had been delighted to find a scion of the House of Saud among their disciples. But they had quickly made it clear to him that he was too valuable an asset to be used as a gun- or bomb-carrying foot soldier. Instead they had given him special skills and training—teaching him how to organize self-contained terrorist cells, intelligence networks, and money-laundering operations. He had been schooled in the arts of command and deceit and then sent back to Saudi Arabia to put those lessons into practice.

Well, Ibrahim thought coldly, he had repaid their investment in him a million times over.

He returned his attention to the task at hand. The Radical Islamic Front's plan to destroy the American undersecretary of state contained a single, troubling flaw—a flaw that would have to be mended before it was put into action.

Ibrahim glanced up from the document in his hands. Massif Lahoud sat across the table, watching him closely.

"Do you approve this venture, Highness?" Lahoud asked carefully.

Ibrahim nodded, then held up a single finger. "On one condition. The Front must first agree to work with Afriz Sallah. You know this man?"

Lahoud shook his head. Usually it was not wise to admit ignorance in front of the prince, but in matters like this there was always much hidden.

"Sallah is a demolitions expert—one who has handled such matters before, usually in Egypt. And the Front lacks the necessary explosives expertise to carry out this operation on its own. I don't want Carleton walking away unscathed because they bungled the mission. Tell the Front we will cover their expenses and Sallah's fee—if they can work effectively with him."

Ibrahim tore off a piece of paper, wrote an address on it, and showed it to Lahoud. "Contact Sallah at this address and arrange a meeting. Understand?"

The older man read the address, committed it to memory, and then handed the paper back. "I will attend to it immediately, Highness."

Ibrahim nodded again. "Good. Hashemi will arrange for your transportation back to Taif."

The meeting was over.

Ibrahim turned his attention back to his paperwork. He had more important matters to manage.

MAY 26

Crash Investigation Base Camp, Near the Ileksa River

Colonel Peter Thorn left the tent being used as a makeshift morgue more shaken than he'd expected. He wiped off the dab of menthol rub from under his nose and took a deep breath of the fresher air outside. The menthol had helped make the nauseating smells inside the tent bearable—but only by a slim margin.

"Jesus, God," he muttered, trying to push the grim sights he'd just witnessed to the back of his mind.

"That was a bad one," agreed a quiet voice from beside his shoulder.

Thorn turned. Helen Gray looked ghost-white, and so did Koniev. The MVD major was busy dabbing at his mouth with a balled-up handkerchief.

Thorn didn't blame the younger man for getting sick. He still felt ill himself.

Two teams of Russian doctors were busy in the tent behind them—racing against the clock to positively identify the dead, and to find out what precisely had killed them. They were operating under extremely primitive conditions—forced to conduct autopsies by lamplight on folding tables, with only boiled riverwater at hand to wash off the tables between corpses. There weren't enough diesel generators available to provide refrigeration yet, so the medical teams were also fighting the rapid decay of the bodies they were trying to examine. Bacteria and other microorganisms were erasing vital physical evidence with every passing hour.

Thorn grimaced. Death was never pretty, but what he'd seen laid out on those autopsy tables was appalling. He sought refuge in routine and turned to Koniev. "So where exactly do we stand, Major? I got lost pretty fast in there. I'm afraid my Russian language skills are limited."

"Dr. Panichev is fairly confident that he and his subordinates will be able to identify everyone aboard the plane," the MVD officer replied slowly. "They've been able to take fingerprints from most of the bodies recovered so far. They may also need dental records, of course. I assume you can provide such information for the Americans on the inspection team?"

"Of course." Helen nodded. The color was just starting to return to her face.

"What about causes of death?" she asked. "My Russian's a little better than Colonel Thorn's . . . but not that much better—especially when it comes to technical terms. And Dr. Panichev is, well . . . he's . . ."

"Cryptic?" Koniev finished for her. He forced a wan smile. "Plain words are not so impressive to laymen, perhaps. Of course, I suspect the good doctor would even use medical jargon to propose marriage."

Helen chuckled. "Probably." She shook her head. "Not like you, I suppose, Alexei?"

"Oh, no." Koniev's smile perked up. "I would be extremely eloquent—even poetic."

Thorn felt faint stirrings of jealousy. Helen and this Russian policeman sometimes seemed entirely too close for his comfort. Especially when the MVD major's honesty was still an unknown factor.

Down, boy, Thorn told himself quickly. Helen and Koniev had been assigned together for several months. It was only natural that they would have established a friendly working relationship by now. Still, he had to admit that he would feel far easier in his mind if the MVD officer was not quite so determinedly charming and good-looking.

"In any event, I fear the autopsy results are slim so far—despite Panichev's best efforts to dazzle us," Koniev continued. He shrugged. "From what I gathered, the predominant cause of death seems to be impact trauma."

"Oh?" Thorn countered. "What about the burns we've noted on every body recovered so far?"

"Mostly postmortem," the younger man answered.

"And the other injuries we observed?" Helen asked. "The puncture wounds and gouges?"

"Panichev says they appear consistent with a crash. There was a lot of torn metal flying about when the plane hit the trees." Koniev frowned. "But the good doctor won't rule out the possibility that some of them might have been inflicted by shrapnel from a bomb or missile."

The Russian officer nodded toward the helicopter landing pad—barely visible through the trees. "He's sent tissue samples to the labs in Moscow so they can be tested for explosive residues. But getting conclusive results will take several days at least."

Thorn and Helen nodded their understanding. They headed toward a large tent adjacent to the landing pad. Maybe the NTSB and Russia's Aviation Authority teams had found something new. Maybe.

Pieces of twisted metal and heaps of twisted, fire-blackened control and electrical cabling covered the tarp floor inside the tent. The piles of wreckage were scattered in separate sections corresponding to different areas of the aircraft—each marked by painted outlines on the floor and signs in both the Russian and English alphabets.

Technicians wearing gloves and sterile surgical garb crouched beside different pieces of debris—intently examining them and taking detailed notes of their findings. Others stood conferring beside large worktables set up along one wall of the tent.

The tall, gaunt head of the NTSB investigative team, Robert Nielsen, was in one of those small groups. Nielsen turned his head when Thorn and the others came in. He immediately broke away from his colleagues and came over to meet them.

Nielsen looked tired and irritated. The higher-ups in Washington and Moscow were all over the investigation, demanding answers instantly. Thorn, Helen, and Koniev had been careful not to joggle his elbow, because they understood the difficulties the crash team was operating under. Distant bureaucrats were not as understanding—or as patient. Still, Thorn and the others needed something, if only a status report.

"Do you have any theories about what went wrong yet?" Helen asked softly.

"Theories, yes. Proof, no." Nielsen hesitated. "The pilot's Mayday calls show he lost both props—one right after the other—before the plane augered in. So right now we're looking pretty hard at some kind of catastrophic engine or fuel system failure. That seems the most likely scenario anyway."

"But you don't have any hard data that would confirm that?" Koniev pressed.

Nielsen shook his head wearily. "No, Major, we don't." He pointed to two marked sections on the floor. Both were nearly empty. "That's where we're going to reconstruct the engines . . . when we find them. So far we've only recovered twenty to thirty percent of the wreck."

Thorn cut in with a question of his own—one that had been bothering him ever since he'd read the English-language transcripts of the An-32's last radio calls. "What are the odds of something going wrong with both engines like that? Accidentally, I mean?"

Nielsen chewed his lower lip for a moment, plainly reluctant to give them a hard and fast answer. Finally, he said slowly, "If this were an American plane flying from an American airport, I'd tell you the odds against losing both props accidentally were high—very high."

Then the NTSB chief glanced quickly at Koniev and said quietly, "But a Russian aircraft? With Russian maintenance? Well, that puts us in a whole new ballpark, Colonel. I can't rule anything out. Not a thing."

FBI/MVD Evidence Holding Area,
Crash Investigation Base Camp

Colonel Peter Thorn slid the contents of yet another black plastic bag out onto a folding table and began carefully sorting through the pile. Scorched wallets. Broken watches. Torn clothing. Razors. Other toiletries. Mangled paperback books. They were all personal effects recovered from the crash site—the belongings of the dozen men who had died when the doomed An-32 fell out of the sky.

He sighed. Cataloging the victims' possessions was a necessary and important part of any investigation. But that didn't make it any easier. It raised too many ghosts. He flipped one of the wallets open and stared down at the happy faces of a man and woman surrounded by four smiling children—three adolescent boys and a much younger girl. It was a picture of Marv Wright, one of John Avery's team members, and his family.

Thorn shut the wallet and closed his eyes for an instant.

He'd met Wright just before the ex-Navy diver shipped out for Moscow. The man had been eager and willing—ready for a new start, a new adventure. Now what was left of him was lying on a slab inside the morgue tent . . .

"Peter?"

Thorn looked across the tent to where Helen Gray sat sorting through her own pile of personal effects. "Yes?"

"Can you take a look at these for a second?" She held up a pair of battered leather-bound notebooks.

Thorn was at her side in seconds. He leaned over her shoulder and gently touched the front cover of one of the notebooks. Despite the scorch marks and mud stains, he could still make out the gold embossed seal of OSIA. It was an arms inspection team logbook.

He nodded. "You just hit the jackpot, Helen."

Helen opened the other logbook, carefully peeling torn and charred pages away from each other. She scanned one page and then another. Her eyes narrowed.

"What's up?" Thorn asked, leaning closer.

She showed him a page filled with row after row of eight-digit numbers. All of them had a check mark beside them. "Are these what I think they are?"

"Bomb identifier codes? Yeah, they are," Thorn agreed.

"Then what do you make of this?" Helen asked, turning the page.

Thorn stared down at more rows of serial numbers. Again, all were checked off. But this time one of the bomb ID codes was also circled boldly. Why? He looked at Helen. "Whose logbook is this?"

"It belonged to John Avery, Peter."

Avery.

Thorn frowned. He'd known the inspection team leader for years—long before either of them wound up working for OSIA. As one of the Special Forces' top nuclear weapons experts, Avery had briefed Thorn and other Delta Force officers on bomb types, security measures, and effects several times. He remembered the former Green Beret's absolute precision—his almost manic attention to detail. Hell, the man had practically charted his own blood/alcohol ratio over drinks at the Fort Bragg Sport Parachute Club. Why would Avery circle a weapon's serial number after he'd already checked it off?

Thorn leafed through the second logbook and stopped on the same page. Again, all the bomb codes were checked off. But none of them were circled. He silently showed it to Helen.

She shook her head in confusion. "What does it mean, Peter?"

"I'm damned if I know, but I'd sure like to find out—"

"Special Agent Gray? Colonel Thorn? I think you need to see this. Immediately!" Alexei Koniev's voice broke their concentration. He sounded strained.

They turned around. The Russian major was on the far side of the tent they'd been assigned as a work space. He'd been going through the larger pieces of luggage recovered so far. Now he stood staring down into an open suitcase.

When they joined him, they could see that Koniev was looking at two clear plastic bags nestled carefully among folded clothes. Both were full of a white, granular powder. He pulled out a penknife and made a small incision at the top of one of the bags.

The MVD major silently offered the bag he'd sliced open to Helen. She dabbed one finger in the powder and studied it closely. Her face wrinkled. "Christ, Alexei! I think that's pure heroin!"

Koniev nodded slowly. "Yes, I think so, too."

Thorn looked down at the bags and then back up at the Russian policeman. "How much is this stuff worth?"

"Two kilos of heroin? On the street?" Koniev grimaced. "Perhaps six billion rubles. Roughly one million of your American dollars."

"Whose suitcase is that?" Helen demanded.

Koniev looked as though he'd swallowed poison. "Colonel Anatoly Gasparov," he said reluctantly. "The chief Russian liaison officer to your OSIA inspection team."

Helen Gray looked up at Thorn, worry written all over her face. "What do you think, Peter?"

He frowned. "I think our lives just got a whole lot more complicated."

CHAPTER THREE

IN TRANSIT

MAY 28

Pechenga, Northern Coast of the Kola Peninsula, Russia

(D MINUS 24)

Rolf Ulrich Reichardt glanced out a dirty window toward the harbor below. Pechenga, he thought smugly again, was perfect for his purposes.

Located twenty kilometers from the Norwegian border, the dreary little town lay huddled between inhospitable frozen tundra and the frigid Barents Sea. Its only asset was the sheltered harbor built for Soviet Army units and amphibious ships based there during the Cold War. When the U.S.S.R. collapsed, the soldiers left and the ships were either scrapped or left to rot at the pier. Now the town's few thousand inhabitants struggled to survive on coastal trade and a meager fishing industry.

With so little activity to distract Pechenga's harbormaster, Reichardt had his full attention as well as the only other chair in the dingy office overlooking the bay. The German lounged casually in the stiff-backed chair, making himself as comfortable as possible in the squalid circumstances. He had left behind his expensive suits and dressed instead in gray slacks and a navy pullover with a black leather jacket to protect him from the chilly winds that always blew off the Barents.

He checked his watch, a Rolex. Expensive, perhaps, but admirably precise. It was also a name people associated with wealth, and power, and success. So much so that many of those Reichardt dealt with saw only the watch—and never the man. And that was useful.

Reichardt tugged his sleeve back over the watch. There was still ample time to begin work. With luck, the ship he was here to see loaded would be underway by nightfall—by dinner, he corrected himself. So near the summer solstice and so far north, the sun would not set until almost 11:00 P.M.

He glanced out the window again.

Star of the White Sea was a small, bulk freighter, sound in hull and engine, though she'd never win any beauty contests. Her dark gray hull had once been topped by a crisp blue-and-white superstructure, but the paint had long ago succumbed to irregular patches of almost leprous rust and grime. A few men milled about on deck, while others, mostly Reichardt's own security force, waited on the pier. The only other vessels in sight were a few fishing boats and an international environmental survey ship.

A muffled cough brought his attention back inside the cramped office.

The harbormaster, a stooped, elderly man named Cherga, was still leafing through Reichardt's papers with evident interest. Manifests, customs forms, and authorizations from the Russian Ministry of Defense covered his battered wooden desk. All except one had been acquired legitimately, though some had needed slight alterations on names, numbers, and dates. Reichardt's own credentials identified him as the shipping agent for a company called Arrus Export, Inc. They were also genuine—although they showed his name as Mikhail Peterhof, a White Russian of German extraction.

He waited while Cherga studied each document intently, usually nodding, but sometimes setting a page to one side.

Reichardt hid his impatience. The Russian might be only a small-town bureaucrat, but he nevertheless wielded considerable power. In a country that still thrived on red tape, examining official documents was part procedure, part beloved ritual.

In any event, the German knew paperwork alone would not be sufficient to move his cargo out of the harbor. Whether lumber or refined metal or jet engines, a few palms needed to be greased first. For that reason the papers on Cherga's desk included a plain envelope containing a wad of dollars and deutsche marks, equivalent to several months' official salary for the older man. At the current rates of exchange, Russia's miserably low wages were an open invitation to graft and corruption.

With a small sigh, the harbormaster opened the seal on the envelope. His fingers riffled quickly through the notes, and he smiled with evident satisfaction. The bribe was big enough to win his cooperation without attracting too much attention. Cherga glanced up at Reichardt. "As always, it is a pleasure doing business with you, Mr. Peterhof."

"Thank you, Harbormaster," Reichardt said sincerely. Three decades of covert work—first for East Germany's feared state security service and later for himself—had taught him to appreciate men whose services could be bought. It made life so much simpler. He nodded toward the papers on the other man's desk. "I assume you have found everything in order?"

"Of course," the elderly Russian bureaucrat said. He carefully stamped the necessary permits and shipping authorizations, gathered all the documents into a neat pile, and then presented them to Reichardt with a flourish. "I wish your cargo a good voyage, Mr. Peterhof."

Reichardt left the office just as the majority of Pechenga's dockworkers and crane operators began straggling into view. He stepped onto the pier and signaled to his security team. Two scrambled up the *Star*'s gangplank, while others fanned out along the dock. All of them were armed, but none carried their weapons openly. His guards were there as a last resort only.

Reichardt nodded to himself. There would be no mistakes today. This phase of the Operation was too close to completion to permit any further errors. Not like that fool Serov at Kandalaksha.

His lips thinned, remembering the Russian Air Force general's pale, frightened face. Reichardt had zero tolerance for incompetence, ideology, or sentimentality. The stakes involved in this venture were enormous. If need be, he would carry out the murderous threats he had made against Serov and his family.

The German suppressed the small shiver of pleasurable excitement evoked by the thought of what he could do to the Russian, his wife, and his daughters before finally killing them. Neither pity nor morality would stop him from punishing those who failed him.

Reichardt had grown up in a system that valued power above any outdated bourgeois virtue. He had seen through the communist party's other lies at an early age—a wisdom his foolish, deluded parents had never achieved. They had lived their whole wasted spans on earth as true-believing "servants of the State." But Reichardt understood that power over life and death was the ultimate power—the nearest approach to divinity possible in a cold, uncaring universe. And he enjoyed every chance to exercise that power.

He turned to watch the first truck roll up to the end of the pier. Two more vehicles followed close behind. Each truck carried two long metal crates. The local longshoremen, grateful for a day's work and the extra bonus promised if they finished early, moved rapidly into position as the ship's crane maneuvered its wire rope down to their level.

Reichardt stood where he could both see and be seen. His alert gray eyes missed nothing as the first crate rose high into the air and then swung slowly toward the *Star of the White Sea*'s forward cargo hold.

"Watcher Two to Control. Unknown crossing security perimeter." The radio message from one of his observers crackled in Reichardt's earpiece.

He turned and spotted a serious-looking young man in a cheap suit and bulky overcoat marching down the pier. After scanning the mix of longshoremen and plainclothes security personnel milling about, the man headed toward Reichardt.

"Mr. Peterhof?"

Reichardt nodded brusquely. "I'm Peterhof."

The younger man inclined his head. "I'm Inspector Raminsky, with customs. I've just received your papers from Harbormaster Cherga. I came down as soon as I could."

Reichardt frowned. What the devil was this? He'd already

dealt with the clerks in customs yesterday. This Raminsky looked like potential trouble—probably fresh out of university and still full of energy and inflated self-importance. A young pup, then, and one too inexperienced to know when not to bark.

Carefully masking his displeasure, Reichardt calmly asked, "How can I help you, Inspector?"

"Well, Mr. Peterhof, as soon as I saw the, ah, nature of your cargo, I knew it would have to be personally inspected."

Reichardt's first impulse was to dismiss him; then he reconsidered. Compliance would attract less suspicion. He called over the head longshoreman, a bearlike man in greasy coveralls.

"Very well. Which crate did you wish to examine, Mr. Raminsky?" Reichardt gestured toward the truck currently being unloaded and two others that waited behind it with their engines idling.

Raminsky, obviously pleased at being given a choice, pointed to the remaining crate on the first truck in line. "That one."

Reichardt nodded his agreement and then issued orders to the head longshoreman. "All right, Vasily. Open it up for the inspector."

The crates were standard Russian Air Force issue. They were designed to allow inspection without being totally dismantled, but it still required care to open the end panel. After several minutes of prying with a crowbar, the panel fell to the ground with a loud, metallic clang.

Raminsky stepped forward and shined a flashlight inside, revealing a bright, concave, metal surface with the center curving into a dark hole. The official shifted his beam slightly, illuminating the turbine wheel at the center.

"This appears to be a jet engine," remarked Raminsky skeptically.

"Of course," Reichardt snorted. "It is a Saturn AL-21 turbojet engine." He tapped the bundle of documents he still held in one hand. "Just as stated on these custom forms. Forms which I must point out have already been signed by your own Minister Fedorov."

If he was impressed, Raminsky hid it well. Instead he merely raised an eyebrow and examined the sizable cargo crate more carefully. It was seven meters long, two meters high, and three meters wide—just large enough to allow a man to squeeze alongside the engine, although the internal bracing required careful movements. Undaunted, the inspector took off his overcoat and crawled inside.

Reichardt resisted the urge to pace or look at his watch while the Russian tapped the jet engine's metal skin and peered into tight spaces. Finally, the customs man clambered out, almost tripping on the brace and catching himself just in time.

After shaking himself off and retrieving his overcoat and paperwork, Raminsky looked the papers over again. He shook his head and announced, "There is no final destination marked on this export form, Mr. Peterhof."

Reichardt eyed him coldly, his patience finally wearing thin. "I am aware of that, Inspector. The reasons for that are explained in the authorization letter from the Ministry of Defense. But again, this has already been approved by your own ministry in Moscow."

Without looking up, Raminsky pressed the matter. "Nevertheless, it is highly unusual not to specify a destination. I may have to reconfirm this authorization with the ministry."

Reichardt decided he'd allowed the loading to be delayed long enough. He stepped close to the young man and spoke quietly, but menacingly. "The destination of these engines is the business of my company, the Ministry of Defense, and no one else's."

The change in Reichardt's tone caused Raminsky to look up with a startled expression on his face.

"You have heard of my employer before?" Reichardt demanded.

Reluctantly, Raminsky nodded.

Arrus Export, Inc. was a major player in one of the fastest growing sectors of the post-communist economy—arms sales. Arrus specialized in buying surplus Russian weapons and military spare parts at significant discounts and then reselling them to various Third World countries. Several prominent former Russian military leaders served on the Arrus board, along with a number of influential Americans and Europeans. From time to time, some of Moscow's new tabloids darkly hinted that substantial Arrus funds often flowed freely into certain government officials' personal bank accounts in exchange for a free hand inside the Russian armed forces. But nothing had ever been proven.

Satisfied that he had gotten the impudent fool's complete attention, Reichardt continued. "These are matters for the State, and the State has promises to keep."

The German paused. "It is not in your best interest to interfere with those promises, Inspector." He glanced away from Raminsky and motioned to two members of his security team who were observing the exchange. They closed in on either side. Raminsky saw them and paled slightly.

"I have instructions to make sure that these engines reach their destination intact and on time. I am also authorized to take any measures necessary to accomplish that task. *Any* measures. Do you understand me?" Reichardt waited for his message to sink in.

With his eyes darting back and forth between the two hard-faced men standing beside him, the young Russian customs official hurriedly nodded again.

"Good," Reichardt said calmly and dismissively. "Our papers are in order, and you have inspected the cargo to confirm that it contains the jet engines we are authorized to export. We will now proceed with the loading."

Without a second glance, he stepped aside and turned away.

Raminsky started to say something more, but it came out only as a strangled cough. Then he turned on his heels and fled quickly down the pier, clutching his paperwork to his chest.

The longshoremen, who had all observed Raminsky's humiliating retreat, returned to their work reenergized. The last crate was secured in the *Star of the White Sea*'s hold by mid-afternoon.

After shaking hands with the captain and wishing him a safe voyage, Reichardt sought out one of his security team, a dark-haired, powerfully built man. "Is the plane ready, Johann?"

"Yes, sir. And your luggage is already aboard." Johann Brandt had served under Reichardt in the Stasi. He was competent, efficient, and completely loyal to his superior. Like his fellow operatives in Reichardt's Revolutionary Movements Liaison Section, Brandt had gone underground just before East Germany collapsed—emerging with a new identity and a much fatter bank account. All of Reichardt's subordinates would obey any command he gave them. They had all made the same Faustian bargain—selling their souls for vast sums of money.

"Good. And our people on the *Star* know what to do?"
Brandt nodded.

"And the others are ready to close our office here?"

Brandt nodded again. "Yes, sir."

For several weeks Reichardt's men had operated out of a rented flat near Pechenga's small harbor—guarding shipments, keeping track of port officials and local law enforcement, and watching for strangers.

Now that this phase of the Operation was complete, it was time to move his men to new posts in other cities. There was other work to be done.

Investigation Base Camp, Northern Russia

Colonel Peter Thorn pushed aside the newest bag of personal effects recovered from the crash site and sat back from the worktable. He stripped off the pair of latex surgical gloves he wore when handling potential evidence and rubbed at sore eyes. Too little sleep and too much close work in bad light had left them feeling gritty, almost raw.

He felt a gentle hand on his shoulder and looked up into Helen Gray's worried face.

"You okay, Peter?" she asked softly.

He nodded. "Yeah. Just tired." He covered her hand with his. "Just like you."

They were all on the edge of exhaustion. Since Alexei Koniev had found nearly two kilos of pure heroin in Colonel Anatoly Gasparov's luggage, the three of them had been working almost around the clock to try to pin down just what had gone wrong aboard the An-32 carrying Gasparov, John Avery, and the rest of the OSIA inspection team. Although neither the NTSB nor the Russian Aviation Authority experts were willing to label the crash as anything but an accident yet, finding a million-plus dollars of illegal drugs aboard the downed aircraft added up to one hell of a potential motive for sabotage.

Helen and the Russian MVD major spent most of their time on the secure communications channel to Moscow or poring over the voluminous police and surveillance files faxed to them. Operating on the working theory that Gasparov might have fallen afoul of a rival drug-dealing *Mafiya* gang, they were trying desperately to trace his most recent movements and any suspicious contacts.

Which left Thorn with the painstaking grunt work of sifting through the rest of the crash victims' personal effects—looking for something, anything, that might shed some light on the situation. He was still puzzled by the discrepancy between Avery's inspection logbook and the other two they'd recovered so far. Faint alarm bells went off whenever he saw the circled weapons serial number, but he couldn't make it connect with Gasparov's apparent heroin smuggling. In any event, both Washington's and Moscow's records were quite clear. Avery and all of his teammates had given the Kandalaksha special weapons storage depot a clean bill of health before boarding the doomed An-32.

Helen pointed her chin toward the bag he'd set aside. "Find anything more?"

"Nope." Thorn shook his head. "A couple more wallets. Part of a key chain. Pieces of a couple of paperback books. Nothing significant." He looked up at her. "How about you? Any progress?"

"Not much." Helen bit her lip in frustration. "Gasparov's arms inspectorate colleagues are saying the same thing. They all knew he was cutting corners—selling government equipment and supplies and so on—to supplement his salary. But they're all 'shocked,' just 'shocked,' that he'd have anything to do with illegal drugs."

Thorn arched an eyebrow. "You believe them?"

She shrugged. "I don't know." She took her hand off his shoulder and started pacing. "Questioning Russian officials is tough enough in person. But I really don't like having to rely on secondhand interrogation reports translated into some Russian cop's idea of English."

"Plus you can't be sure whether or not the cop who's asking the questions isn't a crook himself?" Thorn probed.

Helen nodded grimly. "That, too, Peter. We both know the MVD is riddled with people on the *Mafiya*'s payroll. For all I know, the officers assigned to question Gasparov's associates are working for the same drug ring."

Now that she was on to the subject of police corruption, Thorn decided to risk asking a question that had been on his mind since he'd arrived at the An-32 crash site. "So what about Koniev? How far can you really trust him?"

Helen stared down at him. "Alexei?" She shook her head in disbelief. "You're asking me if Alexei Koniev is dirty?"

Thorn had the sudden feeling he'd stepped on a delayed-action mine. He forged ahead anyway. "Yeah, I guess I am." He outlined his reasoning. "I've seen the pay scale for an MVD major, and there's no way Koniev can afford the clothes he wears—not on his salary. So where's the money coming from?"

"I vetted him myself, Peter," Helen said coolly. "He's clean. As far as the money's concerned, Alexei's older brother, Pavel, just happens to be one of Russia's top entrepreneurs. He's a software wiz who's built himself a pretty good-sized commercial empire. From time to time, he likes to help Alexei out. That's all there is to the mystery money."

"Oh." Thorn winced. He hesitated and then forced himself to admit the obvious. "Guess I look something like a jerk right now, don't I?"

"Yes, you do. Maybe a little jealous, too," Helen replied tartly. Then, seeing the crestfallen look on his face, her tone softened slightly. "Of course, you're kind of cute when you're jealous, Colonel Thorn."

He tried a sheepish smile. "Sorry, I can't help it. Once Special Forces, always Special Forces. Jealousy's just part of my Neanderthal Army training. Sort of 'see my woman, see handsome stranger, bash handsome stranger . . .' "

Helen made a face. "Peter. Oh, Peter . . ." She chuckled and shook her head. "So here you've been keeping one eye cocked at Alexei Koniev—suspecting him of being everything from a *Mafiya* plant to a Muscovite Don Juan who's trying to sweep me off my feet . . ."

Thorn laughed quietly. "Okay, that does sound kinda stupid. But you've got to admit, the guy is pretty slick."

Helen's smile grew wider. "Now, Peter Thorn, if I were interested in somebody suave and debonair, would I be interested in you?"

Thorn laughed and shook his head. "Probably not."

"Right. So stop worrying." Helen leaned over and kissed him.

Suddenly, a snide, perfectly modulated voice washed over them. "Well, well, well. What an interesting investigative technique, Special Agent Gray."

Helen pulled herself upright, already turning red.

Thorn swung around in his chair. He took an instant dislike to the middle-aged man standing leering at them from the entrance to the tent. Everything about the stranger seemed out of place in this rough working camp deep in the Russian wilderness. His perfectly tailored suit, crisp white shirt, and expensive black loafers without a trace of mud on them all shouted "rear-echelon motherfucker" to Thorn—or, worse yet, "politician."

"Who the hell are you?" Thorn growled as he stood up, not bothering to hide the anger in his voice.

"FBI Deputy Assistant Director Lawrence McDowell,"

the other man answered calmly. He came closer. "And I might ask you the same question."

Great, just great, Thorn thought bitterly.

He knew McDowell headed the FBI's International Relations Branch—which made him Helen Gray's Washington-based boss. According to Helen, he was the worst possible mix—intensely ambitious and a prima donna to boot. He spent more of his time toadying to the current administration and to powerful Capitol Hill staffers than he did managing the Bureau's far-flung legal attaché offices. Apparently, he and Helen had also crossed swords sometime in the past—before either of them worked in the same unit. Ever since then the bastard had tried to make her life difficult whenever he could.

And now they'd given him the perfect opening to make even more trouble. Shit.

"I asked you a question"—McDowell's eyes flicked to the rank insignia on Thorn's battle-dress uniform—"Colonel."

"My name's Peter Thorn."

"Thorn." McDowell chewed on that for a second or two. Then it clicked. The FBI man snorted in disgust. "The Delta Force cowboy."

Thorn knew what the other man was thinking. Two years before he'd led a Delta Force commando raid into Teheran to kill Amir Taleh—an Iranian general who'd organized a terrorist campaign on American soil that had thrown the whole country into complete chaos. When the operation started going wrong, the President had gotten cold feet and tried to abort the mission. Thorn had refused. He'd disobeyed a direct order from the commander-in-chief, pushed ahead, and won—though at a high cost in casualties. Success had protected him against the court-martial he'd expected, but it hadn't saved his career from oblivion. And for a climber like McDowell, that was probably the worst of his sins.

McDowell turned back to Helen. "All right, Agent Gray. Now that you're done flirting with Colonel Thorn here, maybe you can fill me in on your progress—or lack thereof— on this investigation." He glanced at his watch. "I've got half an hour before my helicopter ferries me out of this dump and back to Arkhangelsk, so let's not waste any more time."

Thorn felt his hands straighten into killing edges. With an effort, he forced them to relax. This bastard needed a lesson in manners, but it would have to be a verbal lesson. He stepped forward. "Hold it right there, you son of a—"

"Colonel Thorn!" Helen exclaimed.

He stopped and stared at her. Her bright blue eyes were ice-cold now.

"You're out of line, Colonel," she said sharply. "This is an FBI matter."

Thorn suddenly realized what he'd almost done. He'd allowed McDowell's insults to push him to the brink of interfering in Helen's professional life. And that would have been catastrophic for her—and for them.

For all its progress in the past decades, the FBI's upper reaches were still mostly a male preserve. As one of the first women to serve in the Hostage Rescue Team, and now as one of the Bureau's top-ranking legal attachés, Helen was still swimming against the tide. No matter how chivalrous it might feel, jumping in to fight her battle with McDowell would only put everything she'd achieved at peril.

He just hoped Helen would forgive him for dragging her so close to the edge.

Swallowing hard, Thorn spun on his heel and left without another word.

The White House, Washington, D.C.

The Blue Room of the White House was brimming with men in tuxedos and women in designer gowns, mingling with each other and trying to figure out who the important players were. Waistcoated waiters circulated with trays of beautifully presented hors d'oeuvres and glasses of champagne.

The richly furnished room clearly awed some of the guests with its French Empire furniture, luxurious gold drapes, and portraits of early presidents adorning the royal blue walls. It was an elegant and imposing setting, offering a glimpse of power and luxury that came naturally to few Americans.

Prince Ibrahim al Saud sipped a glass of mineral water and studied the glittering crowd through narrowed eyes. He was not one to be impressed by such surroundings. Even though he was only one of thousands of princes in Saudi Arabia, he'd been born to privilege and wealth—and the power that wealth provided.

The prince was relatively inconspicuous among all the other Middle Easterners invited to this reception and dinner for the visiting Egyptian President. Only a few of the guests recognized him on sight, and then usually as the chairman of Caraco.

The ebb and flow in the crowded room brought an elegantly coiffed elderly woman into the small circle of guests around Ibrahim. Diamonds sparkled on her fingers and ears. She looked in his direction, clearly intrigued.

One of the men who headed Caraco's Washington office whispered the pertinent information in his ear: "Mrs. Carleton. Her husband is the Undersecretary of State for Arab Affairs. She's an avid gardener. Famous for her roses."

Ibrahim nodded briefly. Carleton's wife? How ironic. He moved closer to the woman. "My dear Mrs. Carleton, what a pleasure to meet you."

She smiled back, though less certainly. "Thank you, Mr. . . . ?"

"My apologies, Mrs. Carleton. Of course you do not know me. Please forgive my impertinence, but your fame precedes you." He bowed. "My name is Prince Ibrahim al Saud."

Her eyes widened slightly. "Your Highness. The pleasure is all mine." She still seemed uncertain. "But what fame are you referring to?"

"Why, to your garden, Mrs. Carleton," Ibrahim replied. "I'm sure you know that your beautiful roses are the talk of all Washington. Such natural beauty carries a special significance for those of us reared in the barren desert."

She blushed. "Oh, how kind of you to say so, Your Highness. But really, I'm just an amateur, you know . . ."

Ibrahim listened to her prattle on with only half an ear. It was all too easy, really. A quip, a personal greeting, a reference to some favored hobby or interest—they all enabled Ibrahim to more easily play the part of a gracious, but charmingly informal, Arab prince of royal blood. As a young boy watching his father wheeling and dealing with Texas oilmen on their first visits to Saudi Arabia, he had learned the lesson that these Americans, for all their oft-professed egalitarianism, were always delighted to attract the attention of royalty.

Ibrahim smiled at that thought, though his smile never warmed the soul within his lean frame. There were other Americans, uglier Americans, who mocked anyone in whose body the blood of the Prophet flowed. He remembered such

men from his boyhood, too. For an instant, his smile faltered
and his fingers tightened around the stem of his glass. Then
he relaxed. This was not the time, or the place, to allow
those memories free rein.

When the undersecretary's wife had had her fill of his polite attention and moved on, he turned his gaze outward.

From across the room Ibrahim watched Richard Garrett
smoothly working the crowd. Garrett was Caraco's legal
representative for its American division, an unassuming title
for a very important role.

An amiable Yankee who had attended all the right schools
and knew all the right people, the former Commerce Secretary was one of the capital's most familiar and respected
faces. He was also a personal friend of the President and a
darling of the American media.

Before his stint at the Commerce Department, Garrett had
headed an extremely successful law practice in Washington.
His former clients ran the gamut from environmental groups
to tobacco companies to financial organizations to foreign
governments. Each had found their interests advanced in return for sizable fees.

Three years ago, Ibrahim had been introduced to Garrett
by a mutual friend from Harvard. It seemed to the friend
they might speak the same language of prestige and power.
Ibrahim paid Garrett well to advocate free trade, Arab-
American cooperation, and any other cause that might ad-
vance Caraco's business and political needs.

Ibrahim watched the elegantly attired, white-haired lawyer
weave in and out of the crowd, smiling and pumping hands,
laying the groundwork for future deals. He was good at what
he did and was one of the few Americans the Saudi prince
respected. Of course, respect was not trust, so the lobbyist
would never know the true nature and depth of Caraco's
corporate operations.

Garrett worked his way back to Ibrahim and took another glass of champagne. He grinned. "Things are moving our way, Your Highness. We shouldn't have any trouble getting expedited approval for the Kazakhstan pipeline contract."

"Oh?" Ibrahim asked. "So your fabled charm bears fruit again, my friend?"

"Bushels of it," Garrett confirmed. His grin grew wider. "Helped along by generous infusions of Caraco cash, of course. You have many friends in this room, Your Highness."

"Naturally." Ibrahim smiled again to himself, more warmly this time, thinking with pleasure about all those who could not detect the venomous hatred that lay beneath his polished, Western mannerisms. Education did have its uses.

He spotted a young, serious-looking presidential aide in a conservative gray suit making his way through the slowly milling crowd—coming straight toward him. Ah, he thought, at last.

The young man stopped at his side and cleared his throat importantly. "Your Highness? The President asks if you would join him in the Library. If you'll follow me?"

Ibrahim nodded. The social aspects of this evening were over. Now it was time for business. He and Garrett followed the young presidential aide out of the Blue Room, into a short hallway, and then down a flight of stairs. Since both of them had met the President before, they knew where they were headed.

At their destination, the aide stepped aside to open the door and then closed it silently behind them.

The White House Library was less formal than the grand public rooms upstairs, but it was ideally suited for quiet, private meetings. Elegantly proportioned wood chairs and bookcases lined the walls—many inlaid with representations of the American eagle, its wings open full in triumph.

The books on its shelves represented the best of American literature, as well as collections of presidential papers. The Library was intended for the private use of the President and his family. Being invited there was a mark of special favor.

The President himself stood waiting to greet Ibrahim as he entered—flanked by the current Secretary of Commerce. A second man, this one somewhat heavyset and in his mid-fifties, stood off to one side.

Ibrahim shot a questioning glance at Garrett, who whispered, "That's Dan Holcomb. With the CIA."

The Saudi ran his eyes over the stranger with more interest. He welcomed the chance to compare the reports he'd studied with the flesh-and-blood man. Holcomb was the Deputy Director of the CIA—and reputedly the real mover and shaker inside the American spy agency. The current Director was rumored to be more interested in editing position papers than in actively pursuing operations. Left to his own devices, Holcomb had apparently jumped into the leadership vacuum with gusto. His presence at this meeting was a good indication that the administration valued its "special relationship" with Caraco and its founder.

Ibrahim also noted with some amusement the absence of several other men who would have been there just months before. None of the President's political fund-raisers were anywhere in sight. Evidently America's current chief executive and his advisers had learned to be more cautious—though they were clearly still just as interested in amassing campaign and legal defense funds.

He strode forward to shake hands with the President and the other men, then took the offered seat and cup of coffee. He sipped without pleasure. A weak, thin brew—as always.

After several minutes of polite and meaningless chitchat—shared memories of student days at Oxford and Harvard and the like—Ibrahim leaned forward. "I know that your time is limited, Mr. President, so I will try not to waste any of it."

The President's eyes crinkled in amusement. "I appreciate your concern, Your Highness. Don't you worry about that, though. I've got an army of bright-eyed aides who keep me running on schedule."

Ibrahim allowed the polite fiction to pass unchallenged. This American president had a long and well-deserved reputation for tardiness. Choosing his words carefully, he continued. "Very well, then. I'm sure you know how much my companies and I support your administration—in all its endeavors, both domestic and international."

The President nodded seriously. "Naturally. And we're very grateful for your corporation's assistance, Highness."

The CIA Deputy Director, Holcomb, nodded just as seriously.

Much of Caraco's support was financial. Although present American law made direct political contributions from foreign-owned businesses illegal, the President and his party organizations had received hundreds of thousands of dollars of "soft money" donations—all ostensibly made by American-born executives of Caraco and its subsidiaries. The fact that Ibrahim made those contributions possible by paying his subordinates special bonuses was left carefully unstated. Other corporations offered larger sums, but few made their contributions so freely and so discreetly. And campaign finance reforms that would plug the loopholes Ibrahim was exploiting were still bottlenecked in the Congress by partisan infighting.

There was another side to Caraco's relationship with the administration, however—one that Holcomb and the President were both clearly aware of. From time to time, Caraco or its subsidiaries provided quiet assistance to the CIA and other U.S. intelligence organizations. Useful items of economic intelligence gathered in the course of its business operations flowed occasionally into U.S. databases. At other times, Caraco's various enterprises provided convenient cover for covert CIA activities in the Middle East and Eastern Europe.

Enjoying this little dance of deliberate ambiguity, Ibrahim smiled. Bargaining had its own long-established traditions—both in his own country and in the President's native South. Chief among them was that gifts were never true gifts. They always carried a hidden price tag. From the expectant looks on the faces of the President and his advisers, they were waiting for him to name Caraco's price. So was his own man in this room, Richard Garrett.

Idly, he wondered whether any of these American politicians would really care if they knew they had already repaid his modest cash investment in their goodwill a hundred times over. Washington, D.C., was a city that lived on rumor, gossip, and influence. Just the fact that he'd been invited to this private meeting with the nation's top leaders would enhance Ibrahim's reputation and smooth his way in any future dealings with American bureaucrats, regulators, and law enforcement officials.

Shifting slightly in his seat, the Saudi prince decided to move directly to his stated reason for seeking this meeting. He looked firmly into the eyes of the American leader. "Much as it saddens me to say so, Mr. President, I am concerned that the new congressional free trade bill with Russia is not being endorsed by your administration as strongly as it might be. I earnestly hope you will reconsider this position."

The legislation, designed to lower trade barriers with Russia and Eastern Europe, had been sponsored by a bipartisan coalition, but administration support had been lukewarm—at best.

The President and the others in the room nodded gravely. Since the end of the Cold War, Caraco and its various subsidiaries had been expanding rapidly into the territories of the former Soviet Union. Caraco-owned companies were busy pursuing a wide range of enterprises—involving themselves in everything from modernizing Russian oil production and refining to importing Western-made consumer and electronic goods. Given the huge sums his corporation had invested in the region, Ibrahim's acute interest in U.S. policy there was easy to understand.

The President leaned forward, his manner becoming more animated and less formal. He clearly enjoyed discussing and debating even the smallest details of policy. "Well, now, Highness, I'll agree with you that this Russian free trade bill is a fine idea—in principle. But let's speak practically for a moment, shall we? The truth is, most of the old Eastern bloc countries are critically short of the hard currency they'd need to buy our products. And some of my advisers are worried that lifting all trade restrictions now would just open up another source of cheap labor—draining away more American jobs."

In translation, Ibrahim knew, that meant that the American labor unions which were among this administration's most ardent backers were unwilling to tolerate yet another free trade pact they believed would put their members' jobs at risk.

He smiled warmly. "Ah, but Mr. President, you and I both know the benefits of fair and aboveboard trade far outweigh any such risks. Surely you've seen Dr. Wohlmayer's most recent analysis of the subject?"

As Ibrahim intended, that sparked a prolonged debate on the advantages and disadvantages of tariffs and free trade—one that eminently suited this president's tendency both to show off his own knowledge and to micromanage all aspects of his administration.

Fifteen or so minutes later, the Saudi prince noticed the eyes of the others in the room drifting to the clock or to their watches. Without batting an eyelash, he gracefully brought the conversation to a close, leaving the President with a calm, final request that "your administration study the matter intently and offer as much support for this legislation as possible."

"Your Highness," the President responded politely, "you can rest assured we'll do everything we can to accommodate you in this matter."

Which meant nothing, Ibrahim knew. Not that he really cared one way or another. Meeting the President privately—and, more important—*being seen* to meet the President privately—had been his primary objective. His interest in the free trade bill for Russia and Eastern Europe was purely academic. After all, who knew better than he that America's days as the economic and political arbiter of the world were numbered?

Once upstairs in the Blue Room again, Ibrahim said good night to Garrett and asked one of the White House staff to summon his car. He'd done what he had come to do. He had no need to rub elbows with any more American politicians.

Strolling into the warm, Washington night, he spotted his limousine waiting at the curb and got in. As it pulled away, he poured himself a cup of strong Middle Eastern coffee and scanned the faxes waiting for him on the tray. As usual, there were numerous fires to extinguish.

Then one caught his eye.

FROM: ARRUS EXPORT, INC.—
MOSCOW OFFICE
TO: CHAIRMAN, CARACO
TEXT: Goods en route
END MESSAGE

Prince Ibrahim al Saud settled back into the comfortable leather seat and smiled broadly.

May 29—Hotel National, Moscow

FBI Deputy Assistant Director Lawrence McDowell slipped off his suit jacket, examined it for unsightly creases, and then carefully hung it up in the spacious closet of his hotel room. Then he padded across the plush carpet and pulled open the door of the room's minibar. Smiling, he took out a small bottle of Scotch and examined the label. It was Glenfiddich, of course.

Newly renovated and supervised by consultants from Forte Hotels, the Hotel National believed in serving its guests the very best of everything. Originally built in 1903, the National's gilt chandeliers and frescoed ceilings had survived the Revolution intact. And, over the decades, its luxuries had prompted any number of the famous and infamous to stay there—H.G. Wells, Anatole France, and John Reed, to name a few. Even Lenin.

Still amused at the thought of sharing quarters once enjoyed by the founding father of the Soviet state, McDowell dropped ice into a glass and poured two fingers' worth of Scotch over the cubes. Then, savoring his drink, he ambled back to the large windows and stared out across the Kremlin's red-brick walls, gold-domed cathedrals, and palaces. No doubt about it. The Hotel National had the best accommodations and view in Moscow. Well worth the $450 a night price tag. Especially since his bill was being covered by the U.S. taxpayer.

McDowell raised his glass in a mock toast to his absent

fellow citizens and took another sip of the smooth, smoky Glenfiddich. Thank God for his expense account and that ever-useful phrase "necessary official expenditures." He'd been offered a room in the U.S. Embassy's guest quarters— an offer he'd hastily declined. Why suffer through govern-ment-issue State Department hospitality when you could live like a czar? His stay here might even make up for the exhausting, whirlwind trip he'd been forced to make to that godforsaken air crash site.

Well, he thought smugly, at least the trip hadn't been a complete waste. He'd been able to take Helen Gray and her soldier boy down a notch or two. His comments on that re-lationship in her personnel file should make damning read-ing at her next promotion review.

The phone rang, abruptly ending that pleasurable train of thought.

McDowell scooped it up, expecting it to be the concierge confirming his dinner reservation for the evening. One of the National's four restaurants was the Moscow offshoot of Maxim's of Paris.

He was wrong.

"Is this Mr. McDowell? Mr. Lawrence McDowell?" It was a middle-aged man's voice, smooth, assured, educated, and with just the trace of an accent.

"This is McDowell."

"Mr. McDowell, my name is Wolf, Heinrich Wolf. I rep-resent Secure Investments, Limited. I'm calling about your local commodities account."

The FBI official flushed angrily. Jesus, he'd heard that Moscow was turning into a center for wild and woolly cap-italism, but he'd never expected a salesman to get through the Hotel National's switchboard. This guy probably had a standing bribe out to the operators for info on any high rollers who checked in.

Still scowling, he growled, "Look, Mr. Wolf, or whatever your name is, I don't have an account with your company. And I don't want an account. So you can just save your sales pitch."

The man on the other end simply chuckled. "Of course you've done business with us, Mr. McDowell. We worked together years ago. In fact, we invested quite heavily in you—and in your career. Don't you remember your PEREGRINE account?"

PEREGRINE? McDowell paled. It couldn't be. Not now. Not after all these years. He was safe. He should have been safe. He clutched the phone tighter. "What did you say?"

"You heard me very clearly: PEREGRINE," the voice said calmly. "So you do remember us, then?"

Suddenly cold and dizzy, McDowell sat down in a chair. He licked his lips that felt as dry as bone. "But you don't exist anymore! You're all gone. Dead. Finished. Kaput."

"Come now, Mr. McDowell," the other man chided. "Old firms may go under or change hands . . . but you know that debts and obligations never disappear. They must always be paid—sooner or later."

Lawrence McDowell sat silent in his chair, still holding the phone with numb fingers—listening in mounting fear while the man who called himself Heinrich Wolf calmly outlined just what he would have to do to meet his old obligations.

CHAPTER FOUR

DATA STREAM

MAY 29

Crash Investigation Base Camp, Northern Russia

FBI Special Agent Helen Gray stared down at the jumble of scorched tubing and pieces of crumpled metal spread out across a folding table. The NTSB's chief investigator Robert Nielsen, Alexei Koniev, and Peter Thorn stood close by, studying the same pile of debris.

Even without looking directly at him, she could sense Peter's rigid self-control and utterly expressionless face. Ever since that bastard McDowell had walked in on them yesterday, he had avoided anything but strictly professional behavior toward her. Whenever they met, it was "Special Agent Gray" this and "ma'am" that.

It didn't take ESP or a degree in psychology to read his mind. Angry at himself for having caused her trouble, Peter was busy beating himself up—all in the name of some chivalrous, self-denying impulse to spare her further humiliation. It was all very old-fashioned, and also absolutely unnecessary in her opinion.

Helen sighed silently in frustration. One of the things about Peter Thorn that had first attracted her to him was his readiness to admit her competence and to acknowledge her skills. Very few of the men she'd ever worked with—let alone dated—would do that. Even when she'd showed them she could beat them at their own games, most just patted her on the head and drifted off—probably wondering why this strange woman worked so hard to master "masculine" abilities.

Peter had been different. Even after she'd been wounded, he'd pushed her hard to get back on her feet and onto active FBI duty—just as hard as she had ever pushed herself. He'd also known that she had to fight her own battles. She'd loved him more than ever for that.

But he'd changed over these past few months. He seemed more hesitant—less sure of himself and of his place in her heart.

Part of that was her fault, Helen knew. She'd allowed herself to be swept up in the excitement of her new assignment. Tracking illegal drugs, money laundering, arms smuggling, and the other booming ventures of Russia's organized crime syndicates was often a twenty-four-hour-a-day job—one that made maintaining a relationship across eight time zones and thousands of miles immensely difficult.

Of course, the time they'd spent together here hadn't been very conducive to romance, Helen thought ruefully. She and Peter were two birds of a feather. Neither of them found it particularly easy to open their hearts to another person—even under the best of circumstances. Being dead-tired most of the time made that more difficult still. And the lack of privacy only compounded their woes. It was tough to rekindle physical and emotional intimacy when you were liable to be walked in on at any moment. So far, they were exactly .000 for two on that score, Helen realized, blushing as she remembered the knowing leer on McDowell's face.

"Have you seen enough, Miss Gray?" Robert Nielsen's dry, precise voice broke in on her thoughts, tugging her back to the case at hand.

Helen refocused her attention on the wreckage heaped in front of her. She turned to the head of the NTSB investigative team. "So what exactly am I looking at here, Mr. Nielsen?"

"Part of the An-32's port engine." The tall, gaunt man nodded toward the table. "One of the recovery crews found it at the bottom of a pond last night."

"And the starboard engine?" she asked.

Nielsen shook his head. "They haven't recovered it yet."

"But you've learned something about what caused this engine to seize up?" Helen prodded.

"Yes." Nielsen pulled a length of gnarled, threaded sleeve off the table. "This is the housing for the engine fuel filter. Now take a look at what we found inside it."

Straining slightly, the NTSB man unscrewed the sleeve—exposing another, smaller sleeve inside. Then he reached inside and extracted a blackened cylinder.

"That's the filter itself?" Peter asked quietly.

Nielsen nodded. He held it up for closer inspection. "See that?"

"See what?" Helen peered intently at the filter. It looked pitch-black against the light. "I can't see anything."

"That's exactly my point," Nielsen replied. "You should be able to see the light shining through the mesh screens on this filter."

He tapped the cylinder with one gloved finger. "But this filter is clogged, Miss Gray. It's choked with so many contaminants that I'm not surprised this engine seized up."

Alexei Koniev raised an eyebrow. "Contaminants? What kind of contaminants?"

"Dirt. Metal shavings. Rust particles." The NTSB man ticked them off on his fingers. "It's all the kind of crap you expect to find in most aviation fuel—just multiplied about a thousand times over the normal levels."

Helen framed her next question carefully, conscious that she was treading on touchy ground. Like most people in his profession, Nielsen hated being asked to arrive at hard-and-fast conclusions ahead of the evidence. "This fuel contamination . . . do you think it could have happened accidentally? Or does it look deliberate?"

"Was it sabotage, you mean?" Nielsen pursed his lips, looking down at the dirty filter he still held in his hand. Then he shook his head. "I don't know, Miss Gray. Not with any degree of certainty."

"So speculate, then," Helen said sharply, momentarily losing patience. With effort, she reined her irritation in and tried a winning smile instead. "Please."

"Damn it, it's not that simple," Nielsen grumbled. "We've had bad fuel bring down planes in the U.S. And it's an endemic problem here in Russia. What's more, both engines would draw from the same fuel source. So when one engine died of fuel starvation, the second would follow in short order."

"All of which is consistent with the last radio transmissions from the aircraft," Helen reflected.

"Right." Nielsen held the filter up again. "What we're seeing here could just be sloppy maintenance. Contaminants like these always settle out over time. So we may have a case where somebody really screwed up. Maybe they didn't replace an old, used filter when they should have. Or maybe they fueled the plane using aviation gas from the bottom of a tank . . ."

"Or maybe somebody did the same things—on purpose," Peter finished for him.

"That is possible, Colonel," Nielsen confirmed reluctantly. "The mechanics are the same either way. And the equation's the same, too: The more contaminants flow through the filter, the more clogged it gets. Eventually, there's not enough fuel getting through to feed the engine."

Koniev frowned. "Is there any way you will ever know the truth?"

The NTSB investigator sighed. "Maybe. At least I hope so." He nodded at the tangled pile of engine components. "We're shipping all this off to Moscow this evening for more detailed forensic analysis."

Then Nielsen shrugged. "But there's a limit to what we'll learn about this accident through an electron microscope." He turned his gaze on the three of them. "You might have more luck on your end."

"Meaning that whatever went wrong at Kandalaksha had a human component?" Helen said calmly.

"That's exactly what I mean, Miss Gray," Nielsen agreed.

"Very well." Major Alexei Koniev straightened up. He turned to Helen. "So we go to Kandalaksha?"

Helen nodded firmly. "Yes, Alexei. I think that's exactly what we'll do." Her eyes narrowed. "And then we'll take a good, hard look at the maintenance operation there—and at the people who readied this plane for takeoff."

"Good." The Russian MVD officer turned toward Peter Thorn. "Will you accompany us, Colonel?"

Helen held her breath. Peter was already pushing the envelope of his watching brief as a liaison to the crash investigation. Especially since his superiors at OSIA had been reluctant to let him come to Russia at all. And none of the paper pushers in Washington would be happy if they found out that their least favorite ex–Delta Force officer had actively joined the hunt for whatever, or whoever, had brought the An-32 down. That might even give them the ammunition they needed to force him out of the Army entirely. How could she blame him if he opted for the safer course and stayed behind?

But she also knew that would probably spell the end of any future they might have as a couple. If she headed for Kandalaksha without him, they wouldn't see each other again before he had to leave for the States. And if he chose the safer career course, his own wounded pride would always stand between them.

"Well, Colonel?" Koniev asked again.

Peter hesitated, visibly restraining himself from turning toward her, and then nodded decisively. "I'm in, Major."

"You're sure, Peter?" Helen heard herself ask.

"I'm sure." He smiled tightly at her, a fleeting grin that flashed across his tanned, taut face and than vanished. "I wouldn't miss this for the world."

MAY 30

Headquarters, 125th Air Division, Kandalaksha

(D MINUS 22)

Colonel General Feodor Serov reached for the phone on his desk and then stopped. Instead he glanced again at the fax he'd just received from the Ministry of Defense—as though hoping he could find the inspiration for some alternative course of action in its terse directives.

No, he thought somberly, scanning the flimsy sheet of paper for the tenth time, there were no other options left. Much as he hated it, he would have to seek assistance—and quickly.

Without hesitating further, Serov turned back to the phone and punched in the emergency contact number he'd been given. Then, while waiting for the call to go through, he flipped the switch on the high-tech scrambler his "business associates" had assured him would thwart electronic eavesdropping.

"Yes." The voice on the other end was impersonal, emotionless.

Serov grimaced. "This is Colonel General Serov. I need to speak to Reichardt. The matter is urgent."

"Wait."

The line went silent for several seconds while Reichardt's subordinate patched the call through to his superior.

"What is the problem now, Feodor Mikhailovich?" the German asked icily.

Although the emergency number carried a Moscow prefix, Serov knew modern cellular telephone technology meant Reichardt could be anywhere in the world right now. He might be in London, Paris, or New York. He might also be right outside the headquarters building itself again—waiting with murderous intent inside yet another unmarked staff car. The ex-Stasi agent had already shown his ability to move through Kandalaksha's security undetected and unchallenged. It was almost as though the German was a ghost, or a demon.

Serov suppressed a shiver. He was a man, a soldier, and a fighter pilot—not a babe in swaddling clothes to be frightened by old wives' tales of werewolves and witches.

"Well?" Reichardt demanded.

"There are new . . . complications . . . in the crash investigation that may require your action, Herr Reichardt," Serov said slowly, dragging the words through clenched, unwilling teeth.

"Complications?"

"I've received new orders from the Ministry of Defense," Serov explained. "An investigator from the MVD is on his way here now to interview my maintenance crews. I've been directed to cooperate fully with his inquiry."

"I see," Reichardt said coldly. "So Captain Grushtin's foolproof sabotage left traces."

"Possibly," Serov admitted. "Though if the aircraft had gone down over the White Sea as we hoped, we wouldn't have to worry now."

"Don't mince words with me, Feodor Mikhailovich," Reichardt snapped. "You have the MVD about to swarm around your ears, correct?"

"Yes. A Major Koniev arrives tomorrow morning."

"Koniev . . ." Reichardt paused momentarily, clearly pondering the name. Then he continued: "Very well. What is it that you wish of me?"

Serov swallowed hard, hating what he was about to do. Betraying the official trust by dealing with the ex-Stasi agent and his employer had been difficult enough. Betraying one's own comrades was harder still. But then the faces of his wife and children rose in his mind, reminding him of the price of failure. He set his misgivings aside. "There is a potential weak link."

"Grushtin," Reichardt guessed.

"Yes," Serov confirmed. "Nikolai is a talented mechanic and artificer, but I'm afraid he is not a good liar."

"Unfortunate," Reichardt said simply. "So where is the gifted Captain Grushtin now? On the base?"

Serov shook his head unconsciously. "No. I sent him on leave once he finished his work on the project. As a reward, you understand."

"Where is he then?" the German demanded.

"Moscow."

"Moscow," Reichardt repeated. "Where exactly?"

Serov told him.

Reichardt did not even bother to hide the sudden wolfish hunger in his voice. "Excellent, Feodor Mikhailovich. It appears that Captain Nikolai Grushtin may yet perform another service for us, after all."

MAY 31

Maintenance Hangar, Secondary Runway, Kandalaksha

Helen Gray leaned close to Peter Thorn's ear and whispered, "Jesus Christ! If this is an example of Colonel General Serov's full cooperation, I'd sure hate to see him stone-walling."

Peter nodded grimly.

The Russian base commander had set aside an empty, unused hangar for their use. As a place to conduct confidential interviews it left much to be desired. With the doors open, the noise from the Kandalaksha flight line was deafening. With the doors closed, the unheated hangar's thick concrete walls trapped both the nighttime cold and the lingering reek of spilled fuel, oil, and grease. Crude drawings and coarse jokes left spray-painted on the walls by long-discharged Russian conscripts added to the general air of disrepair.

Nor were the other aspects of Serov's "cooperation" much better.

At the Russian general's insistence, one of his top aides, a lean, hatchet-faced colonel named Petrov, sat in on every interview—perched across the table in full view of every hapless enlisted man they questioned. Tough-looking sentries wearing body armor and toting AK-74 assault rifles were also posted at the hangar entrance.

Serov had explained these steps as a necessary precaution, given the presence of nuclear weapons at Kandalaksha. "We take security very seriously here, Miss Gray," he had said, and then, with a sidelong glance at Peter Thorn's U.S. Army uniform, "although it is clear that others in the Ministry of Defense do not share my concerns."

Bull, Helen thought. She'd bet cold, hard cash that the Russian general's precautions were intended to intimidate potential witnesses—not to protect nukes that were stored in bombproof bunkers miles away.

If she was right, the worst of it was that Serov's plan was working. So far all of the ground crewmen they'd interviewed had insisted that nothing out of the ordinary occurred while the OSIA inspection team's An-32 was being readied for takeoff. She didn't believe them. Nobody liked being questioned by the police, but there were too many hesitations, too many nervous glances at Serov's aide, too many dry mouths, and too many sweaty brows for her to buy their stories.

No. Something had gone badly wrong out there on the Kandalaksha flight line. But they still didn't know whether to pin the blame on sloppy procedures or deliberate sabotage.

Frustrated, Helen turned her attention back to the aircraft mechanic Alexei Koniev was questioning. She couldn't follow the rapid-fire flow of Russian, but she could read body language plainly. The mechanic, a private, had flat, Asiatic features that marked him out as a native of Russia's Far East. A nervous tic near the corner of one eye told her he was frightened.

Koniev snapped out a question, listened briefly to the private's hesitant, uncertain reply, and then waved him away in disgust.

"No dice?" Helen asked.

"Nothing," Koniev snorted. He nodded toward the mechanic, already hurrying out of the hangar. "According to that one, the sky was blue. The birds were singing. The flowers were in bloom. And he and his comrades did everything humanly possible to make sure that plane was ready to fly."

Peter Thorn leaned over. "Who's next?"

Koniev glanced down at the unit roster open on the table in front of him. "A Lieutenant Vladimir Chernavin." He frowned. "Perhaps the lieutenant will demonstrate his fitness to be a member of the officer class by telling us something resembling the truth."

Helen shrugged her shoulders. "Maybe."

Despite her skepticism, she had to admit that Chernavin made a better first impression than his subordinates. The lieutenant was short, an inch or so below her own five foot ten, but he was solidly built—carrying enough muscle to show that he did his own share of the grunt work out on the flight line. Close-cropped brown hair topped a round, open, boyish face that proclaimed his youth. He also had a ready, infectious smile.

Chernavin took the chair Koniev indicated. His eyes took in Peter's military uniform and widened. "You are American?" he asked in passable English.

After a quick glance at Koniev, Peter nodded. "Colonel Thorn, U.S. Army." He indicated Helen. "And this is Special Agent Gray of the U.S. Federal Bureau of Investigation."

The Russian lieutenant grinned excitedly. "I am very glad to meet you, Colonel! And you, Miss Gray."

Helen didn't even try to conceal her surprise. "Really, Lieutenant? Then you're the first person I've run across here at Kandalaksha who's happy to talk to us. Most of your subordinates seem to think we're either spies or secret policemen."

Chernavin's open, friendly face clouded over. "Ah." He shrugged. "Then they are ignorant peasants. Their heads are still stuffed full of the old Cold War propaganda. They have not studied America and its marvels as I have."

The young Russian brightened again. "I hope to visit your country one day, you see! So I am not afraid."

"You do know we're here to investigate your unit's work on the An-32 that crashed eleven days ago?" Koniev cut in impatiently. "You understand that, Lieutenant Chernavin?"

"Of course."

Helen fought to keep her face impassive. The Russian Air Force lieutenant seemed blissfully unconcerned by their inquiry. Why? She leaned forward. "It doesn't bother you that an aircraft you worked on went down in the woods shortly after taking off from here—killing everyone on board?"

Chernavin lowered his gaze. "Oh, no. No. I did not mean that." He looked up at Helen. "Of course, I am very, very sorry that all those people died. It is a great tragedy, naturally. A great tragedy."

"A tragedy? Not an accident? Not a disaster?" Koniev said skeptically. "Explain that, Lieutenant."

The young Russian officer spread his hands apart. "I only meant that, whatever caused the aircraft to go down, it had nothing to do with the work performed here at Kandalaksha."

Helen smiled at Chernavin. If Koniev wanted to grab the tough guy spot in the good cop–bad cop routine, she would oblige. "You seem very sure of that, Lieutenant."

He nodded emphatically. "Yes."

"Why?" Koniev rapped out. "Why are you so sure, Chernavin?"

"Because Captain Grushtin handled the preflight check himself," the Russian maintenance officer said confidently.

Grushtin? Helen glanced down at the maintenance records in front of her. She'd spent enough time in Russia to puzzle out the Cyrillic alphabet, and Koniev had scribbled a hasty translation of the Air Force technical terms and jargon. She looked up at the young Russian officer. "Just who is this Captain Grushtin, Lieutenant?"

For the first time, Chernavin seemed unsure of himself. "Captain Nikolai Grushtin is one of the chief maintenance officers on the base." His gaze swiveled from Helen to Koniev and back again. "He is a brilliant mechanic. Brilliant. So you see, that is why I am confident that this crash had nothing to do with our work here."

Koniev slid his own copy of the An-32 maintenance log across the table toward the younger man. "If this Captain Grushtin performed the preflight check himself, Chernavin, perhaps you can tell me why he is not listed in this log . . . or anywhere else for that matter!"

Clearly surprised, the lieutenant stared down at the papers for a moment. Then he snapped his fingers and looked up. "Captain Grushtin is not listed because he was not officially assigned to supervise the ground crews on that day. The log would only show those of us on that morning's flight line roster."

Helen felt her heart rate quicken—aware that it was the same sensation she used to have on the Hostage Rescue Team firing range when the first real target popped up. She shook her head. "So this Grushtin character just showed up unannounced and you let him handle the An-32 maintenance work?"

Chernavin nodded. "Of course. He is my superior officer."

"And that didn't seem strange to you?" she pressed further.

"No . . ." the Russian lieutenant said slowly. He tried to explain. "The captain is a perfectionist and this was an important flight—one with so many foreigners aboard. I thought he just wanted to make certain the aircraft was readied according to his standards."

I bet he did, Helen thought coldly. She sat back while Koniev took the ball.

"And you found nothing unusual in this—even after the plane crashed?" The MVD major glowered across the table at Chernavin. "Why was that, Lieutenant?"

The Russian Air Force officer reddened. He lowered his gaze, unable to meet Koniev's glare. "Well, you see, I . . ."

He wanted to duck any responsibility for the crash, Helen realized suddenly. And Grushtin's intervention gave him a convenient out. If Kandalaksha's most "brilliant" mechanic had missed something in the preflight check, then how could anyone blame a young junior officer like him? Her mouth twisted in distaste as she stared at Chernavin. She'd never been able to stomach people who tried to dodge accountability for their own actions.

"If Captain Grushtin wasn't managing the flight line that day, what was his official duty assignment?" Peter Thorn asked abruptly.

Chernavin looked startled. He glanced quickly at Serov's aide and lowered his voice. "He was in charge of a special project." The Russian lieutenant nodded pointedly toward Thorn's American uniform and said knowingly, "The special *engine* project."

What the hell was this "special engine project," Helen wondered, and why did Chernavin seem to expect Peter to know all about it? Was there any connection at all between Gasparov's heroin smuggling, the cryptic notation in John Avery's inspection log, and this "project"? Or were they looking at a series of unrelated events?

"That's quite enough, Lieutenant!" Colonel Boris Petrov loudly interrupted, breaking her train of thought.

Chernavin fell silent, looking more worried than ever.

Serov's top aide scowled at Koniev. "Your authorization for this inquiry does not include prying into unrelated state secrets, Major! Especially not in front of foreigners! So you will confine your questions to matters involving the An-32 and the ground crews. Is that clear?"

Alexei Koniev stiffened in anger, and Helen braced herself for the explosion. Several months spent working closely with the MVD major had shown her that he had a deeply hidden temper. It rarely showed itself, but interference in the performance of what he perceived as his duty was the one thing guaranteed to set him off.

Koniev's cell phone chirped unexpectedly—heading off his intended reply. Impatiently, he flipped it open. "Yes. Koniev speaking."

The MVD officer listened intently for a time, his face growing angrier by the minute. Finally, he gripped the phone tighter and responded, "I see. You're quite sure? Very well. I'll call you back."

Koniev snapped his phone shut and turned toward Helen and Peter. His lips were compressed in a thin, tight line. "The lab tests on the recovered engine came back. There were fresh tool scrapes on the fuel filter."

"Meaning what?" Helen asked softly.

"Meaning that Captain Grushtin or one of his men changed the engine fuel filter here at Kandalaksha—and deliberately installed a contaminated replacement," Koniev said bluntly. "The evidence is conclusive. The plane carrying Colonel Gasparov, his shipment, and your OSIA inspection team was sabotaged."

He whirled on Serov's aide. "This investigation is now a formal murder inquiry, Colonel Petrov. Do you agree?"

The other man nodded reluctantly. "It appears so, Major. As difficult as I find that to believe."

"I don't give a damn what you believe, Colonel! And I don't give a damn about your so-called state secrets," Koniev said savagely. "I expect your full cooperation—real cooperation—this time."

Petrov stiffened. "Very well."

"Good." Koniev eyed him carefully. "Then you, or Colonel General Serov, will tell us *exactly* where we can find this Captain Nikolai Grushtin. Or you and your commanding officer will explain your refusal to assist us in even less comfortable and less convenient quarters. In Moscow. Is that understood?"

Sitting rigidly upright in his chair, the other man nodded slowly. He seemed completely cowed.

But later Helen found herself wondering uneasily why the hatchet-faced Russian colonel's lips had twitched briefly into what looked remarkably like a self-satisfied smirk.

JUNE 1

Proprietary Materials Assembly Building, Caraco Complex, Chantilly, Virginia

(D MINUS 20)

Caraco's Washington-area regional headquarters lay in the middle of the green, wooded countryside surrounding Dulles International Airport. Broad streets, grassy lawns, and patches of oak and pine forest left standing around homes and office buildings gave the area something of a rural feel—despite the fact that it was only a few scant miles from the western edge of Washington's urban sprawl.

Seen from the outside, the Caraco compound was almost wholly unremarkable. It blended well with the neighboring modern-looking office parks and light industrial complexes fanning out from the airport. Its large, boxy buildings were pleasantly anonymous, practical, and architecturally uninteresting—similar in style to dozens of others bearing different corporate logos and names like "Vortech" and "EDC, Inc."

Even the compound's chain-link fence, perimeter floodlights, and twenty-four-hour guards were not out of the ordinary. Many of the area's high-tech electronics firms had tens of millions of dollars in manufacturing equipment and industrial secrets to protect.

But the fence, lighting, and guards were only the visible signs of a much more complete, almost sentient security system. A network of computer-controlled video cameras and motion sensors had been woven around the border of the compound to detect any unauthorized human or machine intrusion. All incoming phone, fax, and data lines were constantly monitored for signs of electronic eavesdropping, and all the external windows were double-paned and vacuum-sealed to thwart laser bugging.

Two of Caraco's three buildings contained offices, meeting rooms, computer centers, and file storage areas—all the run-of-the-mill trappings of any building owned by a large multinational corporation. But the third building was different—very different.

Guards armed with Heckler & Koch MP5 submachine guns were stationed just inside the main door. Special identification badges were required to gain entrance—something none of Caraco's American-born employees carried.

Inside, the warehouse-sized building was divided into several areas by movable partitions. All the activity was in one area, just off the main entrance. Racks of electronic equipment lined one wall, while the others were covered with wiring diagrams and enlarged photos of a twin-turboprop aircraft.

The floor was crowded with benches, each covered with tools and electronic equipment. Half a dozen technicians sat at the benches—peering at oscilloscope screens, or methodically assembling electronic components.

They conversed easily in low tones, their German mixing with country-western music playing from a boom box on a table next to a coffee machine.

The room had a hard, industrial feel, with nothing personal, no prints or photos, no newspaper clippings anywhere in sight. The only item not related to the workplace was the radio, now belting out a Clint Black tune.

One of the technicians finished wiring a piece of gear, nodded to himself, and called across the room, "Klaus? Unit Number Three is ready."

A man in his fifties, at least twenty years older than the rest of the technicians, balding with gray, close-cut hair on the sides, walked over from another workbench. "You remembered the interlocks this time, I hope?" he asked, half joking and half serious.

"Yes, Klaus. I checked them twice before calling you," the young German technician answered respectfully.

They knew and used only first names in the project, and his was Franz, at least as long as this job lasted. He was in his early twenties with a smooth-shaven head, and he knew the older man still couldn't get used to the small gold loop piercing his left eyebrow. His training was good, however—

the best available from one of Germany's top technical schools. He knew electronics.

Caraco had recruited him straight out of school, promising only foreign work and high pay. Very high. Franz had hesitated only momentarily before agreeing to what he suspected was some sort of illegal activity. After all, he had come to the United States on a tourist visa—not on one that permitted him paid employment. The working conditions inside the Caraco compound were hard, almost Spartan. Security was tight. And his new employers had made it clear that questions, of any kind, were unwelcome—perhaps even dangerous.

None of that mattered much to the young technician. Germany's "miracle" economy had stagnated over the past decade. Most of his peers and friends were still unemployed—reduced to living on the public dole or squatting in abandoned buildings. Well, not him. For this two months' work, he would make enough to live decently while finding a more permanent position. If Caraco wanted to bend a few petty American laws as part of the bargain, so be it.

To demonstrate his success, Franz, humming along with the radio, touched a test probe to several connections inside the device.

The older man watched carefully and then nodded, pleased. "Very good. All right, let's do a navigation check."

Franz disconnected the unit from the bench's power supply and picked it up by two built-in handles. Holding it with respect, he followed Klaus over to a long workbench in the far corner of the room.

Together, they fitted the new device, which had a curved underside, to the top of a similarly curved metal plate. Connectors in the device mated with sockets in the plate.

Referring to a checklist tacked up next to the workbench, Franz pressed a square green button on the front panel. Several small green LEDs lit up, and a display on the front came to life. It was blank for only a moment, then showed the number 1. Another pause and it increased—flickering from 2, to 3, and then on up to 7 in rapid succession. After a few seconds more, an 8 appeared.

Below the green glowing number, several more numbers appeared—latitude, longitude, and an elevation above sea level. They matched the numbers posted prominently on the wall above the workbench, but both men had long ago memorized them.

In theory, it was possible to obtain a good global positioning system (GPS) fix using the signals transmitted by just three satellites, but first-rate accuracy demanded five. The precise number available depended both on the location of the receiver and the orbits of the twenty-four operational GPS satellites. There were always enough above any observer's horizon for a decent fix, and often enough for an excellent one.

Another light glowed on the unit.

"Receiving DGPS correction data," Franz reported.

"Very good." Klaus grinned. "Convey my thanks to the U.S. Coast Guard and all the other companies providing us with such services."

The younger German matched the older man's grin. The signals transmitted by the GPS satellites were carefully degraded so that civilian-owned receivers couldn't match the accuracy of those used by the American armed forces. Differential GPS, or DGPS, was a technique used to correct those errors. Software inside base station receivers matched their precisely known location against that supplied by GPS, and transmitted error correction data to mobile receivers within range. The U.S. Coast Guard and a number of private companies had set up systems of radio beacons across North

America—supplying constant error corrections to anyone with the appropriate equipment.

Standard civilian GPS sets could provide a navigation fix accurate to within one hundred meters horizontally and one hundred fifty meters vertically. Using five satellite signals and DGPS error correction, those same sets could provide a fix accurate to within one meter.

Satisfied that the device's GPS sub-system was on-line and working, the two men carefully checked yet another set of lights above the test panel. All were green.

Franz made a notation. "The computer is up and running, Klaus."

"Good," the older man grunted. He checked a pair of readouts on the workbench. "The processors are in sync. And the data feed is operational."

The two German technicians tested several more functions on the panel, then, satisfied, disconnected the device. Then the man called Klaus watched as Franz placed it on a rack against one wall—next to several other pieces of electronics. He allowed the younger man one moment of satisfaction before ordering him back to work.

Caraco had them on a tight schedule.

CHAPTER FIVE

LOOSE ENDS

JUNE 1

Near Bergen, Norway

(D MINUS 20)

"Bornestangen light bears three two five."

Captain Pavel Tumarev grunted in reply, studying the radar scope. The Don radar set was stepped down to its shortest range setting, for maximum detail. Even then, he could see three other ships, one in the channel ahead of him and two others in the outbound channel approaching him, but separated by a goodly distance. *Star of the White Sea* was in her place, on the starboard side of the crowded channel.

Bergen was one of the busiest ports in Scandinavia—a hub for North Sea oil exploration, fishing, and bulk cargo transport.

Norwegian radar stations watched all the merchant traffic and Channel 13 crackled with directions from Bergen traffic control. Tumarev's ship had been under positive control since passing Sjerkaget light, but if he collided with something, traffic control wouldn't take responsibility for it.

"Bornestangen light bears three three zero," reported the port bearing taker.

"Range to Venten Mountain?" Tumarev asked. There was an edge to his question. The radar operator was supposed to report the range every half minute, but he was late.

"Fifty-three hundred meters."

His first officer looked up from the chart table. "Navigator recommends immediate turn to three three five degrees."

"Come left to three three five," ordered Tumarev. "Watch the current." They were on an ebb tide, and it might push them out of the channel if they didn't pay attention.

Tumarev scanned the bridge, then stepped out on the port bridge wing to watch the ship swing. He sensed someone follow him out and knew it was Dietrich Kleiner, Arrus Export's "senior representative" on board. A nice enough fellow, Tumarev thought sourly, as long as you didn't try to talk to him or mess up somehow.

Kleiner had ridden his ship many times, always into Bergen. He always departed at that port—often without saying so much as a word. When he did speak, he used Russian, but it was clear from more than his name that the man was German.

Tumarev grimaced at his own understatement. Kleiner, he thought, exhibited the same Teutonic craving for precision, lust for power, and contempt for Slavs that had led his damned country into two world wars and ruin.

The German was shorter than the *Star*'s captain, which was saying something, but stocky instead of just small. He weighed at least ten kilos more, and as far as Tumarev was concerned, it was all mean. He was also younger, in his mid-thirties instead of his fifties, and showed none of the traditional respect due a ship's master.

Kleiner didn't make every trip on the *Star*, praise God, but when he did he was everywhere. He seemed to know how a merchant vessel should be run, and wasn't shy about telling the captain when he thought Tumarev or his crew were slacking. Losing their Arrus Export charter was the most pleasant thing he promised.

Satisfied they were back on course, Tumarev risked a glance at his unwelcome passenger. The German was watching him with a scowl—almost as though he were disappointed the Russian hadn't put *Star of the White Sea* on the rocks.

Tumarev shrugged and went back inside. This close to the end of the fourteen-hundred-mile run from Pechenga, he had more important matters to attend to. Kleiner and his superiors at Arrus Export paid him well to carry their various cargoes out of Russia without asking inconvenient questions. But they didn't pay him enough to spend all his time worrying about licking their boots.

Although Bergen lay at the end of a twisted forty-kilometer channel, it was an excellent deepwater port. Ships of every type and size crowded the harbor—with oil tankers and container ships anchored below the same steep slopes that had once seen Viking longships unloading plunder and Hanseatic League merchantmen taking on mounds of salted fish.

Tumarev followed traffic control's instructions to Pier 91A and moored *Star of the White Sea* portside to a weathered concrete pier sheathed with wood and rubber fenders. It was late in the day, nearly 1800 hours, but the captain saw cranes waiting for his ship.

He gave the boatswain his orders.

Almost before shore power was secured, Tumarev saw the hatch covers being removed, with Kleiner standing next to the boatswain like an unwelcome shadow.

The Russian captain lit an American cigarette and, with his ship safely tied up, relaxed for a few moments, curiosity for once eclipsing his natural laziness. He stood in a shadow and tracked Kleiner while the German watched the first jet engine they were carrying being hoisted out of the *Star*'s hold. The ship had other cargo aboard—mostly dried fish and scrap metal—but his contracts with Arrus were always clear. Their shipments always got top priority.

Once the first crate was lifted off the ship, Kleiner hurried to the dock and greeted a tall, dour-looking man in a suit. Tumarev spat to one side. The Norwegian had the look of an inspector or customs official, and he had scant use for either sort. Like their counterparts in Russia, the local bureaucrats often seemed to exist only to make his life difficult and to skim off a percentage of his already meager profits in tariffs, taxes, and fees.

To his surprise, the Russian sea captain actually saw a thin smile cross Kleiner's lips as he shook the newcomer's hand. Then the Norwegian official showed his teeth, too—the kind of greedy smile one often saw on the face of someone about to receive an expected gift.

The German produced a large manila envelope and passed it to the official, then turned away, heading back up the gangplank. Tumarev, absorbed in the transaction, almost forgot to turn away himself, but he was sure he hadn't been seen. He was also sure that whatever Arrus Export's crated jet engines had been listed as on his ship's manifests, they would appear as something else entirely at their ultimate destination.

Tumarev also noticed that the engines were not being unloaded to the pier. Instead, the cargo handling cranes were swinging them—he could see three of the five crates now—directly into the hold of another ship on the other side of the pier, in 91B. He squinted at the name painted below her superstructure. *Baltic Venturer.* She appeared to be both newer than the *Star* and bigger by half. She was also moored port-side to, with her bow out. Line-handling crews and a tug were already standing by.

The Russian snorted. Evidently, Kleiner's employers weren't planning to waste any time in moving their newly transshipped cargo out of Norwegian territorial waters. But then they never did.

Well, it was none of his business, Tumarev reminded himself. He had a ship to take care of. Left to her own devices, *Star of the White Sea* would probably take them all to the bottom in a cloud of rust. He tossed his cigarette over the side and went below to remind the engineer about the need to check their starboard fuel pump.

When he came back on deck an hour later, the *Baltic Venturer* was already underway—steaming back down the narrow, winding channel toward the open North Sea.

FBI Legal Attaché Office, U.S. Embassy, Moscow

Spring was slowly giving way to summer all across Moscow—heralded by blue, cloudless skies and longer, hotter days. Red-tinged sunlight streamed through the window in Helen Gray's fifth-floor office, dancing on dust motes swirling in the warm air.

Colonel Peter Thorn sat in a chair with his back to the window, letting the late afternoon sun relax shoulders that were still stiff from a long day spent in cramped airplane seats and uncomfortable airfield waiting rooms. Covering the thousand miles between Kandalaksha and the Russian capital had required first hopping a military cargo flight to

Arkhangelsk, and then waiting for the once-a-day commercial flight south. For now he was content to wait for Helen to finish the phone call she'd received within minutes of their return to the embassy.

He stretched his legs out and accidentally bumped into Alexei Koniev's feet. "Sorry, Major."

Koniev chuckled. "Don't worry about it, Colonel. Rabbits do not complain about their teeming warrens. Why should we be any different?"

Thorn nodded. The MVD officer's imagery was apt. One person could work comfortably in Helen's narrow office. Two people might squeeze in for a short time without driving each other crazy. But three was very definitely a crowd. When added to her desk, computer, bookshelves, and filing cabinets bulging with case files, two extra chairs left barely enough room to breathe.

His gaze drifted to the framed pictures on Helen's walls and desk. One showed her parents, brother, and two sisters. Two familiar faces smiled back at him from another photo—an older man in U.S. Army dress blues and the stars of a major general and a silver-haired woman wearing an elegant evening dress. Sam and Louisa Farrell.

They were two of the most important people in his own life.

Major General Sam Farrell had been his mentor and commanding officer for most of his years with Delta Force. Thorn knew his old friend had called in every favor he was owed to keep him in the Army after the Teheran raid. Farrell had retired the year before, but he still carried a lot of weight in the special warfare and intelligence communities. And Louisa Farrell had first introduced him to Helen.

Which brought him to the last picture—the one Helen kept prominently displayed on her desk. It was a picture of them together—a picture taken in those heady, happier days when she'd taken her first steps unaided after being wounded. Back in the days when marriage, a life together, had seemed the logical and inevitable next step to both of them.

Thorn shied away from that thought, uncomfortably aware that he didn't have any pictures of Helen displayed in his own barren office at OSIA or even in his empty town house in the Virginia suburbs. They were all packed away somewhere in envelopes. He had lived his whole life as a uniformed nomad—always ready to move on to the next post, to the next duty station. Permanence had never been part of the package. By the time he'd begun to accept the possibility, she was gone—to Moscow and this legal attaché assignment.

"*Khorosho. Da. Spasibo.*" Helen hung up her phone and looked up at her two colleagues.

"So what's the word?" Thorn asked.

She shrugged. "You want the good news first, or the bad news?"

"The good news."

Helen nodded toward the phone. "That was Titenko—the deputy head of the organized crime directorate. He finally ran a militia patrol past Grushtin's dacha earlier this afternoon."

"And?" Koniev leaned forward.

"He's there," she said. "They spotted a brand-new BMW outside. It's registered in Grushtin's name."

Thorn smiled wryly. "Nice car—especially for a guy whose salary is just a couple of hundred dollars a month." He straightened up. "So when do we pay Captain Grushtin a visit?"

Helen frowned. "That's the bad news. Titenko won't let us move without backup from an SOBR team."

Thorn mentally paged through the briefing papers he'd read. SOBR was the Russian-language acronym for the Special Detachments of Rapid Deployment—the MVD's organized crime SWAT unit.

"The SOBR?" Koniev said impatiently. "For God's sake,

why? We're talking about bringing one man in for questioning—not assaulting a drug lord's mansion!"

Helen shook her head. "General Titenko and the rest of your superiors aren't so sure about that, Alexei. After reading the report we filed from Kandalaksha, they've seized on the heroin angle to explain why Grushtin sabotaged that plane. If he is working for a smuggling syndicate, there's no telling what kind of firepower he could have hidden in that dacha."

In theory, Thorn agreed with this Titenko's caution. Rushing an operation without adequate recon or backup was a good way to get yourself killed. And he could understand why the Russians were so eager to believe the An-32 crash was drug-related. Since returning from Kandalaksha, he'd seen some of the reports crossing Helen's desk. Heroin transshipments from Southwest Asia and China through Russia to the West were on the rise. And it would make sense for the smugglers to use Russian Air Force bases as transfer points. With the right officers in their pockets, they wouldn't find it very difficult to slip large quantities of heroin onto cargo aircraft ferrying in supplies, spare parts, and personnel. As chief of maintenance at Kandalaksha, Nikolai Grushtin was ideally placed to recover such shipments from any number of different hiding places aboard the aircraft arriving at the air base.

Of course, Thorn realized, pinning the blame on the *Mafiya* also made good political sense. It made the crash an entirely Russian tragedy—turning away any suggestion that the American nuclear arms inspection team might have been the intended target. Well, he still wasn't so sure. An air base in the far northern reaches of Russia seemed awfully far from the poppy fields of Afghanistan. And the connection between the heroin they'd found in Colonel Gasparov's bag and Captain Nikolai Grushtin was still entirely theoretical. As far as he was concerned, it would stay that way until he had a chance to question the Air Force maintenance officer himself.

He cleared his throat. "Okay, so we wait for backup. Just when is this SWAT team available?"

Helen glanced out the window and then checked her watch. "Not until later tonight—after dark."

Outside Moscow

Colonel Peter Thorn crouched low beside the dark BMW parked outside Grushtin's country home. He risked a cautious glance around the bumper.

Birch trees gleamed silver in the pale light cast by the rising moon. Patches of shadow flickered in and out of existence as a cool wind stirred the trees. The sky overhead was full of stars. Moscow's lights were a distant orange glow on the northern horizon. They were thirty kilometers south of the city. The dacha itself was just meters away—separated from the rutted dirt lane by an unpainted wood fence and a stretch of weed-choked open ground.

Thorn pulled back into cover.

"Anything?" Helen Gray whispered in his ear.

"Nothing new," he reported softly. "The lights are on, but the curtains are drawn."

Koniev appeared out of the darkness, bent low, and dropped to the ground beside them. He unsnapped the holster at his side and drew an automatic pistol—a 5.45mm Makarov PSM. "The SOBR team is almost in place. They will go in first—on my signal. Are you ready?"

Thorn nodded tightly, aware that his pulse was accelerating. He glanced again at Koniev's pistol. His own hands felt empty—too empty. Neither he nor Helen was armed. The Russian authorities frowned on foreigners—even foreigners with military or law enforcement connections—carrying weapons. Koniev had only bent the rules at the An-32 crash site because Helen had been the only woman quartered among hundreds of men. Once they'd come back to Moscow, her sidearm had gone straight back into an embassy lockbox.

The Russian MVD major risked his own look around the BMW's bumper. He clicked the transmit button on a hand-held radio. *"Tri. Dva. ODIN!"*

The shadows came alive.

SOBR commandos wearing dark ski masks, jeans, running shoes, and bulky body armor charged out of concealment— covering the short distance from their hiding places to the dacha in seconds. One smashed in the front door with a sledge-hammer—covered by two more armed with AKS-74U sub-machine guns. The door crumpled, torn off at the hinges, and they poured inside. At the same time, others broke in through the ground-floor windows. More commandos armed with night scopes and sniper rifles swept their weapons through tight firing arcs—looking for targets on the upper floor.

The area fell silent again.

Suddenly, Koniev's radio crackled with a hurried report from inside the dacha. His face fell. He stood up.

Thorn stood with him. "What's wrong, Major?"

"They found Captain Grushtin," Koniev said heavily.

Helen joined them. "Good."

The Russian MVD officer shook his head tiredly. "No, not good. Come with me."

Thorn and Helen exchanged a troubled look before following Koniev inside.

The dacha's front room was packed with evidence of Grushtin's illicit activities. A Japanese-made television set, VCR, and high-end stereo system filled an imported Scandinavian entertainment center on one wall. Personal computer components sat atop a handsome oak desk in the opposite corner. An expensive Persian carpet covered the hardwood floor.

A stepladder lay on its side on the carpet, next to a high-peaked officer's cap and two empty vodka bottles.

Four SOBR commandos were inside the room, cradling their weapons in their gloved hands. All of them were staring up at the ceiling.

Thorn turned his own gaze upward.

Wearing his full Russian Air Force dress uniform—right down to his polished brown boots—Captain Nikolai Grushtin dangled from the rafters of his own ceiling. His face bulged out over the noose tied tight around his neck. Dark stains down the back of his uniform trousers showed where he had voided his bowels in death.

Thorn sighed. "Oh, hell."

"Hell, indeed," Koniev echoed him. He turned away and snapped out a question to the ranking SOBR trooper in the room. The commando stiffened to attention, hurriedly replied, and then carefully handed him a folded piece of paper.

"A suicide note?" Helen asked grimly, turning away from the body dangling above them.

"So it seems," the MVD major said cautiously. "The assault team found it on the desk over there. Right by the computer." Holding it by the edges, he carefully unfolded the piece of paper.

Thorn looked over his shoulder. Scrawled Cyrillic characters filled the page above a signature. The writing looked shaky, uneven. There were splotches where the ink had run. Were they tear stains? Or sweat?

Koniev frowned. "It's dated yesterday." Still holding the note, he began translating. " 'I, Nikolai Grushtin, write this last testament and confession in great turmoil of soul and mind. Once a loyal officer in our noble Air Force, I end my days as a murderer, a drunkard, and a peddler of drugs. I accuse Colonel Anatoly Gasparov of leading me down this evil path. It was he who played on my weaknesses until at last I succumbed—selling my honor for money and the things money could buy. Together, we conspired to smuggle heroin into our beloved motherland—auctioning it off to the highest bidder among Moscow's many criminal gangs.

" 'But then the devil named Gasparov played me false,' " Koniev continued reading out loud. He could not hide the contempt in his voice. " 'He told me he no longer needed me. That he had other men who would do what I had done— and for less. Enraged, I resolved to take my revenge. So I sabotaged his aircraft by installing contaminated fuel filters and by ensuring the fuel itself was impure. I cared nothing for the others whose lives I took.

" 'Now, however, I am haunted by their ghosts and by the knowledge that my crimes must soon come to light. I am ashamed of what I have done, and of what I have become. I cannot live with that shame . . .' " Koniev's voice tapered off. He looked up. "It ends there."

Thorn swung away and stared up at the corpse suspended from the rafters. Was this it? Had John Avery and all the others died simply because of a falling out between two greedy drug smugglers? He'd seen enough combat to know how thin the line between life and death really was—and how often survival depended more on sheer luck than on skill or virtue. But the deaths of the OSIA arms inspection team members now seemed especially meaningless.

He tore his eyes away from Grushtin's body and turned to Helen. "What do you think?"

She looked equally troubled. "It seems plausible. At least on the surface." She glanced at Koniev. "We need other samples of Grushtin's handwriting, Alexei. And an autopsy. As soon as possible."

The MVD officer nodded rapidly. "I will arrange it." He snapped out another string of orders to the senior SOBR trooper and then rejoined them. "The commandos will touch nothing until a crime scene unit arrives."

Thorn nodded toward the personal computer on Grushtin's desk. "You should also have somebody take a close look at the files on that machine, Major. If we're lucky, this bastard may have been keeping track of their suppliers and maybe even their customers."

"Good idea, Peter," Helen said quietly. Her hand rubbed at her left leg, unconsciously tracing the faint scar left by the bullet that had severed her femoral artery two years before.

He knew what she was thinking and remembering. A partially wrecked laptop computer had been the only real prize they'd netted from the raid where she'd been so badly wounded. But her sacrifice had not been in vain. The captured computer had yielded encryption software that had allowed them to tap into a deadly terrorist group's e-mail communications network.

Almost against his will, Thorn found himself staring back up at the grotesquely bloated face of Captain Nikolai Grushtin. Had the dead man told them the truth in his apparent suicide note? Or had he taken other, darker secrets with him to the grave?

JUNE 2

Criminal Investigation Morgue, Militia Headquarters, Moscow

Helen Gray took a shallow breath and looked away from the stainless steel autopsy table—refocusing her attention on cracks in the room's green wall tiles and then on the bright fluorescent lights overhead. She had witnessed many autopsies in her years with the FBI—first as a student at the academy and later as a field agent. But she'd never been able to get used to the cold, clinical butcher's work required to extract useful information and evidence from a corpse.

The attitude of the doctor conducting this autopsy, a bored and cynical militia coroner named Rachinsky, only reinforced her dislike of the whole procedure. Right from the start, he'd made it clear that he regarded the process as a colossal waste of time and effort—and that he intended going through the motions only to keep them off his back.

Helen was also aware that outside observers might reasonably conclude that Peter, Koniev, and she were doing much the same thing—going through the motions. So far all the evidence supported the conclusion the Russian government was eagerly drawing: that Nikolai Grushtin had singlehandedly caused the An-32 to crash as an act of vengeance directed at his fellow drug smuggler, Colonel Anatoly Gasparov. Certainly the story fit all the known facts.

The MVD's experts had compared the suicide note with other samples of Grushtin's handwriting found in his dacha. It matched. They judged the shaky, uneven nature of the writing to be the result of severe emotional distress—probably compounded by the massive amount of alcohol he had apparently imbibed just before hanging himself.

And nothing other experts had found in the dead Air Force captain's personal computer files shed much more light on his dealings with Gasparov. There was no list of heroin suppliers or buyers—no day-to-day journal revealing any more details of their freelance smuggling network. Only a slim file containing his financial records had proved to be of interest. It showed four separate wire transfers of $250,000 each to a Swiss bank account in his name. The first payment had been made in early April, the last on May 24. Unfortunately, none of the file entries indicated the ultimate source of Grushtin's funds.

Helen looked back toward the table in time to see the coroner step back with a disgusted look on his thin, unshaven face. The overhead lights glittered off his wire-rim spectacles.

Rachinsky snapped off the overhead microphone and snorted. "As I knew all along, this man was a genuine suicide." He stripped off his latex gloves and tossed them toward a waste bin in one corner of the room. "You should not have wasted my time. For God's sake, there are three thousand murders a year in Moscow now. That's eight a day! I have better work to do than confirming what should have been blindingly obvious to any police cadet!"

Helen kept a tight grip on her temper. "Nevertheless, we'd all appreciate a more detailed explanation of your findings, Doctor." She glanced across the table at Peter Thorn and Alexei Koniev. "Right, gentlemen?"

They both nodded.

Koniev added an explicit warning. "This is a matter of the highest importance to the government, Rachinsky. I'm sure you would not want any hint that you had done anything less than your best work to reach the wrong ears in the Kremlin . . ."

"Oh, very well," the Russian coroner groused. Moving with an ill grace, he yanked on a new pair of surgical gloves and motioned them closer.

Rachinsky roughly pulled Grushtin's head to one side, exposing a deep groove across his neck where the noose had been. He spread the gouge apart with two fingers. "You see these marks? The black-and-blue speckling along this line?"

Helen studied the groove carefully—noting the tiny marks the coroner had indicated. "What are they?"

"Minute areas of bleeding caused by the rupture of small

blood vessels in the skin." Rachinsky shrugged. "They show this man was alive when the noose tightened."

"What else?" Koniev asked.

"These areas of postmortem lividity." The coroner pointed to purplish areas on Grushtin's face, above the neck, and then to others on his arms and legs. "Again, the areas where the blood has pooled and settled are consistent with a death by hanging."

Helen shook her head. "I'm not questioning the fact that Grushtin died that way, Doctor. I'm asking you what makes you so sure he inflicted that death on himself?"

"What makes me sure of that?" Rachinsky stared at her in disbelief. "The man was drunk beyond description. He must have known he would be arrested soon. There are no signs of other injuries. More to the point, he left a note in his own handwriting! So what else could it be but suicide?"

Helen frowned. Everything the militia coroner said made sense, but something still nagged her about Grushtin's apparent suicide. It seemed so convenient—almost too convenient. It was like being handed a perfectly wrapped package—one the Russian government was only too ready to accept.

She summoned up a mental image of the Russian captain's body dangling from the rafters of his dacha. Something about that image seemed wrong, or incomplete, somehow. Something about the stains on the dead man's uniform trousers . . .

She looked up at Rachinsky. "Captain Grushtin lost control over his bowels while dying, didn't he, Doctor?"

The coroner's thin face registered his distaste. "Yes. He expelled feces. What of it? That's quite common—especially in a death of this kind."

Helen pressed further. "Were there any signs of urine? Any evidence that he lost control over his bladder at the same time?"

"No." Rachinsky shook his head. "But the two things do not always occur together. Usually, but not always."

"Usually . . ." Helen repeated. She let that sink in before going on. Maybe the inconsistency meant nothing, but she wanted to make absolutely certain. "Then I would like you to examine that area again, Doctor—more thoroughly this time."

"I will do no such thing!" Rachinsky said flatly. "Nothing in the facts of this case warrants such an absurd . . . even ghoulish . . . reexamination. I've given you my medical finding, and that should be enough!"

"No, Doctor." Koniev moved closer to the coroner, his mouth tight with barely suppressed anger. "Your finding is not sufficient. Not in this case. Not when it is now clear that your initial examination was incomplete." He stabbed a finger repeatedly into Rachinsky's chest, emphasizing each point. "You will do as Special Agent Gray requests. Is that clear?"

The militia doctor stepped back—away from the MVD officer's prodding finger. He licked his lips nervously, glanced briefly at the three grim faces in front of him, and then shrugged. "Very well, Major. If it will convince you of the perfectly obvious—so be it."

Rachinsky picked up a scalpel and moved slowly down the autopsy table to stand poised over Grushtin's pelvic cavity.

Helen was sure she heard him mutter something about "a crazy, sex-starved American bitch" in Russian before he started cutting, but she chose to ignore it.

After making several short, swift incisions, the coroner leaned forward to take a closer look at his handiwork. Suddenly, he turned deathly pale. "Mother of God!"

"What is it, Doctor?" Helen asked sharply.

Rachinsky stared up at her, still horror-stricken. "There

are massive burns and major scarring inside this man's urethra. It's completely obstructed."

Helen fought down a sudden sense of triumph. Her instincts had been on target. "What might cause injuries like that?"

The militia doctor shook his head slowly in dismay. "I have not seen such things for a long time." He stopped, and quickly checked the overhead mike to make sure it was still switched off before going on. "Not since the Chekists . . . you understand?"

Helen nodded, knowing Rachinsky was making a coy reference to KGB torture during the Soviet era. Russia had still not come to terms with the atrocities routinely committed under its abolished communist government. Too many of the same people were still employed by the KGB's successor agencies. "We need specifics, Doctor."

The coroner nodded rapidly, now apparently eager to make up for his earlier intransigence. "Of course." He flipped on the mike again, dictating his new findings onto tape. "Upon closer scrutiny, it is now clear that the subject, Nikolai Grushtin, was tortured for a prolonged period of time. Perhaps by means of severe electrical shocks applied to the inside of his genitals. Or possibly by a superheated wire inserted into the same region."

Helen winced at the gruesome images evoked by Rachinsky's dry, matter-of-fact evaluation. Grushtin's involvement in the downing of the An-32 certainly warranted punishment, and probably even the death penalty. But no one deserved the kind of agony the Russian Air Force captain had apparently suffered before dying.

Moving with more energy and interest than he'd shown before, the coroner examined Grushtin's legs and arms more carefully, turning them first one way and then another under the bright lights. He reddened.

"Find anything else, Doctor?" Koniev asked dryly.

"Perhaps," Rachinsky admitted reluctantly. "It is difficult to tell with the postmortem lividity, the pooled blood, but there may be faint traces of bruising around the wrists and ankles. Very faint. As though whoever bound him took great pains to avoid leaving evidence."

Helen motioned Peter and Koniev off into the corner, leaving the now thoroughly embarrassed militia coroner to continue his work. She lowered her voice. "Well, now we know why Captain Grushtin wrote and signed that suicide note."

Koniev nodded grimly. "Somebody is covering their tracks. Somebody capable of great evil. Somebody with enormous resources. Somebody who found out we were interested in Grushtin almost as soon as we knew ourselves."

"But is that somebody here in Moscow? Or back at Kandalaksha?" Helen asked.

Koniev's mouth turned downward. "Who can say? All we know now is that this affair is far more than a murderous quarrel between two heroin smugglers." His shoulders slumped. "Grushtin was our only solid suspect. Even now that we know he was murdered, I don't know where to begin looking. There are more than two hundred *Mafiya* syndicates in Moscow alone—any one of which might be involved in this matter."

"Kandalaksha," Peter said suddenly.

"Kandalaksha?" The MVD officer looked curiously at him. "You seem very certain. Explain that, please, Colonel."

"Gladly." Peter ticked his reasons off one by one. "Okay. Kandalaksha is at the center of everything we've investigated. First, the OSIA inspection team plane takes off from there—and it crashes. Second, one of the men killed aboard that plane is carrying two kilos of pure heroin—which he apparently picked up somewhere on the base. Third, the man who sabotaged the plane was stationed at Kandalaksha."

"But not as a regular maintenance officer," Helen chimed in abruptly, remembering their interrogation of Lieutenant Chernavin. "Grushtin was supposed to be working on some kind of secret project, right, Peter?"

He nodded, smiling crookedly at her. "Exactly. A special *engine* project. One Chernavin seemed to believe an American military officer should know about. But General Serov's aide certainly seemed mighty pissed when the kid mentioned it to us."

"You think there is a connection?" Koniev asked. "That this project is somehow tied in to Gasparov's heroin smuggling?"

"I really don't know, Major," Peter admitted. "Not for sure. What I do know for sure is that something big and nasty is going down at that air base. Something Grushtin was willing to kill to conceal . . ."

"Something that meant he had to die once we started zeroing in on him," Helen finished for him.

"Yep."

Koniev nodded slowly. "It makes sense." He sighed. "I will file another request with the Ministry of Defense this evening. We will need its authorization to conduct an in-depth investigation on the air base."

"I really wish you didn't have to do that, Alexei," Helen said slowly.

"Yes," the MVD major agreed sadly. "It seems evident that the men we are hunting have allies somewhere inside my own government. And that they will doubtless know of our decision to return to Kandalaksha within hours. But we must have permission to enter the base. How else can we proceed?"

Helen nodded her reluctant agreement and saw Peter doing the same thing. She had the uneasy feeling that following the proper channels was keeping them at least one step behind the bad guys, but what other options were open to them? Once you started cutting corners to obtain results, you were on a slippery slope—headed toward the dangerous paradox of breaking the law to uphold the law. No. She and Koniev were officers of the law—and that meant obeying the law, even if that put their investigation at risk.

Kalitnikovskoe Cemetery, Moscow

(D MINUS 19)

Rolf Ulrich Reichardt leaned forward from the back seat to check the time on the dashboard clock of his Mercedes-Benz sedan. It was nearly midnight. He sat back—staring out the window at the rows of tombstones crowding the cemetery to his right. During the 1930s, Kalitnikovskoe had been infamous as a dumping ground for the bodies of those murdered in the KGB's Lubyanka Prison. Did the man he had come to meet remember that? The German rather suspected he did. Felix Larionov, "the Lariat," was known for his heavy-handed sense of irony.

Johann Brandt, acting as his chauffeur and bodyguard for this covert meeting, stiffened suddenly. "They're here."

Reichardt peered through the windshield and saw two cars pull up and park just across the darkened street. Both were brand-new Mercedes. Russia's criminal classes had a well-developed appreciation for fine German automotive engineering.

Three hard-faced men in black leather jackets and slacks climbed out of the first car and fanned out—scanning the immediate area for any signs of trouble. They were heavily armed. One carried a shotgun. The other two cradled Uzi submachine guns.

Satisfied, one turned and flashed a thumbs-up toward the second Mercedes. Its high-beams flashed once.

Responding to the prearranged signal, Reichardt and Brandt climbed out of their car and walked slowly toward the middle of the street. Except for a briefcase carried by Brandt, they were unencumbered, and they were careful to keep their own hands in plain view. The rear doors of the second Mercedes popped open. Two men stepped out and came forward to meet them.

Both were well dressed and middle-aged, but one, a wiry, white-haired man, bore jagged scars on his face that testified to a hard life. A brightly colored tattoo on the back of his left hand showed he had spent time in the Soviet prison system.

Reichardt recognized Felix Larionov from earlier business dealings. The *vory v zakone,* the "thief professing the code," controlled several of Moscow's most powerful and active criminal gangs. The second man, fleshier and softer-looking, was Larionov's *sovetnik,* his "adviser"—a term meaning everything from legal counselor to second-in-command.

Larionov stopped just out of arm's reach. He nodded once. "Herr Reichardt."

"Vor," Reichardt said politely, carefully masking his irritation at having to come hat-in-hand to this criminal for help. The unexpected persistence of Major Alexei Koniev and his two American colleagues was proving extremely troubling. Gasparov's heroin smuggling had proved a remarkable stroke of luck—one he had been quick to seize on. Ordinary police investigators would have been quite satisfied to close their case with Grushtin's apparent suicide.

The memory of the Russian officer's screams brought him a brief moment of pleasure. Orchestrating Grushtin's death had seemed a masterstroke—the capstone on the intricate heroin smuggling cover story he had so rapidly contrived to blind the official inquiry into the An-32 crash.

Reichardt's mood darkened again. But Koniev and these two Americans had not taken the gift he offered them. Instead, they were coming dangerously close to piercing the security screen he had erected around his activities at Kandalaksha. That could not be tolerated or ignored. Not any longer.

It especially irked him to involve others outside his control in the Operation, but time was short, and his resources, though enormous, were not inexhaustible. He looked steadily at Larionov. "Can your people handle the disposal of these packages for me? The ones we discussed over the phone?"

The Russian smiled thinly. "They can." Then he held up a cautionary hand. "But the proper question, Herr Reichardt, is whether or not I *will* order them to undertake such a task."

"Of course. My apologies." Reichardt gritted his teeth. Beggars could not be choosers, he reminded himself coldly. His own security teams were still scattered around the world. He needed the Russian *Mafiya* chieftain's assistance and manpower—for now. "*Will* you accept this commission, *Vor?*"

"You can assure me this work is not done at the behest of any government?" Larionov asked. The refusal to perform any work for the authorities was an integral part of the Russian thieves' code.

"Yes," Reichardt said firmly. "This is a private endeavor. And so I swear it."

"Then so I accept it," Larionov agreed. He motioned toward his adviser. "I believe Kiril told you our price?"

Reichardt nodded slowly. Two hundred thousand American dollars plus expenses was well over the ordinary fee for such services, but it was reasonable—given the short notice, relative importance of the targets, and the fact that he insisted on having one of his own men in direct command.

At his signal, Brandt stepped forward and opened the briefcase he carried for the Russian's inspection. It contained bundles of small-denomination greenbacks and a stack of airline tickets.

"Good." Larionov smiled more broadly, showing a set of yellowing, tobacco-stained teeth. "Then our business here is concluded. My boys will rendezvous with this man Kleiner of yours in Murmansk tomorrow evening."

Near Taif, Saudi Arabia

Prince Ibrahim al Saud looked up impatiently as his personal secretary, Hashemi, brought Massif Lahoud into his private office.

The Egyptian-born head of the Persian Gulf Environmental Trust looked weary. He had traveled half the night from Damascus to Riyadh and from there to Taif. Under other circumstances, Lahoud's report could have been made in a five-minute phone call, but Ibrahim maintained a single, inflexible rule in these matters. Where possible, his subordinates would never discuss their involvement in terrorist activities electronically. Phone calls, faxes, and electronic mail could all be intercepted, and Ibrahim had a high regard for the code-breaking abilities of intelligence organizations like Israel's Mossad and the American National Security Agency.

"Well?"

"The Radical Islamic Front agrees to your condition, Highness. One of our freelance Syrian operatives attended the meeting. They have contacted Afriz Sallah and hired him for this operation. Everything is proceeding according to plan."

Ibrahim smiled. "Very good, Mr. Lahoud. Then I authorize you to release the necessary funds from the trust's private account. Take the usual security precautions."

Lahoud nodded. "Of course, Highness."

When he was gone, Ibrahim sat back in his chair. A single prearranged order from Lahoud would set events in motion. The funds released from the trust's account would flow through an intricate network of dummy accounts set up in half a dozen banks—some in the Middle East, some halfway around the world. By tomorrow, the Radical Islamic Front would have the cash it needed to arrange the assassination of the American Undersecretary of State for Arab Affairs. And if anyone ever tried to trace the ultimate source of the Front's money, they would find only the equivalent of an empty desert—with all the tracks filled in by the wind.

CHAPTER SIX

MANIFEST DESTINY

JUNE 4

Surplus Engine Storage Depot, 125th Air Division, Kandalaksha

Colonel Peter Thorn pivoted slowly through a full circle, carefully checking their immediate surroundings. Broken windows stared back at him from the abandoned buildings visible in every direction. The rust-eaten Lada staff car that had brought them here was parked in front of a large, metal-roofed concrete building enclosed by a sagging chain-link fence. Railroad tracks ran parallel to the fence for a hundred meters before angling off toward the woods around the base perimeter.

Nothing was stirring. Nothing except the hairs on the back of his neck. They were nearly four kilometers from the busier portions of Kandalaksha, and this place was too quiet—too isolated. He glanced at Koniev and shook his head meaningfully. "I don't like this, Major. Not one goddamned bit."

"Neither do I," Koniev agreed. He jerked a thumb toward the sullen-faced Russian sergeant who had picked them up at the airfield's main gate. "But this man insists that General Serov himself ordered him to bring us here."

"Yeah," Thorn said. "That's what worries me."

Nearly two full days had passed since they'd learned that someone had faked Grushtin's suicide. First, the higher-ups in Russia's Ministry of Defense had taken their own sweet time—nearly twenty-four hours—to authorize another probe of the officers and men of the 125th Air Division. Hours more had been lost covering the sheer distance between Moscow and Kandalaksha.

Thorn wished again that Russian law allowed foreigners to carry weapons. Whoever had killed Grushtin had been given plenty of warning that they were coming back to this base. And plenty of time to arrange a warm and deadly welcome if that was judged necessary.

He shook his head silently, knowing his concerns might seem ridiculous, maybe even paranoid, to some. But there were too many dead bodies floating around for him to ignore the danger they might be in. Somebody connected with Kandalaksha was playing a game for very high stakes.

Thorn came to full alert as a big black Zil limousine with tinted windows turned onto the access road and roared toward them. Red command flags fluttered from its hood.

He stepped back—putting the bulk of the Lada between himself and the approaching car. Out of the corner of one eye, he noticed Helen taking the same precaution. If this was an ambush, the rusting staff car wouldn't offer much protection—but he lived by the credo that some cover was always better than none when bullets were flying. As a veteran of the FBI's Hostage Rescue Team, Helen had the same instincts and the same training.

The Zil pulled up and parked within a few feet.

Thorn relaxed only slightly when the tall, trim figure of Colonel General Feodor Serov climbed out of the limousine's back seat. He hadn't liked the Russian base commander much when they'd first met, and he liked him less now. Although Serov had the usual fighter jock arrogance coming out of his ears, that wasn't what really bugged him about the Russian. It was something else.

Thorn had used the Ministry of Defense–imposed delay to study the OSIA dossier on Serov. Nothing he'd read gave him a high opinion of Kandalaksha's commander.

The Russian had a long track record of backing those he perceived as winners—no matter who they were or what they professed. When Yeltsin was on the way up, Serov supported him. When it seemed the communists might reclaim power in Russia's first contested presidential election, the general had hurried to proclaim his renewed faith in Marxism. But then he'd turned his coat back to the side of the government just as quickly once the election results came in. Pure and simple, Feodor Mikhailovich Serov struck Thorn as a first-class opportunist—a careerist who always looked out for himself. And that made the Russian the antithesis of everything he thought a soldier should be.

"Major Koniev. Special Agent Gray. And Colonel Thorn." Serov tried a smile. It flitted nervously across his face and disappeared. "I am grateful that you agreed to meet me here."

"I was not aware we had a choice, General," Koniev said flatly. He'd read the same files and evidently come to the same conclusions about Serov's character. "Perhaps you could explain why we've been brought to this godforsaken place. As you know, we have a number of people to question in connection with Captain Grushtin, his murder, and this secret engine project of yours."

Thorn watched Serov flush an angry red at the MVD officer's dismissive tone. He hid a grin. Given a whip hand over the Air Force general by Moscow's orders, Koniev had evidently decided to push him hard. Atta boy, Alexei, he thought coldly. Keep the arrogant SOB off balance and on the run.

With a visible effort, the base commander regained control over his features. He forced another thin, humorless smile. "I understand your mission, Major. And, as I promised Defense Minister Ulanov, I will cooperate fully with this investigation." Then he shrugged. "I merely thought starting here would save you precious time and effort."

"How so?"

Serov motioned toward the weather-stained concrete building beyond the chain-link fence. A nearby gate stood ajar. "It would be quicker to show you, Major."

"Very well," Koniev said wryly. He waved the base commander toward the gate. "After you, General."

Frowning, Serov led them through the gate and then an unlocked metal door into the cavernous building. Enough sunlight filtered in through dirt-encrusted windows to reveal dozens of massive metal cylinders lying in rows across the floor. Some were covered by canvas tarps. Others were left exposed to the drafts wafting in through the ill-fitting doors and windows. Turbine wheels, thrust nozzles, and mazes of piping and wiring around the outside identified the cylinders as jet engines.

The Russian general stopped by one of the enormous engines. He patted it. "This is a Saturn AL-21 turbojet. Two of them power each of my Su-24 fighter-bombers. And each engine produces nearly twenty-five thousand pounds of thrust.

"But these . . ." Serov patted the vast cylinder again, less affectionately this time. "These Saturns produce nothing— not an ounce of thrust. They are worn out and inoperable. Useless. All of them."

"And they're just sitting here—gathering dust?" Thorn asked, eyeing the rows of silent engines in front of him dubiously. No U.S. Air Force commander he'd ever met would have allowed so many defective power plants to pile up. "Can't they be repaired?"

The Russian general nodded. "Certainly, they could be repaired, Colonel Thorn." Then he shrugged. "If my government supplied the trained manpower or the money to run an adequate maintenance operation. Unfortunately Moscow provides me with neither. So here they wait and here they rust—just so much useless scrap metal."

He turned his gaze on them. "Do you understand the situation here at Kandalaksha? Do you know the difficulties we face every day? The fuel shortages? The budget cuts? The pay shortfalls?" Serov scowled. "My pilots are lucky if they get four hours' flying time a month—barely enough to learn how to take off and land safely. Fewer than half my planes are flight-ready—"

Koniev stepped closer, interrupting him. "Spare me the litany of your woes, General. There are many other commanders with similar problems."

The MVD officer sharpened his tone. "But your real problems go far beyond slow pay and budget restrictions, General! At the moment, one of your officers is dead—apparently murdered by others involved in a heroin smuggling ring operating out of *your* duty station. The very same officer we believe sabotaged a plane carrying the American arms inspection team and their Russian counterparts. If you wish to avoid a court-martial for incompetence or worse, I suggest you start discussing this secret project of yours—now!"

Serov hid a scowl. The arrogant, insubordinate young pup! He fought the temptation to cut this interrogation short by pulling rank on the MVD officer. But Reichardt's telephoned instructions had been explicit.

"Give Koniev and the Americans some of the truth, Feodor Mikhailovich," the German had ordered. "Not all of it. Just enough to convince them they're on the right trail. I will handle the rest."

The Russian general grimaced. Even the partial truths he was about to tell revealed too much of his own wrongdoing for his taste. But Reichardt had made it clear that he had no choice—none at all. He was caught in a vise between the German on the one hand and these meddling investigators on the other.

"You have thirty seconds," Koniev warned.

"Very well," Serov said bitterly, surrendering to foul necessity. He would obey Reichardt's instructions. He nodded toward the rows of unrepaired engines. "You are looking at the raw materials for a venture, Major . . . a private business venture. One that involved several of my ranking officers and myself—including Captain Grushtin."

Koniev cocked his head. "A business venture? Using state property? Perhaps you had better explain yourself more fully, General."

"Yes. I suppose I must." Serov sighed. "Very well. You should know that I have never been a rich man—not on the pittance the State pays me. And even that meager amount will shrink further once I retire."

He spread his hands in a mute appeal. "My wife and I have two daughters in school, Major. Their fees had drained every ruble of my savings, and we were growing increasingly desperate with every passing month. I knew our finances would only get worse once I could no longer rely on government housing and rations. I even considered resigning my commission early to try and earn a proper living in some other way. Perhaps even as a menial laborer for one of the new private companies." He looked down at his feet. "Then several months ago I was approached by a man named Peterhof. He was the representative of a major arms export company—a company called Arrus Export, Incorporated."

Arrus? Colonel Peter Thorn glanced at Helen.

"I've heard of it," she whispered. "It's a big player in the Russian arms market. Moves tanks, artillery, spare parts, and other military gear all over the globe."

"This man wanted to buy working Su-24 engines for export out of Russia," Serov continued. He shifted uneasily. "Naturally, I refused."

"Naturally," Koniev said cynically.

Serov flushed again. "Call me what you wish, Major, but I am no traitor. I need every engine in working order just to keep some of my aircraft flying!"

"But then you thought of the engines stored here?" Helen prompted.

"Exactly!" Serov nodded vigorously. "Since Moscow will not provide the resources to repair them, they are all destined for the scrap heap sooner or later. So I decided to make some profitable use of them."

"How?" Koniev demanded. "Surely this arms merchant, Peterhof, did not pay you for useless jet engines?"

"No." Serov shook his head. "That is where Captain Grushtin and the others came in. Especially Grushtin."

"You cannibalized some of the engines to provide the parts to repair some of the others," Thorn realized suddenly.

"Yes," the Russian general confirmed. "Captain Grushtin led the work crews we used to rebuild working Saturns from the wreckage of others."

"And just where did these rebuilt engines go, General?" Koniev asked.

"I don't know," Serov said slowly. "It was never discussed. And I never asked. It was made clear that such a question would be unwelcome."

Thorn frowned, running over the most recent defense bulletins he'd read in his mind. Which countries flew the Su-24? Iran? Iraq? Libya? Didn't China have its own homebuilt copy of the Su-24, the Hong-7? Any of them would welcome the chance to obtain spare engines for their expensive, advanced attack jets. And none of them were exactly members of the friends of America hit parade.

There was another possibility, he realized. One that was even more disturbing. Since the collapse of the U.S.S.R. both the CIA and the Defense Intelligence Agency had been engaged in projects to acquire top-grade Soviet weaponry for evaluation and training. Did the U.S. Air Force Red Eagles Squadron based at Nevada's Dreamland have Su-24s in its inventory now? Jesus. What if this was some kind of CIA-sponsored covert purchase gone wildly wrong? Langley would go ape if it had been sucked into a drug smuggling operation by accident.

Thorn spoke up with a question of his own. "Exactly how many engines did you sell, General?"

"Twenty," Serov answered. "We transferred four separate shipments of five engines each."

"When?"

The Russian general frowned. "I have the exact dates in my office, but the first shipment was made sometime in April. The last left by train late last month—around the twenty-sixth, I believe."

Thorn suppressed a whistle. The engine shipments roughly coincided with the wire transfers they'd found in Grushtin's financial records. He stared hard at Serov. "And how much were you paid for these rebuilt engines?"

The Russian general glanced uneasily at Koniev.

"How much?" the MVD major ground out.

Serov capitulated. "Two hundred thousand American dollars per engine," he admitted softly.

"And precisely how much of that did you pocket for yourself, General? In your *impoverished* circumstances, I mean?" Koniev asked in disgust.

"Half," Serov whispered.

Helen took up the hunt. She turned toward the base commander. "Then how much did the other officers earn? Captain Grushtin, for example?"

"Grushtin?" Serov's lips pursed in thought. "Perhaps ten thousand dollars an engine. Something like that. Not more."

Thorn arched an eyebrow. If the Russian general was telling the truth, Grushtin's four $250,000 wire transfers were wildly over the amount the murdered maintenance captain could have earned from refurbishing the Su-24 engines. Five times as much, to be exact. So what else had he been paid for?

He looked more closely at the massive Su-24 engines laid out across the bare floor in front of them. You could hide one hell of a lot of heroin in any one of those babies. Was that what Grushtin's game had been?

"You say the last shipment left by train on May 26?" Koniev said.

Serov nodded. "Yes."

"Do you know where that train was headed?" the MVD major asked.

"Pechenga," the Russian general said eagerly. "I remember that Peterhof wanted those engines due in Pechenga no later than the morning of May 28."

After he'd ordered Serov back to his headquarters to assemble both his records and the other officers involved in his scheme, Koniev turned back to Helen and Thorn. "Well," he asked wearily, "what do you think? Did that corrupt swine tell us the truth?"

Thorn thought about that for a moment, running Serov's answers over in his mind. "Yeah. Some of it, anyway. A lot of what he said rang true."

Helen nodded. "He may be holding something back. But the basic story seems to fit what we already know."

"Then we talk to the rest of his officers now?" the MVD officer said.

"Yes." Helen narrowed her eyes. "Before they have any more time to coordinate their stories. And if they confirm what Serov says . . ."

"We head for Pechenga," Thorn said flatly.

"Uh-huh," Helen agreed. "And we hope the trail hasn't grown too cold in the meantime."

Satisfied, Thorn turned to Koniev. "Just one more question, Major. What's likely to happen to Colonel General Serov? When you report this to Moscow, I mean?"

Koniev's mouth turned down. "Probably nothing."

"Nothing?"

The MVD officer shrugged ruefully. "Perhaps a slap on the wrist, if he's unlucky." He grimaced. "Compared to the recent activities of other senior officers in my country's armed forces, I suspect his crimes will seem unimportant to my superiors."

Thorn nodded. In one case he'd read about, the commander of Russia's entire Far Eastern Strategic Air Force had been arrested for using his long-range bombers as an air freight service.

"In any event," Koniev continued sadly, "Serov is no fool. I would be very surprised if a portion of his newfound fortune hasn't already made its way up the ladder in Moscow."

Christ, Thorn thought grimly, contemplating the prospect that high-ranking officials could so easily be bribed—and worse, that a ranking police officer like Koniev could so easily imagine such a thing. He had the sudden, uneasy feeling they were walking into quicksand here—and that nobody would be standing by with a rope to pull them out if they started sinking.

JUNE 5

Wilhelmshaven, Germany

(D MINUS 16)

Just thirty miles east of the Netherlands and eighty-odd miles southwest of Denmark, Wilhelmshaven was one of several ports along Germany's low, waterlogged North Sea coast. The city and its harbor lay just inside the mouth of a large, sheltered bay, the Jadebusen.

Once home to warships of the Kaiser's High Seas Fleet and Hitler's Kriegsmarine, Wilhelmshaven had been eclipsed as a port in recent years by Bremerhaven, but supertankers still arrived regularly to offload oil destined for the heavy industries of the Ruhr.

The city, often cold and wet with North Sea weather, wasn't a big tourist draw. That suited *Baltic Venturer*'s owners perfectly. Shortly after she arrived from Bergen, harbor workers shifted the five steel cases to another Caraco-owned ship, the *Caraco Savannah*. This time, facilitated by a liberal exchange of deutsche marks, the cargo manifests were again magically altered. Instead of titanium scrap metal bound for a German metals-recycling company, the crates now contained "gas turbines," the sort used in factories and oil refineries to produce auxiliary power.

Caraco Savannah was larger than *Venturer.* She was a thirty-knot container ship, modern in equipment and gleaming in a coat of white-and-red paint.

Her destination was Galveston.

CHAPTER SEVEN

RED STAR

JUNE 5

Yegorova Railway Station, Pechenga

Dmitry Rozinkin leaned against the station's rough, cement block wall, scanning the passengers coming off the Murmansk train while pretending to read the local rag. He flipped through the thin, poorly printed pages and sneered to himself. It was pathetic, a weekly with fewer than ten pages. Why, Moscow had dozens of daily newspapers now—some of them pretty slick-looking. He didn't read any of them himself, but he saw them stacked up at newsstands.

He shifted uncomfortably, feeling the shoddy workman's cloth coat he wore tighten across his shoulders. He'd be damned glad once this job was over and he could get back into his city clothes—the brown leather bomber jacket and

American-made blue jeans that marked him as a young man on the way up. As one of the "new class"—those with enough guts and the right connections to prosper in today's Russia.

Rozinkin glanced up from a sports article, stared indifferently at the passengers alighting from the closest car, and then quickly lowered his eyes. There they were! Right on time. They were making his life easy.

Two of the three were relatively inconspicuous. Just a well-dressed man and woman. Although the woman was a real looker, the Russian decided. He licked his lips. She was trim, lithe, and curvy. Just the way he liked them.

The second man walking close by her side stood out like a sore thumb. Before he'd wound up in prison for theft, Rozinkin had done a short-lived stint in the armed forces. He could spot a military uniform two hundred meters away. But this man's uniform was not Russian, it was American.

Something about the American soldier caught Rozinkin's attention as the trio walked right by him. It was his eyes, the Russian realized. They were the eyes of someone who had seen Death come in many guises. Someone who had stared back at Death without blinking.

He shivered slightly—suddenly glad that he had drawn lookout duty only for this job.

He folded his newspaper under his arm, settled an old blue cap on his head, and swung in behind them. They headed straight for the taxi stand—or what passed for one in this miserable flyspeck of a town. Two cabs sat idling outside the station—both weather-beaten sedans that were probably being held together with baling wire and chewing gum. He was close enough to them to hear the youngest, the Russian man in civilian clothes, tell the lead taxi driver their destination.

Rozinkin waited until the beat-up cab turned the corner, then took out a portable phone and punched a button.

"Yes."

"They're on the way," he reported. "And they're alone."
He broke the connection.

Pechenga Harbor

Major Alexei Koniev let the door to the harbormaster's office swing closed behind him. Still angry, he strode out onto the pier to where Helen Gray and Peter Thorn stood waiting.

"Any luck?" Helen asked.

Koniev frowned. "Not much," he admitted.

Harbormaster Cherga was all too typical of Russian officialdom, he thought sadly—corrupt, lazy, and amoral. There were such people everywhere they turned in this case. People who would sell their honor or their country without batting an eyelash.

Koniev shook his head tiredly. He'd become a policeman to help pull Russia out of its wicked past. To make the words "law and order" stand for something more than tyranny and mass murder. But sometimes it seemed a futile task—something akin to mucking out a stable with the aid of a toothbrush and nothing more.

What must Helen and this Colonel Thorn of hers think of his country and his countrymen? They both came from a nation where public officials generally respected the rule of law. He felt the hot flush of shame on his forehead.

"Alexei?" Helen Gray asked again.

Koniev pushed his emotions to the side and refocused his attention on the case in hand. "According to Harbormaster Cherga, Arrus Export loaded the last consignment of jet engines aboard a freighter called the *Star of the White Sea*." He nodded toward the ship berthed at the end of the pier. "That's it. The ship has just returned from Bergen."

"Bergen, Norway?" Helen wondered. "Why there?"

"It's a major port," Koniev said. "One with many vessels entering and leaving each day."

"A place where a small cargo could get lost in the shuffle?" Thorn suggested.

"Perhaps." Koniev shrugged his shoulders. "This Cherga also claims he dealt with a man named Peterhof."

"Imagine that," Helen said flatly. "Any description?"

"Gray hair. Gray eyes. Middle-aged. Distinguished-looking." Koniev snorted. "At least it matches what Colonel General Serov told us about this Peterhof."

"Which wasn't much," Thorn commented dryly.

"True, Colonel."

With that, Koniev turned on his heel and led the way down the pier. This was his investigation, and the tramp freighter Arrus Export had chartered was the next link in the chain they were building.

The hull of the old ship loomed over them as they drew nearer. *Star of the White Sea* looked more like an abandoned building than a merchant ship to Koniev. It was big enough, and gray and dirty enough. Inch-thick mooring lines held her to the pier, while a gangplank near the stern led up to the main deck. A forest of cranes covered the front two thirds of the deck, while the superstructure sat almost all the way back on the stern.

Koniev went up the gangplank first. It angled steeply up to the main deck. The *Star of the White Sea* was empty, and with the tide in, they climbed almost two stories crossing the gap between the pier and the side of the ship.

A dark-haired man in worn overalls and a filthy jacket lounging against the bulkhead straightened up as Koniev reached the top.

Koniev flashed his identity card. "Major Koniev. MVD." He nodded toward the superstructure. "I want to see the captain of this ship."

The sailor, unsmiling, nodded silently and sauntered over to an intercom built into the bulkhead. He punched one of the buttons. "There's an MVD officer here to see you, Captain."

The sailor had a thick Georgian accent, Koniev noted. Odd. Few natives of that mountainous republic went to sea.

He heard Helen and Thorn reach the top of the gangplank. He wondered how much of the conversation the two Americans were going to catch if this ship captain didn't speak English fluently. Few people outside Moscow and the other major cities did. It was inconvenient.

The intercom squawked something unintelligible.

"Yes, sir." The sailor turned to Koniev and muttered, "He's in his cabin. Come with me."

He led the three of them to a set of steeply sloped stairs on the aft end of the ship's superstructure and climbed up to the second deck.

The three decks of the superstructure were arranged like the layers of a wedding cake, each smaller than the one below it. Glancing up to the third deck, Koniev could see a glassed-in space—almost certainly the bridge—topped by a small mast, radio aerials, and a radar antenna. A small funnel for the engines' exhaust grew out of the aft end of the superstructure.

The entire superstructure was painted white, with the funnel in blue. Close up, he could see the effects of the harsh Barents and Norwegian Seas on the vessel. Rust, dirt, and grease streaked the sides. More used to the signs of neglect than his American friends, he still wondered about that. Was this captain abnormally sloppy or careless? If so, that could be a useful clue to the man's character.

Their guide opened an exterior door in the center of the second deck and entered, with Koniev close behind.

Down a short corridor, they came to a passageway running fore and aft the length of the deck. Doors lined both sides. Stenciled signs showed that they were in the crew's quarters. The smell of burnt grease and overcooked potatoes wafted out from under the door marked "Galley."

The captain's cabin was at the forward edge of the second deck, right under the bridge, Koniev realized. Logical.

The Georgian sailor rapped three times on the door, then waited until a gruff voice from inside called, "Come." Then he opened the door and stepped aside—allowing Koniev and the two Americans in first. He followed them inside and shut the door.

The cabin was fairly large but sparsely furnished. A cot bolted to one wall showed where the ship's captain slept. A desk and single chair in the middle of the compartment showed where he handled his paperwork when he wasn't on the bridge.

One sailor, a thin and rough-looking sort with dirty blond hair, stood facing the desk holding his cloth cap in his hands. A second man got up from behind the desk when Koniev and the others came through the door. He offered his hand. "I am Captain Tumarev."

Again, Koniev caught the faint trace of another accent underlying the Russian words. Was Tumarev from one of the Baltic States?

Certainly the captain of the *Star of the White Sea* contrasted sharply with his crewmen. Better dressed, he was also better groomed. He was short, even shorter than Koniev, and powerfully built. He was also younger than the MVD officer would have expected, in his late thirties at most.

Was this ship his first command?

Automatically, Koniev shook the other man's hand, aware that Helen and Thorn were right at his back. Large by shipboard standards or not, six people crowded the cabin.

He showed his identity card again. "My name is Major Alexei Koniev, Captain."

The man calling himself Tumarev smiled, showing a mouthful of perfect teeth. "And what can I do for you, Major?"

"You carried a shipment of jet engines from this port on May 28," Koniev stated.

The other man nodded. "Yes, that's true." He shrugged. "What of it?"

Koniev frowned. Tumarev's informal, indifferent attitude irked him. He should show more respect to an officer of the law—especially one asking questions about a shipment that, at best, skirted the edge of legality. Perhaps it was time to show this seaman who was in charge here. He sharpened his tone. "Then I want to see your manifest for those engines, Captain. And I want the name and address of the firm you delivered them to in Bergen. Immediately. Understand?"

Tumarev seemed unfazed. Instead, he simply nodded. "Of course, Major." He moved back around his desk and pulled open a drawer. "I have those records in here."

But the ship captain's hand came out of the drawer holding a pistol aimed squarely at Koniev's midsection.

The MVD officer heard Helen gasp and reflexively reached for his own weapon.

"Don't move, Major!" Tumarev said sharply. He included the two Americans in his next order. "Put your hands up! All of you! Now!"

Koniev obeyed slowly, mentally cursing himself for his carelessness—for focusing so much on the hunt that he forgot that one's prey could sometimes turn and fight. He should have asked the local militia for backup. Out of the corner of his right eye, he could see another pistol in the dark-haired Georgian's hand.

Tumarev nodded pleasantly. "That's better." He motioned toward the MVD officer with his empty hand. "This pig first."

The thin, blond-haired sailor, moving quickly and efficiently, roughly frisked Koniev—first taking his identity card and then yanking the Makarov out of his shoulder holster.

Grim-faced now, Koniev stood motionless as the man vanished behind him. Rustling cloth and a muttered American swear word told him Helen and Thorn were getting the same treatment. He tried frantically to sort through the situation—looking for some way out. What the devil was happening here? What was Tumarev's game? What did he hope to gain by taking a law officer and two foreigners captive? The man was acting more like a bandit chieftain than a ship's captain.

More like a bandit chieftain. The phrase echoed in his mind. Koniev studied Tumarev more carefully, suddenly chilled to the bone.

The blond-haired sailor moved back into his line of sight, still holding Koniev's gun. "That's all. The others were clean." He looked at Tumarev expectantly.

The captain shook his head. "No, not here." He smiled coldly. "Use the tape."

The sailor slid the pistol into his pocket, produced a roll of duct tape, and took a step toward Thorn—the nearest of the three to him.

Colder than he'd ever been in his life, Koniev half turned to look at Helen and the American colonel. They looked surprised, angry, and somewhat baffled. But did they truly understand the peril they faced? Tumarev's brutal, dismissive "not here" could have only one meaning.

Koniev breathed out, his thoughts suddenly reaching toward his older brother. Their parents were dead. And now perhaps Pavel would be left all on his own. The possibility of that pierced him with regret, but there were no options left—no other doors to open. He must act. Or none of them would make it out of here alive.

Flatfooted, Koniev launched himself across the desk—straight at Tumarev. He was counting on surprise, on doing something totally unexpected. He was also counting on the fact that a bullet would have to hit something vital to kill him quickly. With luck, he could give Helen and Peter Thorn a chance to react.

Thorn exploded into action—spinning to the left, poised for a round kick with his right leg. He glimpsed Helen moving at the same time, whirling toward the dark-haired sailor who'd brought them here from the gangplank.

Three deafening gunshots erupted—two in rapid succession, the third a split second later.

His foot missed its intended target—slamming into the blond sailor's hip instead of his stomach—but the kick still had enough energy to knock the man down. The roll of tape skittered away across the steel deck.

Thorn threw himself across the sailor, pinning one arm. He chopped down hard twice—aiming for the man's exposed throat. Something crunched on the second blow, and he saw the sailor's eyes widen in horror.

The man suddenly stopped fighting and gasped, struggling desperately for oxygen that couldn't get through the larynx Thorn had smashed. His arms and legs quivered as he flopped on the deck like a dying fish tossed into the bottom of a boat.

Another pistol shot rang out.

Thorn crouched low as the round whined over his head, ricocheting off the metal bulkhead in a shower of sparks. Jesus! His hands tore through the dying sailor's clothing. Where the hell was Koniev's Makarov?

There. His hand closed around the shape of the pistol inside a jacket pocket. He tugged frantically, feeling the cloth give way.

Yet another gunshot erupted behind him.

Come on! Come on! Thorn worked the slide—chambering a round. He rolled, bringing the Makarov up, looking for a target. The dark-haired sailor Helen had attacked was down—lying twisted and broken on the deck. He rolled further . . .

Too late he saw Tumarev swinging toward him, weapon in hand.

Three more shots cracked out—one right after the other. One round slammed into the freighter captain's chest. The second hit him in the throat. The third caught him in the forehead.

His face a red, ruined mask, Tumarev fell back and slid down behind his desk. He left a trail of blood smeared across the metal bulkhead.

Helen Gray lowered the Tokarev pistol she'd seized, breathing hard. She checked the room swiftly. Nobody was moving. Nobody but Peter.

They exchanged glances, unspoken communications that said "We're both all right," before simultaneously turning to Alexei Koniev.

The young Russian lay slumped over Tumarev's desk. Two separate red patches covered most of his back. Oh, God . . .

Helen moved toward him, aware of Peter doing the same thing. They each took an arm, turned Koniev over, and gently laid him on the deck. She knelt beside him, cradled his head, and pressed her fingers to his neck—searching for a pulse.

"He's gone, Helen," Peter said grimly.

His voice seemed far away, and Helen realized she'd known there was no pulse for some time—only a minute, probably, but it seemed much longer.

Still cradling Koniev's head, she looked down at his chest and saw the dark red ruin where two bullets had struck him, spaced only inches apart. A third opening, this one an ugly exit wound, showed where the dark-haired sailor had shot him in the back while he struggled with Tumarev. That bullet should have been fired at her, she knew.

Alexei Koniev had bought them time with his own life.

She stared down at the young Russian major. Why had he done it? He must have known the price he would have to pay. She heard Peter searching the compartment, gathering weapons and spare clips. She looked up.

Peter was right to force his emotions to the side for now. They were still in danger. If they survived, she would have time to mourn later. But knowing that didn't make it any easier to let her grief over Koniev's death go, to close it off for a while longer. Helen fought for control, and took a deep breath.

As she stood up, Peter came over to her and pulled out a handkerchief. Taking her face in one careful hand, he tenderly wiped her cheeks dry. She hadn't even known she was crying.

Then he offered her Koniev's 5.45mm Makarov and two spare magazines.

Helen shook her head quickly, fighting back more tears. "You keep it."

She picked up the pistol she'd used to kill Tumarev. Three shots there plus the bullet the dark-haired sailor had fired at

Koniev added up to three 7.62mm rounds left in the magazine and one in the chamber. Not enough. She tore it out and snapped in a fresh magazine.

Some people would have called the Tokarev she carried a piece of obsolescent junk. It was single-action, not double, and it didn't have a real safety—just the half-cocked hammer. Still, she'd scored three-for-three with it against that son of a bitch Tumarev. And right now, that made this pistol the sweetest piece of hardware she'd ever fired.

Peter handed her three extra magazines and watched as she tucked them in her jacket pocket. "Ready?"

Helen nodded.

He grimaced. "We've got to get off this damned ship and get the militia out here, pronto."

True, she thought. Staying put meant ceding the initiative to any bad guys left outside the cabin. It was high time to get out of this blood-soaked rat pit. "You think the whole crew's in on this thing?"

Peter shook his head, more in puzzlement than disagreement. "I dunno anything for sure right now." He prodded one of the dead sailors with his foot. "But somehow I don't think we're going to have an easy stroll back out to the pier. Whoever planned this wants us dead real bad."

Helen joined him near the door to the passageway. She glanced back at Koniev's body, then turned away.

"The feeling's mutual," she said grimly.

Thorn took a deep breath and then let it out slowly, readying both his mind and body for instant action.

Now.

In one smooth motion, he pulled the door open, ducked forward, scanned the passage, and then pulled his head back in. Nothing. He glanced at Helen. "Clear."

She nodded tightly, holding her pistol ready in both hands. "Go."

Thorn glided out into the corridor, keeping low. It ran straight aft to a door standing wide open into the sunshine. Helen followed right behind him, sliding off to the other side.

Feet clattered on the metal stairs leading up from the main deck. A man's head and shoulders appeared in the open door.

"Watch left!" Thorn warned softly. He dropped into a shooting stance, but kept his finger off the trigger. Years of Delta Force training had taught him the art of discriminate shooting. The guy coming up the stairs could be anyone—all the way from the ship's cook to a Russian militia officer.

Instead, he focused on the man, quickly noting a shaggy haircut, a dark leather jacket, and a thin, pale face.

Halfway up the stairs, the stranger spotted them in the passageway and called out something in rapid-fire Russian. Something about wanting to know where "Kleiner" was, Thorn thought wishing his own Russian were good enough to give him an answer.

Suddenly the pale-faced man got a better look at them. He froze for a single instant, then turned, and dropped back down the stairs out of sight.

"Well, that was useful," Helen remarked dryly.

They came to a junction. A second passageway crossed theirs, running across the ship with doors to the port and starboard—both closed.

Thorn hesitated. "Portside's the way out," he suggested.

"And probably the first place they'll be waiting for us," Helen countered.

"Good point."

They turned the corner into the second corridor.

Helen reached the starboard door first. It was a heavy metal watertight hatch opened by a long handle connected to clamps on both sides. Pull the handle and the clamps would unlatch. They would also make noise. A lot of noise.

She stopped, pressing her ear against the door and testing the handle.

Thorn controlled the urge to tell her to throw it open, to get moving. He had to trust Helen's judgment. He put one hand on the metal wall of the corridor. Shit. He could feel the vibration made by running feet.

"We've got company," he said quietly, already starting back toward the intersection.

The portside door flew open—revealing another man, this one in grease-stained overalls. He held a pistol in his right hand.

Thorn dropped to one knee and took rapid aim—still holding his fire. Was this one of the bad guys or just somebody investigating all the shooting?

The sailor's eyes opened wide. His pistol swung up.

Bad choice, Thorn thought coldly. He squeezed the trigger once, then again. Hit by both rounds, the gunman folded over and flopped onto the deck—half in and half out of the door.

He risked a quick glance over his shoulder. Helen had the starboard hatch open now, and she was scanning the outside of the ship.

A voice called something from the aft. Maybe a name? Or maybe an order? Thorn couldn't tell. He felt more footsteps through the freighter's metal skin.

"The natives are getting restless, Helen," he said bluntly.

"I can hear," she shot back. "Don't rush me."

All of Thorn's instincts told him to move and move fast, before they were cornered. The two shots he'd just fired had echoed throughout the entire ship.

"Okay, it's clear," Helen finally announced. She stepped out onto the walkway that ran around the outside perimeter of the deck and turned toward the ship's stern.

Thorn followed close behind her, pulling the hatch shut behind him to buy them some extra time. He turned, blinking in the bright sunlight, and immediately saw why she'd been so cautious.

The catwalks surrounding each deck were a maze of metal boxes, hose reels, and other objects he couldn't recognize. Hell, he thought, you could hide a platoon out here.

Without pausing, Helen slid forward—moving smoothly from cover to cover. Thorn came after her, keeping his pistol trained behind and above them, while she searched for enemies ahead.

They were heading for the gangplank, one deck down at the aft end of the superstructure. That was their only real way off the ship. Diving off the side into the oil-stained harbor wasn't an option—not with armed men waiting above to pick them off while they were in the water. Going off on the pier side would be even worse. That was a long way down. Jump far enough to hit the pier, and they risked breaking legs, arms, or their necks. Jump too short and they'd wind up in the drink anyway—only this time trapped in the shadowed space between the ship and the pier.

No, Thorn thought grimly, it was the gangplank—or nothing.

Helen Gray poked her head around the aft corner of the *Star of the White Sea*'s superstructure—straining to see the gangplank through the tangle of gear cluttering the freighter's stern. There were four men standing close to it—all arguing excitedly. At least two had guns in their hands. She couldn't see the others clearly enough to tell whether or not they were armed.

Before she could draw back into cover, one of them caught a glimpse of her movement and snapped off a shot. It whipcracked past, missing her face by about a foot.

"Shit!" Helen yanked her head around the corner of the superstructure and backed up fast.

"How many?" Peter asked urgently.

She held up four fingers, listening intently for the sound of feet clattering up the stairs toward them. If the bad guys were completely stupid and rushed them . . . she crouched lower still, aiming toward the corner. Eight rounds in the magazine, she decided. That ought to be enough.

They weren't stupid.

Instead of men running, she heard only shouted commands in Russian—and then silence.

"We've got to move!" Peter whispered urgently in her ear.

It was hell having the same kind of counterterrorist training, without ever having worked as a team before, Helen thought. Both of them were highly skilled in the combat arms and in close-quarters tactics. But they were each used to leading teams that had lived, practiced, and fought together long enough to know each other's moves instinctively.

Helen rapidly ran their options through her mind. They were outnumbered by at least two to one. Given the disparity in numbers, constant movement was the best way to keep pressure on the bad guys—to make the bastards dance to their tune.

Staying on this deck was the worst option. That was "horizontal thinking" and too obvious. Combat in a built-up environment was often a lot like an aerial dogfight. Sometimes it paid to go vertical.

She glanced up at the third deck. Moving there would give them better visibility and better fields of fire. But it would also leave them more exposed—and it would limit their ability to maneuver. She shook her head. The day she treed herself was the day somebody could declare her brain-dead and pull the plug.

Helen looked down. Heading for the main deck would cut their fields of fire, but it would give them more running room. And that made it the best choice of all. Close-range firefights were the best matchup for the pistols they were carrying. She hadn't seen any of the bad guys carrying long arms, but she couldn't ignore the possibility.

Peter arrived at the same conclusion in the same instant. "Down to the main deck?" he suggested.

"Yeah," Helen agreed impatiently. "I'm with you, Peter."

"Never doubted it, Special Agent Gray." Then he was up and running lightly back the way they'd come.

She came out of her crouch and followed after.

There were stairs leading down to the main deck right outside the hatch they'd come through. They took the stairs two at a time, staying as quiet as possible while moving as fast as possible. They needed to put some distance between themselves and the place where she'd been spotted.

When they reached the forward end of the freighter's superstructure, Helen could see an open deck stretching hundreds of feet toward the bow. Even with the forest of masts, winches, and other cargo-handling equipment, moving out there would leave them too exposed. It was a ready-made killing ground. Besides, she thought, their salvation—the gangplank—lay in the other direction.

Thorn eased around the forward corner of the superstructure carefully—scanning for any signs of movement on the deck ahead. Nothing. With his left hand he signaled the all-clear to Helen and slipped ahead—careful to stay close to the metal bulkhead.

His plan was simple. Head for the gangplank, eliminate anyone guarding it, and run like hell for the cover offered by the warehouses at the land end of the pier. Anything more complicated was likely to go wrong—especially since they knew so little about the ship's layout and the people they were up against.

With his senses extended, and staying as low as possible, Thorn advanced a step at a time—listening, watching, trying to guess where the enemy might be lurking.

Nothing stirred. Nothing except the wind off the Barents Sea whining through the *Star of the White Sea*'s cargo cranes and radio antennas. And the sound of water lapping around her hull. He frowned. They were trapped in a nightmare killing house scenario: fighting an unknown number of enemies on unfamiliar ground.

Something scraped against the metal above and ahead of them.

Thorn froze.

Another footfall came a second later. He flattened himself against the bulkhead, listening as the cautious, careful footsteps approached a point directly over his position. There were two men moving on the walkway above. Evidently they still expected to find their prey on the second deck. Not smart, he thought.

Thorn waited until the Russians were past his position and over Helen before moving. He swung around, tracking them by sound. If either of them leaned over the walkway railing, he'd have a good shot.

But he couldn't wait for that. Fighting defensively wasn't going to get them out of this jam. His hunter's instinct told him to take these men down now—while he could catch them by surprise. The only question was, how? Should he make a deliberate noise to lure them into looking over the edge? He discarded that idea immediately. If only one of the Russians fell for it, the other would be alerted, above them, and in a position to pin them down.

The need for speed pushed at him, too. There were at least two other gunmen hunting them. And what were they doing while he crouched here?

Helen was watching him, waiting for a signal.

Thorn spotted a fire hose coiled around a large metal bracket bolted to the bulkhead between them. The bracket looked strong enough to hold his weight. Perfect.

He pointed at the bracket, then at his foot, and finally toward the men above.

Helen nodded her understanding.

Thorn set one foot on the bracket and slowly shifted more of his weight onto it. It held.

He exhaled slowly, running through a mental countdown. Three. Two. One. Now!

Thorn stood up on the bracket, grabbing for the edge of the second-deck walkway with his left hand. He steadied the Makarov, aiming for where he guessed the two Russians should be.

The bracket groaned under his full weight.

Both men were already turning toward the source of the sound, weapons at the ready. They were only yards away.

The closest Russian appeared over Thorn's front sight. He squeezed the trigger. The man fell to the deck, clutching his stomach.

The second gunman, a big man with thinning hair, fired back before he could shift targets. The round clipped the deck near Thorn's face—spraying sharp-edged paint chips in a stinging arc across his left cheek.

Moving fast, Thorn swung his pistol toward the second man and squeezed the trigger again. Sparks flew off the railing instead. Damn it, he'd missed! Suddenly, the coiled fire hose shifted beneath him. The Makarov wavered off target. Shit!

Smiling now, the big Russian leaned out over the railing to get a clearer shot. The smile vanished. Helen's bullet took him under the jaw and blew off the top of his skull. He staggered, then toppled over the railing and fell to the main deck below.

Thorn stood poised on the bracket long enough to make sure the first man he'd shot was still down. Satisfied, he dropped to the deck. Blood trickled down his cheek. Impatiently he wiped it off.

Two more of their enemies were down—dead or dying. But that left at least two more to go. And they couldn't stay lucky forever. He glanced at Helen. "Straight on?"

She nodded calmly. "Let's press it."

Thorn took the lead again, moving quickly to the portside of the freighter's superstructure. He peered around the corner. There was no one in sight—not even near the gangplank. Sure. Somehow he doubted the bad guys would leave the only exit unguarded. At least one of them had to be out there somewhere—sprawled in cover, waiting and watching.

He ducked around the corner and dropped behind a large metal box, an equipment locker of some kind. They were going to have to flush out their enemies the hard way.

Helen Gray followed Peter around the corner.

A pistol shot cracked from somewhere ahead and above. The bullet slammed into the deck at her feet and whirred away—tumbling through the air. She went down on one knee, firing rapidly in the direction the shot had come from, trying to keep the shooter's head down until she could spot him.

Another round hit the bulkhead above her.

There! Helen saw the gunman. He was on the second-deck catwalk, lying prone behind a stanchion. She frowned.

With only part of one arm and his head exposed, the Russian was a difficult target. She fired again, mentally counting off her shots. Two more were left in the magazine.

Out of the corner of her eye, she noticed Peter lifting his head above the equipment locker, trying to spot the man who had her pinned down.

Five meters from the gangplank, Mischa Chabenenko lay flat behind a metal fitting on the rusty steel deck. He saw the American man rise slightly, looking up toward the super-structure towering above—toward Yuri's firing position.

Chabenenko felt his heart pounding. Sweat trickled down his forehead and puddled under his arms. This was supposed to have been an easy job—a piece of cake. Instead it had all gone wrong. Kleiner, the German bastard who'd masquer-aded as Captain Tumarev, was dead. And so were most of his comrades—all of them killed by these two Americans. Except for that gutless worm, Rozinkin, already on his way back to Moscow, Yuri and he were the only ones left.

All he'd been told was that the two Americans and an MVD major were poking their noses into places they should not be. And that the *vor*, Larionov, wanted them stopped—permanently.

Chabenenko muttered an oath under his breath. Someone should have checked into just who they were trying to stop.

What should he do? It would be easy to let the Americans escape, he knew. All he had to do was just stay in hiding here, let them get clear, and then flee down the gangplank himself. He might have a slim chance of making it safely back to Moscow before the militia picked up his trail.

But then he'd have to answer to the *vor*.

A bead of sweat rolled down his nose and dripped onto the deck. Felix Larionov did not tolerate failure. Or cow-ardice.

Chabenenko shook his head. He'd rather take a bullet here than die screaming under the Lariat's knife. Besides, if he could just take these two, he and Yuri would share the pay once meant for eight.

Driven by fear and greed, he took careful aim, centering his pistol sights on the American man's head. He pulled the trigger.

Superheated air tore at Peter Thorn's face as a slug screamed past, only an inch away—way too close. He dropped back behind the locker.

Shit! There was a second shooter out there, near the gangplank—one he couldn't see.

The gunman above them fired again.

Helen screamed—a terrible, rising wail that tore at his soul. He whirled around, expecting to see her writhing in agony on the deck.

So did the Russian who'd been shooting at her. He poked his head further out from behind the stanchion—trying to see whether the woman he'd hit needed a second bullet to finish her off.

Instead, Helen still knelt there, perfectly poised and aiming for the upper deck. She fired twice, coolly paused, and then snapped a fresh magazine into her weapon.

She glanced at Thorn and nodded contemptuously toward the upper deck.

He followed her nod and saw the gunman's shattered head lying cocked at an odd angle over the edge of the catwalk.

Thorn swallowed hard, forcing his breathing back to a normal pace. She'd scared the hell out of him with that stunt. Another bullet tore across the top of the metal locker he was using for cover, reminding him that at least one of their enemies was still alive and fighting.

Helen rolled in beside him. "Spotted the guy. He's close to the gangplank—about four or five meters back, behind some kind of rusted-out fitting."

Thorn ran through the memory of what he'd seen before the latest round of shooting started and nodded. He knew the spot she was talking about. Remembering the round that had nearly taken his head off, he frowned. They didn't dare move forward. This Russian was too good a shot to risk rushing him.

But they couldn't wait here indefinitely. If there were any more bad guys left alive aboard the *Star of the White Sea*, huddling behind this metal locker was a good way to wind up getting shot in the back.

The gunman fired again.

Why? Thorn wondered. Neither he nor Helen had offered him a target. So why was he still shooting? Was he trying to keep them pinned here long enough for his friends to close the net?

Another steel-jacketed round punched into the equipment locker.

Thorn suddenly realized the Russian was firing at fairly steady intervals—once every several seconds, almost in a pattern. Acting instantly, he rose above the locker with his pistol braced in both hands, aiming just above the metal fitting—right where the shooter would be . . . now!

He had the fleeting impression of a pale white face, an open mouth, a dark gun.

Thorn fired three times in rapid succession, holding the Makarov down and on target as it bucked upward.

Hit at least twice, the gunman slumped over the fitting. His pistol clattered to the deck. Blood pooled beneath the dead man, blending with the rust, grease, and dirt coating the steel surface.

Silence fell over the corpse-strewn freighter. Nothing moved. Nothing at all.

Thorn breathed out and looked at Helen. She smiled wanly back. Her hands were shaking now as reaction set in and the adrenaline wore off. He looked down. So were his.

He set his jaw and rose to his feet. It was time to get off this damned ship. Time to start finding out why they'd been ambushed. To find out why Alexei Koniev had been murdered.

It seemed to take an eternity to reach the gangplank and dash across. Nobody fired at them. They stepped onto land just as they heard the sirens screaming—drawing ever closer to the docks. Pechenga's militia force had apparently woken up.

Peter Thorn and Helen Gray waited until they saw the patrol cars skid around the corner of the harbormaster's office, then very carefully laid their weapons down on the ground. With their hands out and empty, they went to meet the approaching militia.

CHAPTER EIGHT

TERMINATIONS

JUNE 6

Commanding Officer's Quarters, Kandalaksha

Phut.

The muffled pop brought Colonel General Feodor Mikhailovich Serov fully awake. What the devil was that? He opened his eyes and started to reach for the bedside lamp.

He froze—suddenly aware of the cold metal cylinder pressed hard against his mouth.

"Very good, General," a dry voice commented. "You show sense."

A gloved hand reached past him and flicked the lamp on—flooding the bedroom with light.

Serov blinked rapidly, staring down the enormous muzzle of a silenced 9mm Makarov pistol. Sergeant Kurgin—his orderly and Reichardt's watchdog—looked back at him, stony indifference written across his narrow face. He was dimly aware of another man, blond-haired and broken-nosed, standing close by the side of the bed.

"Do not move, General," Kurgin ordered calmly. "This won't take long."

Dazed by the sudden reversal of his fortunes, Serov obeyed, lying rigid while Kurgin's companion quickly and efficiently strapped his wrists and ankles together with tape. Leaving him trussed like a hog readied for slaughter, the broken-nosed man stepped back.

Kurgin pulled the pistol away and stood waiting, still staring down at him.

Something wet and warm trickled off the headboard and dripped onto Serov's forehead—something that smelled oddly like heated copper. He flinched, remembering the muffled sound that had first wrenched him into this waking nightmare. Elena!

He turned his head sideways and moaned aloud.

His wife lay dead in bed beside him. Her eyes seemed closed in peaceful sleep, but the neat, puckered hole in her forehead told him they would never open again. Powder burns etched her fair skin black around the wound. The exit wound was messier. Bright red blood and gray brain matter had sprayed across her pillow and onto the headboard. He retched suddenly, desperately turning his own head away as his stomach heaved.

When the shivering fit passed, Serov looked up at Kurgin. His mouth felt as though it were filled with sand and ashes. "Why?" he croaked. "Why are you doing this? I don't understand. Reichardt promised me I would be safe once Koniev and the two Americans were dead."

Kurgin shrugged his shoulders. "It seems someone else made a small mistake this time. The Americans are still alive." His lips twitched into the ghastly parody of a smile. "And so Herr Reichardt must sacrifice another pawn to fend them off for a while longer."

Serov swallowed hard, staring death and utter disaster squarely in the face. Kurgin's bad news spelled out his own death sentence. Reichardt had used him to bait the hook for Koniev and the Americans. But by pointing them toward the trap waiting for them in Pechenga, he had left himself vulnerable to further interrogation—if they lived. So now that Reichardt's ambush had failed, he was of no further use and of considerable potential danger to the German and his mysterious employer.

"And my wife? Why kill her? She knew nothing of all this," he said bitterly.

His onetime orderly shook his head and smiled in mock amusement. "Now how could we be sure of that, General?" He stroked the silenced pistol in his hand gently. "In any event, you should be grateful that Herr Reichardt ordered me to kill her quickly. He is not ordinarily so gracious and forgiving."

Serov winced. He tried to moisten his dry lips and failed. "And what of my daughters?"

"Them?" Kurgin shrugged again. "I have no orders concerning them."

For the first time since opening his eyes, Serov felt a small measure of hope—though none for himself. Perhaps Reichardt would leave his children unmolested at their schools in France and Germany. They might be left penniless and alone, but at least they would be alive.

He nerved himself one last time to stare up at Kurgin, fighting hard not to show the panic bubbling up inside. As a younger man, he had flown high-performance MiGs to the edge of the envelope and beyond—cheating Death to win praise and promotion. Now Death had come in a different guise. He had lost his final gamble.

Well, so be it, he thought wearily. At least a bullet in the brain would be quick. Perhaps it would even be painless.

Serov hawked, turned his head, and spat toward the floor in one last, futile gesture of defiance. "All right then, damn you! Get on with it!" He nodded toward the silenced pistol in Kurgin's hand. "You have your weapon. Use it."

"This?" Reichardt's agent glanced down at the pistol in surprise. He laughed softly. "No, no, General! This is not for you. After all, we do have appearances to maintain."

Before Serov could move, Kurgin's companion gripped his right arm in a vise grip and tore the pajama sleeve up above his elbow.

Gasping now, Serov rolled his eyes toward Kurgin.

The sergeant had set his pistol aside. Moving with deadly precision, he reached into his tunic and took out a hypodermic needle and a length of surgical tubing. He held the needle up to the light, tapped it gently, and then smiled cruelly. "No bullet for you, Colonel General. Nothing so easy, no. I'm afraid you will be taking a long and painful trip to hell."

Serov started screaming even before the needle touched his skin.

King Khalid International Airport, Riyadh, Saudi Arabia

Grateful for the air conditioning that kept the blast furnace heat of the Saudi summer at bay, Anson P. Carleton, the U.S. Undersecretary of State for Arab Affairs, strode forward to a podium inside the King Khalid Airport's official reception area. His aides, U.S. Secret Service agents, and Saudi security personnel trailed after him and then filed off to either side.

Outside, the honor guard and band that had greeted him on his arrival began dispersing. Heat waves distorted their figures as they marched away under a merciless sun that baked the tarmac like pottery in a kiln.

Carleton noted the brand-new mural decorating the wall behind the podium—a stylistic rendition of a map of Saudi Arabia, its flag, and a verse from the Koran. It hadn't been there on his last visit to Riyadh. The Saudis must be sprucing up their airport—yet again. He shrugged mentally. His hosts always seemed to have the money for bold and lavish interior decorating. Now it was his job to persuade them to move boldly in other, more important areas—to continue the process of making a full peace with Israel.

He looked down at the notes of his prepared arrival remarks. His words would be carefully chosen and indirect, as was usual when dealing with sensitive political issues in Arab countries. But they would leave his real audience, the ruling Saudi elite, in no doubt that the United States was committed to yet another serious and sustained effort to reconcile Jerusalem and its Arab neighbors.

Carleton cleared his throat, looked straight up into the unwinking lenses of the dozen or so television cameras assembled to record his statement, and opened his mouth—

The mural behind him erupted in flame.

The fiery blast enveloped Carleton a millisecond before the fragments thrown by the explosion tore him to pieces and then sleeted outward—killing or maiming dozens of the aides, security guards, and reporters clumped near the podium.

Two rooms away, Yassir Iyad, an airport maintenance worker, felt and heard the short, sharp concussive thump that told him the explosive charge planted inside the new mural by the Radical Islamic Front had detonated. He smiled broadly and then wiped the smile off his face.

Working swiftly, the young Palestinian guest worker detached a small controller from the piece of wire hanging out of an electrical conduit inspection plate. He concealed the controller in his pocket. Next, he tugged on the wire—pulling it out through the conduit. Since the wire had only been attached to the bomb's trigger mechanism, it came out easily. If it had hung up on the wreckage, Iyad had come prepared to cut it off and conceal it in place. Fortunately, that wasn't necessary.

Instead, the Palestinian simply reeled the wire in—all twenty meters of it—gathering it up on the same spool it had come from. Then he clipped off the scorched, twisted end and dropped that in his pocket beside the controller. He planned to drop both pieces of incriminating evidence somewhere deep in the desert outside the Saudi capital.

After replacing the access plate, Iyad left the storage room—locking the door behind him.

Then, donning a look of anguished concern like a mask, the Palestinian hurried, along with everyone else, toward the scene of the tragedy.

Near Taif, Saudi Arabia

(D MINUS 15)

"Officials have characterized this as the most serious terrorist attack on the United States in two years—pointing out that Undersecretary of State Carleton is the highest-ranking U.S. official ever assassinated on foreign soil. The White House is preparing a statement . . ."

Prince Ibrahim al Saud snapped the television off. A slight smile graced his lips. Carleton's death was only a fraction of what he hoped to accomplish, of what he planned to accomplish—but the Americans had suffered today.

JUNE 7

MVD Holding Area, Sheremetevo-1 Airport, Outside Moscow

The MVD holding area at Sheremetevo-1 showed signs of hard usage. Its black-and-white checkerboard linoleum floor was scarred, scuffed, and still showed mud and other stains tracked in during the last spring rainstorm. Several of the overhead fluorescent lamps were burned out, and some of those that were left flickered at irregular intervals. Puke-ugly, lime-green plastic chairs bolted around the walls provided the room's only seating.

Colonel Peter Thorn sat stiffly upright in one of those hard plastic seats, studiously ignoring the young MVD private standing nearby. The kid looked barely old enough to shave, and Thorn earnestly hoped he'd been given enough training to know how to work the safety on the AKSU submachine gun he held cradled in both hands. From the way the private twitched whenever Thorn so much as shifted in his chair, he seemed to think he was guarding Bonnie and Clyde.

Thorn looked across to where Helen Gray sat. Another soldier stood watching her, and a burly, hard-faced MVD captain occupied the chair right next to hers.

She looked pensive, sad, and utterly weary. There were shadows under her blue eyes—shadows that had darkened in the two days since Alexei Koniev had died.

He sighed inaudibly. Losing a partner was one of the toughest things that could ever happen to anyone in law enforcement or the Special Forces. It was something you never really got over. He knew that only too well. One of his closest friends, his old sergeant major, had been killed in the Delta Force raid on Teheran. He still had occasional nightmares about that—nightmares that lingered on in a sadness that was hard to shake when he woke up.

Thorn shook his head somberly. This investigation had already exacted a bitter price from the woman he loved—and they still weren't much closer to the truth they'd been seeking. He leaned toward her, hoping he could find the right words to tell her how sorry he was. "Helen, I—"

"Silence!" the MVD captain barked in heavily accented English. "No talking! It is forbidden."

Thorn bit down on a savage curse. Damn it. This was ridiculous. He rubbed angrily at his wrists, fiercely massaging the abrasions left by handcuffs that had been locked down too tight for too long.

He hadn't been very surprised when the first militia units arriving on the scene at the *Star of the White Sea* put them under arrest. That had been a reasonable precaution for any policeman faced with a shipload of corpses and two armed foreigners. But what followed next hadn't been reasonable. Not by a long shot.

They'd been held under lock and key at the Pechenga militia headquarters for hours, denied any contact with the American embassy, and ignored whenever they demanded information on the state of the investigation down at the docks. When this MVD captain and his men showed up earlier today, Thorn had at first thought the wheels of Russia's ponderous bureaucracy were finally starting to spin in the right direction.

Big mistake, boyo, he thought bitterly. If anything, their situation had gone from bad to worse. He and Helen had been hustled out of militia custody, handcuffed like common criminals, and plopped onto a military transport plane bound for Moscow.

And now they'd been left sitting in this dingy, godforsaken waiting room for more than two hours. He grimaced. What kind of game was the MVD playing here? Somebody, probably that smug son of a bitch Serov, had set the three of them up, and every minute that passed gave whoever it was more time to either cover his tracks or vanish.

Thorn swiveled slightly in his chair as the door to the holding area swung open.

A young man cautiously poked his head through the opening. Wary brown eyes blinked owlishly behind his horn-rim glasses. "Captain Dobuzhinsky?"

"*Da.*" The MVD captain lumbered to his feet. "You are from the American embassy?"

"Yes." The young man nodded rapidly. He strode forward. "My name is Andrew Wyatt. I'm with the administrative affairs section."

It was about time the pinstriped cavalry rode over the ridge, Thorn thought sourly.

Wyatt turned toward them. "Special Agent Gray? Colonel Thorn? I've been sent to bring you back to the embassy." He glanced at the MVD officer. "I assume that's all right, Captain?"

Dobuzhinsky nodded dourly. "First, you must sign for them." The captain held out a clipboard and watched impassively while the young embassy staffer hurriedly read through the official form attached to it—moving his lips as he sounded out some of the Russian legal jargon.

Once Wyatt scrawled his signature across the bottom of the form, the MVD officer uncuffed them—first Helen and then Thorn. He scowled at them and then nodded abruptly toward the door. "Very well. You are free to leave. But only to go with this man from your embassy. Nowhere else. You understand?"

Thorn restrained his anger until they were outside the terminal and on their way to the embassy car waiting at the curb for them. Then he swung around on Wyatt. "What the hell is wrong with the Russians? First, we're almost aced by some of their frigging *Mafiya* types and then they throw *us* in the slammer! Don't they give a damn about why one of their best officers was murdered?"

The young embassy staffer spread his hands apart. "I'm afraid that's out of my bailiwick, Colonel. My orders were to bail you out and get you back to the embassy—pronto. The Deputy Chief of Mission wants to see you in his office ASAP."

Partly mollified, Thorn pulled open the rear door on the embassy car and held it for Helen. "Fine." He slid in beside her and said, "Maybe the State Department can light a fire under those idiots in the Kremlin."

Helen simply shook her head and stared out the window of the car as they sped out of the airport—heading southeast for Moscow.

U.S. Embassy, Moscow

Randolph Clifford was the Deputy Chief of Mission, the number two man at the American embassy in Moscow. His office, richly furnished with carefully selected czarist-era and American colonial antiques, was meant to endorse his authority, to remind visitors of his position as a high-ranking representative of the U.S. government. It was not meant to serve as the setting for a shouting match.

Colonel Peter Thorn supposed that Clifford, a portly man with a thick mane of white hair, might be called distinguished under less stressful circumstances. Right now, though, the bad-tempered twist of the diplomat's mouth and the vein throbbing dangerously on his temple ruined his image as an urbane shaper of American foreign policy.

"Look, Special Agent Gray," Clifford said in exasperation. "As far as Washington is concerned, the only thing that happened aboard the *Star of the White Sea* is that two of our citizens stumbled onto a Russian *Mafiya* drug buy that went sour. It was just an unhappy coincidence that you, the colonel here, and Major Koniev went aboard the ship at that particular time and got caught in the crossfire." His tone was final, almost dictatorial, but then he was used to having the authority to back up his dictates.

"Is that the story the MVD's trying to peddle?" demanded Helen angrily, glaring back at the red-faced diplomat with unblinking eyes. "If so, only a moron would even pretend to believe it!"

Thorn hurriedly tamped down a wry grin. He'd wondered what it would take to shake Helen out of her depression over Alexei Koniev's death. He should have guessed it would be contact with one of the State Department's "best and brightest" at his most obnoxious. Now Thorn was just glad she didn't still have the Tokarev automatic she'd picked up aboard the Russian freighter. If she'd been armed, he had the feeling Randolph Clifford might already have been on the receiving end of a full eight-shot magazine.

Clifford bristled, and then visibly relaxed his facial muscles. He adopted a more soothing, almost fatherly, tone. "I'll overlook that unfortunate comment, Miss Gray. You're overwrought. And I know you've been through hell—"

"Don't patronize me, Mr. Clifford!" Helen interrupted. "What I'm overwrought about, if anything, is the way we, the U.S. government that is, seems to be papering this whole thing over."

Evidently too mad to sit still, she got up and started pacing the room.

Thorn leaned forward. It was time to stick his own oar in. "What happened in Pechenga wasn't an accident, sir. It was a cold-blooded ambush. They were waiting for us."

"Perhaps so," the embassy official replied, and clearly glad to talk to him while Helen cooled off. "But the MVD claims that the ambush could have been set up in thirty seconds when one of the *Mafiya* lookouts spotted you coming down the pier." He shook his head. "Given the odds against you, I'm still amazed you managed to escape at all."

Helen snapped, "I'm sure that whoever planned all this is even more amazed!"

Clifford ignored her remark and went on. "You have to view this matter from the Russian perspective, Colonel. The evidence the MVD found aboard that tramp freighter seems quite clear."

He tapped the bulky manila folder he'd told them contained the official Russian government crime scene report. "First they discover nearly fifty kilos of what looks like heroin in one of the ship's storage lockers. Then they find out that these drugs are really just milk sugar laced with a small percentage of the real stuff. And finally, they stumble across all nineteen of her crew, including the real Captain Tumarev, gagged and bound with duct tape, shot in the back of the head execution-style, and then dumped in a cargo hold!"

The diplomat shuddered involuntarily, evidently remembering the photographs he'd said were included in the MVD report. He was a bureaucrat, not a man of action.

Helen, who'd seen worse sights in her tour with the FBI's Hostage Rescue Team, stopped pacing and shrugged. "All of which proves nothing." She leaned over the diplomat's desk. "Except that whoever arranged that ambush was willing to go to extraordinary lengths to put an end to our investigation before we got any closer to the truth. And now you and the MVD are giving the bad guys what they want on a silver platter!"

Clifford turned red with anger. "Listen, Miss Gray, your investigation has done more to strain U.S.-Russian relations than you can possibly imagine." He scowled, speaking plainly and candidly for a change. "Somebody in the Pechenga militia already blabbed to the Moscow press corps. And only Undersecretary Carleton's murder yesterday has kept this off the front pages in the States. But the local boys are running wild, and they're embarrassing the hell out of the Kremlin. The press is playing every angle it can dream up—Russian organized crime, lousy Russian aircraft safety, Russian drug smuggling, corruption in the Russian military . . ."

"I don't give a damn about the press, Mr. Clifford—or the Kremlin," Helen said forcefully. "My job is finding out the truth about what happened in Kandalaksha and why my partner was killed."

Clifford shook his head just as firmly. "That's where you're wrong, Miss Gray." He included Thorn in his baleful gaze. "As it stands, you two have managed to anger almost every faction in the Russian government. Most of them were never very happy with the idea of Americans investigating crimes on Russian soil. Now they're furious!

"Your original charter covered the OSIA plane crash only," the diplomat continued. "But once you started poking around into *Mafiya* drug cartels and their ties to the Russian Air Force, the MVD claims you crossed the line into 'impermissible interference.'"

That was too much for Thorn. "That's bullshit," he growled. "Alexei Koniev had permission from his higher-ups every step of the way."

"And Major Koniev is dead," Clifford reminded him brutally. "Which brings me to another problem. The MVD is having trouble believing that one of their best men was killed in that ambush while you two walked away without a scratch—even if the major did die a hero." He shrugged. "Not everyone believes your story about what happened aboard the *Star of the White Sea*."

Helen glared and Peter opened his mouth to protest, but the diplomat held up a conciliatory hand. "Don't worry. I believe you. At least I think I do. I've read both your personnel files."

Clifford sighed and turned to face Thorn directly. "But your Special Forces background makes you very hot, diplomatically, Colonel." He gestured vaguely toward the window. "There are a lot of people here in Moscow who don't see you as a simple soldier, Colonel. To the Russians, the closest thing to Delta Force is the old Soviet Spetsnaz. And that means you're a trained assassin in their eyes—a paid U.S. government killer. So your presence here makes them nervous. They were willing to let it lie as long as things stayed relatively quiet, but you're in the spotlight now."

Thorn tensed. He knew that what Clifford said was true. Officially, he'd been on very thin ice from the beginning, and now the ice had cracked. He looked over at Helen, hoping she was on firmer ground.

As if on cue she sat down in the chair next to him and

crossed her arms. "Colonel Thorn's background has proved an extremely valuable asset during this investigation," she said steadily.

Clifford snorted. "That depends on your perspective, I suppose. Others might reasonably argue your whole effort has been an unmitigated disaster from beginning to end. This Pechenga fiasco is simply the last straw."

Jesus. Thorn shook his head, trying desperately to think of a way out of the bureaucratic box he saw being built around them. "I don't accept that, Mr. Clifford. As far as I can see, we've made substantial progress. We've established beyond a shadow of a doubt that the OSIA transport plane was sabotaged. And we know that this Captain Grushtin carried out the sabotage—though we don't know yet why, or on whose orders."

"That's no longer any of your concern," Clifford said bluntly.

"What?" Helen exploded.

The diplomat drew a deep breath, then stood up and walked around his desk to face them. "All right, I'll spell it out for you. Your role in this investigation is over. This is now solely a Russian matter, involving Russian nationals on sovereign Russian territory. As a result, any further inquiries will be handled by the Russian government and *only* by the Russian government. Is that understood?"

Helen's eyes blazed. "No, it is not understood, sir," she ground out through gritted teeth. "As an FBI legal attaché, this case still comes under my jurisdiction. Or have you forgotten the Americans who also died when that plane went down?"

Clifford rounded on her, his patience evidently at an end. "That's the second part of my message, Special Agent Gray. As of now, you're no longer a legal attaché at this embassy. The FBI is transferring you back to Washington—at the request of the Russian authorities and the ambassador as well."

Oh, hell, Thorn thought, watching the color drain from Helen's face. That's torn it. These sons of a bitches have just flushed her career down the toilet.

"It's for your own good, Miss Gray," Clifford explained, more calmly now that he'd dropped his bombshell. "Your usefulness as an investigator here is now nil. No official will ever talk to you." He spread his hands. "Besides, there's the matter of your own physical safety. After what you did aboard the *Star of the White Sea*, the *Mafiya* may come after you personally."

"I can take care of myself, Mr. Clifford," Helen said tightly. "And I can find people who'll talk."

The Deputy Chief of Mission shook his head. "You have your orders, Miss Gray. I suggest you obey them."

He turned toward Thorn and arched an eyebrow. "As for you, Colonel, you've been ordered back to D.C., too. You'll be assigned to temporary duty at the Pentagon—pending your imminent retirement."

Thorn sat motionless. He told himself he wasn't surprised—not really. Egged on by a White House still angry at him for disobeying the President, the brass hats had been looking for a chance to toss him out of the Army for two years now. Only his old commander's pull had kept them at bay for this long. Well, he'd been living on Sam Farrell's nickel ever since Teheran and it looked like he'd just spent it. The one thing he hadn't expected was to pull Helen down with him.

Clifford turned his back and looked out the window. "You both have forty-eight hours to get your personal affairs in order, to pack, and do whatever else you need to do. But you will not leave Moscow. And you will check in here at the embassy by phone at 0700 hours and 1900 hours each day.

Finally, you will keep your contacts with Russian nationals to the absolute minimum necessary to prepare for departure."

"In other words, we're under house arrest," Helen muttered.

Clifford looked over his shoulder at her. "On the contrary, Miss Gray," he countered. "I've given you the freedom of the city. And you should be damned grateful to me. I'd be within my rights and my authority to confine you to the embassy grounds or ship you out on the evening flight—with your personal effects to follow."

Then he shook his head. "But I won't do that. You've created a nasty incident—one that my staff and I are going to have to bend over backward to smooth over. But you've committed no crime, per se—no matter what some of the MVD's hardliners are claiming. So for God's sake stay low, keep your mouths shut, and steer clear of any more trouble!"

Without waiting for any further argument, Clifford turned back to the window in a clear dismissal.

Thorn stopped in the hallway outside Clifford's office, aware that he still felt numb, almost completely disconnected from his own body. No matter how many times he'd told himself his days in the Army were numbered, the diplomat's cold announcement that he was being forcibly retired had still hit him with the force of a hammerblow. He'd spent most of his adult life in uniform. What could the civilian world offer him now?

Thorn frowned, remembering friends who'd opted out of the Special Operations Command during the Army's recent waves of downsizing. Two or three had joined defense firms as managers. A couple had tried to set themselves up as security consultants. One was a teacher at some high school in the Midwest. They were making a living, supporting themselves and their families, but they all missed the Army's close-knit camaraderie, excitement, and sense of a larger purpose.

He glanced at Helen. Her face mirrored his own stunned disbelief. She clearly didn't harbor any illusions about her own long-term prospects in the FBI. The legal attaché job had been a plum assignment—one that had put her in the running for further promotion. But the FBI hierarchy was notoriously unforgiving and notoriously touchy about bad publicity. Screw up once and you'd find yourself in hot water. Screw up once, *in the public eye,* and you were likely to spend the rest of your career either in some podunk town in the middle of nowhere, or, worse yet, trapped in the drearier confines of the J. Edgar Hoover Building.

Without thinking, Thorn slipped his arm around her shoulder. Normally Helen was prickly about public displays of affection, especially on her professional turf, but she welcomed his touch now. She sighed deeply and half leaned against him as they headed back toward the elevators that would take them to her office.

"Jesus, you two sure don't look like the superhuman Amerikanski secret commandos I've been reading about in the afternoon paper! More like folks who've been caught out in a tornado."

Thorn stiffened and swung around toward the short, balding man who'd come around a corner behind them. He'd taken just about enough crap from the U.S. State Department for one day . . .

Helen laid a cautionary hand on his arm. She tried smiling and almost made it. "Hello, Charlie."

The newcomer looked ready to embrace Helen, but he settled for pumping her hand. "Christ, Helen! I'm sure glad to see you alive and well. When we heard about that business in Pechenga, we were all horrified."

He turned to Thorn and extended his hand. "And you're Peter Thorn. I'm Charlie Spiegel. I work here at the embassy."

Helen explained. "Charlie and I worked together on a couple of cases. I can't tell you who he works for, but he's good at his job." The implication was obvious: Charlie Spiegel worked for the CIA.

"She's too kind, Colonel," Spiegel said. He flashed a quick grin. "Mostly I just sit around and file reports claiming credit for whatever paydirt Helen digs up."

"But not this time," Thorn said quietly.

Spiegel's grin faded. "No, not this time." He shook his head sorrowfully. "Man, I'm afraid you two have taken one hell of a long walk off a short pier. I hate to say it, but I think the ambassador's right to get you out of Russia before anything else hits the fan—and the quicker the better."

He saw the surprise on Thorn's face and shrugged. "Helen said I was good, and it's my job to keep plugged in. Look, why don't you come to my office? While His Nibs in there gave you the forty lashes with a wet tongue, I've been keeping my ear to the ground. There are some new developments I think you should know about."

The CIA agent's office was on the floor above Helen's, and it was just as cramped and a lot messier. Books, periodicals, and printouts cluttered Spiegel's battered desk, every shelf, and much of the floor space.

Thorn shook his head wryly as he and Helen cleared stacks of reference works off chairs so they could sit down. This guy seemed to live on paper.

Spiegel didn't wait for them to get settled. He flopped into his own swivel chair and started explaining. "First, I don't think you folks fully understand the flap your gun battle in Pechenga has created. You're both front-page news here. Hell, Clifford's people had to do some pretty fast footwork to keep the media away from you. That was part of the reason for that little covert handoff out at Sheremetevo Airport."

Thorn considered that grimly. The only thing worse than sitting in MVD custody would have been getting caught by a mob of eager-beaver reporters and cameramen. Everything in his nature and his Delta Force training taught him the importance of staying out of the glare of TV lights.

"The forty-eight hours you've been given isn't just to let you pack, it's mostly to give the story time to cool off," Spiegel said confidentially. He lowered his voice. "You didn't hear it from me, but the embassy is even making sure you don't arrive home at a commercial airport. You'll take a regular flight to Germany, but then they're transferring you to a military passenger flight to Andrews Air Force Base."

"Arriving in the dead of the night, I suppose?" Helen asked bitterly.

"You got it," Spiegel confirmed. "And I wouldn't be a bit surprised if you're listed on the manifest as PFCs John and Jane Doe. The last thing anyone wants is more news coverage."

Thorn nodded. He agreed with the precautions the State Department was taking on that score, if on no other.

"What about our work, Charlie?" Helen asked. "Can you or your people dig any further? I don't want this investigation to fall through the cracks once they've shipped us off. We've paid too high a price to let it go so easily."

Spiegel looked blank. "Jesus, Helen. That's gonna be a problem. I mean, the word's come down from on high: Steer clear of the Kandalaksha mess. It's a Russian-only situation. If my people start asking too many questions, I'm going to trip all kinds of alarm bells all over the damn place—both here and in D.C." Then he shrugged. "Besides, with this Grushtin character dead and that freighter a bust, I wouldn't really know where to start looking. Seems to me you've run this thing into a dead-end—no pun intended."

Thorn frowned. He wasn't going to let this guy off the hook so easily. He claimed he was a friend of Helen's. Well, let him prove it. He shook his head. "Not true. We know one of the people who set us up. Have somebody put the squeeze on Colonel General Feodor Serov. That son of a bitch knows a hell of a lot more than he told us."

Spiegel sighed. "That's one of the new developments I mentioned. Somebody took out both Serov and his wife yesterday—probably very early in the A.M. Whoever did it was a pro. The wife took one bullet to the brain. Serov went a little harder. Somebody pumped him so full of heroin that the stuff was practically pouring out of his eye sockets."

Thorn felt his jaw muscles tighten. Every time he thought they were close to the inner core of this mystery, somebody got there first and cleared out all the evidence and witnesses. He looked hard at Spiegel. "I suppose Serov's murder is all over the evening papers, too?"

The CIA officer shook his head. "Not a peep. Nada. The MVD and the Russian Air Force have clamped down a complete security blackout around Kandalaksha. Nothing's getting in or out. They're damned serious about it, too. Finding out one of their highest-ranking officers was involved in drug trafficking has them rattled."

"Oh?" Helen looked skeptical. "Then how did you find out about it?"

"Well . . ." Spiegel smiled slyly. "Let's just say that Russian counterintelligence isn't as good as they'd like to think."

"All right, so Serov's dead," Helen said slowly, thinking aloud. "That still leaves one more trail you could follow."

"Oh?" Spiegel said. "Fill me in. I've never claimed omniscience."

"Arrus Export," Helen said. "Both Serov and the customs agent at Pechenga claimed they were dealing with a man named Peterhof."

"Yeah," Spiegel said. "I read your report." Then he shook his head again. "That's another dead-end, I'm afraid."

"Why?"

The CIA man shrugged. "We checked with the Arrus office here in Moscow. They've never had anyone named Peterhof working for them. And they claim they've never run an Su-24 engine acquisition program like the one you described."

"What makes you think they'd admit something like that so easily?" Thorn challenged. "Christ, we're talking about black-market arms sales here!"

"I understand that, Colonel," Spiegel said. He checked to make sure the door was completely closed, then lowered his voice slightly. "Look, Arrus is a clean operation, okay? It's on the side of the angels."

Helen stared at him. "Are you telling us that Arrus Export is a Company asset? That it's a front organization for the CIA?"

"Not exactly," Spiegel said hastily. "But Arrus has done some significant favors for us in the past. And it's very well connected back in the States. The owners are fair-haired boys in Langley's books."

Helen looked forward, her eyes glittering. "I'm going to ask you one more question, Charlie." Her lips thinned. "And I expect a straight answer."

"If I can," Spiegel temporized.

"No ifs, Charlie," Helen said coldly. "And no screwing around with maybes . . . or other covert op double-talk. You owe me. Remember?"

The CIA officer flushed. "Ask your question."

"Is this engine smuggling operation tied into the Agency

somehow?" Helen said carefully. "Or to some other U.S. government outfit?"

"No."

"You're sure?" Thorn asked skeptically. Spiegel's denial meant nothing if he was out of the loop. All covert operations were run on strict need-to-know principles.

"I'm sure, Colonel," the CIA man said. He looked Thorn squarely in the eye. "I went straight to the top of the Operations Directorate when I saw Helen's preliminary report from Kandalaksha. I even asked about the drug angle. Hell, I know this wouldn't be the first time someone's tripped over one of our ops, but I'm telling you this was not one of them."

Spiegel shook his head yet again. "Look, I don't know who the hell was buying Su-24 engines on the sly, or running heroin, or whatever the real story is. But I do know the CIA is clean. We're not involved here."

He glanced at Helen and frowned. "Christ, Helen, I know what you're going through. Hell, I liked Alexei Koniev, too! But face facts: You've pushed this thing as far as you can. You've already put your whole career on the line, and you were damned lucky to get out of Pechenga in one piece. So let the Russians sort out their own messes!"

Thorn knew Spiegel was offering them good advice, but he didn't need to see the stubborn set of Helen's shoulders to know that she wasn't prepared to let the matter drop so easily. Unfortunately, he didn't see what choice either of them really had. Once they were out of Russia their ability to pin down the truth of what had happened at Kandalaksha would drop to precisely zero.

JUNE 8

U.S. Embassy Residential Compound, Moscow

Helen Gray surrendered any hope that she could persuade herself to sleep. Her body was tired—beyond tired, in fact. Every muscle ached. And whenever she moved, she could feel every separate scrape, cut, and bruise she'd collected during the desperate firefight aboard the *Star of the White Sea*. She could have ignored the pain. Training and sheer exhaustion would have allowed her to do that.

But now her mind and memory betrayed her.

The image of Alexei Koniev lying dead rose before her, and then fled back into the darker recesses of her mind— chased away by old ghosts and new fears. All her life she'd pushed herself hard—striving always and everywhere to be the best, to win every game and every contest. Now it looked as though she'd finally met a puzzle she couldn't solve and an unknown enemy she couldn't beat.

Helen opened her eyes in the darkness and lay staring up at the ceiling of her small bedroom.

When she was just thirteen, she'd set her heart on becoming an FBI agent. Her parents, her brother and her sisters, and even some of her teachers had tried to convince her that she was on a wild-goose chase. But she'd persisted. She'd weighed every class, every hobby, and every interest by how far it moved her toward her goal—the FBI Academy at Quantico.

Once in the FBI itself, she'd clawed her way up and into the elite Hostage Rescue Team by sheer ability and hard work—disdaining the various affirmative-action shortcuts that had been dangled in front of her. To Helen, the way to smash the sexist bias of the Bureau's old boy network was to prove it flat-out wrong—not to give them a chance to fall back on the tired, old cop-out that women couldn't make the grade without special help.

Her jaw tightened. There would be celebrating in some corridors of the Hoover Building once the news that she'd been yanked out of Moscow filtered through the rumor mill. Larry McDowell for one must be as pleased as punch. And there were plenty of others like McDowell scattered throughout the FBI.

Of course, Helen knew that she had friends and mentors in the Bureau's hierarchy, too. Men who trusted her. Men who would stand by her. But what could they do for her now? Incurring the wrath of the Russian government while solving an important case might have been acceptable. Pissing off the Kremlin just to come up with a jumble of unintelligible clues—all leading nowhere—was another story.

On the surface, Charlie Spiegel was right. Their investigation had reached a dead-end. Every witness and every potential suspect they'd turned up had been murdered—first Grushtin, then the entire crew of that Russian tramp freighter, and now Serov. And, with Alexei Koniev dead, she and Peter had not only lost a partner and friend, they'd also lost their access to anybody they could trust in Russian law enforcement. So what else could they do but slink home to America with their tails between their legs?

Helen sat bolt upright in bed and thumped her fist onto the mattress with a muttered, "No way!"

"Thought you were awake," Peter Thorn said softly, pushing himself up to sit beside her.

Peter had visited the broom-closet-sized room offered him as temporary accommodations by the embassy staff just long enough to drop off his travel kit. Then he'd come straight to her own cramped quarters to help her pack. Several hours of steady work had left her life in Moscow jumbled up in cardboard boxes all over the floor. At her invitation, he'd stayed for the night. Both of them were too drained and exhausted to make love, but neither wanted to leave the other's side. And neither of them gave a damn anymore about the gossip that might race through the chancery building.

Helen turned her head toward him, seeing his eyes gleaming in the dark. "You can't sleep, either?"

"Nope." Peter sighed. "I just keep running things over and over in my mind—trying to see where we screwed up." Then he shrugged ruefully. "And trying to avoid thinking about what happens next. Once we're home, I mean."

Helen sat silent, struck by a sudden sense of shame. She'd been thinking too much about herself. No matter where they stuck her—whether in Mudville or the Hoover Building's basement records office—she would still carry a badge. She would still be an FBI special agent. But Peter . . . Peter had lost everything.

The United States Army had been his home—his real family, in fact—for all of Peter Thorn's life. His father had been a career soldier, a highly decorated senior sergeant in the Special Forces. Peter's boyhood had been spent on military bases around the country and around the world. And, after his wayward mother abandoned them when he was eleven years old, he and his father had grown still closer—closer to each other and closer to the Army they both loved.

Now he was forty and faced with the prospect of . . . what? Helen wondered. Retirement? Shuffling papers as a manager in some corporate hive? Living hand-to-mouth as a freelance counterterrorism consultant in a world crowded with other ex-soldiers chasing the same degrading contracts?

She felt tears well up in her eyes and turned toward him. "Oh, Peter . . ." she whispered brokenly.

His arms tightened around her. One strong hand softly stroked her hair. He kissed her forehead gently, brushing his lips across her skin. "It'll be all right, Helen," he promised. "We'll see this thing through together. No matter what happens."

"Side by side?" she asked.

"Come hell, high water, earthquake, or congressional committee," Peter said flatly.

Helen felt her fatigue, her pain, all her doubts, and all her fears fly away—vanishing in a single, convulsive instant. Her lips met his fiercely and parted. Her body molded to his in a flowing, moving, pulsing rhythm that swept time and trouble aside.

Sometime later, exactly how long she wasn't sure and didn't really care, she lay still in the comforting circle of his arms. She ran her fingers through the hair on his chest, feeling her eyelids growing heavier by the second. "Wow."

"Wow, yourself," Peter agreed gladly. But then he shifted slightly beneath her. "Who knows? Maybe retirement won't be so bad, after all."

Helen heard the worried undertone in his voice and felt sleep fade out of her reach again. She raised herself up on one elbow and tapped him on the ribs. "You don't mean that, Peter, do you?"

He sighed. "No, not really." His eyes looked over her head—off toward a horizon she couldn't see. "I know what I am, Helen. I can't dodge it. I was born to follow the fife and the drum—not the lute and the tambourine. If I can't be a soldier . . ." He fell silent.

"Then we have to find a way to beat these guys. To win our honor back. To prove we were right to chase after

Grushtin and Serov, and whoever murdered them," Helen said angrily, feeling her mind starting to come fully alive for the first time since she'd left Randolph Clifford's ornate office.

"Nice sentiment in theory. But probably impossible to carry out in fact," he said reluctantly. "I think we're licked, Helen."

"You don't really believe that."

"No," Peter said finally. Then he shrugged. "But I really don't know where the hell we go from here."

"Back to the basics," Helen suggested.

"Okay," he said. He sat up in bed again. "The basics being: What's worth sabotaging a passenger plane, murdering a high-ranking Air Force officer, and slaughtering an entire ship's crew to keep secret?"

"Heroin?" she speculated. "Bulk quantities of heroin? Stashed inside one or more of those Su-24 engines Serov and his officers sold?"

"Maybe. It fits most of what we know," Peter said slowly. "And the Russians and our own people have sure bought that as the motive behind all this."

She heard the doubt in his voice. "But you haven't?"

He shook his head. "Christ, Helen, I don't know. Not for sure." He grimaced. "All I do know is that I'm really tired of having heroin smuggling shoved in my face as a motive at every possible opportunity."

She nodded. The same thing had been bothering her. The ambush aboard the *Star of the White Sea* made it clear that the bad guys had been one step ahead of them all the way. If that were so, and they were smuggling drugs, why hadn't they tried harder to clear away the evidence?

When she asked that question aloud, Peter nodded himself. "Good point. God knows those guys had plenty of time to themselves aboard that freighter—once they murdered the crew." He leaned back against the pillow. "No, the more I think about it, the less I believe this whole thing is really about heroin smuggling."

"But what about the stuff we found in Gasparov's suitcase?" Helen asked.

"Coincidence?" Peter suggested. "It could be a coincidence that the bad guys have been running with ever since—leading us down a bunch of blind alleys."

Helen thought that over. "Maybe. The only real link we had between Captain Grushtin and Colonel Gasparov was that suicide note . . ."

"Which they forced Grushtin to write under torture," Peter finished for her.

Helen grimaced. "Well, then, if we're not chasing smuggled heroin—what the hell are we looking for?"

"Something else kept at Kandalaksha. Something valuable."

"Su-24 bombers, maybe?" Helen wondered. "What if General Serov wasn't just selling engines? What if he was selling whole aircraft?"

Peter shook his head. "I doubt it."

"Why?"

"Because Avery and his team weren't there to count planes. They'd have no reason to go anywhere near the flight line or the hangars. If Serov and his commanders were selling off their aircraft inventory, John and his inspection team would never have spotted it."

"So there'd be no reason for Serov to have Captain Grushtin sabotage their transport plane," Helen concluded.

"Exactly."

"Then what do you think the inspection team could have uncovered that spooked Serov?" she asked again.

Peter hesitated for several seconds and then said, "Well, I keep thinking about that circle in John Avery's inspection logbook."

Helen remembered the strange notation they'd seen scrawled around one of the nuclear weapon identifier codes. She shivered suddenly. "Jesus, Peter. You think we might be tracking a loose nuke?"

He nodded, slowly at first and then more decisively. "Yeah. It's possible. Maybe John spotted something during his inspection—something he wasn't supposed to see."

"But he and his team signed off on the Kandalaksha storage site before boarding that plane," Helen pointed out. "Why not call a treaty violation right then and there?"

Peter shrugged his shoulders. "Maybe he wasn't sure." His voice sharpened. "Or maybe he thought it would be too dangerous to say anything at Kandalaksha. Even in Russia, nobody can just back a truck up to a weapons bunker for a quick pickup. What would you do if you suspected the base commander and some of his top officers had sold one of the bombs in their care?"

"My God." Helen swallowed hard. It sounded crazy at first—until you realized that nuclear weapons were the only commodity at Kandalaksha more valuable than a shipment of drugs. "Would anyone believe us if we tripped the alarm?"

"Now? After Pechenga?" Peter asked. He shook his head grimly. "Not a chance. Between the MVD, our own government, and whoever set us up, we've been pretty thoroughly discredited. We'd need hard evidence to set the nuke-hunting teams in motion—not just some doodles in a notebook."

His shoulders slumped. "And there's the rub. We can't get that kind of evidence. Once we're on that flight to Andrews, we're out of the picture."

Helen knew he was right. Whether the people who'd tried

to kill them in Pechenga had been smuggling drugs or a nuclear weapon, she and Peter needed more information, and they weren't going to get it if they kept playing by the rules. She lay awake for hours, long after Peter had slipped into a fitful sleep, trying to decide just how far outside the regulations and the law she would be willing to go to discover the truth.

CHAPTER NINE

BREAKING STRAIN

JUNE 9

Tegel International Airport, Berlin

The captain's announcement came over the loudspeaker in Russian, German, and, finally, English. "We are now on final approach to Tegel International Airport. Please remain in your seats with your seat belts fastened until we have reached the terminal and you are instructed to release them."

Colonel Peter Thorn felt Helen Gray grip his hand tightly.

"You still want to do this?" he asked. He tried to put as much feeling into the question as he could, as if extra emphasis could pull Helen's real desire out of her.

"We don't have any other choice, Peter." She was equally emphatic, but that didn't reassure him. "You know that nobody else is going to do a damned thing more about this case. There's just us, and we owe it to Alexei. Hell, we owe it to ourselves."

Thorn shook his head. They'd had the same discussion, and the same arguments, for the entire two-hour flight from Moscow. What had seemed reasonable late at night in the privacy of her empty apartment seemed a lot less sensible in broad daylight. His theory that they might be chasing a loose Russian nuclear weapon suddenly appeared the stuff of nightmares—and about as substantial.

The worst of it was that all the real risk of what Helen proposed would fall on her shoulders. Following his travel orders to the letter wouldn't change his own fate one iota. No matter what he did, he was slated for the Army's dust heap—for forced retirement. But failing to report on time might give Helen's own enemies inside the FBI hierarchy the excuse they needed to bounce her out of the Bureau altogether. He was risking a minor black mark on a service record already headed for the inactive list. She was risking her paycheck, her pension—everything that was left of her whole career.

It seemed a huge bet to make—especially when the odds against getting to the truth were stacked so high. If they failed, or if the smuggled jet engines proved to be just that, smuggled jet engines, she was facing an unalterably bleak professional future. And even if they faced it together, that wasn't a future either of them could look forward to.

The passenger jet shuddered as its wheels touched concrete. Thorn took a deep breath. The first leg of their journey home was over.

He stood up, pulled a sport coat out of the overhead compartment along with his travel bag, and handed Helen her own carry-on suitcase. At the embassy's insistence, he was traveling home in civilian clothes. And from long habit, they were both traveling light.

They got off the plane and cleared German customs quickly. No German bureaucrat felt much like wasting time on American travelers—not when they were confronted by a planeload of Russians, Ukrainians, Georgians, Kazakhs, and a host of other ex-Soviet ethnic minorities.

As always, Tegel was packed, jammed wall-to-wall with arriving and departing passengers.

Thorn took his stamped passport back and suddenly felt Helen nudge him gently in the ribs.

"George Patton, Jr., at five o'clock," she muttered.

He looked up, spotting who she meant with ease. A young Army captain wearing a crisply starched Class A uniform stood to one side of the hall leading to customs—craning his head as he searched the crowd. The captain was their ride to Ramstein Air Base, where they'd be spirited into the States aboard a military passenger plane.

Thorn squared his shoulders instinctively and then relaxed. It was time to doff the military habits of a lifetime. He glanced at Helen. "Right, here we go." He motioned her ahead. "You first, Miss Gray."

She nodded and merged with a clump of other passengers—careful to stay on the far side of the group.

Thorn waited another thirty or forty seconds and then did the same thing. He walked right past the young captain without making eye contact and turned the corner.

Their would-be escort never saw them. He was looking for a man and woman traveling together—not apart. More to the point, Thorn realized, the younger man was expecting them to be looking for him just as hard as he'd been searching for them.

Helen joined him right around the corner. "How long have we got?" she asked.

"Unless they've bred all initiative out of junior officers,

I'd say we've got about five minutes before he starts looking for us," Thorn replied with a wry smile.

Helen started walking even faster.

It took them another few precious moments to sort through the welter of signs for Scandinavian Airlines System once they reached the main terminal and ticketing area. Thorn glanced back the way they'd come. No sign of pursuit. Not yet, at any rate.

He shook his head. It felt damned strange to be relieved *not* to see an American army uniform. He didn't like it. Like Helen, he'd always been secure in his actions—taking risks, but always sure of his course. His years of service with Delta Force had offered him the chance to escape the dull, grinding routine of the peacetime Army, but he'd still had the sense of being part of a larger whole. But now they'd both jumped completely outside the hierarchies that had provided purpose and direction for so much of their adult lives.

They got into line at the SAS ticket counter and scanned the monitor showing the airline's scheduled departures.

Helen nodded toward the flickering display. "There's a direct flight for Bergen at eight."

"No good." Thorn checked his watch. "We're not going to get away with hanging around here for two hours. If we're going through with this, we need to put some airspace between ourselves and our Army watchdog back there." He jerked a thumb over his shoulder toward customs.

"True." Helen narrowed her eyes. "There, Peter." She pointed to a string of letters and numbers at the top of the monitor. "There's a flight to Oslo in half an hour. It'll be boarding any time now."

Thorn reached out and gently turned her to face him. She didn't pull away. "Look, Helen. This is where it gets real. We can still find that captain and make up some excuse for missing him at customs. We'd be home by tomorrow morning."

"There's no time for this, Peter," she protested softly. "I've made up my mind." Shifting in his grasp slightly, she pulled him toward the counter as the line moved forward.

Office of the Deputy Chief of Mission, U.S. Embassy, Moscow

"What?" Deputy Chief of Mission Randolph Clifford stared at Charlie Spiegel in disbelief.

Spiegel could only restate what he'd already said. "I saw them to the airport. I saw them board the plane."

"Then why weren't they on the plane when it landed in Berlin?"

The CIA officer shrugged. "I can't answer that, sir. If the Army's telling the truth about having somebody there to meet them, then Colonel Thorn and Special Agent Gray obviously got past him somehow."

"Why? And where did they go?"

Spiegel grinned. "I understand Bavaria's nice in the summer."

Clifford was not amused. "You assume this disappearance was voluntary. What if they were abducted?"

Spiegel turned serious. "Unlikely, given their background. You saw my report on Pechenga, sir. If somebody tried to take Helen Gray or Thorn off that plane against their will, believe me, we'd have heard of it by now."

Clifford nodded stiffly. He rubbed at his temples, evidently fighting the beginning of a world-class headache. "I can't believe this. A senior Army officer. Hell, and a senior

FBI agent! Violating travel orders, vanishing off the face of the earth . . ." He looked up at Spiegel in disbelief. "Have Thorn and Gray both gone crazy?"

"It doesn't sound like they've got much to lose by going off on their own," the CIA officer responded. "Have you notified the German authorities?"

"No." The diplomat rubbed harder at his forehead. "We won't get any help there. Thorn and Gray haven't committed any crimes—none that matter to the Germans anyway. The most I could do was get our own embassy and military to agree to report to us if they turned up." The frustration in Clifford's voice was clear.

"If I'd been through what they've been through, I'd take some time off before going home to face the music," Spiegel said flatly. "This may be their way of telling us all to go to hell."

Clifford reddened. "I suggest you get back to work, Mr. Spiegel." He nodded toward the door. "Just figure out what Thorn and Gray are doing. And why."

Spiegel headed back to his own office suspecting that the other man wasn't going to like the answers he would probably come up with. He'd worked long enough with Helen Gray to appreciate just how stubborn and determined she could be once she had her sights on an unsolved puzzle—or an enemy. What he couldn't figure out was what she hoped to accomplish. Drug trafficking was a major crime, but it was so widespread that blocking one smuggling route just pushed the stuff somewhere else. Trying to stop it completely was as futile as good old King Canute ordering the tide back with a wave of his royal hand. Besides, Helen and Peter Thorn weren't going to be allowed back into Russia—not legally. So where were they going to pick up the trail they'd followed so disastrously to Pechenga?

The CIA officer closed the door to his office and turned toward the wall map pinned up behind his desk. His eyes fell on Norway and he nodded to himself. He'd bet that Helen and the colonel were on their way to the only link left in the chain they'd been tracing—to Bergen.

Well, Spiegel decided, he'd take some time before reporting back to Clifford. The Agency didn't have many people on the ground in Norway—certainly not enough to waste their time and efforts looking for a couple of government employees who'd only broken a few travel regs. Besides, he thought, Helen Gray might just get lucky.

JUNE 10

Bergen, Norway

The high northern sky over Bergen glowed a deep, rich golden orange—a color that touched the steep green slopes above the city with fire. The same golden hue danced across the waters of the harbor—softening the outlines of the oil tankers, container ships, and fishing trawlers packed along Bergen's piers. Although it was already evening, only a few lights gleamed from the windows of the city's red-gabled houses, shops, bars, and restaurants.

Helen Gray glanced toward the moored ships and then back along the narrow street stretching up from the harbor toward the mountains. The season was working to their advantage. This close to the start of summer, Norway's warm eighteen- and twenty-hour days attracted streams of tourists. To the casual observer, she and Peter would be just two more vacationers—eager to take in the spectacular scenery and amble through the historic sites.

She turned to Peter. "All set?"

He showed his teeth in a quick grin and tapped the Canon EOS camera he'd purchased that afternoon. "You bet."

With Peter tagging along a couple of steps behind her, Helen walked toward the first waterfront tavern they'd located earlier in the afternoon—after arriving by train from Oslo. They'd waited until now, after the dinner hour, when the men they were looking for would be relaxing, gossiping, and griping after their day working on the docks.

The Akershus was named after the historic fortress that guarded Oslo's harbor. This was no tourist attraction, though. The bar's exterior was weathered, clearly not painted since the winter's passing, and winters in Norway could be very hard. Aside from the sign, a small anchor and a Viking longship painted on the front window were the only decorations. Still, it looked clean, and large enough to give them a good chance of finding the witnesses they needed.

Inside, a bar ran along one wall, down the full length of the room. It was surfaced with scarred dark wood. The room was paneled in matching wood, and ten or twelve tables filled the rest of the space.

Even this early in the evening, it was already half full. Some of the men were finishing meals, others were playing cards, and a few were already into their third beers, to judge from the empties. Helen noticed that there were no women in the room at all. This was clearly an all-male preserve. Only two men stood at the bar, talking soberly to each other and the barkeep, a large, blond, bearded man, who only needed a horned helmet to resemble one of his Viking ancestors.

Helen and Peter drew a few long looks from the patrons when they first entered. But once they'd ordered beers and taken a table in the corner, they were ignored.

Helen sipped her beer and studied the customers over her raised glass. A few were young—in their twenties, perhaps. The others ranged up to sixty or so. Most were solidly middle-aged. And all of them were dressed in work clothes—dark-colored overalls, often stained, or ripped and mended. Their scuffed boots and the hard hats dangling from the chairs behind them hinted that these were exactly the sort of men the two Americans were looking for.

Finally, Helen nodded to Peter and got up, approaching a man in his mid-fifties. He sat alone at a table, nursing a beer. "Excuse me, do you speak English?"

"*Nei.*"

Well, so much for him. She turned to a younger man at the next table, scruffy, but with an alert look. "Do you speak English?" she repeated.

"*Ja,* a little."

Helen offered her hand and flashed a smile, trying to turn on the charm without making it too obvious. "I'm Susan Anderson, with the ETS News Service." She handed him a business card, imprinted with the false name she was using, the name of the fictional news service, a phone number, and an Internet address.

She still felt somewhat awkward about operating under a phony identity. But years as an FBI agent had taught her the annoying truth that witnesses who often clammed up when questioned by someone with a badge were only too happy to spill everything they knew to the first journalist who came strolling along—especially one who was an attractive woman. Besides, flashing her American FBI credentials in a Norwegian port city was far more likely to generate the kind of official interest they wanted to avoid.

The airport hotel they'd checked into immediately after arriving in Oslo catered largely to international businessmen. Its facilities included a fully equipped computer center—complete with PCs for rent, laser printers, and the latest software. So an hour's work with some word processing and graphics programs had produced a small set of what appeared to be professionally printed business cards for each of them—Helen's as a journalist and Peter's as a photographer.

"You are a reporter?" The young Norwegian dockworker seemed curious, and a little interested, although she couldn't tell if he was responding to her smile or her occupation.

"I'm doing a story on a tramp freighter that sailed from here to Russia a week ago. Have you heard of the *Star of the White Sea*? She was moored at Pier 91A." Helen and Peter had spent the afternoon puzzling over back issues of the local newspaper's Shipping News section to dig up that piece of information.

"So? What is so special, this ship?" The man was interested, but seemed cautious.

Helen ignored his question and pressed on. Telling him that the entire crew had been murdered might make him clam up altogether. "I just want to talk to men who might have seen her." She let the corners of three hundred-kroner notes show in her hand. At current exchange rates, that was worth about fifty dollars—enough to loosen a few tongues without raising too many eyebrows, she judged.

He waved it back. "Knut and Fredrik, they work on the docks. I am inside, in a warehouse." He fired a string of Norwegian at a pair of men sitting three tables over. They perked up, obviously curious about the attractive foreigner, and answered.

The first man broke off the conversation after about three exchanges and turned back to Helen. "I am sorry. They do not know this ship."

She smiled again. "That's all right. But do you know anyone else we can ask? It would be a real help to my story. We could even take his picture for the article," she added, gesturing to her photographer. Peter fiddled with the Canon's lens, trying to look professional.

The Norwegian looked around, then asked another older man, and then another group of three. All replied, *"Nei."*

He shrugged and smiled at Helen. "I am sorry."

Helen smiled back, grateful for his efforts. "Never mind. Thank you anyway."

Peter had already gotten up. She turned toward the door, then changed her mind and went over to the bar. The Viking bartender took the bill she offered, and evidently understood her instructions to get her translator another beer and make it the best he had. No point in leaving sour feelings behind them.

Once outside on the street again, they turned toward the harbor.

Helen shook her head. "Well, that was a bust."

"Isn't this what you law enforcement types call legwork?" Peter asked. He shrugged. "Hell, we knew this wasn't going to be fast, Helen. This place must see dozens of ships come and go in the space of a week. Finding some of the guys who unloaded the *Star*, and who remember doing it, could take some time."

She drew a deep breath. "Yeah, I know. I just think of how easy it would have been to go straight to the port authorities, flash my badge, and ask to see the *Star of the White Sea*'s cargo manifests."

"We can still do that. You're still an FBI agent," Peter reminded her.

Helen grimaced. "Jesus, I get bad vibes at the thought. The last time we went barreling into a harbormaster's office, we got shot at."

They went on to another tavern, misnamed the Grand Café. Smaller than the Akershus, its clientele was similar.

Workingmen gathered around tables to play cards and drink. This time, Helen was immediately successful in finding someone who spoke English.

Arne Haukelid was a college student, studying literature, who'd taken a job at the docks to earn money between semesters. He also watched the news, and was well versed on current affairs.

"You want to know if any of us saw the *Star of the White Sea*, Miss Anderson? The one where they killed everyone and they found the drugs?" His voice carried in the quiet room, and Helen winced inwardly, then remembered Haukelid was still speaking English.

The young Norwegian let her buy him a beer, then circulated around the room, asking here and there. She couldn't follow the conversations, but headshakes and *"Nei"* were easy to understand. Another bust.

Peter and Helen left the Grand Café and headed for another bar, Ole Bull, and after that a place called Sjøboden. By this time it was almost ten at night, and she was getting worried that anyone with a day job would be heading home.

Sjøboden was another pub with nautical decorations scattered around. It looked a little rougher than the other places they'd been in, but it was also the most crowded, nearly filled with strong-looking men.

The buzz of conversation did not change when Peter and Helen entered, and a few of the dockworkers, sizing Helen up, even greeted her with *"Goddag"* and a smile. It looked to her like they'd had more than a few beers, but they still had an eye for a pretty woman.

One of them spoke English, but to Helen's consternation he'd heard all about the *Star of the White Sea*, and the fate of her crew. To her relief, though, her informant knew someone who actually helped unload her.

He pointed to a pair of men who willingly made room at their table for Helen and Peter when they came over. She let the conversation run on for a while, hoping to steer the talk in a useful direction.

The oldest, Olaf Syverstad, had the most to say. "This is a bad business. We haven't had too much drugs here. But soon these criminals and smugglers will be squeezing us." In his sixties, Olaf was concerned more for his son, Karl, who still worked at the docks.

Karl Syverstad had been translating for his father, and was delighted to have a chance to practice his English. Blond like his father, Karl's back and shoulders were as broad as a house. He'd been a longshoreman for five years.

"*Ja*, I worry now. Now that I know what is going on. Then, I liked working on the *Star*. They paid us overtime to stand by, and unload her as soon as she came."

"What did she carry?" asked Helen.

"Mostly scrap metal and fish," the younger Syverstad answered.

"And they were in a hurry to unload that?" Helen didn't have to act puzzled.

"Not all of it," the big Norwegian said. "There were five metal crates that came off first. They went straight across the pier to another ship, and that ship left right away—less than an hour, I think."

"What ship was that?" Helen forced herself not to sound too eager. Her story was supposed to be about the murders on the *Star*.

"*Baltic Venturer*. She was bound for Wilhelmshaven. In Germany."

"How do you know that?" Helen asked.

"It was her home port. Painted on her stern. And I heard the crew talking."

Helen looked over at Peter, who was listening intently,

but seemed content to let her do the talking. She continued. "So you only saw them unloading scrap metal, fish, and these crates?" She held out her hands, as if to describe the size of a box.

The younger Syverstad nodded. "*Ja,* pretty much. But those crates were big things, big enough for an auto maybe."

Bingo, Helen thought. His description matched the rough sizes of the Su-24 engines Serov had showed them. She leaned forward. "And what did the *Star* carry back to Russia?"

The Norwegian shook his head. "Nothing, she went back empty. I was on her for two days unloading. I saw nothing."

His father tapped the table for emphasis. "And a good thing, too, boy. Or you might have wound up dead—just like those poor Russian sods."

Helen let them talk for a while longer, about drugs, other ships to Russia, crime in Bergen, but finally found a graceful pause in the conversation and made their good-byes.

It was chilly outside, the midsummer twilight holding only a little warmth and a sea breeze from the west stripping even that away. Helen shivered slightly, but then glanced at Peter. "Well, what do you think?"

"I think we head for Wilhelmshaven, don't you?" he replied quietly.

"Yep." She couldn't hide the satisfaction in her voice. The trail left by the people who'd ambushed them and murdered Alexei Koniev hadn't grown completely cold after all. They'd found another link in the chain.

"What do you think about passing this information back to the Bureau?" Peter asked.

Helen thought about that a moment. She doubted they had enough hard data to penetrate the FBI's bureaucratic inertia yet, but that shouldn't stop them from trying to prod Washington into taking official notice that *something* very strange was going on with whatever material Serov and his officers had smuggled out of Kandalaksha. At a minimum, it wouldn't hurt to leave a paper trail of their findings—just in case they ran into trouble somewhere along the line.

She looked back at Peter and nodded. "Fine. But I'd rather not give the Bureau a chance to zero in on us just yet."

He slipped an arm around her shoulders. "Not to worry, Special Agent Gray. We'll be the very soul of discretion."

JUNE 11

Office of the FBI Director, Washington, D.C.

Lawrence McDowell handed the fax he'd received only an hour before to the Director, careful to hide his resentment from the other man. David Leiter had been a hotshot prosecutor before he'd been picked by the President to head the FBI, but he'd never served a day as a field agent. McDowell was prepared to kowtow to anyone above him, but it irked him to realize how far down the FBI's totem pole he still was—despite all his years of service and ass-kissing.

Leiter, a trim, telegenic man in his early forties, read the document intently.

> *From: Special Agent Helen Gray*
> *To: Deputy Assistant Director Lawrence Mc-*
> *Dowell, FBI International Relations Branch*
> *via fax: (202) 555-9987*
>
> *Jet engines described by SEROV as possible*
> *contraband were transferred in BERGEN,*

*NORWAY, from freighter STAR OF THE
WHITE SEA to freighter BALTIC VEN-
TURER, which immediately left for home port
of WILHELMSHAVEN, GERMANY. Strongly
recommend you investigate re: ultimate destination of engines, precise contents of
crates, etc.*

Gray

"That's it?" demanded Leiter.

McDowell felt his palms starting to get damp. The Director had a reputation for backing his subordinates to the
hilt—as long as they were producing. But he had zero tolerance for inefficiency. McDowell knew if he didn't give
Leiter the right answers, he could be on his way to Billings,
Montana, as a junior G-man before the day was out.

He cleared his throat. "The cover sheet was from a commercial fax service in Berlin, sir. It was sent earlier today,
which places Special Agent Gray and Colonel Thorn in Germany some forty-eight hours after they missed the meeting
with their Army escort."

Leiter frowned. "I can read a calendar, Assistant Director
McDowell." He slapped the fax down on his desk. "Do you
have any goddamned idea about what they've been doing in
the meantime?"

"No, sir. Not exactly," McDowell reluctantly admitted.
"But I've dispatched an agent from our Berlin office to this
fax service. We're also checking out airline and passport
records to see if they actually went to Bergen to obtain this
information—or if Agent Gray is simply trying to pull rabbits out of her hat to save her own hide."

Leiter's eyes narrowed. "Exactly what do you mean by
that, Mr. McDowell?"

"What I mean, sir, is that Special Agent Gray is obviously still chasing after this Russian drug smuggling ring—despite the fact she's been pulled off that case. So now, having violated your directive to return here, she's running around Europe—presumably with her Army boyfriend." McDowell grimaced. "I'm afraid that she's completely out of control."

"You're her supervisor. Are you telling me you didn't see any sign of this coming?"

McDowell tried to sound concerned and distressed. "I believe Special Agent Gray is under massive stress, sir. She hasn't done very well in the Moscow office"—the poor performance reviews he'd given her would document that—"and then she involves herself in that crazy shoot-out in Pechenga."

He shook his head. "Add that together with her memories of that bloody counterterrorist raid here in the D.C. area two years ago, and I think we've got an agent who may be coming apart at the seams."

Leiter nodded gravely, clearly remembering the details. The HRT section under Helen Gray's command had lost four out of ten agents while successfully attacking a heavily fortified terrorist safe house. She'd been badly wounded herself. Nobody could walk away from a bloodbath like that psychologically unscathed.

McDowell pressed his point. "Plus there's her association with this guy Thorn, whose only real ability seems to be to disobey orders." He frowned. "Frankly, I think she's become a liability to the Bureau and to you, sir. You'll remember I recommended revoking her law enforcement powers when we recalled her from Moscow—"

Leiter broke in. "And I still won't approve it, Mr. McDowell. Agent Gray hasn't committed any offense serious enough to justify such action—especially when we haven't heard her side of the story."

McDowell shrugged. "What can she say in her own defense?"

"That's for Agent Gray to establish, not you," Leiter growled. "In the meantime, I want all FBI offices to watch for her and Colonel Thorn. If they're found, I want them escorted back here. They're not to be arrested or placed in custody of any kind. Is that clear?"

"Yes, sir." McDowell knew when to get out. The meeting hadn't gone as well as he'd hoped, but at least Leiter had been diverted from asking specific questions about the fax's contents.

Five minutes later, McDowell closed the door to his own office and moved to the window—staring blindly down at Washington's bustling streets while pondering his situation. He was uncomfortably aware that his neck was in a noose— a noose largely of his own making.

He scowled. It had seemed so easy back in the 1980s. His salary as a field agent hadn't been high enough to match his expensive tastes. After all, why drive a Chevrolet when you could take a spin in your very own Porsche or BMW? So he'd gone looking for a little extra something to pad his paycheck. And he'd found it.

McDowell found himself wanting a drink. He turned away from the window and found the bottle of bourbon he had stashed in his bottom desk drawer. He poured a generous dollop into a water glass and downed it in one go.

When East Germany's secret intelligence service, the Stasi, offered him fifty thousand dollars—as a simple retainer, but with the promise of more to follow—he'd jumped at the money. And why not? Pure patriotism was for suckers, the kind of all-American idiots he'd left gasping in his tracks ever since entering the FBI Academy. East. West. Communism. Capitalism. None of the grand causes mattered much. Not when you were looking out for the only interests that were really important in the end—your own.

Besides, McDowell thought angrily, he'd never done a damn thing wrong for the money. Since the East Germans hadn't contacted him again before the Wall came tumbling down, he'd never actually betrayed his country. All he'd done was redistribute a little wealth from an enemy spy agency into his own back pocket. And where was the real harm in that?

He grimaced, pouring another slug of bourbon. But now this ex-Stasi son of a bitch Heinrich Wolf, or whatever his real name was, had come crawling back from the shadows to blackmail him. The man's confident use of the code name the East Germans had assigned McDowell, PEREGRINE, proved he had access to their secret files. He swallowed the liquor, feeling the warm glow burn down his throat and into his stomach.

His orders from Wolf were clear—report back on the movements of Helen Gray and deflect her inquiries whenever possible. McDowell shook his head. He certainly didn't mind throwing a stick into that bitch Gray's spokes. And he didn't give a damn about the heroin Wolf and his men must be smuggling inside those Russian jet engines—although he wouldn't have minded a cut of the money they were likely to make. Let the dope addicts drip the goddamned poison into their veins. It was no skin off his nose.

But what he really didn't like was the knowledge that an ex-Stasi drug trafficker had him by the balls. McDowell was under no illusions. No matter what happened to Helen Gray or Peter Thorn, Wolf wasn't going to back off—not now. The bastard too clearly enjoyed having a senior FBI official at his beck and call.

McDowell shoved the bourbon bottle back into his desk. Maybe he should start asking a few questions of his own about this *Baltic Venturer* and its mysterious cargo. The more he knew about Wolf's covert business arrangements, the more chance he might be able to figure out some way to turn the tables on the double-dealing German.

Near Middleburg, Virginia

(D MINUS 10)

Prince Ibrahim al Saud glanced out the window of his speeding limousine. They were still several minutes away from his estate deep in the heart of Virginia's hunt country—a lush green landscape of rolling hills, woods, horse farms, quaint historical towns, and luxury homes. It was an alien vista to one raised in the vast, arid reaches of the Arabian Peninsula. All the land around him was a single, all-encompassing oasis of peace and plenty. But it was a soft, weak land—without the harsh, intervening stretches of rock and sand that tempered a man's soul and taught him endurance and faith in God.

His eyes fell on a group of horses contentedly cropping grass in a field by the side of the road. What magnificent beasts, he thought, admiring their proud profiles. Once again he regretted the march of time and technology that had rendered the horse a luxury—a plaything for the idle rich, instead of a weapon of war. Images of the Prophet's cavalry galloping to victory over the infidel floated across his mind—the green banners of Islam fluttering in the wind, scimitars flashing in the sun, the clatter of hooves, the dust rising heavenward in great billowing clouds.

With regret, Ibrahim pushed those heady images back into his subconscious. Wars were waged with other weapons now—explosives, automatic rifles, rocket launchers, and, most of all, with the money that purchased those weapons. The funds and the orders he dispatched could hatch plans to blow up an Israeli school bus one day, and to down an American airliner the next.

Ibrahim leaned forward and poured himself a glass of mineral water from a carafe kept carefully chilled and waiting for him whenever he used this car.

He frowned. Despite the joy he felt when his enemies grieved, he could not hide a growing belief that the secret war he was waging was being lost.

The West had proved more resilient than he and those under his control had ever imagined. Over the past several years, terrorists had struck hard at Israel, the United States, and their allies—planting bombs in cars, buses, buildings, and airplanes around the world. And yet, already the scars were healing.

Ibrahim shook his head and took another sip of his water.

He had learned from his earlier failures. America could not be brought to its knees solely by plastic explosives, assault rifle bullets, or shoulder-launched missiles.

The limousine turned off onto the tree-lined private road leading to his estate—driving through a rippling sea of sunlight and shadow.

Five years ago, Ibrahim had purchased a substantial parcel of prime Virginia countryside. Since then, he'd lavished considerable sums on architects, interior decorators, and landscape designers to ensure that the house and its grounds reflected his intellect, his will, and his traditions. The Middleburg estate would never be more than one of several residences he owned around the world, but it pleased him to occupy ground so close to America's political and military nerve center.

In total, the grounds covered thirty acres—all walled and patrolled. Sturdy steel gates barred access to the estate proper—gates manned by armed guards belonging to his own private security force. None were American. All were fellow Arabs—veterans of Saudi Arabia's Airborne Brigade released into his service by royal command. Their residence visas and weapons permits came courtesy of his intimate political ties to the current American administration.

The limousine stopped just inside the gates.

Ibrahim watched in satisfaction as two guards moved in on either side of the vehicle—carefully inspecting both driver and passenger to make sure they were who they claimed to be. A third man checked the trunk, exempting only his personal baggage from his search. Still another ran a handheld monitor over the car, scanning for any electronic eavesdropping devices that might have been planted while it sat at Dulles International Airport.

Prudence was the Saudi prince's watchword in matters pertaining to personal safety. He believed himself unknown to his enemies. He saw no point, however, in staking his life and fortune and future on that belief.

Once the guards had finished their security sweep, the limousine pulled away—heading uphill toward the main house. The heavy steel gates swung shut behind it and latched. As a further security measure, a row of sharpened spikes whirred up from the pavement.

The house itself sprawled across one hilltop, almost reaching another nearby crest. Dazzling white walls, a red-tiled roof, and arched promenades gave it a Mediterranean appearance. Smaller outbuildings had the same design features. Flower gardens covered the lawns immediately surrounding the house. They not only suited his personal tastes, but served as better concealment for the battery of electronic warning devices that guarded the building.

The key members of Ibrahim's household staff were lined up outside the main entrance—waiting to greet him. Two personal assistants, his majordomo, the groundskeeper, the head of his maintenance staff, his stable manager, and the estate's security chief bowed in unison when he stepped out of the limousine.

Ibrahim coolly acknowledged their deferential greetings and then dismissed them. But two, the groundskeeper and the security chief, lingered.

The prince arched an eyebrow. Anything that needed his personal attention this quickly must be a problem, and a serious one at that. He studied the two men for a moment.

The head of security, a tough, former Saudi paratroop captain named Talal, stood confidently—waiting for permission to speak. From his body language, he evidently didn't think himself to be in any trouble.

On the other hand, the groundskeeper, a young Egyptian, was clearly worried—almost frightened.

Ibrahim had seen nothing on the drive in that would imply the man had been derelict in his duties. The flowers were in bloom. The trees were trimmed. And the lawns were immaculate. This problem must be a personnel matter. He summoned one of his assistants. The aide hurried back out from the house, took his briefcase, bowed deeply, and hurried away.

He turned back to the two men, still waiting silently for his commands. "Very well. What is it?"

The groundskeeper stepped forward, moistening his lips. "Highness, I am afraid that one of my workers, a Pakistani, tried to leave the compound last night."

So it *was* a personnel matter.

Ibrahim turned to his security chief.

"The man was caught almost immediately," Talal reported calmly. "Our security cameras spotted him leaving the dormitory area, and one of the dog patrols apprehended him before he could cross the wall."

"You have questioned this man?" Ibrahim asked coldly.

Talal nodded. "Thoroughly, Highness." The security chief continued his report. "We've also searched his personal effects and interviewed the rest of the grounds staff."

"And?" Ibrahim demanded. "Why did he attempt to flee?"

"He's been here for one and a half years, and now he says he just wants to go home," Talal replied. "I found nothing in his letters or other possessions that would indicate another motive."

Ibrahim considered that a good sign. Harboring an ungrateful wretch was bad enough. Harboring an enemy spy would have been much worse—especially now, with his plans coming to fruition.

Most of the estate's groundskeepers, house staff, and other menial workers were illegals hired in Pakistan, Jordan, Syria, Sudan, and other Islamic countries—ostensibly on one-year contracts. They were slipped into the U.S. on student or tourist visas. The Immigration and Naturalization Service turned a blind eye to this activity—again thanks to his generous support of the American political establishment. After all, if a wealthy and well-connected Saudi prince wanted to surround himself with fellow Muslims as his servants, why rock the boat?

Ibrahim made sure his servants were given reasonably good quarters and decent meals. But most of their pay was sent home, and when their year-long contracts were up, they found it very difficult to leave. Expenses were charged against their pay, or the promised immigration papers were delayed, or they were simply threatened with arrest by the local police if they strayed off the estate. Poor, undereducated, and utterly ignorant of American law, they stayed put. Those few who tried to steal away were always caught.

"Where is this Pakistani?" Ibrahim snapped.

"In the equipment shed, Highness," the groundskeeper said nervously.

"Very well. Then get back to your work. Talal and I will handle this matter ourselves. Nothing more will be said. Nothing. Is that understood?"

"Yes, Highness!" The groundskeeper bobbed his head, obviously relieved, and then disappeared.

The equipment shed housed the gardening tools used by the grounds staff. It stood well off by itself on one side of the main house, screened from view by a stand of trees.

Talal unlocked the door. "I've confined the grounds staff to their quarters, Highness. They believe we are conducting a search for missing items believed stolen by this Pakistani."

Ibrahim nodded his approval. It was a good cover story— one that would discourage any sympathy for the missing man. Theft was a serious crime in the Islamic world.

The shed's interior was all steel and fiberglass on a concrete foundation. Workbenches lined two walls with pegs and tools for maintaining the other equipment, while the floor was taken up by several tractors and power mowers. Bags of fertilizer and grass seed were stacked against one wall.

The Pakistani lay facedown on the concrete floor—huddled against the bags. He was bound hand and foot. The young man raised his head weakly when Ibrahim and Talal came in, but he didn't speak. His eyes were unfocused— though whether from fatigue or from the security chief's "questioning," the Saudi prince couldn't tell at first. One side of his face looked wrong somehow.

Talal stepped over and roughly pulled the Pakistani up to a sitting position—propping him against the stack of fertilizer and seed bags. Now Ibrahim could see that his security chief had been *very* thorough in his questioning. Blood matted one side of the young man's head, and the eye on that side was puffy and swollen.

Ibrahim's anger, so carefully controlled in front of his subordinates, now sprang to the surface. He was a scion of the Prophet and a prince of the royal blood. And yet this worm, a man who had eaten his salt, had defied him—challenging his authority, abusing his hospitality. No excuse could justify such betrayal or mitigate the punishment he must exact.

In a cold rage, Ibrahim stepped closer to the Pakistani. He grabbed one shoulder and threw the dazed young man flat on his back. Without stopping to think he snatched one of the bags from the neatly stacked pile nearby, felt himself stagger slightly under its weight, and then hurled it down on top of the prostrate Pakistani.

The man screamed as the bag slammed into his chest.

Ibrahim looked more closely at his handiwork and smiled icily as he considered the hundred-pound bag of grass seed he'd just thrown onto the traitor.

The Pakistani struggled vainly to escape the weight slowly crushing the breath out of his body. "Forgive me, Highness," he whispered painfully. "I beg you . . ."

Ibrahim ignored him. He picked up another heavy bag with both hands and tossed it on top of the first. The added weight drew another scream of agony from his victim. A third bag—this one hurled onto the man's face—muffled his cries. Blood trickled out onto the concrete floor.

Sweating now, and enjoying the exertion, Ibrahim piled a fourth and fifth bag atop the writhing Pakistani. By now only the young man's legs were visible. They kicked at the floor, wildly at first, and then slower and slower.

Ibrahim stood back, watching and waiting. Even after a full minute by his watch, the Pakistani's legs still quivered spasmodically. It took another thirty seconds before all movement ceased.

He turned to Talal. The security chief stood impassively waiting by the door. "Clear this mess up. And get rid of the body tonight."

There were plenty of lonely places in rural Virginia, and Ibrahim knew Talal would bury the body deep.

"What do we tell the rest of the workers, Highness?" the security chief asked quietly.

"That he was caught stealing, and that we have turned him over to the American police."

Talal nodded silently and bent to begin hefting the bags back into place.

Ibrahim stepped past him and headed for the main house—eager to read Reichardt's latest report. Pleasurable or not, he'd wasted enough time on trivial matters for now.

CHAPTER TEN

EXECUTION DOCK

JUNE 11

Berkeley County Airport, Outside Charleston, South Carolina

(D MINUS 10)

Berkeley County Airport was a small, single-strip field twenty-five miles north-northwest of Charleston, just one mile from the town of Moncks Corner. Church spires dotted the town's skyline. To the northeast loomed the swampy forest of cypress and scrub pine that had sheltered Francis Marion, the "Swamp Fox," during the American Revolution. The olive-green waters of Lake Moultrie glittered in the distance.

Buildings clustered north of the runway, linked by dirt and gravel roads. The facilities of the general aviation firms based there—aircraft rental companies, an aerial surveyor, a flying school, and an air charter service—were dwarfed by Caraco's three brand-new steel-frame hangars and two smaller buildings. A forbidding chain-link fence surrounded the compound.

Rolf Ulrich Reichardt emerged from one of the hangars and stood blinking in the bright morning sunshine. He mopped impatiently at his forehead, already finding the Southern heat and humidity oppressive. A small plane—a single-engine Cessna—droned low overhead, touched the runway, and trundled past, taxiing toward the rows of other private aircraft lined up on the lush green grass. Another Cessna circled lazily off in the distance—waiting its turn to land.

Berkeley had no control tower. Pilots using the field listened to a common radio frequency, Unicom, and worked out any traffic control problems among themselves.

Reichardt turned to his escort, who stood waiting patiently at his side, completely attentive to his superior's needs.

Dieter Krauss was one of Reichardt's men from the old days. He was reliable, if utterly unimaginative. Once he'd headed a Stasi Special Action squad, used to beat dissidents whose activities the State found inconvenient or irritating. But Krauss had aged poorly, and his strength had faded. Too many vices. Now in his early fifties, he looked like a man fifteen years older. He was still useful in a supervisory role, and in an operation of this magnitude, Reichardt needed every agent he could lay his hands on.

"You have had no trouble from the locals?" Reichardt asked. He inclined his head toward the small shed that housed the airport manager. "No difficult questions?"

Krauss shook his head. "No. They have all accepted our cover story."

Reichardt nodded. The county officials who ran the airport had been informed that Caraco intended its new facility as a transfer point for corporate executives flying in from its other U.S. enterprises to Charleston. Given the high landing, maintenance, and aircraft parking fees at Charleston International, none of them were surprised that Caraco viewed their field as a low-cost alternative. In any event, no responsible local official would turn up his nose at the promise of added revenues flowing into the airport coffers.

His pager buzzed. He checked the name and number displayed and pursued his lips. Interesting.

With a single, sharp nod, Reichardt dismissed Krauss and sent him back to work. Then he turned on his heel and stalked back through the gate to where he'd parked his rental car—a sleek, comfortable Monte Carlo.

Even though he'd parked in the shade, the car's interior was already sweltering. Despite the sticky heat, the German pulled the car door firmly shut behind him. There was no point taking a chance that a local might overhear him, and absolutely no sense in allowing the man he was about to call to hear anything that might let him guess Reichardt's location.

The Monte Carlo came equipped with a car phone, but Reichardt ignored that. Instead, he opened his briefcase and removed his own digital cellular phone. It contained an encryption chip that would prevent either casual or deliberate eavesdropping.

He keyed in a code and then the phone number displayed on his pager. An automated system routed his call through several dummy numbers before dialing his contact—vastly complicating any attempt to trace the call.

A cautious voice answered. "McDowell."

"This is Heinrich Wolf," Reichardt said smoothly. "From

Secure Investments, Limited. What can I do for you, Mr. McDowell?"

"You've got a problem," McDowell said. "Two problems, in fact."

Reichardt listened in silence and mounting irritation while the American FBI official filled him in on the fax he'd just received from Berlin. Although they'd survived Kleiner's abortive ambush in Pechenga, he'd thought Special Agent Gray and Colonel Thorn were out of the picture—on their way home to the United States in disgrace. But now here they were again—popping up with data he'd believed completely secure. One of the loose ends he'd gone to enormous lengths to tie up had come unraveled again. Somehow the two Americans had tracked the cargo transfer in Bergen.

"Where are they now?" he demanded.

"I don't know," McDowell reluctantly admitted. "The fax is six hours old already. And they could have arranged for a delayed transmission."

Reichardt scowled, thinking fast. With at least a six-hour head start, these two American troublemakers could be well on their way to almost anywhere. Chasing them would be futile, he realized. This would have to be an entirely different sort of hunt.

He gripped the cellular phone tighter. "I need more information on Thorn and Gray. Immediately."

McDowell hesitated—but only for an instant. Both he and Reichardt knew who held all the aces in the game they were playing. "I have photos and personnel files on both of them."

"Good. Then you can fax them to me now." Reichardt gave the American one of the dummy numbers that would ultimately connect with his phone, disconnected, and plugged a cable into the cell phone.

Within minutes, the portable fax machine he carried in his briefcase spat out two photos and several pages of personal and professional data—all stamped "FBI Confidential." He rang McDowell back. "You've done good work, Mr. McDowell. I think I can promise you a high return on your latest investment."

"I don't want more money," the FBI agent said shortly. "I want out. I'm running too many goddamned risks here."

"We all run risks, PEREGRINE," Reichardt mockingly chided. "There are no rewards without them. True?"

There was silence on the other end, and Reichardt knew McDowell was cursing himself. Every act he committed tightened the noose around his neck, giving the German more control. Time to dangle some cheese in front of the rat. "Don't worry so much, Mr. McDowell. Your assistance is valued. It reduces your debt to us. Soon, you will hear no more from me."

The FBI official couldn't hide the desperate hope in his voice. "When?"

"Soon," Reichardt repeated. He snapped the phone shut.

Ignoring the sweat trickling down his forehead in the stifling car, he scanned the papers he'd been sent. One eyebrow went up as he paged through the official records of the two Americans' past exploits as members of the FBI's Hostage Rescue Team and the U.S. Army's Delta Force. No wonder they'd bested poor Kleiner and his hired Russian bandits in combat.

This Peter Thorn and Helen Gray were dangerous, Reichardt reflected. Too dangerous. And too damned persistent. They'd already pierced three layers of the elaborate veil he'd drawn over the Operation. If he left them on the loose much longer, they might get too close to the core—and draw too much official attention with them.

At least he now knew where they were headed next. The

Americans had discovered that the ship they were chasing, *Baltic Venturer*, had sailed to Wilhelmshaven. From what he had learned from their files, Thorn and Gray would not abandon the chase. Not when they were hot on the scent.

Reichardt considered his options carefully, and then made several phone calls. The first was to his security team leader in Wilhelmshaven. There would be no subtlety this time. The time was too short. This time he would demand certainty.

Wilhelmshaven

Heinz Steinhof alternated between pacing up and down Weserstrasse and standing across the street from the Port Authority office. It was late in the afternoon, but he couldn't bet on the two Americans arriving today—or ever. In fact, for all he knew, they'd already come and gone, and his men would be watching and waiting until the end of time.

Which they would, or at least until Reichardt told them to stop.

Reichardt's phone call earlier that afternoon had surprised Steinhof. The security team was almost through with its job of "sanitizing" the temporary Caraco export office in Wilhelmshaven. Two of his best operatives had already left for the United States. Now all their work had to be set aside so they could hunt for two American snoopers.

It wasn't the job that bothered Steinhof. Find two people and kill them. Easy enough. He'd done it before.

When Reichardt had found him almost thirty years before, he'd been an unwilling conscript in the East German National People's Army. Steinhof had been working as an enforcer for a gambler in the barracks—something that had brought him to the attention of his military superiors, and, as it turned out, to the Stasi as well. Reichardt had solved the People's Army's discipline problem by recruiting Steinhof for secret work himself.

In the years since, the ex-soldier had conducted many different missions for Reichardt—murders, assassinations, bombings, and smuggling operations of different kinds. Most had been dangerous. All had been difficult.

But Reichardt had carefully planned and painstakingly researched all those assignments. It was the other man's strength and safeguard. By the time Steinhof tightened a wire garrote around someone's neck, he not only knew the perfect time and place to do it, but why the garrote was better than the knife or the gun.

Now, though, all he had to work with were a pair of names and two photos—faxed once and then faxed again, growing muddier with each transmission. Reichardt apparently knew nothing about when this Thorn and Gray would arrive in the city, or indeed, if they would come at all. It was unsettling, but Steinhof knew better than to press his superior for more information. Men who called Rolf Ulrich Reichardt's imperfections to his attention tended to have short life spans.

At least, he knew the two Americans would be seeking news of the *Baltic Venturer*. That gave a focus to Steinhof's surveillance plan.

With just six men left, counting himself, the ex-Stasi agent could only cover the Port Authority office and the Customs House. But that should be enough. Assuming they came to Wilhelmshaven at all, the Americans would have to go to one or the other if they were interested in information about *Baltic Venturer*.

Steinhof glanced down at the pictures he still held in his

hands. Reichardt had warned him to handle this man and woman with care. And their records made it clear that they were deadly close-combat fighters.

He smiled thinly. If he and his men did their jobs right, the two Americans would never realize they were in a fight— not until that last instant before the light and life faded from their eyes.

Port Authority Office, Wilhelmshaven

Helen Gray took a deep breath, filling her lungs with Wilhelmshaven's salt-scented air and trying to wake herself up. The forty-eight hours since she and Peter Thorn had ditched their ride home to the States had been a blur of short-haul plane flights, long train rides, and restless sleep snatched wherever and whenever possible.

After flying back into Berlin from Bergen, they'd passed what little was left of last night in a tourist hostel in one of the German capital's cheaper districts. This morning they'd hopped the first passenger train heading here. They'd left their bags in a locker at the Wilhelmshaven train station. Neither of them wanted to stay any longer than was absolutely necessary.

She caught Peter suppressing a yawn of his own and nudged him gently. "You up for this? Or do you want a nap first?"

He shrugged. "Aged, ancient, and weary as I am, I think I can hobble on, Miss Gray. How about you?"

Helen shook her head, checking her pockets for the fake business cards that identified her as an American journalist named Susan Anderson. Satisfied, she squared her shoulders and led the way across the street.

The Port Authority office occupied the entire ground floor of a commercial building on the south side of the Weser-strasse. Inquiries at the front counter finally produced a drab brunette named Fräulein Geiss, who spoke enough English to answer their questions.

The German woman tapped the counter impatiently. "How may I help you, Fräulein Anderson?"

Helen did all the talking again. "We're looking for information on a Wilhelmshaven-registered ship, *Baltic Venturer*. Specifically, the dates of her last arrival and departure, where she docked, and what cargo she carried."

The brunette studied Helen's business card curiously. "You are a reporter, yes?"

"That's right." Helen nodded.

"May I ask, why do you want this information?"

"Of course." Helen smiled politely. "We're doing research for a business news story on the North Sea trade—analyzing the effects of the new open markets in Russia and Eastern Europe. I'm especially interested in seeing how the growing competition from former Soviet bloc merchant ships is affecting established Western routes and customer relationships . . ." She watched the German woman's eyes glazing over and hid a smile. Answering potentially awkward questions with a flood of information—all of it boring—was often an effective way to make sure no more awkward questions were asked.

After several more seconds, Fräulein Geiss held up her hand. "Enough, please, Fräulein Anderson. I understand your need. Allow me to check for you."

The German woman turned to a computer mounted on the counter and typed in a few lines. Numbers and letters flashed onto her screen. "*Ja*, we have that ship in our database." She tapped the screen with a pen. "She arrived six days ago—on the fifth—and docked at S43."

Helen leaned over the counter. "Is the ship still in port?"

Fräulein Geiss entered another code and studied the new set of symbols on her monitor. She shook her head. "No. She sailed again on the seventh—bound for Portsmouth in England."

"Can you tell us what cargo she offloaded?" Helen asked, quickly scribbling the ship's berth and her arrival and departure times on a notepad.

The German woman shook her head stiffly. "I do not have this information. That is not our function here. You must obtain that from the Customs Office."

Helen thought fast for a moment. There were three possibilities facing them. First, that the crew of the *Baltic Venturer* had unloaded her cargo of contraband jet engines here in Wilhelmshaven. Second, that she'd carried them away with her on the next leg of her journey. Or, the third possibility: that whoever controlled the engines had shifted them to another vessel—just as they'd apparently done in Bergen.

She flipped to another page of her notebook. "Do you have some way to find out what other ships were berthed next to her while she was in port?"

"Of course." Fräulein Geiss nodded humorlessly, apparently a bit nettled that an American reporter would doubt the efficiency of the Wilhelmshaven Port Authority office.

This time the German woman produced two lists. One was for S42, the berth to port of the *Venturer*. The other was for S44, to starboard.

S44 had been empty when the *Baltic Venturer* arrived, but a "reefer," a refrigerated cargo ship, had steamed in the next day. She'd unloaded her goods for the next three.

S42, the portside berth, had been busier. A container ship, the *Caraco Savannah*, had been moored there, but she'd left almost immediately. Another ship had taken her place later that same day, taken on cargo, and then sailed right after *Baltic Venturer* on the seventh.

Fräulein Geiss waited until Helen's pen stopped moving. "Is that all, Fräulein Anderson?"

Helen smiled at the dour woman. "That's all, Fräulein. But I do want to thank you for your time and effort." She put a hand on her pocketbook.

The German shook her head primly. "Such thanks are not necessary. I do my work, that is all. Now, if you will excuse me . . ."

"Of course," Helen said. "So the Customs House is . . ." She produced the pocket map they'd picked up at the train station's tourist kiosk.

With a barely suppressed sigh, Fräulein Geiss circled the location for her.

From across the Weserstrasse, Heinz Steinhof watched the serious-looking man and pretty woman emerge from the Port Authority office. They stood on the pavement, studying something the woman held in her hands. A map?

He turned to the big, dark-haired young man beside him. "You were right to signal me, Bekker. This looks promising."

Sepp Bekker grunted in reply. Steinhof had recruited him several years ago from the dissolving ranks of East Germany's Border Command. Bekker was just short of two meters tall, with broad, almost Slavic, features. He was in his early thirties, strong, quick, and utterly without principles. He also had wild tastes, evidenced by the cobra's head tattoo that peered over the edge of his shirt collar.

The ex–border guard bragged about his tattoos whenever he could—idly boasting to his fellows that he had one for every would-be escapee he'd shot before the Berlin Wall crumbled. Steinhof thought he needed seasoning.

Steinhof himself was almost as tall as the younger man, but his own hair had turned silver and he kept it close-cropped. A casual observer might mistake the two of them for father and son, but the older man's face held more intelligence than the young, tattooed thug's ever would.

The two Americans had turned away now—walking west toward the Customs House.

"Wait here."

Bekker nodded, settling back into the shadow of the building.

Staying on his side of the street, Steinhof passed them at a rapid clip, then crossed over at the next intersection. This close to the end of the working day, there was plenty of foot traffic, and he was one of a half dozen others waiting at the light when the two Americans reached it.

He studied them carefully at close range—making sure he stayed out of their direct line of vision. No doubt about it. These two were the quarry Reichardt had assigned him— Thorn and Gray in the flesh and within easy reach.

Steinhof shifted slightly on the balls of his feet. He could feel the weight of the Walther P5 Compact hidden by his jacket. There they were, less than two meters away, totally unaware and unguarded. He had the sudden urge to draw his pistol and kill them now, here, immediately.

The urge passed.

Murder on a public street in broad daylight was far too risky. No matter how badly he wanted these Americans dead, Reichardt would not thank him for getting himself locked up by the police.

Steinhof lagged further and further behind Thorn and Gray—watching as they turned off the sunlit street and entered the Customs House. He spotted the man he'd placed outside the building and casually signaled him over. Their watching and waiting were over. It was time to begin setting the stage for the last act in the two Americans' lives.

Friedrich-Wilhelm-Platz, Wilhelmshaven

Holding the heavily laden tray in both hands, Colonel Peter Thorn carefully maneuvered his way through the crowded, noisy tables at the little outdoor restaurant overlooking the Friedrich-Wilhelm-Platz—a small park separated from the Wilhelmshaven waterfront by a few short blocks. Across the way, a stern statue of Kaiser Wilhelm seemed to stare disapprovingly down at the frivolous antics of his former subjects. When they weren't busy working, Wilhelmshaven's citizens indulged their three favorite pastimes—eating, drinking, and boating.

Thorn neatly dodged an overweight German businessman with an overflowing beer stein exuberantly making a point to his dining companions and sat down across from Helen Gray.

With a dramatic flourish, he waved a hand over the tray he'd set between them. "Two coffees, madam. Black. No cream. No sugar. And for nourishment—a delicious assortment of breads, cheeses, and hard salami."

A twinkle crept into Helen's eyes—replacing the hunted, worried expression he'd seen all too often since they'd cut out on their own. She reached for one of the coffees. "You do show me the nicest places, Peter. I've got to say this is exactly how I dreamed of taking the grand European tour."

Thorn grinned back. "Touché."

Helen put her cup down and started paging through the

information they'd gathered at the Customs House. The types of cargo carried by ships entering and leaving German ports were a matter of public record—although the owners, final destinations, and tonnage remained closely held proprietary data. She shook her head, clearly frustrated by something.

"What's the problem?" Thorn asked.

"This." Helen slid the page she'd just read—a copy of the cargo manifest for the *Baltic Venturer*—across the table to him. "According to that, the ship wasn't carrying jet engines. Not one." She frowned. "Could she have stopped somewhere else between Bergen and here?"

Thorn scanned the form himself and shook his own head. "I don't think so. Her last port of call is listed here. And it was Bergen." He pointed to a line halfway down the page.

"Then where the hell are Serov's engines?"

Thorn couldn't see them listed anywhere on the sheet, either. According to German customs, the *Baltic Venturer*'s cargo consisted entirely of timber, paper pulp, and titanium scrap.

His mouth twisted downward. Had the Norwegian dockworker in Bergen sold them a bill of goods? Had the man just made up a story to please a pretty American woman reporter? Were he and Helen really just on some kind of self-inflicted snipe hunt?

He rubbed his jaw, still studying the cargo form. "The engines could have been brought in covertly. Maybe they weren't reported to customs at all," he speculated.

"Possibly," Helen acknowledged.

Thorn nodded, as much to himself as to her. "Look, I'd rather believe a human being than a piece of paper. Karl Syverstad was damned positive when he described those crates he saw shifted from the *Star of the White Sea* to the *Venturer*. Dozens of ships go in and out of this port every week. How much time do customs inspectors really have to dot every I and cross every T on these forms, anyway?

"Not much," Helen said slowly.

"What else have we got?" Thorn asked.

She pushed over the rest of the forms.

Three other ships had been berthed alongside the *Baltic Venturer* at one time or another during her stay in Wilhelmshaven. The reefer moored at S44 had carried beef from Argentina as its sole cargo. The first of the two ships anchored at S42, the *Caraco Savannah*, had brought in iron ore and bauxite—and she'd left carrying automobiles and auxiliary electric generators. The second had arrived empty, and then sailed with a cargo of machine tools.

Not much help there.

Thorn slid the papers back to Helen's side of the table. "Say the engines aren't listed anywhere on those forms. Where does that leave us?"

She looked up from the notes she'd taken at the Port Authority office. "Looking hard at *Caraco Savannah*, I think."

"Why?"

"Because she left Wilhelmshaven roughly three hours after *Baltic Venturer* pulled in," Helen argued. "The pattern's the same one we found in Bergen. Bring the contraband in, offload it right away, and get it back out of port before anyone official starts poking around."

"Easy to say, but damned hard to prove. It's just as likely those jet engines were offloaded straight into a truck," Thorn countered.

Helen's theory made sense to him, but playing devil's advocate was the best way he knew to make sure they stayed on track. They were trying to analyze this situation with far too few solid facts—something he found akin to playing pin the tail on the donkey in a pitch-black room you weren't even sure had a donkey in it. Their training taught them to be intuitive, to look for links and hidden relationships. But their training also taught them the need to confirm hunches with hard evidence. So where was that confirmation?

While Helen riffled through the customs forms, Thorn sat back in his chair—trying different pieces of the puzzle in different combinations.

Suddenly she looked up at him. "*Baltic Venturer* was carrying titanium scrap, right?"

"Right."

"Don't jet engines contain a lot of titanium?" Helen said slowly.

The light dawned. "They just changed the label! Jesus, it's simple. Grease a palm somewhere and one tiny line changes on one lousy form."

"And then changes again when the engines are transferred for the second time?" Helen asked.

"Maybe," Thorn said. He pulled the customs forms back again. "Let's take a closer look at exactly what the *Caraco Savannah* was carrying when she left port."

This time it stood out like a sore thumb. The remarks column of the German manifest described the "auxiliary electric generators" more fully as gas turbines.

Helen followed his pointing finger. "A jet engine could also be called a kind of gas turbine, couldn't it?"

"Yep," Thorn agreed. He scanned the report again. "Now let's see where she was taking those generators."

He was silent for a moment, then turned his head to look directly at Helen. "Galveston. Whatever Serov and his boys put in those engines, it's headed for the U.S."

Helen stared back at him. "Christ, Peter. If that ship sailed on the fifth, she could already be close to the States right now."

Thorn nodded grimly, considering the possibility that a

freighter might be drawing ever nearer to the U.S. with a smuggled Russian nuke on board.

"We've got to call this in, Peter," Helen said flatly.

"Yeah." He glanced at his watch. "It's after quitting time on the docks. And we're going to need confirmation before Washington will take any action. We've got to find somebody who saw those crates shifted from ship to ship with his own eyes. Somebody who'll swear to it under oath, if it comes to that."

Helen nodded. "So we go pub crawling again?" she asked.

"Uh-huh." Thorn drained his cold coffee in one gulp and stood up. "In a tearing hurry, Helen. I've got a really bad feeling that we're running against the clock now."

The last light was fading across the Jadebusen by the time they settled on a likely spot to begin their search—a waterfront bar close to berth S43 named Zur Alten Café.

The bar turned out to be one large room laid out with long tables running almost its entire length. What little light made it through the smoke was soaked up by the dark paneling and dark wood floors. Knots of men sat close together at the tables, eating from plates piled high with food and drinking from massive glass beer steins.

Helen Gray stood in the doorway for a moment, blinking as she felt her eyes starting to smart from all the cigarette smoke hanging in the air. She was instantly aware that once again she was the only woman in the whole place, and that her light-colored business suit stood out like a beacon against the rough, oil-stained work clothes worn by the longshoremen crowding the room. Even Peter's jeans and sweatshirt looked out of place in here.

She slipped through the crowd to the bar itself, aware of Peter pushing right behind her. The bartender spoke only a little English, enough to understand that she was American and that she was interested in a "*schiff*"—a ship. Anything more complicated faded into mutual incomprehensibility.

Helen swung around as one of the other patrons, an older, silver-haired man, came to her rescue.

"Excuse me, please, but I speak a little English. May I help you?" he asked, speaking loudly over the hubbub in the packed room.

Helen turned on the charm, favoring the German with a dazzling smile. "That would be wonderful, Herr . . . ?"

The silver-haired man smiled back. "Steinhof. Heinz Steinhof."

He listened intently to her explanation, but held up a hand as soon as she mentioned berth S43 and the *Baltic Venturer*. "I am a supervisor for cargo, but that is not one of my berths. However, my friend Zangen handles that area of the harbor. He is a meticulous and thorough man. So I am sure that he would remember this ship and what she loaded and unloaded."

"Where can we find Herr Zangen?" Helen asked. "Is he here this evening?"

Steinhof seemed amused. "Zangen?" He shook his head. "Oh, no. Fritz Zangen is a most responsible man—a family man. He will be at home with his wife and children at this hour."

Damn. Helen hid her disappointment. "Is there any way we can contact Herr Zangen? Perhaps make an appointment to speak with him? Tonight, if possible?"

"This is a matter of some urgency, then, Fräulein Anderson?" the older German asked, clearly curious now.

"It is, I'm afraid."

Steinhof looked at his watch and seemed to consider something. Then he looked up. "Zangen and his family live close by. Why don't I take you to his apartment myself? I am certain he would not mind."

"You're sure it's not too much trouble?"

"No trouble." The silver-haired man shook his head. "Less beer for me tonight means less fat here tomorrow," he said, patting his stomach.

"Come." Steinhof gestured toward the door. "A ten-minute walk and then you can ask Zangen all your questions."

With a nod to the bartender, the two Americans followed Steinhof out of the door. He immediately turned north, away from the waterfront.

This close to sunset the traffic was heavy along Banter Weg Strasse, but they soon turned off onto a smaller street, Bremer, and then a still smaller one, Kruger. The car and foot traffic thinned with each turning. Most of Wilhelmshaven had been leveled by American B-17 bombers trying to hit Nazi sub pens during World War II. Now they were in a part of the city that had not been bombed out or reconstructed, and the streets twisted and curved. The buildings were older, too—sometimes in need of work, but more often neat and well maintained.

They crossed into a residential area—mostly larger nineteenth-century town houses that had been broken up into flats—and it was getting difficult to keep their bearings. Helen made the effort, though, because it would be dark by the time they finished talking to Steinhof's friend.

She spotted a man following them while craning her head around to double-check a landmark for later reference. He was tall, dark-haired, and no more than twenty feet behind them. She'd caught him in the midst of turning his own head—swinging around to look back the way they'd just come.

Helen felt the hairs on the back of her neck stand up. She knew exactly what the stranger was doing. She'd done it herself on a dozen different close surveillance assignments. The man behind them was making sure they weren't being followed.

Her gaze swept out in an instant—tightly focused on the area around them. Shit. Besides the big man behind, there were at least three others. Two were out in front, strolling casually while conversing. The third was across the street, easily keeping pace with them while pretending to read the evening paper.

She and Peter were caught in a moving, ready-made ambush—pinned in plain view. She grimaced, angry at herself for getting sloppy. After Pechenga, she should have realized that paranoia was the only sane course.

The only other person in sight was well behind them and across the street—an old woman tottering homeward under the weight of a single grocery bag. No help there. They were on their own.

Helen turned her head forward. Peter was a little ahead, still chatting with the ever-talkative Steinhof. It didn't take a genius to realize that the seemingly helpful German had set them up. How he'd known where they would be wasn't important. Not at the moment. What mattered most was where she and Peter were being led now.

She took an extra half step forward, catching up with the two men, and slipped her arm through Peter's. After a few more steps, she casually laid her head on his shoulder. He glanced down at her.

"Trap. Box pattern," Helen whispered softly. "Four, plus Steinhof."

She felt Peter stiffen momentarily, then his hand slipped down into hers and squeezed.

Steinhof turned his head toward her, still smiling. "You said something, Fräulein Anderson?"

"Just that it was awfully nice of you to bring us all this way, Herr Steinhof," Helen lied, forcing herself to sound cheerful.

Their guide smiled broadly. "It is no trouble at all, I assure you. We in Wilhelmshaven pride ourselves on treating our visitors as honored guests."

Helen gritted her teeth. Somehow she doubted that the average tourist was slated for a bullet in the back of the skull and a quick, anonymous burial somewhere out in the North Sea. It was agony to walk casually down the street, knowing that they were in the jaws of a trap that might close at any moment.

Peter let her hand go, but not before exerting a gentle pressure against her palm—pushing her back behind him. He was getting ready to move.

Helen dropped back half a pace.

Steinhof nodded to a narrow, dimly lit side street just ahead. "There we are. Zangen and his family live only a few doors down."

The two men pacing them in front turned left and headed down that street—disappearing around the corner. Helen tensed. They must be nearly in the planned kill zone.

Thorn saw the first two men vanish around the corner. For the next several seconds, it would be two against three—instead of five. They weren't going to get a better chance. He spun toward Steinhof, yelling, "Now!"

Helen whirled toward the man following right behind them and disappeared out of Thorn's field of view.

Despite being taken off guard, Steinhof blocked his first strike easily—sweeping it away with his left arm. And then the German's own right hand flickered out—as quick as a striking serpent.

Christ! Thorn yanked his head aside, feeling displaced air slap him in the face as Steinhof's rigid palm flashed right past the bridge of his nose. A fraction of an inch closer and he would have been dead.

Attack followed attack, and parry followed parry, all in a dizzying blur of instinctive actions and reactions, too fast for conscious thought. A second passed. Another.

Thorn drifted toward the street, sweeping his open left hand in defensive circles—ready to strike with his right the instant he saw an opening. The other man mirrored his movements. Part of Thorn's brain knew that he was running out of time and options fast. He had to move—to break clear before the rest of the ambush team closed in. But he didn't dare leave Steinhof alive and whole behind him. The German was deadly at close quarters.

Helen Gray sprinted straight toward the big, dark-haired man who'd been tailing them. He was already reaching under his coat for a weapon. No time for anything fancy, then. Just close the distance and pray . . .

She slammed straight into the younger German's stomach. It was like hitting a concrete wall. His arms tightened around her waist and heaved.

Helen felt herself being lifted off the ground and thrown toward a parked Audi. She curled into a ball in midair, hit the side door, and rolled away—aware of the fire running all down her side and left leg.

She scrambled to one knee and froze, staring into the big man's drawn Walther P5 pistol. He was barely a foot away—so close she could smell the sweat on him and see the tattooed cobra's head poking above his shirt collar.

He smiled nastily at her and tightened his finger on the trigger. " *'Wiedersehen, schön Fräulein*—"

Helen chopped at her attacker's hand, knocking the pistol away just as it fired. A 9mm slug tore into the pavement by her knee and screamed away. Before the big German could pull his weapon back on line, she struck again—this time aiming for his empty left hand.

She jammed her fingers into the fold of skin between the dark-haired man's left thumb and index finger, and *squeezed*, crushing the nerve ending there with every ounce of strength. Her left hand gripped the wrist of the hand holding his pistol.

The tattooed German's eyes opened wide in shock and agony as he screamed.

Using her grip as a lever, she rose from her knees—simultaneously forcing the screaming man downward. His broad, flat-featured face bent closer.

Now!

Helen shoved his weapon hand out of the way, spun back, and then drove her left elbow straight into his nose with all her might. She felt the crunch as shards of sharp-edged cartilage speared upward and into his brain. He dropped like a stone and lay facedown in a spreading pool of blood.

Thorn tried another strike, felt Steinhof's left arm drive him off target, and gave ground. The older German countered instantly—driving in with lightning speed, aiming for his throat this time. He blocked it and fell back further.

Steinhof followed, still attacking—hammering against his defenses, probing for that one weak spot that would let a killing blow slip through.

Thorn deflected another strike with his left arm and felt the German's jacket brush past his open fingertips. He grabbed desperately, curling his hand around the other man's sleeve. Cloth tore through his fingers as Steinhof wrenched the arm out of his grip.

But for an instant, the older man staggered off balance, open, and vulnerable. Thorn lashed out—throwing his entire weight into the attack. His palm slammed heel-first into Steinhof's forehead. Blood sprayed out of the German's nose and eyes as his brain ruptured under the massive impact. He crumpled to the pavement—dead before he even finished falling.

Recovering quickly, Thorn spun around, heading toward Helen.

The whole melee had lasted less than ten seconds.

Helen looked up and saw Peter sprinting toward her . . .

Crack!

And ducked as safety glass sprayed through the air from the shattered windshield of a parked car. The third German in Steinhof's ambush party—the one flanking them from across the street—had his pistol out and was shooting.

Bent low, Peter raced up to her. "Let's move! Move!"

Still breathless, Helen scrambled up and took off down the street the way they'd come—crouching to keep the row of cars between her and the gunman. She could hear more shouts behind her. The rest of Steinhof's team must have finally tumbled to the fact that their plan had gone sour. She also saw the little old lady standing rigid with shock, spilled groceries jumbled at her feet. The woman was pointing straight at them—screaming something in high-pitched, frantic German.

Another pistol round tore past her head—showering brick dust and fragments across the pavement.

They rounded a corner and kept running, faster now. There were no more shots.

Two more corners brought them out onto a major street—

Bismarckstrasse. Mercedes, Fiats, Audis, and Volkswagens roared past in both directions.

After snapping a quick look back in the direction they'd come, Peter flagged down a passing cab and bundled Helen inside.

He rapped on the partition separating them from the driver. "The *Bahnhof! Schnell, bitte!*"

Then he swung around to face her. "You okay?"

Still breathing hard, Helen nodded.

"You're sure?" Peter persisted.

Truth be told, her left leg hurt like hell. The sudden explosion of violent hand-to-hand combat had strained her old injury. But she was alive.

"I'm fine," she insisted. "What about you? Who the hell was that guy Steinhof?"

He grimaced. "Definitely pro."

"You think we should leave Wilhelmshaven . . ." Helen let her voice trail off.

He nodded again, still grim-faced. "Yeah. Don't you?"

Helen ran over the events of the last few minutes in her mind. They'd left two men lying dead in the street. Plus, they'd left a witness—the elderly German woman—whose testimony was bound to indicate that she and Peter had made the first hostile moves in the brief, bloody confrontation. She frowned. "You don't trust the German police?"

"Not much. Not under the circumstances." Peter looked out at the brightly lit buildings flashing past. "It might take days to clear up exactly what happened. And I don't think we have many days left. Even if the embassy managed to spring us sooner, home we'd go, under airtight security this time—looking like fools."

"Plus, we know there are still at least three of those bastards alive out there—alive and looking for us," Helen said slowly. "And they'll be waiting for us out at the docks."

The cab stopped in front of the busy, bustling train station, and they hurried inside to retrieve their bags from the lockers. The next train for Berlin wasn't due to leave for another few hours—far too long to loiter inconspicuously, even on the crowded station concourse. Instead they hopped the first train out—one headed for Hannover.

By the time the Wilhelmshaven police started interviewing witnesses, they were rolling south at eighty kilometers per hour.

CHAPTER ELEVEN
SAFE HAVEN

JUNE 12
Pension Wentzler, Lichtenberg Borough, Berlin

Helen Gray gingerly peeled down her jeans and dispassionately studied the varicolored bruises running down the length of her left thigh. She shrugged after a moment. Painful, yes, but she hadn't suffered any serious injury. Nothing that some aspirin, cold washcloths, and a few hours' rest couldn't handle.

Rest would be welcome in any case. She and Peter Thorn had been on the move almost constantly for nearly seventy-two hours now, and they were running a little ragged. They'd each managed to grab a couple of hours of fitful sleep on the early morning train from Hannover to Berlin, but that wasn't really enough to fully recharge their batteries.

She rebuttoned the jeans, turned to face the tiny bathroom's little mirror, and brushed her hair back into place. Satisfied with her appearance for the time being, she stepped quietly out into the equally tiny bedroom and closed the door behind her.

Peter Thorn looked up from the documents he'd been studying for what must be the twentieth time. "Feeling better?"

"Yeah."

Peter scooted over to make room for her on the narrow bed. The bed, a single, straight-backed metal chair, and a use-battered wooden wardrobe were the only pieces of furniture in their room.

Helen took in their surroundings and shook her head in amusement. This hotel wasn't exactly the Ritz. On the other hand, they did have a private bath—an uncommon luxury among small, family-run pensions. And the Pension Wentzler had several other things going for it from their perspective—it was relatively inexpensive, inconspicuous, and so small that days might pass before its owners delivered their guest registers to the police as required by German law. The pension was also in what had once been East Berlin—far enough away from the glitz and glitter of the West Berlin shopping districts to be fairly quiet.

Of course, there was some irony implicit in their choice of sanctuary, she knew. The hotel was just a few blocks away from the once-feared Normannenstrasse headquarters of East Germany's disbanded Ministry of State Security—the Stasi.

"You still think we should phone home?" Peter's question brought her out of her reverie.

Helen nodded. "Yes, I do." She ticked off her reasons. "First, we've followed the trail as far as we can on our own. And whatever's hidden inside those smuggled jet engines could be arriving in Texas in the next day or so. If we're chasing a stolen Russian nuke, that's a risk we can't run. We have to push the Bureau's wheels into motion—now, not later."

"All true," Peter admitted. "But I still hate the thought of relying on Larry McDowell for anything . . ."

"So do I," Helen said. "Like it or not, though, he's my boss. If we want to send our data up the chain of command, he's the guy we have to start with. And, as much as I hate it, the weasel has the kind of clout we need to get out of Germany without being asked too many inconvenient questions."

Peter nodded reluctantly.

Helen knew he was remembering their earlier assessments of the situation they were in. After the carnage they'd left on that quiet Wilhelmshaven residential street, Germany's highly efficient law enforcement agencies were undoubtedly looking for them. Not by name. Not yet. But the police were sure to have obtained fairly accurate descriptions of the two Americans last seen in Herr Steinhof's company. With those in hand, putting real names to their faces was only a matter of time.

The longer she and Peter stayed out on their own, the higher the odds they'd be arrested and charged with manslaughter—or its equivalent in German law. They'd achieved a lot operating on their own—without a legal safety net—but it was time to come in from the cold.

Helen checked her watch, mentally subtracting six hours to arrive at the local time in Washington, D.C.

Washington, D.C.

Deputy Assistant Director Lawrence McDowell tossed his briefcase to one side and plopped himself down in the plush chair behind his desk. He scanned quickly through the overnight reports from the FBI's overseas offices, looking for anything particularly urgent or interesting. Nothing struck his eye.

With that out of the way, he turned to the one-page memo on top of his internal action pile. It was a draft of his latest press release—listing the most recent accomplishments of his outfit, the FBI's International Relations Branch. Grist for the media mill, it would be shotgunned out to more than a hundred newspapers, radio stations, television networks, wire services, and interest groups. With luck, the release would catch some editor's eye somewhere and become part of tomorrow's news. If it did, the circle would be completed—because a clipping of that story would land on the Director's desk.

McDowell ran his finger through the draft, scowled, reached for a marker, and then scrawled "Redo!" across the top in large red letters. His name appeared only once in the release and that was in the last paragraph. He drew a red circle around that section and then a line pointing to the front. He also crafted several sentences ascribing the field office successes to the personal leadership of both McDowell and the Director himself.

Any complaints from his underlings would be met with his usual reminder that "RHIP"—rank hath its privileges—followed by an insincere invitation to lunch or dinner the next time they were in D.C.

Satisfied now, McDowell buzzed for Miss Marklin, his secretary. The tall, good-looking blonde came in quickly, almost at a run. She'd learned early on not to keep him waiting.

He handed her the draft press release. "Give this back to Thompson and tell him I want the final version on my desk before lunch."

"Yes, sir."

McDowell turned back to the rest of his morning paperwork, looking up in irritation when his secure phone line buzzed. He grabbed it. "McDowell."

"This is Gray."

The sound of Helen Gray's voice struck him like a thunderbolt. "Where the hell are you?"

"Berlin, sir," she said coolly, using the calm, utterly unimpressed tone of voice that never failed to get under his skin.

"Then I suggest you stop screwing around and report to the embassy there, pronto!" McDowell snapped. His hand reached for the button that would initiate a phone trace, hovered for an instant, and then withdrew. Tracing an international call was a major endeavor, and besides, from all the traffic noise he could hear in the background, she was using a pay phone.

"That might be . . . difficult, sir," she said. "We've run into a snag while tracking this shipment of smuggled jet engines . . ."

"Outside your jurisdiction and without Bureau sanction," McDowell reminded her, his anger barely under control. Her little escapade had him in hot water with both the Director and that ex-Stasi son of a bitch, Heinrich Wolf.

"Yes, sir. Nevertheless, Colonel Thorn and I have obtained information you need to hear."

McDowell reined in his temper. Gray was right—though for more reasons than she knew. "I'm listening."

He took notes while she ran through the sequence of their lone-eagle investigation and brought him up to date on their latest finding. He drew a sharp line under "Galveston." "You're sure this shipment is headed for Texas?"

"Yes, sir."

"Fine. I'll pass the word on to the local DEA office," McDowell lied. "Now, Agent Gray, I suggest you get yourself on the first available flight to D.C. I understand the Director wants to personally chew you out—"

"This isn't about heroin trafficking, sir," Helen Gray interrupted. "Colonel Thorn and I believe the *Caraco Savannah* may be carrying a stolen Russian tactical nuclear weapon."

McDowell felt his blood run cold for a moment.

A stolen nuke? Was that what Wolf's game was? McDowell could turn a blind eye to a little drug running. Tons of heroin and cocaine washed up on American shores every day—no matter what he did or didn't do. And there was always the chance he could muscle in for a cut of their action. But nukes were a whole different ball game. If Wolf and his cronies really were smuggling a nuclear weapon into the U.S., and anybody ever found out he'd helped them . . .

McDowell gripped the phone tighter, feeling his palms sweating profusely. He cleared his throat. "Just what hard evidence do you have to back up that rather extraordinary claim, Special Agent Gray?"

McDowell listened intently while she ran through their chain of suppositions, feeling himself relaxing as it became clearer and clearer that she and Thorn were simply grasping at straws. His anger came roaring back at the same time. The bitch had scared the hell out of him over a simple doodle in some dead OSIA inspector's logbook.

The corners of his mouth turned down. Trust a borderline case like Helen Gray to go off half cocked over the worst-case scenario—especially when it required ignoring every bit of real evidence they'd acquired.

But it wouldn't do to let her know that he thought her wild-eyed theory was completely full of crap. If she thought he wasn't taking her seriously, she and this Thorn character were likely to try an end run around him—and that would blow his only chance to keep a lid on this whole can of worms.

"All right, Agent Gray," McDowell said after she'd finished. "I'll run your theory past the Director, pronto. In the meantime, I want you and Thorn out of Germany."

"As I said earlier, sir, that may present a problem," she countered.

What now? McDowell wondered. He drummed his fingers on the desk impatiently. "Go on."

"We were ambushed again near the Wilhelmshaven docks. Five hostiles were waiting for us. They knew exactly what we were looking for."

Wolf's men, McDowell suddenly realized—using the information and photos he'd passed on the day before. Too bad the Stasi bastards had failed. It would have made his life so much simpler. "And?"

Helen Gray's voice dropped an octave. "We killed two of them while making our break. I suspect the German police are looking for us now."

It was getting worse and worse. McDowell grimaced. He needed time to sort through this mess—and to reach Wolf. That bastard would never forgive him if he allowed Thorn and Gray to slip through his fingers after they'd made direct contact.

He sighed. "All right, then. I'll try to see what I can work out. In the meantime, just sit tight and stay off the streets." He let his tone grow rougher. "And God help you if you screw up and get arrested before I've had a chance to smooth things over! Call me back in six hours. Understood?"

"Yes, sir."

This time McDowell could hear the anger in her voice. But that anger was combined with a reluctant acceptance.

Much as she must hate it, she clearly knew how dependent she was on his help.

Good, he thought. That would make whatever action he took that much easier.

Shafter-Minter Field, Kern County, California

(D MINUS 9)

Ninety-odd miles northwest of Los Angeles, the flat expanses of California's agricultural heartland—the Central Valley—stretched as far as the eye could see in all directions. Crop-dusters, heavily laden with pesticides or fungicides, lumbered down Shafter-Minter Field's main runway at periodic intervals. Outlined against the fiery glow of the rising sun they lifted off into the air and turned—roaring off toward the vast fields surrounding the airport.

Two new hangars and several other buildings, painted dazzling white in the bright California sunshine, sat just off the main runway—secure behind a high steel fence. A discreet sign on one of the buildings identified the compound as the "Caraco Corporate Aviation Training Center."

Rolf Ulrich Reichardt stood just inside one of the two hangars—watching as sweating workers continued modifying the interior. They'd walled off part of the floor space—building living quarters large enough to house several men for a week or more. Another crew was hard at work in another area of the hangar building another enclosure—this one out of heavy steel. Welding torches sputtered and burned, filling the hot, stuffy hangar with acrid smoke, but the big central doors were kept closed as a safeguard against prying eyes.

The construction crews were working almost around the clock to meet the Operation's tight timetable.

Satisfied by what he saw, Reichardt slipped outside and strode into the second hangar. Technicians were hard at work there, too, inspecting a sleek, twin-engined Jetstream 31 turboprop. Others were busy unloading crates filled with extra tools and spare parts next to the area marked out for a second Jetstream still en route to the field. Their orders were clear: When the word came down from on high, the aircraft based at Shafter-Minter would be ready to fly—or else. There would be no exceptions, no excuses, and no delays.

Reichardt turned as the door behind him opened. Johann Brandt stepped through it, his face serious.

"What is it, Johann?" he asked.

"Another message from PEREGRINE."

Finally. Reichardt swung away from the organized chaos filling the hangar and followed Brandt outside onto the airport tarmac. The twin-engined Cessna executive jet that Prince Ibrahim al Saud had put at his disposal sat waiting for him. Reichardt hurried up the steps into the Cessna's luxurious interior—all solid cherry, dark leather, and gleaming brass. A powerful computer workstation and communications center now occupied the aft end of the six-passenger compartment.

Reichardt dialed McDowell's direct line.

The FBI agent sounded almost happy. "You missed them again, Herr Wolf. Your people in Wilhelmshaven blew it. Thorn and Gray are still alive."

Reichardt scowled. "I'm already well aware of that fact, Mr. McDowell."

He'd received the first panicked report from the survivors of the Wilhelmshaven security team barely an hour after their ambush went disastrously wrong. He shook his head. That tattooed young idiot, Bekker, was no great loss. But Heinz Steinhof had been one of his best and most trusted operatives. First Kleiner and now Steinhof. His losses were mounting. These two Americans were even more dangerous than he'd first thought.

Well, Reichardt thought sourly, at least this time he'd had the foresight to take added precautions against possible failure. The cover story he'd so painstakingly built over the past few weeks should hold water for long enough.

The German turned back to the conversation at hand. "You've been in contact with Special Agent Gray, then? Another fax, I assume."

"Not a fax," McDowell said. "A phone call. From Berlin."

Reichardt raised an eyebrow. Interesting. Perhaps the two Americans were even more rattled by their narrow escape than he'd hoped. "Go on."

He listened intently while the FBI agent ran through the details of his talk with the American woman, Gray—frowning only when he heard that she and Thorn knew the *Caraco Savannah*'s final destination. He made a mental note to push the work in Texas even further ahead of schedule.

McDowell's dismissive tone made it clear that he didn't believe their nuclear story. That was fortunate. Still, the FBI agent already knew more about the Operation than he should. At some point in the not-too-distant future, he could easily become a liability.

The American's next question confirmed that. "Is there some part of the Galveston waterfront you want me to steer any potentially embarrassing investigations away from? A warehouse, maybe? I've got some contacts in the Drug Enforcement Agency I could use to help you out—if need be."

"Don't let your beak grow too much, PEREGRINE!"

Reichardt growled. "You know the bounds of your orders. Stay within them!"

"Well, then . . . what action should I take?" McDowell asked plaintively. "About Gray and Thorn, I mean."

Reichardt ran through his options, knowing they were far more limited than he would prefer. Most of his special action teams had already left Europe—bound for the United States. In any event, too few of his people were close enough to Berlin or its environs to make an aggressive move against the two Americans. He rubbed his jaw. How else could he make sure they were taken off the chessboard until it was too late for them to interfere further?

The answer struck him suddenly. Why strive for the complicated solution when a simple plan would work just as well—and with fewer risks?

Smiling now, Reichardt said, "Very well, PEREGRINE. Here are your new instructions. You will follow them precisely, and without deviation. Clear? . . ."

Outside the Europa Center, Berlin

Inside the phone kiosk, Helen Gray turned her back on the *Wasserklops*, the gigantic fountain outside the towering Europa Center. She glanced at Peter Thorn. "Any sign of trouble?"

He continued scanning the crowded, neon-lit square and streets around them for a moment longer before shaking his head. "Nope. A few cops on patrol—but they don't seem to be looking for anyone in particular."

Helen nodded—relieved but not especially surprised. Even if the Berlin police were hunting for them, they'd have a hard time picking out two particular foreigners from among the tens of thousands milling along the Kurfürstendamm—the German capital's busiest and most prosperous boulevard. The Europa Center behind them was a hive of activity—housing everything from fine jewelry stores to overpriced restaurants and even a pallid imitation of a Monte Carlo casino.

She punched in McDowell's office number, waited for the automated operator, and then swiped the phone card they'd purchased at a local store through the electronic reader. Glowing digits on the phone's display showed how many long-distance minutes her German marks would buy. Thank God for modern technology, she thought while waiting for the call to go through. In an earlier day, she and Peter would have needed a satchel to carry all the coins necessary to call overseas using untraceable cash.

This time McDowell's secretary patched her straight through.

"McDowell here."

"This is Gray," Helen answered steadily. "We're ready."

"You should be," her boss said. "You were right. The German police are looking for both you and Colonel Thorn. Or at least two Americans matching your physical descriptions."

Helen sighed. "Damn."

"Exactly," McDowell agreed icily. "The Berlin field office has obtained a copy of the Wilhelmshaven police report. It doesn't make pleasant reading. The German authorities don't exactly approve of so-called tourists dropping corpses all over their nice clean streets."

"Have they identified the bodies yet?" she asked.

"One of them. The older guy carried a walletful of ID and credit cards made out in the name of Heinz Steinhof. The local police say he apparently owned some kind of export-import business in Hamburg."

Helen snorted. "Sure. And John Gotti just ran a little mom-and-pop pasta shop in Brooklyn."

"There's one more thing you should know, Special Agent Gray," McDowell said, sounding smug.

Helen didn't like the sudden shift in his tone of voice. "What's that?"

"The German cops found a plastic bag containing fifty grams of pure heroin sewn into Steinhof's jacket. In case you can't handle the math, that's worth roughly twenty-five thousand dollars on the street. So they're assuming this was some kind of mid-level drug buy that went sour."

Helen made a face. More heroin. More misdirection for anybody in authority eager to jump on the easiest and safest explanation for everything they'd discovered. Terrific.

"You still there, Agent Gray?" McDowell said.

She fought down the urge to let her temper flare. "I'm still here."

"Good. Anyway, whatever the hell you and Thorn have stuck your big dumb feet in, it's pretty clear we've got to scoop you out of Germany before you wind up in the slammer. God knows, the FBI, the U.S. Army, and I personally don't need the kind of bad PR that would generate."

That rang true, Helen thought. Trust McDowell to worry more about his image than about the truth of their story. She took an even firmer grip on her temper. "So, what do you suggest, sir?"

"Nothing fancy. Just make your way to the following intersection," McDowell said, rattling off a couple of street names in badly pronounced German. "That's in some district called Neukölln. Can you find it?"

Helen flipped through the city-guide map book she'd picked up on their first pass through Berlin. Neukölln lay just east of the city's old Tempelhof Airport. "Yeah. What happens there?"

"You'll meet Special Agent Crittenden. He works out of the Berlin office. Do you know him?"

Helen ran through her memory quickly. She had the impression of a tall, broad-shouldered man with the beefy look of a former football player. "Yeah. I met him once, I think. Either at the academy or at one of our conferences."

"Crittenden will be waiting there at 2030 hours, local time."

Helen glanced at her watch. That gave them a little under an hour and a half to make the rendezvous point. Plenty of time.

"He'll have a car with embassy plates," McDowell continued. "You and Thorn pile in. He'll drive you to the Air Force base at Ramstein where you'll both meekly trundle aboard the first available flight heading to Andrews—just like the lost little lambs you are."

Gritting her teeth, Helen nodded into the phone. "Got it."

"You'd better get it, Agent Gray," McDowell said. "We'll sort out your story once you're back here in D.C. In the meantime, make sure you're at the rendezvous point on time. *Capisce?*"

Almost against her will, Helen forced out a terse, "Yes, sir." Then she hung up.

Neukölln Borough, Berlin

Colonel Peter Thorn stepped out of the S-Bahn car onto the Neukölln station platform—quickly scanning the surrounding area for signs of any watchers. Only four other passengers left the crowded three-car electric tram and they immediately headed for the nearest station exit. He signaled the all-clear.

Helen Gray followed him out onto the platform just before the car doors closed.

With a low electric hum and a hiss of hydraulics, the S-Bahn train slid away from the platform and sped off down the aboveground tracks. It disappeared around a bend in seconds—lost in the darkness and urban sprawl.

Thorn strode toward the exit, still keeping a wary eye out for anyone who looked out of place. He went through the turnstiles and came out onto the poorly lit street.

Neukölln was not one of Berlin's more scenic neighborhoods, he decided. Half the street lamps were out—evidently smashed by vandals and left broken by an overworked city bureaucracy. Trash and dog excrement littered the pavement. Most of the tenement-style buildings packed close together in all directions were liberally daubed with graffiti, soot, and torn and tattered political posters.

Most of the cars in sight were old and cheap—a mix of Volkswagens, Fords, Renaults, and even a few dented Trabants. Except for a few elderly men and couples out walking dogs, there weren't many pedestrians on the streets.

"What do you think?" Helen said, skeptically eyeing their surroundings herself.

Thorn shook his head. "I don't like it. It's too damned quiet. This isn't the kind of neighborhood I'd have picked for a rendezvous. There's not enough traffic. We'll stick out like a sore thumb."

"Maybe the RP itself is busier," Helen said.

"Yeah . . . maybe." He summoned up a mental picture of the street map he'd memorized before they set out to meet McDowell's man. The S-Bahn station was about five blocks north of the intersection they were aiming for. About a five-minute walk if they headed straight there. Not that he had any intention of doing anything that stupid.

If nothing else, the ambushes at Pechenga and Wilhelmshaven had again pounded home all the old lessons he'd learned as a combat soldier: Never move blind in unknown country. And never, *ever*, do the expected or the easy.

He turned back to Helen. "Feel like a little stroll?" He nodded up the street—directly away from the rendezvous point McDowell had specified.

She flashed a quick, thin smile. "My thoughts exactly, Mr. Thorn."

Together, they turned and walked north—back the way the S-Bahn tram had brought them—pausing often to check windows or the sideview mirrors of parked cars for any signs that they were being followed. At the first opportunity, they turned right down a narrower side street and picked up the pace. From time to time, they stopped suddenly—hoping to flush out anyone trailing them.

Nothing.

Ten minutes of hard, fast walking and several more turns brought them out onto a wider north–south avenue—one running just a block east of the intersection they were heading toward. There were even fewer cars and fewer pedestrians out on the streets now.

Thorn took Helen's arm and pulled her into a shadowed doorway with him. He nodded toward the next corner. "I should be able to take a quick look at the RP from there."

"Oh? What's this 'I,' Peter?" she asked quietly.

"This is where we split up," he said. "If anybody unfriendly is out there waiting for us, they'll be looking first for a couple. So I'll just mosey on over there—run a fast recon—and then swing back. In the meantime, you keep an eye on my back . . . just in case we missed somebody on our tail. Okay?"

Helen's eyes narrowed. "You really don't trust Larry Mc-Dowell, do you?"

Thorn shrugged. "From what you've told me about him, and from what I saw at the crash site, I trust him to be a lying, slimy, incompetent asshole."

She laughed softly. "I'd say you have the man pegged just right. Okay, Peter, you go run your sweep. I'll watch your back."

He kissed her once and then stepped out of the doorway. He sauntered off, whistling softly under his breath—determined to look and act as much as possible like a local making his way home from one of the several pubs they'd passed.

At the corner, Thorn stopped briefly—looking both ways before crossing the street. He let his eyes sweep west down the block toward the intersection McDowell had picked out as the rendezvous point, scanning for anything and anyone out of the ordinary.

Nothing. Nothing.

There! His eyes lingered for an instant on the dark Mercedes sedan with Berlin plates parked halfway down the block under a burned-out streetlight. That's too nice a car for this neighborhood, he thought grimly. And he'd bet a month's pay there were a couple of guys sitting inside that car—hidden behind tinted windows. His senses went on full alert.

Without breaking stride, Thorn crossed the street, putting a graffiti-smeared apartment building between him and the Mercedes. It took him another five minutes to circle his way east and then north again to get back to the doorway where he'd left Helen on watch.

"Well?" she asked.

"We've got trouble," Thorn said. He filled her in on the car he'd spotted.

"Might just belong to the local Lotto winner . . ." she said slowly.

Thorn grinned. "Why, yes, Virginia, there is a Santa Claus . . ."

"Very funny, Peter." Helen tapped her watch. "We've still got fifteen minutes before Crittenden is supposed to show. You want to scope this out a little further?"

He nodded. "Let's say I'm kinda curious to find out who may be gunning for us this time."

She shook her head. "Jesus, Peter, I sure hope you're just being paranoid."

They headed east for several blocks before turning south again. Once they had gone far enough that way, they swung back west down a trash-filled alley. It took them the better part of ten more minutes to work their way closer to the target intersection—approaching it from the south this time.

They were within a hundred meters of the rendezvous point when Thorn felt Helen stiffen slightly. Her hand closed around his arm—and tugged him off the street into another alley between two brick tenements.

"Shit," she said under her breath. "I don't frigging believe it." She looked up at him, eyes wide in the darkness. "There are two more up ahead fifty meters or so. Standing in a doorway on our side of the street."

"Describe them," Thorn said.

"Dark leather jackets. Jeans. One's wearing a baseball cap. The other's bareheaded." Helen shook her head in disbelief. "How the hell did they know where to find us?"

Thorn spread his hands. "Maybe there's a leak in the Bureau's Berlin office. Or in D.C. somewhere. Hell, maybe McDowell's phone's being tapped . . ."

She grimaced. "I can't believe that. The phone lines into and out of the Hoover Building are checked and rechecked practically every day."

"Well," he said slowly, "all I know is that these people have been all over us every time we get close to their goddamned operation. As to how exactly they're doing that . . ." He shrugged. "We should start doing some serious thinking about it later. After we get ourselves out of this fix we're in right now."

Helen nodded.

Thorn looked intently at her. "So, if you were setting up a tight surveillance net around that intersection, how would you do it?"

She didn't hesitate. "I'd cover all four approach routes, and I'd use at least two foot teams and two cars to do it. That way I'd be set, no matter how my targets entered the zone."

"So we're facing around eight hostiles here," he concluded.

"At least." Helen looked troubled. "We're outside the net now, Peter. We could just back off quietly and slip away. God knows, that would be the smart move."

"Yeah." Thorn knew she was right, but somehow the idea stuck in his craw. Fading back meant ceding the initiative to their unknown adversaries—again. And it would leave them right where they'd started: stuck in Germany while what they suspected was a stolen Russian nuke was sailing into an unsuspecting American port city.

He suddenly realized that Helen was watching him closely.

"You getting tired of playing it safe, Colonel Thorn?" she asked quietly.

"Playing it safe's not exactly our forte, is it, Special Agent Gray?"

"No, I guess not."

He nodded toward the unseen intersection. "Okay. Pretend you're running that op out there. One of your teams spots someone who *might* be one of the two people you're after—but this person is heading *away* from the place you've staked out. What would you do?"

Helen hesitated for only a split second before answering. "I'd detach a team to investigate."

"But not your whole force?" Thorn pressed.

She shook her head. "No way. Not with so many variables still in play. I'd want confirmation first." A wolfish smile crept across her face. "You want a little personal contact with a couple of these folks, Peter?"

He nodded grimly. "You could say that."

Two minutes later, Thorn waited alone inside the dark alley—near the opening to the street. He could feel the damp, dirty brick wall right at his back. A dog barked somewhere off in the distance. Soon now, he thought.

Helen strode right past the opening—heading straight toward the intersection they knew was under surveillance. Her eyes didn't even flicker in his direction.

Good work, he thought.

She left his field of view. Her footsteps faded.

Thorn ran a slow countdown in his head. She must be forty meters from the closest two-man surveillance team. Thirty meters. Twenty.

Adrenaline flooded into his bloodstream—distorting his sense of time. Seconds passed with agonizing slowness. Doubts crept in and multiplied. Had they spotted Helen yet? Would they react the way he hoped?

Helen came back into sight, walking faster now. She stopped, looked toward the alley as though seeing it for the first time, and then darted in. She slipped into the shadows beside him.

"Two on the way," she whispered.

Thorn listened carefully—trying to screen out the dull rumble of background traffic noise to pick out the sound of any nearby car engine starting. If the people out there looking for them started pulling the whole surveillance net around them, he and Helen would have to bug out fast. He listened harder. There. He heard the sound of footsteps ringing on the pavement, coming closer.

Soon. Soon.

Two men appeared at the entrance to the alley. Both wore leather jackets and jeans. One had a baseball cap pulled down right over close-cropped hair. Without hesitating, they plunged into the narrow, dark, trash-strewn passageway. They walked right past him.

Now!

Thorn lunged out of the darkness, grabbed the closest, the one wearing the baseball cap, by the scruff of his neck and the back of his jacket, and whirled him around—slamming him face-first into the brick wall. A quick neck chop dropped the moaning man to the pavement—out cold.

A rapid glance showed him that Helen had put her target down and out in that same split second.

Moving quickly, they dragged the two unconscious men further into the alley, behind a row of overflowing trash bins.

Thorn knelt beside his victim, rapidly frisking the man for weapons and ID. Helen did the same.

"Jesus, I feel like a mugger," she muttered.

"Yeah. But at least we're highly efficient muggers," Thorn said with a wry grin. He set the Walther P5 pistol he'd found in the unconscious man's shoulder holster down on the ground and kept searching.

The smile slipped off his face as his hand closed around a small leather wallet, thin but stiff, in the man's jacket pocket. He flipped it open. One side held a photo identity card of the man he'd knocked out. The other held a badge. The word "*Polizei*" practically leapt off the ID card.

"Oh, shit," Thorn said softly. "Now we are well and truly fucked . . ."

"No kidding." Helen showed him the police credentials she'd found on her own man. "And there's more." She handed him a crumpled sheet of paper. "I found this next to the badge. Take a look."

Thorn glanced down at the paper. He couldn't read all the German but the two Xeroxed black-and-white photos—one of Helen and one of himself in his U.S. Army uniform—were clear enough. He frowned.

"That's my FBI file photo," Helen said.

"That son of a bitch McDowell set us up," Thorn growled.

"Looks that way." Helen shook her head. "I'd guess he decided to have us locked up before we could do any more damage to his precious reputation inside the Bureau. He must be betting he can do enough spin control so that we come out of this smelling real bad—and he gets the credit for shopping us to the German authorities."

"I think McDowell and I have a few things to sort out," Thorn said.

"After me, Peter. After me." Helen dropped the ID card on top of the man she'd attacked and jumped to her feet. "In the meantime, we've got maybe two minutes before their boss runs a radio check and all hell breaks loose. I suggest we skedaddle while the coast is still clear."

"Amen to that." He scrambled upright. "Back to the hotel?"

Helen shook her head, leading the way east down the alley toward the next street over. "No. Too dangerous. If the Berlin police are on the ball, this'll hit the news in minutes. So we leave our bags here and start running now."

"To where? Not the train station," Thorn said.

"Same problem," Helen agreed. "The cops will have men

on watch at every train station, bus terminal, and all the airports before we could even get close."

She didn't bother hiding the despair in her voice as she continued. "Thanks to McDowell, we're about to become the targets of a major manhunt. The *Polizei* aren't going to be very happy that we just put two of their plainclothes detectives in the hospital. And I don't have the faintest idea of how we're going to get out of this damned city—let alone the country."

Thorn kept his mouth shut as they left the alley and kept heading east—deeper into the city. There wasn't any point in trying to cheer her up with false optimism. He was already feeling the walls close in around them himself.

CHAPTER TWELVE

CONNECTIONS

JUNE 13

Vienna, Virginia

Major General Sam Farrell, U.S. Army, retired, had finished writing for the day when the phone rang. He clicked the television off in mid-CNN interview. Who the hell would be calling him after midnight?

He pushed himself upright out of the recliner and reached for the phone on his desk. The desk, like his study, was almost impossibly neat—with everything in its place and spotlessly clean. Farrell blamed his compulsive neatness on the thirty-plus years he'd spent in the Army. Louisa, his wife, said he just had too much free time.

He got to the phone on the third ring. "Farrell."

"General, it's Peter Thorn."

Farrell's irritation changed to pleasure. "Pete! It's damned good to hear your voice."

He'd known Thorn for most of the younger man's military career. The special warfare community was a small, tightly knit fraternity—one that built lasting friendships.

Since his retirement, he'd heard from Thorn once a month or so—a postcard, e-mail, or phone call. And always a card on holidays. Farrell wouldn't call it a father-son relationship, but then he'd served with Thorn's dad, too—long before Pete had been born. Nobody was going to replace big, tough John Thorn in his son's affections. Still, he suspected their friendship bridged some of the emptiness Thorn had felt after his dad passed away.

Somehow, though, Farrell doubted this call was a social one. He knew Thorn too well. "Where are you, Pete?"

"Berlin, sir."

"Berlin?" Farrell wrinkled his brow. "After that business in Pechenga, I'd have thought you'd be back home by now."

"You heard about Pechenga?"

"Hell, Pete. Hear about it?" Farrell smiled wryly. "Anybody with a TV or radio heard about it. Louisa and I keep expecting to see you and Helen on *Oprah* on a show about 'Men and Women Who Date Under Fire.'"

He'd never admit it to Thorn, but he'd also been greedily following any news about the OSIA plane crash and the ensuing events in Russia. It was an interesting and intriguing story, but, more important, he'd known that Thorn was involved.

Farrell turned serious. "I'm real glad you both came through that mess unscratched. It sounded like a bad one."

"It was, sir," Thorn said.

This time Farrell caught the faint undercurrent of very real desperation in the younger man's voice. He frowned. He'd never heard Peter Thorn desperate before. Angry, yes.

Determined, always. And sometimes as stubborn as a mule. But never desperate. He gripped the phone tighter. "Okay, Pete. What the hell's going on?"

There was a long pause—long enough to make him wonder whether he'd lost the connection to Berlin.

Finally, Thorn said, "Helen and I need your help, sir. But frankly I'm not sure you should give it to us."

What? Farrell's frown grew deeper. "Try me."

"Okay, sir," Thorn said. "Here's the situation we're in . . ."

Farrell listened intently as the younger man outlined what he and Helen Gray had done since escaping the carnage aboard that rusting freighter in Pechenga. He found himself shaking his head in growing astonishment at each successive scrape that the two had plunged themselves into.

He'd thought that Thorn's ability to run himself into trouble doing the right thing had reached its peak during the Delta Force raid on Teheran. By rights, his refusal of a direct presidential order to abort that mission should have resulted in a court-martial. Even after Thorn and his troops returned home to a hero's welcome it had taken every ounce of pull Farrell possessed to keep him on active duty. And since then the general had heard whispers around the Pentagon that his own retirement had been hastened by running interference for the younger man.

Farrell snorted silently, correcting that thought. He knew full well that holding his second star and command of the Joint Special Operations Command was as high as he could ever have gone.

No, he'd never really regretted backing Pete Thorn. But, Jesus, he thought, his former subordinate could sure find ways to make his own life difficult. Violation of movement orders. Unauthorized travel. Leaving the scene of a crime. Nobody at the Pentagon was going to be able to sweep that stuff under the rug this time.

Suddenly, Farrell stood bolt upright—still holding the phone to his ear. "You and Helen just *mugged* a couple of German policemen!"

"Not intentionally, sir," Thorn said, sounding moderately contrite. "Helen's boss at the FBI must have sicced them onto our trail after she asked him for help getting out of the country. We thought they were more of the same people who've been gunning for us ever since Pechenga."

"Christ on a crutch, Pete!" Farrell rubbed a hand through his graying hair in distraction. "What the hell are you both doing? I don't care how many kilos of heroin those bastards are smuggling in, you've gone way overboard here! For God's sake, you're in the U.S. Army, remember—not the DEA!"

"We're not chasing heroin, sir," Thorn said firmly. "We're chasing what we think is one loose Russian nuke. And it's already on its way to the States."

Farrell felt the hair on the back of his neck rise. Ever since the Soviet Union came crashing down, every Western government's nightmare scenario had revolved around the uncertain safety and security of the old U.S.S.R's massive nuclear arsenal. And now Peter Thorn was telling him that the nightmare might be turning into a reality.

He took a deep breath. "Do you and Special Agent Gray have any hard evidence to back that assertion up, Colonel?"

This time Farrell waited until Thorn finished detailing their entire chain of evidence and reasoning. Then he let out a low whistle. "That's mighty thin, Pete. Mighty thin. A lot of people—good, smart people, too—would say that's just a lot of half-assed speculation."

"Yes, sir."

Farrell checked a smile. Damn it. Peter Thorn was just as stubborn, and as painfully honest, as ever. So was his conviction the product of sound reasoning? Or just an act of faith? "Have you run this by anybody official yet?"

"Everybody seems to have bought the drug smuggling story hook, line, and sinker," Thorn said. "Helen bounced it off her boss—and he tried frog-marching us into a German jail cell."

Farrell shook his head. "It sounds like you're out of friends, Pete."

"I hope not, sir."

Farrell knew that Thorn would never outright beg or plead, but there was a note in his voice that he didn't hear often. "What do you want me to do, Pete?"

"Two things, sir. The most important is to get somebody official to take a hard look at the *Caraco Savannah* and her cargo. If we're right, there's one hell of a nasty surprise hidden inside one of those jet engines."

Farrell pondered that. Could he risk his hard-earned reputation as a straight-shooter by asking people in authority to take a flyer on one of the wildest theories he'd ever heard a junior officer espouse? The smart move would be to wish Thorn well, advise him to find a good lawyer, and hang up now.

The trouble was, he instinctively believed what Thorn had told him. It explained a lot of otherwise unconnected events—the OSIA inspection team plane crash, the murders of General Serov and Captain Grushtin, and the ambushes at Pechenga and Wilhelmshaven. The heroin smuggling ring story fit the same facts, of course, but it *did* seem too convenient—a little too precisely tailored to satisfy American and Russian bureaucrats who wouldn't want to believe that the unthinkable had happened on their watch.

And damn it, he wouldn't forget this was Peter Thorn, he thought almost angrily. Whatever else the younger man had done, he was a top-notch officer—one of the best Farrell had ever commanded.

So act on your belief, he told himself. He sighed. "All right, Pete. I'll see who I can prod into gear. Now what's the second thing I can do for you?"

Thorn hesitated for another long moment before answering. "To chase these bastards down, Helen and I need to get out of Germany and back to the States. Preferably without seeing the inside of a *Polizei* cell."

Even though he was half expecting it, the request still surprised Farrell. He whistled softly again. "That's a tall order for an old soldier, Pete."

"I know, sir," Thorn said. He cleared his throat. "I'll understand if there's nothing you can do. You've already risked a lot on my behalf—more than I can ever repay you for—"

Farrell cut him off. "You're a damned fine officer, Pete. And a hell of a good man. You don't owe me anything." He grinned crookedly. "Besides, Louisa would kill me if I let anything happen to you and Helen. She's been planning your wedding reception for two years now."

"She might have to change the venue to the nearest federal prison," Thorn said soberly.

"True." Farrell shook his head. "Look, Pete, I'll dig where I can. It's a long shot, though. And being right about this is probably the only way you're gonna save your hide this time."

"Frankly, sir, I'd rather be wrong," Thorn said. "If Helen and I *are* right, that nuke could already be on U.S. soil. And if that's true, we may never find it—not until the damned thing goes off."

Farrell shook off the horrific image of a fireball incinerating an American city, focusing on the more immediate problem. "Right now let's worry about getting you two home safe and sound. Where are you exactly?"

"An all-night Turkish coffeehouse in the Prenzlauer Berg district. I'm using a pay phone in the back . . ."

Farrell jotted down the location and phone number on a scrap of paper. "Can you stay there for another couple of hours or so?"

"Yeah," Thorn replied. "From the looks of some of the other customers, Helen and I could probably live here for a while—as long as we kept paying for coffee, that is."

"Okay, Pete. You hang tight and stay low. I've still got a friend or two in Europe who might be able to pull you out of this jam."

"Thank you, sir." Thorn sounded relieved and grateful. "I really appreciate it."

"Then do me a favor," Farrell said.

"Anything."

Farrell grinned into the phone. "You're not in uniform now, Pete. And neither am I. So drop the 'sir' and call me Sam. Okay?"

"Yes, sir—" Thorn caught himself. "I mean, okay, Sam."

"Better," Farrell said. "Now watch your back, Pete. Meantime, I'll try to round up the cavalry."

He waited until Thorn hung up and then replaced the receiver.

Farrell stood thoughtfully by his desk for a moment. The full implications of Peter Thorn's claim were just beginning to emerge. Where should he go to kick somebody into a serious investigation? Not the Russians. That much was certain. Moscow wasn't going to rock the boat—especially now that any smuggled weapons were off its own soil. And from what Thorn said, the FBI, the OSIA, the CIA, and the State Department were also nonstarters. So who did that leave?

He shook his head. Time enough for that later in the morning. For now, he had two friends who were in serious trouble. The first step was getting them out of Berlin before the German police rounded them up. Slipping them back to the States would be an even bigger job. He started flipping through his Rolodex. Who did he know in Berlin? And who could he trust to shelter a couple of fugitives?

Prenzlauer Berg, Berlin

Colonel Peter Thorn cautiously poked his head around the corner of the back booth—checking the front of the dingy coffeehouse for the tenth time. It was full light outside.

"Anything?" Helen Gray asked.

He turned back to face her. "Nope. Still looks clear."

She nodded, took another sip from the small, steaming cup in front of her, and made a face. "I swear to God, Peter, this stuff is getting stronger. I think it's more grounds than coffee now."

Thorn smiled. "It's an acquired taste."

He drained the remnants of his own cup in one gulp and ran his eyes over the other patrons seated nearby. Most of them had the shaggy, unkempt look of an artsy crowd who tended to gravitate toward coffeehouses after a busy night partying at trendy nightclubs and alternative music houses. They seemed to be relying on coffee, cigarettes, and conversation just to stay conscious. Certainly none of them were paying any attention to the two tired-looking American tourists who'd parked themselves in the far corner booth.

Nobody except the proprietor, that was. But Thorn doubted the swarthy-faced Turk behind the counter went much out of his way to help the Berlin police. There wasn't much love lost between Germany's native-born population and the immigrants who'd flocked there seeking work over the past couple of decades.

He fought down the urge to check his watch again. If Sam Farrell said to sit tight, he'd sit tight. Anyway, their odds of staying undetected by the authorities were better in here than out on the street. By now, their pictures could be plastered across the front page of Berlin's daily newspapers and the screens of the morning TV shows.

"Peter . . . I think we've got company."

Helen's soft warning brought his head around. A man wearing a perfectly tailored business suit had come through the coffeehouse's front door and stood near the entrance—clearly surveying the tables. Thorn had the quick impression of a tough, wiry build, alert blue eyes, and neatly trimmed gray hair.

Without much trouble, the newcomer spotted them and made his way over to their table. He stopped a few feet away, taking evident care to keep his empty hands in plain view.

"Peter Thorn? Helen Gray?" His accent was British—and impeccably upper-class. "My name is Griffin. Andrew Griffin. General Farrell asked me to give you a lift."

Thorn felt himself relax slightly. The name Griffin rang a bell somewhere. He searched his memory for an instant and then looked up at the Englishman. "Colonel Griffin? Of the SAS?"

He remembered seeing the name Griffin while reading classified reports on some of the British 22 Special Air Service Regiment's covert operations. Delta Force and the SAS cooperated closely—often sharing training, intelligence, and tactical tips.

Griffin shook his head. "Ex-SAS. I retired a year ago."

"You ran the FORAY exercise at Cheltenham, didn't you?" Thorn asked.

"Yes. But the code name was FORTITUDE," the Englishman said steadily. His eyes twinkled. "As I'm sure you knew, Colonel. I hope that you're now satisfied I am who I say I am."

Helen smiled. "Won't you sit down, Mr. Griffin? The coffee's . . ."—she tilted her cup to show the dark sediment liberally coating the sides—"available."

The Englishman smiled back. "No, thank you, Agent Gray." He nodded toward the door. "My car is just outside . . . and I understand you two are rather eager to get out of the limelight."

"You could say that, sir." Thorn rose from his seat, caught the owner's eye, and counted out a wad of deutsche marks onto the table. "It's been a very long night."

Together he and Helen followed Griffin through the front door and out onto the street, where a gray Mercedes sedan with tinted windows sat waiting. The ex-SAS officer unlocked the car, ushered Helen into the back seat, offered the front passenger seat to Thorn, and then slid behind the steering wheel himself.

Griffin pulled smoothly out into traffic, heading west. He glanced at Thorn. "I've a sizable flat in Charlottenburg, Colonel. Our mutual friend has asked me to put you and Miss Gray up until he can make other arrangements."

"I'm grateful, sir," Thorn said. "I know you're taking a big risk."

The Englishman shook his head. "It's no trouble." He smiled thinly. "I'll admit that you and Special Agent Gray are rather . . . infamous . . . at the moment, but I think the risk involved is minimal. Or at least controllable."

Helen leaned forward to join the conversation. "How do you figure that, Mr. Griffin?"

Griffin lifted his eyes to the rearview mirror. "I run a security consulting firm here in Berlin, Miss Gray. We specialize in advising British and American corporations on how to cope with terrorist threats—and with the East European and Russian organized crime syndicates. So, you see, I maintain rather good ties to the local German law enforcement authorities. They consider me a very solid businessman and a friend of the police. Given that, I hardly think they'll spend much time considering the possibility that I would offer sanctuary to two such notorious villains."

Thorn winced. "It's that bad, then?"

Griffin nodded. "You put two Berlin police detectives in the hospital, Colonel. Although not permanently, I'm happy to say. And the authorities here do tend to frown on outsiders waylaying their policemen in dark alleys." He glanced at Thorn again. "I assume it was necessary?"

Thorn shook his head grimly. "Not as it turned out." He frowned. "We were suckered in."

The ex-SAS officer nodded. "So General Farrell indicated." He shrugged. "At any rate, as the poet said, these things 'gang aft a-gley.' Who knows, you may even have done those policemen a bit of a favor. Their broken heads will mend. And perhaps the next time they won't traipse so blithely into an ambush."

Helen forced a pained-sounding laugh. "Seems like a tough way to learn a lesson, Mr. Griffin."

For just an instant, the ex-SAS officer let the mask of the civilized businessman fall away—revealing the hardened warrior beneath. "Bruises are often the only way to teach such lessons, Miss Gray. And action—even hasty action—is always preferable to vacillation and delay. But I suspect you and Colonel Thorn already understand that. Which is why you are still alive—and so many of your enemies are not."

Thorn sat in silence for the rest of the short trip to Griffin's flat—mulling that over. The retired British soldier was right about the need for rapid, decisive action. But until Sam Farrell could find a way to get them out of Europe, he and Helen would be forced to play a waiting game.

Washington, D.C.

Lawrence McDowell sat in a chair facing FBI Director David Leiter's desk, watching his superior discreetly as the other man skimmed through his hastily prepared report on last night's fiasco in Berlin. You're in a strong position, he told himself nervously, just stick to your story. Thorn and Gray aren't here to contradict you—so stay cool.

After an agonizingly long minute, Leiter raised his eyes from the report. He scowled. "Damn it. This situation is completely out of control, McDowell. What the hell were you thinking about?"

McDowell decided to play dumb. "Sir? I'm not sure I understand you completely."

"You violated my orders, damn it!" the FBI Director growled. "I told you specifically that I didn't want Special Agent Gray or Colonel Thorn arrested!"

"You told me not to have our people arrest them," McDowell fudged. He licked his lips. "The German police took matters into their own hands."

"Cut the crap!" the other man snapped. "You set this whole thing in motion."

McDowell spread his hands. "To be honest, sir, I really don't see that I had any other choice—not after Agent Gray briefed me on their illegal actions in Wilhelmshaven. The German authorities already had good descriptions of them."

He shook his head sorrowfully. "I'm sure you wouldn't have wanted me to condone possible manslaughter and flight to avoid prosecution."

Leiter pursed his lips. "That's how it's stacking up?"

"The situation is . . . ambiguous," McDowell suggested artfully. "Certainly, Thorn and Gray's overreaction last night suggests either guilt—or complete paranoia. Both the German policemen they attacked are in the hospital suffering concussion. And one of them has a broken jaw."

The FBI Director frowned. "You should still have cleared this with me, McDowell. Damn it, you've completely overstepped your authority here."

"Under the circumstances, sir, I thought it best to handle this matter at a lower echelon," McDowell replied. "Given the current climate in Congress, it seemed unwise to give your critics any more ammunition. This way whatever happens to Special Agent Gray is my responsibility—and not yours."

That should hit a nerve, he thought.

Fed up with a succession of FBI blunders, overreaching, and unproven allegations of corruption in some of the Bureau's administrative sections, several congressional committees were conducting in-depth probes of the organization. In fact, the Director had spent most of the previous day testifying under oath—and in front of television cameras—about several of those incidents. Having a senior field agent on the run from German law enforcement agencies would be the icing on the cake for the Bureau's hungry congressional watchdogs.

For a terrifying second, though, he was afraid he'd pushed the wrong buttons. Leiter's face reddened dangerously.

McDowell decided to play his last card. "If you wish, sir, I'll be happy to submit my resignation over this whole affair . . ." He let his voice trail off, leaving the rest of his intentions plain, but unspoken: If you don't back me up, I'll go running to those same congressional committees—and I'll tell them the Director of the FBI was willing to turn a blind eye to potential felonies committed by one of his agents while overseas. Given all the toadying he'd done to ingratiate himself with the ranking members in both political parties over the years, McDowell was confident they'd listen to him.

He watched the Director's anger fade into resignation and breathed an inward sigh of relief. The other man must have made the same calculations and come to the same conclusion.

"All right, Assistant Director McDowell," Leiter said slowly. "We'll play this your way—for now. Your actions regarding Agent Gray are, reluctantly, approved." He scrawled a signature across the bottom of the report in front of him.

"Thank you, sir." McDowell paused briefly to savor his win before continuing. "I do have two other suggestions."

The Director's eyes narrowed. "Go on."

"I think it's time we revoked Agent Gray's law enforcement powers and issued our own arrest warrants for her and for Colonel Thorn. The odds are the Germans will pick them up sooner rather than later—but it would look better if we were moving off the dime on this end."

Leiter sat stone-faced for a moment, and then nodded abruptly. "Very well, Assistant Director McDowell. Get it done."

McDowell left the Director's office with a heady sense of relief and triumph. He'd survived Heinrich Wolf's little ploy—survived and come out on top. And now, with Thorn and Gray almost out of his hair forever, he could concentrate on finding some way to free himself from that blackmailing bastard's clutches.

Leiter's voice stopped him in his tracks. "McDowell."

He turned. "Yes, sir?"

The Director glared back at him. "From now on you keep me fully informed. I don't want any more ugly surprises like this. Is that clear?"

McDowell smiled blandly. "Of course, sir. You can count on it."

Caraco Transport Division, Galveston, Texas

(D MINUS 8)

The two-story concrete-block building leased by Caraco Transport—one of Caraco's several subsidiaries—was close to Galveston's waterfront. It had a three-bay loading dock at the rear, a single steel door in front, and glass-block windows high on three of the walls.

Like all the other buildings in the area, Caraco Transport's warehouse was surrounded by a fence topped with razor wire. Security lights and cameras covered every approach. None of the neighboring businesses found that at all unusual. Port warehouses were a magnet for thieves.

The extraordinary security measures were kept inside—well out of public view.

The building's front office had been taken over by a highly trained eight-man security force. A gun rack on one wall held half a dozen H&K G-3 automatic rifles. Other weapons lockers held grenades, Russian-made RPG rocket launchers, and handguns for a dozen men.

The security troops were all Germans—veterans of East Germany's now-disbanded People's Army or the Border Command denied further gainful employment after the Wall fell. Their commander, a taciturn ex-commando named Schaaf, was a specialist in urban combat tactics—especially SWAT assault methods and other raiding team techniques.

His expertise was reflected in the facility's defenses. Although already considered burglarproof, the warehouse doors had been strengthened with welded metal plates and steel bars. They would resist any battering ram attack indefinitely. Demolition charges and directional mines were deployed to cover the major avenues of attack.

His men were equally well protected. Masks were provided for use against tear gas. Helmets with built-in hearing protection offered a defense against the flash-bang grenades favored by Western counterterrorist forces.

Four of the eight were always on duty. One continuously monitored a battery of police scanners, intrusion alarms, and TV surveillance cameras. Another patrolled the building—looking for signs of intrusion, whether physical or electronic. The rest were stationed to watch the work on the warehouses's vast, open main floor.

All of them ate, slept, and lived in the building. And, according to Schaaf, if they failed to protect its secrets, they'd be buried in it as well.

Werner Kentner took a quick break from his work, flipped the goggles off his face, and glanced up at the catwalk above the main floor. One of Schaaf's men was in view there—prowling back and forth with an assault rifle cradled casually in his arms.

Kentner mopped his sweating face with a rag and turned back to the job at hand.

One of his men, a young Palestinian from the Gaza Strip,

gave the ready signal and scrambled out of the large metal shipping container.

Kentner nodded. "Hoist away."

A third man, this one a fellow German, spun the controls of the overhead crane poised above the open container. Chains tightened as the slack came off—hauling a jet engine into view.

Almost as soon as it was clear, the fourth member of Kentner's team, an Egyptian by birth, moved in with a cutting torch. Sparks flew as he attacked the shipping container, slicing it into irregular shapes of random size—all of which would be too small to give any clue to the container's original identity. As the pieces dropped free, the fifth man, an older Palestinian, checked them, and then tossed them into a man-high bin to one side. A dozen similar bins were already full.

Kentner turned back to watch the crane operator expertly lower the engine into a specially prepared cradle. Once it was in place, he moved forward—followed by the young Palestinian. The other German shut the crane off and joined them.

Working smoothly, with practiced movements, the three of them began dismantling the engine's outer shell—using wrenches for the easy parts, and hydraulic cutters and power saws for the rest. Preserving the engine intact was not part of their mission.

It took them roughly half an hour to remove the upper half of the outer shell, revealing what should have been a series of turbine wheels and combustion chambers. Instead a TN-1000 nuclear weapon lay inside—carefully braced by a series of welded steel supports. A thick layer of polyethylene covered the bomb. The plastic had not only padded the TN-1000 during its long rail and sea voyage, it also absorbed stray radiation emitted by the bomb's plutonium core.

Kentner stepped back again. "That's it, comrades," he murmured. "The last little beauty."

He patted the TN-1000 affectionately. He'd served in the East German Air Force as an ordnance specialist. He'd seen these Soviet-made monsters before, and he knew how to care for them properly. The nuclear weapon was shaped like a conventional bomb, streamlined with a bluntly pointed nose. With a yield of 150 kilotons, it was roughly fifteen times more powerful than the bombs dropped on Hiroshima and Nagasaki.

After stripping off the polyethylene covering, Kentner carefully inspected the weapon for signs of damage or mishandling. Twenty years of military service had taught him that some Russians were too lazy even to wipe themselves properly. He saw no reason to assume the boys at Kandalaksha were competent.

Using a tech manual printed in Russian, the ordnance specialist checked the TN-1000's safety devices, and then tested the internal circuits. Everything came up green. Reassured, he gave the signal for the crane operator to lift the bomb clear of its concealment and went back to work—this time inspecting the underside.

His two assistants went back to tearing apart the Su-24 engine—throwing various chunks into several different scrap bins. The work went on for hour after hour—a furious maelstrom of cascading sparks and the ear-splitting screech of power saws.

The air was thick with smoke, and they were all half deaf by the time they finished.

Stage Two was quieter, but even more intricate.

Kentner slid the polyethylene sheath back over the TN-1000, and then used the crane to swing it over to a prepared case. Inside, a metal base and cradle supported the weapon. The ordnance man and his team anchored more supports over the bomb—locking it into place. A light aluminum cover, designed to look like a machinery housing, bolted easily onto the frame.

When complete, the entire assembly fitted onto a wooden pallet and then inside a crate.

Finally, Kentner guided the crated 150-kiloton nuclear bomb over to a section of the warehouse where four identical containers waited all in a row.

The five-man work crew exchanged quick grins and then moved rapidly to pack up their tools. They'd barely begun when the first deep klaxon sounded at the rear of Loading Bay One.

Schaaf and three of his men double-teamed into the warehouse—taking up concealed firing positions. When they were ready, the former commando gave Kentner the thumbs-up. "Our first garbage man has arrived," he quipped.

The ordnance man nodded and moved to unlock the loading bay door.

Tommy Perkins was an independent trucker—a road gypsy who didn't mind working late hours. Traffic was lighter after dark anyway. He also didn't mind hauling cargo for Caraco Transport. The big boys often contracted with independents—especially during a crunch when they needed extra rigs. Besides, these Caraco fellas might be foreigners, but they paid on time and in cash—which was mighty convenient when tax time rolled around.

And he had to admit they worked damned hard. They'd loaded his rig with five bins of mixed scrap and processed his paperwork almost before he'd had time to take a leak in the port-a-john they kept out back.

Perkins was on the road in forty-five minutes—headed for a scrap yard outside New Orleans.

* * *

Three other trucks arrived right after he left. Two were independent haulers who took the rest of the scrap metal—this time destined for dumping grounds in Missouri and Georgia.

The driver and co-driver of the third eighteen-wheeler waited inside while the others were being loaded. Both spoke passable English and carried valid U.S. driver's licenses. Both were armed.

After the independents left, they backed their truck up to the loading dock and waited while Kentner and his men slid the five crated "compressors" into the back and secured them in place.

It was well past dark by the time the third semi turned out of the warehouse yard and roared onto a highway heading inland. Schaaf's security detail settled down into a normal nighttime routine. Werner Kentner and his men fell into an exhausted sleep.

The next thing Kentner knew his shoulder was being roughly shaken. He heard a muffled voice speaking to him urgently. "Get up. *Raus mit ihr!*"

Groggy, his vision blurred, he rolled over and looked up at the men standing over him without comprehension. He managed to mutter "What?" just before cold water was thrown on his face.

Spluttering, Kentner struggled to his feet, angry now and ready to deck the swine who had—

His vision cleared and he saw Rolf Ulrich Reichardt holding an empty pitcher, a tight, controlled smile on his face.

"Are you awake now, Werner, or do you need another drink?" Reichardt asked with deceptive mildness. "If so, I'm sure Herr Schaaf can bring me a second container."

Schaaf, the hard-as-nails soldier, stood meekly, one step back and to the side of the ex-Stasi operative.

"What's going on?" Kentner knew better than to challenge Reichardt, but he was still confused—still trying to get his bearings. The warehouse windows were dark. He glanced at his watch. My God . . . he'd only been asleep for an hour or so.

Elsewhere in the makeshift bunk room, men stirred—awakened by the sudden commotion. Reichardt took them all in at a glance and ordered, "Get up, all of you! You have more work to do! Now!"

His voice was equal parts anger and impatience.

Kentner wiped at the water still dripping off his chin. "I don't understand, Herr Reichardt. We are on schedule. Why the rush?"

The ex-Stasi man spared him a terrible, chilling glance. He leaned closer and lowered his voice. "Schedules change, Werner." His eyes grew even harder. "You will not question me. Not now. Or ever again. Do you understand?"

Dazed, Kentner hurriedly nodded.

"Good," Reichardt said coldly. "Then I suggest you get moving. Now."

CHAPTER THIRTEEN
RELAYS

JUNE 14
Charlottenburg, Berlin

Colonel Peter Thorn stepped out of the shower and quickly slipped into the short-sleeved shirt and slacks he'd borrowed from their host. Luckily, he and Andrew Griffin were much the same size. Then he left the bathroom, still toweling his wet hair—moving quietly out of long habit and hard training. He paused in the doorway to the living room.

The ex-SAS officer's Charlottenburg flat occupied the entire top floor of an elegant house that had once belonged to a wealthy industrialist. Large windows looked down onto a wide, tree-lined avenue—now a sea of leaves waving gently beneath a wide, cloudless blue sky. The ornate facades of the houses across the avenue rose above the bright green leaves like wind-sculpted cliffs rising from the ocean. Summer was close at hand.

Helen Gray stood gazing out the window, silhouetted by the mid-morning sun. The light cast a dazzling halo around her dark hair and brought the perfect profile of her face into sharp relief.

Thorn watched her in silence for a moment longer, committing the breathtaking image to his memory forever. He was always aware that she was a beautiful woman—but there were still times when the sheer power of her beauty rocked him back on his heels. This was one of them.

"I've got a penny . . ." he said, at last daring to break the spell she'd cast over him.

Without looking around, Helen shook her head. "My thoughts aren't worth the price, Peter."

"That's my call, I think," Thorn said.

She moved away from the window, ran her right hand lightly over the polished wood of a baby grand piano, and then turned to face him with a small, sad smile playing across her lips. "All right. I was thinking about the future."

Thorn let the damp towel fall around his neck. "Oh? Any future in particular?"

"My future. Your future." Her voice dropped low. "Our future."

So that was it. Thorn joined her by the piano. "Sounds like a sensible subject." He slipped an arm around her waist. "So why the long face?"

Almost against her will, Helen's smile grew a little more genuine. Her eyes regained some of their old sparkle. "Gee, Peter, I don't know. Just because we're being hunted by the German police, tracked by trained killers, and stand to lose our jobs on top of everything else . . ."

"Just that?" Thorn shook his head. He forced a lopsided grin. "And here you had me worried."

"Oh?" she said dryly. "You don't think my catalogue of woes is all that bad?"

Thorn shrugged. "Well, the way I see it we're facing three possibilities. One: We get killed. Now, I'm not planning on that. Two: There's always the second alternative—we go to jail."

"And you see problems with that option, too, I suppose," Helen prompted.

"Yep. Too embarrassing. And the food's usually lousy."

"So your third alternative is . . ."

Thorn shrugged. "We survive. We prove our case. And then we live happily ever after."

Helen sighed. "Sounds nice, Peter. It really does. It's too bad I'm feeling a little too old to believe in real-life fairy tales." She looked away.

"Helen . . ." He turned her toward him and held her. "We'll get out of this. I promise you that."

"Damn it. Cut the pep talk," she said, pulling away slightly from his encircling arms. "I'm not one of your soldiers."

"No, you're not," he said more seriously. He gently tugged her closer and stared straight into her bright blue eyes. "You're the woman I love."

Helen briefly blushed a faint red, then shook her head. "And I love you, too. But as wonderful as that is, it doesn't change the fundamental equation."

"I think it does." Thorn took her by the hand, aware suddenly that his heart was pounding faster than if he'd just finished a five-mile run.

Helen stared back at him. "Peter, this isn't—"

The sound of a key turning in a lock stopped her in midsentence. She swung toward the front door. "Oh, *damn*."

Thorn hurriedly released her.

"This is getting ridiculous," he muttered. He could feel his ears burning bright red. First Alexei Koniev, then Mc-Dowell, and now Andrew Griffin.

Griffin came into the living room seconds later. The ex-SAS officer set his briefcase down on the floor and eyed them carefully. "I hope I haven't interrupted anything important?"

"No, not at all," Thorn said abruptly.

"I see," Griffin said, clearly not believing him. Quiet amusement danced in the corners of his eyes. "I'm sorry for barging back so soon in the day, but I received a call from General Farrell at my office."

"He's up awfully early," Thorn commented. Christ, it couldn't be much past 5:00 A.M. Washington time.

Griffin nodded. "I gather he's flying down to North Carolina later today, and he was rather eager to reach me as soon as possible."

"With good news, I hope?" Helen asked.

The Englishman nodded again. "Very good news. He's found a way to slip you out of Germany without alerting our rather overzealous hosts." The ex-SAS officer turned toward Thorn. "Do you know a Colonel Stroud? One of your Special Forces chaps?"

"Mike Stroud?" Thorn said. "Yeah, I know him. He's with the Tenth Special Forces Group. Stationed at Panzer Kaserne in Stuttgart."

"Ordinarily, yes," Griffin answered. "But right now he's on a rotation through the joint staff at Ramstein."

Thorn whistled softly. That was a piece of luck. Ramstein was the largest U.S. Air Force base in Europe. It was also the hub for military passenger flights to and from the States. "And Mike's agreed to take us in?"

"He has," the ex-SAS officer confirmed. "Apparently General Farrell has a long reach—and many good friends."

"When do we leave?" Helen asked quietly.

"I'll drive you there tomorrow morning," Griffin said. "I gather Colonel Stroud will need some time to arrange the necessary papers. Still, I should think you'll be home in America in short order."

Home, Thorn thought.

He listened to Helen thank their host for the good news and then watched her turn away—moving back to stare out the window again. They were going home. But home to what?

Joint Special Operations Command Headquarters, Fort Bragg, North Carolina

Sam Farrell entered the outer office and nodded to the pleasant-faced, middle-aged woman manning the desk. "Morning, Libby."

"Good morning to you, General!" Her reaction was a mixture of surprise and pleasure. "We weren't expecting you down here."

Then she grinned mischievously. "Or did I miss something on my calendar?"

Farrell grinned back. Libby Bauer had been his administrative assistant before he retired—and she'd worked for his predecessor as well. That made her something of an institution around JSOC headquarters. "Not a thing, Libby. Is the boss in?"

"You're in luck, sir. He's in the building, so I can track

him down for you." She picked up a phone. "This'll only take a minute. Why don't you go ahead and wait inside?"

"Appreciate it, Libby." Farrell nodded. He went through the open door behind her.

Although the room beyond was familiar, the details jarred. It still had the same wood paneling, the same ratty carpet. The big oak desk was also the same, and so were the flags on either side and the JSOC crest on the wall behind it. But there were different mementos on the desk, and the plaques clustered on one wall belonged to his relief, Major General George Mayer.

Mayer appeared before he'd even had time to take it all in. "Sam! This is a pleasant surprise! Jesus, it sure looks like retirement agrees with you."

Farrell shook his outstretched hand. "Hell, George, you look too happy yourself! You must not be working hard enough."

Both men were of a type: sturdy and in excellent physical condition. Neither wore glasses—though Farrell needed them now to read. Mayer was just a smidge taller, and his narrow, angular face contrasted sharply with Farrell's broader, friendlier features.

They shared a common background and common experiences. Mayer had served under Farrell at several points in his career, times both looked back on fondly. While he wasn't as close to Mayer as he was to Peter Thorn, Farrell liked him—the way you like a good son-in-law. In fact, he'd strongly recommended Mayer as his own replacement as head of the Joint Special Operations Command—the headquarters controlling all U.S. military counterterrorist units, including the Army's Delta Force and the Navy's SEAL Team Six.

Mayer called out to Libby Bauer for coffee and motioned his predecessor toward a chair. In short order, she appeared with two steaming mugs, then disappeared—closing the door behind her.

"So how's the book going, Sam?" the current JSOC commander asked. Rumor said that Farrell was working on a novel, supposedly a thinly veiled autobiography.

"Pretty good. I sit at my desk and tell lies all day. Not a bad way to earn a living," Farrell replied.

"But you didn't come all the way down here to discuss literature, did you?"

"No, George. I didn't."

Farrell set his coffee aside. This was the moment of truth. He'd promised Peter Thorn he'd try to kick the U.S. government into gear on the wild-assed story the younger man had told him. Now it was time to honor his promise. He just hoped Thorn wasn't barking up the wrong tree. "There's a container ship headed for Galveston—maybe already there. I believe someone's trying to smuggle a nuclear weapon into the United States aboard that ship."

Mayer grinned. "Look, Sam, you can't run drills like that anymore, you're out of the—" He stopped, studying Farrell's expression more closely. His grin faltered and then vanished. "Jesus, you're really not kidding, are you?"

"No," Farrell said. "And this is no drill, George."

He ran quickly through all the information Thorn had given him.

"Christ." Mayer stood up and started pacing—as though he could work off the horrible implications of what he'd just been told by walking. "You really think this *Caraco Savannah* has a nuke on board?"

"Yes," Farrell said simply. He was committed now.

Mayer spun on his heel. "Who else knows about this, Sam? Have you taken this to the FBI or anybody else?"

Farrell shook his head. "Not yet. You're the first."

"Jesus."

Farrell understood his successor's confusion. The military, the FBI, the CIA, the State Department, the Department of Energy, and almost every other arm of the U.S. government had given a lot of long, hard thought to the potential threat posed by a nuclear weapon smuggled onto American soil. Procedures had been established, organizations created, and yet here he was bypassing the whole establishment in the blink of an eye.

"Just what the hell's going on here, Sam?" Mayer asked. "What's your source for this data?"

"HUMINT," Farrell said, using the acronym for human intelligence—a fancy term that meant an agent, someone who'd acquired the information the hard way.

"What kind of HUMINT?"

"Someone reliable," Farrell said.

"Meaning you can't tell me? Or won't?" Mayer asked.

"Unfortunately, maybe a bit of both, George." From what Thorn had told Farrell, Thorn's name was probably mud around all of official Washington. So there wasn't any point in attributing the data directly to the younger man. The armed forces and the political establishment had missed the boat before—all because they'd viewed an intelligence source with suspicion.

"But you're convinced that this isn't just some cock-and-bull story spun by somebody who's had one too many drinks?" Mayer asked again.

"I think this is gospel, George," Farrell said, hoping like hell that his faith in Peter Thorn wasn't misplaced. "And if I thought I could get action through the normal channels, believe me, I'd be filling out all the proper forms faster than Libby Bauer can make coffee."

"Uh-huh," Mayer grumbled.

Farrell knew what his successor was thinking. Farrell

hadn't exactly been known as a stickler for Army regulations during his time as head of the JSOC. But then nobody in the special warfare community was especially proficient at genuflecting before all the established bureaucratic icons. And Mayer was no exception.

"Okay, Sam." The other man sighed. "If you're so damned sure about this, I'll send up a flare and we'll see what scurries for cover."

Farrell nodded silently. That was more than he had any real right to ask. He just hoped it would be enough.

Fort Bragg, North Carolina

EMPTY QUIVER ALERT—FLASH PRIORITY

From: Joint Special Operations Command Headquarters.
To: Director, FBI

SITUATION:
Reliable HUMINT indicates possible nuclear weapon contained in cargo aboard container ship CARACO SAVANNAH. Vessel departed WILHELMSHAVEN, GERMANY, on JUNE 5. Destination—GALVESTON, TEXAS. Weapon believed concealed inside smuggled Russian-make jet engines shipped as auxiliary generators. Urgently suggest immediate investigation.

JUNE 14

On Interstate 135, Near Salina, Kansas

(D MINUS 7)

Ninety miles north of Wichita, the driver of the big eighteen-wheeler yawned and opened his window a crack. Cold early morning air whipped through the cab, rustling the papers and maps scattered across the dashboard. Feeling slightly more awake, he took his eyes off the road for just a moment and glanced back toward the cot rigged up in the space behind the two front seats.

The driver spoke up. "We're almost to the junction."

His partner rolled over and sat up, rubbing the sleep out of his own eyes. "Good." He climbed forward into the passenger seat and peered out through the dirty windshield.

"More of nothing?" he asked.

The driver nodded, looking out at the same flat landscape of fields and isolated farmhouses he'd been watching go by ever since the sun came up.

The two men had been driving almost continuously since leaving Galveston late the previous day—taking four-hour shifts behind the wheel, and stopping only for quick meals at the diners and fast food restaurants liberally sprinkled up and down American highways. Whenever they stopped, one man always stayed behind to guard the truck and its precious cargo—the five crates loaded at the Caraco warehouse.

A big green road sign loomed up on the shoulder of the highway—announcing that they were approaching the junction with Interstate 70. I-70 ran east and west across the cen-

tral portion of the United States. Turning east would take
them through St. Louis, Indianapolis, Columbus, and eventually all the way to Baltimore. Going west would set them
on a road toward the Colorado Rockies, Denver, and the
whole network of highways crisscrossing the Western
United States.

The big rig turned west and accelerated.

JUNE 15

Caraco Transport Division, Galveston, Texas

The loading door lock turned slowly—so slowly that the
noise it made was almost impossible to hear just a few feet
away. The second the latch cleared the frame, two men
slammed the loading door up and whirled aside. Half a
dozen black-clad figures instantly poured inside through the
opening and fanned out across the warehouse. Each man
carried an MP5 submachine gun at shoulder level, ready to
fire.

Shouts of "FBI!" filled the building—echoing and then
gradually trailing off as the assault force realized the warehouse was unoccupied. And not only unoccupied. The whole
building was completely empty—stripped down to the bare,
freshly painted walls.

FBI Special Agent Steve Sanchez heard the "all-clear"
over his tactical radio and entered the warehouse. He tugged
off his gas mask and cradled it under his arm. His nose wrinkled at the overpowering smell of new paint permeating the
building. The assault force leader saw him coming and

joined him near the entrance to the building's small front office.

"Nothing?" Sanchez asked.

"*Nada,*" the other agent replied. He nodded toward the vast empty open space around them. "You sure this is the right address, Steve?"

"Yeah." Sanchez slowly scuffed at the concrete floor with the toe of his boot, adjusting to the new situation he and his team faced. It was a frustrating end to a very long night. The EMPTY QUIVER alert passed to the Houston field office from D.C. had caught him at his son's soccer game.

Rounding up the other agents assigned to the field office had taken time. Rousting enough port officials to confirm that the *Caraco Savannah* had offloaded cargo in Galveston had consumed several more hours. By the time his people had tracked the generators, or jet engines, or whatever they were, to this address on Meridian Street, it was well past midnight. Organizing this raid and securing the necessary warrants had pushed the clock forward to near dawn. To now.

And for what? Whatever had been stored in this warehouse was long gone.

Frowning, Sanchez turned to one of his subordinates. "Get the Caraco operations manager in here—right now!"

Frank Wilson, Caraco's Galveston port operations manager, was a big man—nearly a head taller than Sanchez. He was fighting both hair loss and a growing potbelly. Right now he was also fighting sleep. FBI agents had come hammering at his door at four in the morning.

Sanchez swung toward the disheveled Caraco executive. "Well, Mr. Wilson? Would you care to explain what was going on in here?"

Wilson blinked, staring at the empty warehouse around

him. He turned innocent eyes on the FBI agent. "Explain what, Agent Sanchez?" He shrugged. "As I tried telling your people earlier this morning, I've never set foot in this building in my life."

"Now how is that possible?" Sanchez asked sarcastically. "You are the top dog for your company in Galveston, right?"

Wilson nodded. "That's right. But Caraco's a big corporation, Agent Sanchez. Very big. We've got more than half a dozen subsidiaries here in the States alone—and more overseas. I run the port operations for the company. We mostly handle shipments of refinery and pipeline equipment for our energy division."

He shrugged and continued. "But this warehouse was leased by Caraco Transport. That's a separate outfit entirely."

"How separate?"

"Different personnel. Different chain of command. Different procedures. Hell, diffcrent pay scales, for all I know!" Wilson said. "That's the way the higher-ups like it, Agent Sanchez. It's part of the whole new wave in corporate management—less top-down direction, more bottom-up innovation."

Sounds more like a recipe for potential chaos and ducked responsibility, Sanchez thought cynically. He was a Bureau man through and through, and good or bad the FBI ran on procedure and centralized control. He tried again. "Did you ever meet any of the people working at this facility, Mr. Wilson?"

The Caraco executive shook his balding head ponderously. "Nope. But then I never had any reason to. Like I said, we're separate outfits—and I've had a ton of work on my plate these past few weeks. We've got a big contract to build a pipeline in Central Asia coming up."

"What about any of your other employees, sir? Did any of them have any contact with the people running this warehouse?"

"You'd have to ask them that question, Agent Sanchez. I sure don't know." The big man shrugged again. "I suppose some of my guys might have run across these folks in the bars after work, but I don't make it my business to pry."

"I can see that."

"Look, Agent Sanchez," Wilson said kindly. "If you want to know more about this operation, why don't you contact Caraco Transport's headquarters directly? I'm sure they'd be happy to answer your questions."

"I'll do that, Mr. Wilson," the FBI agent replied. "Any idea where exactly that might be?"

"Sure. They're based in Cairo."

"In Egypt?" Sanchez heard himself ask.

Wilson chuckled. "Like I said, we're a big company."

Already imagining the tangle of official forms, mounting phone bills, and foreign language translators he was about to wade into, Sanchez signaled one of his subordinates to take the Caraco executive away and get a written statement from him.

He turned back to face the warehouse. Caraco employees or not, he knew the characters who'd leased this place weren't just model tenants when they'd stripped this place down to the bare floor. They'd systematically tried to destroy any trace of their presence. Nobody did that without a damned good reason—like hiding illegal activity.

The sixty-four-thousand-dollar question was: What kind of illegal activity? An FBI addendum added to the EMPTY QUIVER alert questioned JSOC's HUMINT source—implying the goods being smuggled were far more likely to be some kind of illegal drugs than nuclear weapons.

Well, Sanchez sure hoped the higher-ups in the Hoover

Building were right, and the Army was wrong. Missing a big shipment of coke, heroin, or pot was bad. Missing a smuggled nuke . . .

He waved his section leaders over and started issuing orders. "Okay, let's start tearing this place apart. Check the Dumpsters. See when the trash was last collected. Calder, you start interviewing the businesses nearby. Find out what they've seen. I want every license number of every car or truck that's ever been parked within a hundred yards of this place. And get the physical evidence teams in here ASAP!"

An agent speaking into a cell-phone caught his eye. "Do you want NEST?" she asked.

The highly trained specialists of the Department of Energy's Nuclear Emergency Search Team were standing by on high alert. If the FBI raid had turned up any evidence at all of illicit nuclear material, NEST would have come swooping in to find the stuff and remove it safely.

Sanchez shook his head. "Tell NEST there's nothing for them to do here."

He didn't know whether that would make the DOE folks happy or unhappy.

Sanchez moved outside—away from the fresh-paint stink and the maddeningly empty building. For now, he suspected they'd run into a dead-end. The *Caraco Savannah* herself was halfway across the Atlantic, bound for Germany again. It would be days before her crew could be questioned.

Whoever these people were, he thought, they're pros. But nobody could vanish into thin air. They'd made the job of tracking them harder—but not impossible. If he had to, he'd interview everyone in Galveston until they found somebody who could give them a name or a description. Hell, if need be, he and his agents would scrape that goddamned paint off the walls a square inch at a time.

Sanchez narrowed his eyes. Somewhere, somehow, they'd find something. It might take days, maybe even weeks, but he and his fellow FBI agents would find the trail. He pushed the thought that it might already be too late far to the back of his mind.

JUNE 15

Middleburg, Virginia

(D MINUS 6)

Prince Ibrahim al Saud's habit after morning prayers was to check his e-mail, listen to the BBC news, and get caught up on the night's developments in his various business enterprises. He never forgot that the world kept moving while he slept.

The private study in his Middleburg home was actually a suite, with an office for his personal secretary, a meeting room wired for satellite teleconferencing, and his own palatial inner sanctum.

Ibrahim's desk faced a wide picture window that overlooked the lush, green Virginia countryside. Bulletproof glass ensured his personal security. Double panes and vacuum sealing offered protection for his personal secrets—thwarting any attempted high-tech eavesdropping.

Like the rest of the house, the study reflected his heritage, position, and wealth. Priceless handwoven Hamadan rugs covered the floor—matched by other rugs on the walls.

Dozens of precise, colorful geometric patterns covered the rugs and wall hangings—each hiding a single flaw that served to remind the viewer that only Allah could attain true perfection. Tables of beaten, handworked brass held bowls of fruit and dates, and a coffee urn.

Ibrahim scanned the front page of the *New York Times*. Nothing of great interest, he thought. Only one item caught his eye. Algeria's Islamic rebels had slaughtered another four French nuns—this time in the capital city itself. He made a mental note to funnel more money into the rebel leadership's secret accounts. Even civil wars were expensive, and good work should be rewarded.

The phone rang. He snatched it up. "Yes."

"This is Reichardt. We've had some trouble."

Ibrahim slid the newspaper aside. "I'm listening, Herr Reichardt."

"The FBI raided our Galveston facility an hour or so ago."

Ibrahim felt a cold calm settle over him. "And?"

"The Americans found nothing, Highness," Reichardt assured him. "I took the precaution of accelerating our operation there two days ago. I've prepared a full report."

Ibrahim swiveled in his chair to face the low table behind his desk. It held a high-speed fax machine. "Send it."

Within moments of his order, the fax machine clicked and hummed—spitting out several typed sheets. Reichardt remained silent during the transmission, and Ibrahim quickly skimmed each page of the report before dropping them, one at a time, into the shredder next to the machine.

Reichardt's report was thorough at least. It summarized everything the ex-Stasi officer had learned about the progress and intent of the FBI's investigation. But very little of the news was good.

Caraco Transport's Cairo headquarters reported receiving an urgent query from the American embassy about the Galveston warehouse. They were requesting instructions. And the master of the *Caraco Savannah* had radioed that he had received orders from both the American and German authorities to proceed at his best possible speed to Wilhelmshaven—where agents of the two governments would board his ship and interview his crew. Worst of all was the news from Reichardt's contact inside the FBI itself. The Americans had been looking for a smuggled nuclear weapon, and the initial alert had come from a source reporting to the U.S. DOD counterterrorist command—the JSOC.

"So this Colonel Thorn is still causing trouble for us," Ibrahim said softly. "Despite your best efforts to silence him."

Reichardt hesitated. "Yes, Highness. It appears so."

"And where are this irritating American and his woman now? Still on the loose somewhere in Germany?"

"Yes," the ex-Stasi officer admitted. "But they are being hunted by the German police—and now by their own people as well."

Ibrahim frowned. "And yet somehow they seem able to bring all our plans to an end. I find that . . . interesting. Don't you, Herr Reichardt?"

"The weapons are safe, Highness," Reichardt replied. "And I promise you that this latest FBI investigation will hit a dead-end."

Ibrahim felt his temper flare into rage, stung beyond restraint by the German's smug self-assurance. "These investigations should have hit a dead-end at Wilhelmshaven, or Pechenga, or Kandalaksha!" he roared.

A shocked silence greeted his sudden outburst.

Ibrahim wrestled for self-control, anger at Reichardt warring with anger at himself for showing such weakness before the other man. "Your failures are endangering my plans, Herr Reichardt," he said icily at last. "I will not tolerate that."

"I understand, Highness," the German said stiffly.

"When your government collapsed in ruin, I took you and your people under my protection. I provided you with employment, with power, and with a new purpose," Ibrahim said. "In return, I expect success—not excuses."

"I understand," Reichardt said again.

"Good." Ibrahim swept the pile of shredded paper into a wastebasket. It would be burned later in the day. "Now then, you agree that this FBI investigation could be . . . inconvenient?"

"Yes, Highness," the other man said. "I believe the time is too short for the Americans to learn anything significant, but their inquiries could put pressure on us at an awkward time."

"Very well." Ibrahim swiveled back to his desk. "Perhaps I can repair the damage your overconfidence has caused."

Reichardt wisely said nothing.

"Have you finished your round of inspections?" Ibrahim asked.

"I have, Highness," Reichardt replied. "Everything is in order. All will be ready on the appointed day. I fly back to Dulles this evening."

Ibrahim nodded. "Confer with me on your return." He hung up and buzzed his private secretary. "Connect me with Richard Garrett. At once."

He leaned back in his chair, contemplating the rolling landscape outside with hooded eyes. It was time to tighten the chains.

CHAPTER FOURTEEN

POWER PLAYS

JUNE 15

Kaiserlautern, Germany, Near Ramstein
U.S. Air Force Base

Colonel Peter Thorn saw the red Jeep Cherokee swing off the main road and into the parking lot adjacent to the restaurant. He glanced across the table at Andrew Griffin and then at Helen Gray. "That's got to be him."

The ex-SAS officer nodded, watching the sport utility vehicle pull alongside his Mercedes. "So it appears."

A short, wiry man popped open the Cherokee's driver's side door, slid out from behind the wheel, and dropped lightly onto the pavement. He wore a camouflage fatigue uniform, the sort the Army called BDUs—or battle dress uniform—and settled a green beret firmly atop his head.

He turned neatly on his heel, spotted the trio seated at one of the restaurant's outdoor tables, and headed straight for them.

When the soldier came within spitting distance, Thorn pushed the fourth chair out from under the table with his foot. "Take a pew, Michelito."

Colonel Mike Stroud grinned. "Thanks, Pete. Don't mind if I do." He sat down and signaled the nearest waitress. "*Ein Bier, bitte.*"

With his beer in hand, the Special Forces officer turned his dark-eyed gaze more fully on his companions. "You're looking good, Andy. The security consulting business must be booming."

Griffin nodded at Stroud. " 'Booming' is precisely the word, Colonel. There are more villains roaming around Central and Eastern Europe than ever before. And some of them have an unfortunate affinity for explosives. If you ever get tired of swashbuckling around in those fancy uniforms of yours, I can always use more good partners." The Englishman turned to Thorn. "The same goes for you, Peter."

Thorn tried smiling, instantly aware that it wasn't his most convincing expression. "Once I'm out from under my legal troubles, you mean?"

"Well, that would make it easier, of course. But I'm quite serious. I'd be very proud to have you on my team."

"Thanks," Thorn said. He meant it. Under the circumstances, Griffin's offer of future employment was extremely generous—no matter how much he hated the thought that his days in the Army were numbered.

Stroud smiled across the table at Helen. "And you must be this desperate character's gun moll. Sort of the Bonnie to his Clyde, I hear?"

Helen's return smile was also forced. "That's me, I'm afraid."

Thorn concealed a frown. Helen's behavior worried him. She'd been abnormally quiet during the past two days. She was her usual self around Andrew Griffin. But she'd kept mostly to herself whenever the Englishman was out of the flat—spending long hours staring out the window or off into space.

He pushed his concerns away for the moment. It was time to show some manners. "Mike, this is FBI Special Agent Helen Gray."

Stroud shook his head. "I never heard that name, Pete. Or yours for that matter." He reached into one of his chest pockets, fished out a pair of Department of Defense identification cards, and slid them across the table. "These'll get you through the main gate at Ramstein with me. From now on, you're Chris and Katy Carlson. If anybody asks, you're a couple of number-crunchers working out of the Pentagon. I've already booked you into a room at the base BOQ."

Thorn glanced down at the ID card. It bore a reasonable likeness of him—no doubt courtesy of Sam Farrell.

Helen frowned and held hers up. "If you don't mind my asking, Colonel Stroud, where did you get this? Phony DOD IDs don't usually grow on trees."

"Nope, not on trees," Stroud acknowledged. "We usually keep ours in locked filing cabinets."

Thorn knew the other man wouldn't say anything more. Like Delta, Special Forces teams often tried to keep a low profile during their assignments overseas. And anonymous, low-ranking civilian government employees arriving at an airport in some war-torn foreign country were far less newsworthy than uniformed Green Berets making the same trip.

He put his own new card away. "How long do you think you'll have us on your hands, Mike?"

"Well, from what Sam Farrell said, the sooner you're off German soil, the better. So I hope you won't be staying at

Ramstein long." Stroud sipped his beer appreciatively and then explained. "I'm wangling space for you on a Mobility Command cargo flight. With a bit of luck, you'll be heading back to the States in the next day or so. Probably to Dover Air Force Base."

"I don't know how we're going to thank you, Mike," Thorn said. "Not with all the risks you're running for us."

"Shoot." Stroud grinned. "I'm only helping you obey your original orders to head home. Aren't you planning to report in once you're back?"

Helen nodded.

"Then I'm just doing my sworn and solemn duty," Stroud continued. "Nobody could fault me for that, could they?"

Andrew Griffin arched an eyebrow. "Sounds a bit Jesuitical to me, Colonel."

Stroud laughed. "Hey, then I guess I learned something during my misspent youth at St. Ignatius Loyola High School, after all."

Thorn grinned. For the first time since he'd left Delta Force, he had the real sense of being among friends. The jokes were pretty bad, but the camaraderie was very real— and that meant a lot to him right now. With Farrell sounding the alarm around D.C. and Mike Stroud ready to shepherd them through the gates at Ramstein, he and Helen finally stood a good chance of putting their hard-won data in front of the proper authorities.

The White House

Richard Garrett waited until the outer office door swung shut behind him before abandoning the affable smile he usually wore. The former Commerce Secretary turned Caraco lobbyist dropped his briefcase beside the chair he'd been offered and sat down. Then he scowled darkly. "Goddamnit, John, what kind of idiot games are you people letting the FBI play here?"

John Preston, the current White House Chief of Staff, held up a conciliatory hand. "Whoa, Dick! I'm not quite sure what you're talking about. What's all this about the FBI?"

"Save the 'I'm innocent and ignorant' horseshit for the press and other suckers," Garrett growled. "We both know you were on the phone to the Hoover Building right after I called you this morning."

Preston held up both hands now, this time in a gesture of surrender. "Okay, okay, I give. I assume you're referring to the raid on that Galveston warehouse?"

"No kidding." Garrett shook his head in disgust. "So what prompted that piece of lunacy?"

"The FBI had a hot tip, Dick. The Army called a priority one alert—claimed somebody was smuggling a nuclear weapon through there."

"Through a Caraco Transport–leased warehouse? Some pointy-headed general hit the panic button with that as the premise?" Garrett asked sarcastically.

"That was apparently the story," Preston admitted.

"And you let them do this?"

The White House Chief of Staff shook his own head. "We didn't *let* anybody do anything, Dick. Hell, this was an FBI operation. They don't clear that stuff with us. Christ, I didn't even know anything about it until you got on the horn!"

Garrett asked, "So John, you mind telling me precisely what this rogue FBI raid on one of my client's legitimate business enterprises turned up?"

Preston looked distinctly uncomfortable.

"Well?" Garrett pressed.

"Apparently nothing," Preston said reluctantly. "The agent in charge reported the place was stripped down to the bare walls."

"Then I can assume that the FBI's preparing a written apology to Prince Ibrahim al Saud, and that they've called off the dogs?" the former Commerce Secretary pressed further.

"Well . . ." Preston picked up a fountain pen from his desk and began repeatedly pulling the cap off and then putting it back on. "Not exactly."

"Uh-huh." Garrett leaned back in his chair. He steepled his fingers. "Let me see if I add this up right, John: Acting on some wild-assed story about a black-market nuke, the FBI raids a warehouse leased by a respectable international corporation. A corporation that's been damned generous to this president and his party. A corporation headed by a Saudi prince who's known far and wide as a loyal friend of the United States, for Christ's sake! Jesus, the President himself sat down for coffee with Prince Ibrahim just a couple of weeks ago! You with me so far?"

Without waiting for the White House Chief of Staff's reaction, Garrett drove on. "Now, then. The FBI finds precisely, exactly *nothing* during this raid of theirs. No nuclear weapon. No stolen blueprints for Plan 999 from Outer Space. *Nothing.*

"But instead of slinking home in disgrace, the Hoover Building boneheads are still out there—ripping my client's duly leased property to pieces and exposing his good name to a possible media scandal." The former Commerce Secretary leaned forward. "Does that about sum it up, John?"

Preston spread his hands. "I've checked, Dick. There's no media interest in this story. Not yet."

"And I thank God for tiny favors!" Garrett said. He snorted. "The publicity hounds at the FBI usually don't make a move without putting on their TV makeup."

Preston colored. "Jesus, Dick. What the hell do you expect me to do? I run the White House staff. I don't run the Department of Justice or the Bureau. They're out of my bailiwick."

"Bullshit." Garrett looked steadily at the other man. "We both know you and the President have the Attorney General right smack in your back pocket. You say 'jump' and she'll ask you what flavor of moon cheese you want."

The White House Chief of Staff ignored that. "Leiter's got an independent streak, though."

"The FBI Director?" Garrett shook his head. "Use your brains, John. Leiter likes his job. Hell, he loves his job. But he's got five or six congressional committees gunning for him right now. You think he's going to want the White House piling on, too?"

"Maybe not."

The former Commerce Secretary shook his head mournfully. "Maybe not. C'mon, John. We've been friends for twenty years. Get with the program! Do the right thing! You and I both know the FBI's gonna wind up with crap all over its face if it presses this pointless investigation any further. And we also both know that dragging Prince Ibrahim's name through the press won't exactly help you, the administration, or the President."

Garrett sat back, watching as the other man digested his implied threat. Adding the raw details of Caraco's political contributions to the stories already in print might finally tip even a cynical public into giving a damn about the way the current president ran his fund-raising operations. If the water got too hot, Ibrahim could always jet off to Riyadh, the French Riveria, or one of the other homes he had scattered around the world. The President and his closest aides would be left hanging—faced by yet another congressional investigation and ever-higher legal bills.

Preston sighed. "You're certain there's nothing to this rumor the FBI's following up?"

Garrett chuckled. "That Caraco employees decided to smuggle a nuclear weapon into Texas?" He laughed again, more scornfully this time. "I mean, think about it, John. The FBI's all hot to trot . . . and why? Because some of our people got a little overzealous when they cleaned the place up before turning it over to the next tenants. Boy, that sure sounds like a criminal conspiracy to me . . ."

"I see your point," Preston said slowly. "Put that way . . ."

Garrett nodded. "I suggest you do put it that way, John. Exactly that way." He reached for his briefcase—conscious of another job well done. Prince Ibrahim al Saud paid him well to run interference for Caraco's business operations in America, and the lawyer-lobbyist believed strongly in providing value for the money.

JUNE 16

FBI Field Office, Houston, Texas

Special Agent Steve Sanchez grabbed the phone on the second ring, narrowly missing a teetering pile of reports. He'd flown back from Galveston only half an hour before, and he was still trying to dig down to the surface of his desk. "Sanchez."

"This is Leiter," the brusque voice on the other end said.

As in Director of the FBI David Leiter, Sanchez realized. He sat up straighter. "Yes, sir."

"Are you alone?"

Still holding the phone, Sanchez moved around his desk and closed his office door. "I am now, sir."

"Good." Leiter took a deep breath. "Agent Sanchez, do you have any—and I mean, *any*—hard evidence of wrongdoing inside that Caraco Transport warehouse?"

"Not yet, sir," Sanchez said. Hadn't the Director read his latest report?

"Then I'm ordering you to close down your probe. Pull all your people off the case and inform the Galveston police that we've determined there's no basis for any further investigation."

Sanchez couldn't hide his surprise. "What? You call an EMPTY QUIVER and then cancel it just two days later?"

"That's exactly what I'm doing, Agent Sanchez," Leiter said. "Shut it down and send every scrap of paper and computer disk you've generated to this office immediately."

Sanchez sat down, still stunned by the order he'd just received. The Bureau lived on procedures and regulations, and the Director's instructions bordered on the illegal. He felt pulled in two directions at the same time. Part of him, the "good soldier" half, just wanted to shut up and do as he was told. The other side, the stubborn truth-seeker that made him a top-notch detective, wanted to demand an explanation.

Leiter must have sensed, or guessed, his indecision. "I can't tell you much, Agent Sanchez, but it appears that we've stumbled into a hornet's nest here. Caraco has a lot of friends in very high places—and none of them are very happy with what we're doing."

The Director's voice dropped a level. "The universal word I'm getting—from the Agency, the White House, and the Attorney General's office—is that we're barking up the wrong tree. Nobody believes Caraco would involve itself in any illegal activity, let alone something of this magnitude. And frankly, I think the source that triggered this EMPTY QUIVER is highly suspect. I'm tracking that back with the JSOC myself."

"Sir, I—" Sanchez said.

"The bottom line, Special Agent," Leiter interrupted, "is that this investigation is more trouble than it's worth. Without good, solid evidence of wrongdoing, we're walking a high wire without a net. Do you understand what I mean?"

"I understand that somebody at Caraco is pulling some high-priced strings," Sanchez said bitterly. He tamped down his temper. This was the perfect end to a perfect couple of days, but blowing up at the Director of the FBI wouldn't be wise, polite, or career-enhancing.

"Then you apprehend the situation perfectly," Leiter replied. "So close it up, and call me when the material is on its way."

Sanchez acknowledged and hung up. He paced back and forth in his tiny office, counting to ten, then counting again. Should he obey the order or not? If he really believed Caraco Transport had slipped a nuke into the U.S., the answer was obvious. He'd have to disobey the Director—even at the cost of his own career. But did he really believe that?

The FBI agent considered what he'd learned. The news that Leiter considered the EMPTY QUIVER source tainted wasn't very reassuring. It wouldn't be the first time that somebody had tried using the FBI to stick a shiv in a rival corporation's ribs. Was that what was going on here? What if Caraco Transport had only cleaned out its warehouse so thoroughly to protect some sort of trade secret? That seemed rather thin, but then so did everything else about this crazy case.

Sanchez grimaced. He just didn't know enough. And that being the case, he decided to obey orders. Ultimately, Leiter was the boss, and it was his call. If the FBI Director didn't think investigating Caraco more thoroughly was worth the price of admission, Sanchez would just have to trust his superior's judgment.

Tysons Corner, Virginia

"They're shutting the Galveston investigation down?" Farrell said incredulously, staring across the table at the CIA analyst he'd invited to lunch.

Mark Podolski nodded. "I wish I'd known sooner what you were up to, Sam. I would've headed you off at the pass before you went galloping off to Fort Bragg." He took a slug from his diet cola before explaining. "Caraco has connections all over town. So when the FBI hit that warehouse, their top guy in D.C. started screaming bloody murder at the top of his lungs. And believe me when Dick Garrett gets pissed, the White House listens."

"You think I jumped the gun?"

Podolski nodded. "Yeah." He drank more of his soda. "I ran the data you gave me past my team. They all agree. There's not enough solid stuff there to support the conclusion that somebody inside Caraco has his hands on a Russian nuke."

Farrell pondered that. Podolski was one of Langley's best analysts. He never papered over holes in the data or ignored anomalies. "So you don't think anything strange is going on?"

The CIA officer shook his head. "I didn't say that, Sam."

He folded his napkin and laid it beside the mostly untouched meal on his plate. "There is a funny pattern there. And I buy the premise that those Su-24 engines were retagged and transshiped all over Europe—and probably into Galveston. But I just don't see the motive for Caraco to smuggle nukes. If anything, the company's Russian weapons subsidiary, Arrus Export, may be doing a little aviation side business they'd like to keep quiet."

Farrell frowned. "What about the possibility that those engines contained heroin?"

"That's certainly more conceivable," Podolski admitted. Then he held up a cautionary hand. "But I can tell you one thing for certain: Whether it's drugs or nukes, I don't think it's something Caraco's top echelon knows about."

"How can you be so sure of that?"

"Do you know much about Caraco, Sam?" the CIA analyst asked.

"Not as much as I'd like," Farrell said. He nodded toward the cooling plateful of food in front of Podolski. "That's why I'm picking up the tab at this fancy diner, Mark."

Podolski looked down at his uneaten pasta, then continued. "Well, the head honcho is a guy named Ibrahim al Saud—he's literally a prince, a member of the Saudi royal family. And he's down in our books as a straight shooter."

"A Saudi prince?" Farrell shook his head and frowned. He'd paid a number of official visits to Saudi Arabia as head of JSOC. Some of his contacts with the royal family there had left a bad taste in his mouth. A few of the princes were energetic. A great many more were either indolent or just amiably corrupt.

"Ibrahim's not typical," Podolski insisted. "I pulled up his dossier before I came here. He's sharp, shrewd, and tough. Caraco's his baby—from start to finish. Together with all its subsidiaries, the company's probably worth somewhere on the order of ten to fifteen billion dollars. He's not going to rock the boat to smuggle in heroin."

"And he's pro-Western?"

"Totally," Podolski said. "He ran a little close to the radical edge as a university student at Cairo, but his family straightened him out—sent him off to Oxford, and then to business school at Harvard. Since then, he's been a consistent supporter of our interests."

The CIA analyst idly poked at his pasta dish with a fork and then looked up. "Look, I wouldn't invite Ibrahim to an Israel Bonds fund-raiser, but he's a solid guy otherwise. There was even a rumor a couple of years ago that one of the homegrown Saudi terrorist movements had him on a death list."

Farrell sat up straighter. "Rumor? Or fact?"

"Nothing ever happened. But just in case, he's built up a pretty reliable little private security force—mostly out of the best troops in the Saudi Royal Army. I'm telling you, Sam, Ibrahim al Saud is not your mysterious Mr. X smuggler."

Farrell pushed his own virtually untouched plate away. "Okay, I see what you mean. But if Ibrahim hasn't got a motive to run drugs or nukes into the U.S., who else in his company does?"

Podolski shrugged. "You tried the backdoor route with Mayer and the FBI and wound up with nothing. This time, why not just knock on the front door and ask? Caraco has an office in downtown D.C. If somebody on their payroll is padding his salary by running a smuggling operation, they're gonna want to find the guy and shut him down—before it hits the front pages and sends the shareholders screaming for the exits."

Farrell nodded slowly. What the CIA analyst said made sense. Why not give Caraco's top management the information they needed to track down their own bad apples?

JUNE 16

Planning Cell, Proprietary Materials Assembly Building, Caraco Complex, Chantilly, Virginia

(D MINUS 5)

Prince Ibrahim al Saud surveyed the busy room—one of the two large working spaces in the building's basement—with a measure of satisfaction. Desks and computer consoles filled the center of the room, and all four walls were lined with maps—maps of the entire United States and detailed plans of individual cities and towns. Most of the activity right now centered on a giant black-and-white weather map.

He watched closely as the planning cell's meteorologist began updating the chart with the next day's predicted weather. Until now, the former East German Air Force meteorology officer had only been able to provide statistical information. Now the man was dealing with near-term forecasts—ironically using data supplied by the U.S. National Weather Service.

Ibrahim swung around on Reichardt, who stood close by his shoulder. "You're sure that Major Schmidt can provide the accuracy we need?"

"Yes, Highness." Reichardt shrugged. "But America is a vast country—with widely variable weather. It might be better if we could provide Schmidt with another qualified assistant for this last phase."

Ibrahim considered that. The German's suggestion was logical—if a bit late in the game. For an instant, he wondered uneasily what else Reichardt had let slip while going after those interfering Americans, Thorn and Gray. "Very well. Assign one of the pilots. Who better to ensure that the major fully understands our requirements?"

Reichardt nodded.

Ibrahim turned back to check the work of the rest of his staff with a careful eye. Several of the computers were set to monitor the Internet and other information services continuously—constantly tracking the routine movements of American military forces and the operations of the major state and federal law enforcement agencies. Members of the team evaluated the raw information they gathered at regular intervals—discarding any clearly irrelevant data immediately and sifting the rest for any news that might affect his master plan.

"Highness, a phone call has been forwarded from the estate," announced the clipped, British-accented voice of Hashemi, his chief private secretary. "Mr. Garrett is on line one."

Ibrahim grunted a reply and waved Reichardt over to one of the other phones so that he could listen in. Whatever news Garrett had would surely be of interest to both of them.

Ibrahim lifted the phone in front of him. "Yes?"

"I'm sorry to trouble you again so soon, Your Highness," Garrett said smoothly. "But I've just had a very interesting call from a retired Army officer. He claims to have important information about this supposed large-scale smuggling ring operating through some of our subsidiaries."

Ibrahim turned away from the planning cell. "Oh? Who is that?"

"A Major General Samuel B. Farrell, Highness. He headed the Joint Special Operations Command until a year or so ago."

Ibrahim exchanged a significant glance with Reichardt. Now they knew who Thorn had used as a conduit to the

American authorities. He cleared his throat. "This is interesting news, Richard. I suggest you invite General Farrell to your office this evening to discuss his information."

Garrett hesitated. "Are you sure that's wise, Highness? We've already gone to considerable trouble to quash these rumors. Meeting Farrell may lend them unnecessary credence."

Ibrahim shook his head, looking straight across at Reichardt. "That's a risk we must be willing to run, my friend. Rumors or not, these are extremely serious allegations. I don't want to paper them over. Let's act as the good corporate citizens that we are and offer General Farrell a fair hearing."

Caraco Offices, Connecticut Avenue, Washington, D.C.

Caraco's Washington offices occupied the two top floors of a twelve-story building right in the city's nerve center. The elevator only went up to the eleventh floor.

Sam Farrell stepped off and found himself confronted by both a receptionist and an armed security guard. The receptionist was a stunningly beautiful Asian-American woman. The guard, with a crew cut and in his mid-thirties, looked like a professional—definitely a step above the usual moonlighting policeman or cop wannabe.

"Good evening, General Farrell," the receptionist said. "Mr. Garrett is on the phone at the moment, I'm afraid. If you'll wait in the lounge, I'll let you know as soon as he's free." She indicated a door to the right.

The lounge was designed to impress visitors—and it worked.

One entire wall was glassed in, offering a spectacular view of the White House, the Washington Monument, and Lafayette Park. The taupe carpet was so thick that Farrell left footprints, and the other walls were covered with original oils by contemporary American artists—Hopper, Wyeth, Stella, and Thiebaud—not the generic corporate prints for sale at office furniture stores.

Farrell had just started picking out landmarks in the city below when the receptionist appeared at the door. "Mr. Garrett can see you now, General."

She led him through the reception area, through a pair of double doors, and then up a spiral staircase.

Garrett's penthouse office had the same magnificent view. The man himself, white-haired and perfectly attired in a crisply tailored business suit, turned away from the window and strode over to greet him.

"I'm very glad to meet you, General Farrell," the lawyer said. He gestured toward a small group of chairs clustered around a coffee table. "Please take a seat."

Farrell followed him over and sat down. "I appreciate your taking the time to see me, Mr. Garrett. Especially under the circumstances."

The other man showed a set of perfect white teeth in a quick, humorless smile. "But the circumstances are what bring us together, General." He leaned back in his chair. "I can assure you that we take your allegations regarding Caraco Transport and its employees seriously—very seriously indeed. In fact, I've—"

Suddenly, Garrett broke off and got to his feet, facing the spiral staircase. "Your Highness! This is an unexpected honor . . ."

Farrell turned his head and then followed suit.

A tall, slender man with jet-black hair and dark, hooded eyes had just appeared at the top of the stairs.

Garrett hurriedly introduced him. "Your Highness, I present Major General Farrell. General, this is His Highness, Prince Ibrahim al Saud, the chairman and chief executive officer of Caraco."

The Saudi prince waved them down as he drew nearer. "Please, sit down. I'm very sorry to interrupt."

Another man followed him into Garrett's office. He was about Farrell's height and weight, with graying dark hair. Gray eyes gleamed behind a pair of black-frame glasses.

"General, this is Heinrich Wolf," Ibrahim said, nodding toward the newcomer. "Herr Wolf is the chief of security for our European enterprises. I hope you don't mind my including him in this meeting."

"Not at all, sir." Farrell held out his hand as Wolf stepped closer.

Rolf Ulrich Reichardt deliberately softened his grip as he shook hands with the retired American soldier. He wanted to project the image of a business executive or a bureaucrat. Or just another harmless paper pusher. Let Farrell think he was the only warrior in the room.

After they were all seated, Ibrahim leaned forward slightly in his chair. "Now, perhaps you could give us more details of these claims of yours, General Farrell. From what little I've heard, you've made some very grave charges against several of my subsidiary companies."

Farrell nodded somberly. "That's true, Your Highness. But I'm afraid there are very real indications that some of your people are involved in either illegal arms or narcotics smuggling . . ."

Reichardt listened carefully as the American outlined the evidence he must have been given by his protégé Thorn and that damned woman FBI agent. Farrell's version dovetailed reasonably well with the information already provided by

McDowell. Nevertheless, it was irksome to hear again in detail just how deeply his operational security had been breached.

When Farrell had finished, Ibrahim sat back, shaking his head in apparent dismay. "I see your point, General. This certainly looks bad." The Saudi turned toward Reichardt. "This unpleasant situation seems to fall mostly in your jurisdiction, Heinrich. Do you have any comments or questions?"

Reichardt nodded. "One or two questions, Highness." He looked intently at Farrell. "Your evidence seems compelling, General, but I would like to know the source of this information. Naturally, we need to verify its accuracy."

Farrell answered him flatly. "I'm afraid that's impossible, Herr Wolf. You'll have to take my word that I consider my source unimpeachable."

"I see." Reichardt looked down at his fingertips. "I only wondered whether or not your source might be a man named Colonel Peter Thorn. I've studied the Russian police reports on the original Pechenga incident, and I know that the colonel served under your command just before you retired. The logic seemed inescapable. But then two and two do not always add to four in the human equation." He looked up. "Have you spoken with Colonel Thorn recently?"

"No." Farrell's tone was steady and he looked Reichardt straight in the eye.

The German shrugged. "No matter." He glanced at Ibrahim. "I assure you, Highness, if there is such a smuggling ring operating within our bounds, my men and I will ferret them out for you."

"See that you do," the Saudi said coolly.

Farrell cleared his throat. "Not that I want to interfere, Herr Wolf, but I'd like to know how exactly you intend to proceed. Now that you've been instrumental in pulling the FBI off the case, I mean."

"A fair question," Ibrahim commented. He smiled broadly in Reichardt's direction. "What precisely *are* your plans for this investigation, Heinrich? This unimpeachable source of General Farrell's already seems to have done half your work for you."

Reichardt ignored the dig. "I've ordered Arrus Export's Moscow office to cease all operations while we audit their accounts and question every employee. If one of our workers provided this Peterhof with his false Arrus credentials, I'll have his skin."

Ibrahim nodded his approval. "Good. I will not countenance corruption—anywhere."

"Of course, Highness."

"You should also contact the master of the *Caraco Savannah*. Tell him to hold his crew aboard ship once they dock in Wilhelmshaven. I want them all interrogated," Ibrahim ordered.

"Sir."

"And dispatch investigators to Bergen to try to pin down the connection between the cargoes carried by the *Star of the White Sea* and *Baltic Venturer*."

"Of course, Highness," Reichardt said.

Ibrahim glanced at Farrell. "I hope our plan of action meets with your approval, General."

The American nodded. "It seems thorough enough, Your Highness, but . . ." His voice trailed away.

"But you must still wonder why we asked your FBI to stop carrying out the same work?" Ibrahim finished for him.

Reichardt froze in his chair. The prince was playing dangerously close to the edge—too close for his own tastes.

"I prefer to clean up my own messes, General Farrell," the Saudi continued. "You say that some of my people have abused my trust and engaged in a criminal conspiracy. If that is so, then I am ultimately at fault—and I must be the one to take action. It is a matter of personal honor. Can you understand that?"

Farrell nodded again, firmly this time.

Reichardt felt himself starting to relax. Trust Ibrahim to find the avenue of approach best guaranteed to appeal to the American military man. He listened while the Saudi steered the conversation away from contraband cargoes and toward his worldwide enterprises. By the time the prince was through with Farrell, the American would probably be ready to buy Caraco stock.

After all, Ibrahim's persuasive abilities had worked on Reichardt himself.

As head of the Stasi's Revolutionary Movements Liaison Section, Reichardt had worked with dozens of different terrorist groups—providing them with false identity papers, safe houses, weapons training, and special equipment. Although there were no formal links between most of the different terrorist organizations, there were places where their paths crossed. Communist East Germany had been one of those places.

The desperate need for money was another common ground. Every group needed it—for recruitment, training, intelligence, supplies, operations, everything. Terrorism might be "the poor man's nuclear weapon," but it still wasn't cheap.

One source of funding for many of the various movements had been a man known only as "the Paymaster"—a shadowy figure who'd provided huge sums of cash, but always at arm's length. The money handed out to pay for bombings, hijackings, and murders all over the world always came through a different front organization—an organization that vanished once the gift was accepted. For years, Reichardt had kept his ear to the ground—hoping to learn the Paymaster's identity.

His search had taken on a new urgency after East Germany collapsed under the weight of its own inefficiency and corruption. He and his fellow Stasi operatives had taken considerable sums of cash with them when they'd gone underground, but not enough to last them forever. To Reichardt, the so-called Paymaster seemed like somebody who might value a man with his rather specialized skills.

Somewhat to his surprise, Ibrahim had contacted him first—arranging a series of preliminary meetings between go-betweens. Still hiding behind his agents, the Saudi prince had hired Reichardt and his team to organize a number of smuggling operations, terrorist attacks, and assassinations in Russia and Western Europe. In retrospect, the ex-Stasi officer realized those operations had been tests of his ability, ruthlessness, and reliability.

At last, apparently satisfied by the results, Ibrahim had introduced himself directly—to Reichardt's admitted astonishment. He'd never imagined that the Paymaster might actually be the CEO and founder of a large, Western-oriented international conglomerate. It was the perfect disguise—the ideal masquerade.

A subtle change in Ibrahim's tone signaled his intention to end this meeting. The German turned his full attention back to the present.

"So you must understand, General Farrell," the Saudi prince said. "I have every incentive to keep my own house in order. Caraco's prosperity—both now and in the future—depends upon its absolute reputation for honesty and integrity. Rest assured that Herr Wolf and I will get to the bottom of this matter."

Ibrahim smiled grimly. "If our findings confirm your suspicions, I promise you that heads will roll." He rose to his feet. "But now, if you and Mr. Garrett will excuse us, Herr Wolf and I have a number of calls to make."

Their farewells took a few minutes more, but Reichardt and Ibrahim were soon down the spiral staircase. A door marked "Private" opened up into a long hallway lined with offices. Another door, this one locked and unmarked, let them into a small space filled with wire recorders and other electronic equipment. A German specialist named Jopp sat at the only chair in the tiny room—turning ceaselessly back and forth between one of the recorders and the laptop computer it was connected to.

Jopp acknowledged their arrival with a bare nod but kept working.

Reichardt's voice filled the room, coming from a speaker next to the computer. ". . . spoken with Colonel Thorn recently?"

"No." Jopp killed the tape after Farrell's reply, then studied the wave pattern displayed on his computer screen.

The technician spun around to face them. "The American is lying."

"You're sure?" Reichardt asked.

"Positive," Jopp said. "He's talked to Thorn since Pechenga." He punched a key, focusing the display on a smaller part of the voice pattern. "Judging from the spike in emphasis here, I would guess they've been in contact within the past several days."

That was good enough for Reichardt. Jopp was a master of sound, of voices. When they'd both worked for the Stasi, he'd watched the little electronics technician change a man's voice into a woman's—and the words of a loyal servant of the State into those of a traitor. Telling whether an American was telling the truth or not was child's play for Jopp.

Ibrahim nodded. "Excellent work, Herr Jopp. Finish up here and then return to your normal assignment."

Jopp bobbed his head, clearly pleased by the compliment. The Saudi prince was generally sparing in his praise.

Ibrahim crooked a finger, summoning Reichardt back out into the deserted corridor. "So Thorn has told Farrell, and Farrell has told the American military, and through them, the FBI. Where will this news of our plans travel next? The *Washington Post,* perhaps?" The prince's tone hardened with every word. What had started as a summary ended as an indictment.

Reichardt said nothing, knowing that anything he said would only be turned against him.

"You are satisfied that Farrell is the conduit for the information obtained by Thorn and that woman of his?" Ibrahim asked finally.

"Yes."

"Very well," the Saudi said coldly. "You know what to do. Handle the matter promptly and efficiently this time."

CHAPTER FIFTEEN
MOVEMENT TO CONTACT

JUNE 17

Ramstein Air Force Base, Germany

It was nearly four in the morning and Helen Gray found herself pacing again—striding back and forth across the thin brown carpet. The small, Spartan Bachelor Officer's Quarters room Colonel Stroud had booked for them would never have been mistaken for a luxury hotel suite at the best of times. For two highly active, urgently motivated people unable to risk setting foot outside, it was starting to turn into a tiger cage.

Being forced into hiding also left her far too much time to think about the bleak professional and personal future she and Peter faced—despite his brave words and bold declaration of love back in Andrew Griffin's Berlin flat. The truth was that they were confronting grave danger and almost certain disgrace. Even if they somehow managed to come out of this mess with their careers intact, they'd only be separated again—sent off to new assignments in different parts of the country or the world.

Helen sighed. The past year or so away from Peter had been hard enough. She wasn't sure she could stand another period of enforced loneliness. It might be better to make a clean break and say good-bye forever rather than go through that again.

No. She couldn't do that, she realized suddenly. Even the thought of losing him sent a wave of anguish through her heart. But what alternative was there? Could he leave the Army to stay by her side? Could she leave the FBI to follow him? She shook her head. Neither option seemed acceptable. She wanted a lifetime of joy together. Not a life filled with hidden regrets and lingering doubts.

Helen spun on her heel again, nearly barking her shins on the cheap, government-issue desk that came with the room.

The light knock on the door came as an enormous relief.

It was Mike Stroud. He was alone.

Once in the room, the Special Forces officer dumped a pair of camouflage fatigue uniforms, two pairs of boots, and a couple of camouflage field caps out of the duffel bag he'd brought to hold their civilian clothes.

Peter looked down at them. "We're on?"

"You're on," Stroud confirmed. He tossed a set of BDUs to Helen. "Hope these fit, Mrs. Carlson. I had to guess at sizes."

She went into the bathroom to put them on. When she came out, Peter was already dressed. Although neither uniform carried any rank insignia or unit patches, they now looked like just two more of the thousands of American personnel stationed at Ramstein.

"How'd I do?" Stroud asked.

"Not bad," Helen admitted. Her fatigues were tight in a couple of places, but otherwise they felt fine. "You have a keen eye, Mike."

The Green Beret colonel shrugged immodestly. "It's a gift."

Peter grinned—almost against his will. Helen felt her heart lift momentarily as the smile crinkled the tiny crow's-feet around his serious green eyes.

Stroud hustled them out the BOQ door and into the waiting car—this time an official vehicle, a dark blue Air Force van. As he drove, he explained. "We're going straight to the flight line." He checked his watch. "I'm deliberately cutting this right to the bone. That way nobody has time to take a long look at you—or to ask any inconvenient questions."

Helen heard the worry in his voice. "There's more trouble, Mike?"

Stroud nodded, still keeping his eyes on the road. "The word came in from D.C. this afternoon. All U.S. military bases in Europe are being asked to keep an eye out for two wanted fugitives—to wit, one Thorn, Peter, Colonel, U.S. Army; and one Gray, Helen, Special Agent, FBI."

"Shit," Peter muttered under his breath. "This come down from the Germans?"

"I wish," Stroud said quietly. "The order's signed by the Director of the FBI personally."

Helen felt her insides knot up. Their worst nightmare had come true. Their own people were under orders to arrest them. She clenched her fists tight, forcing herself to think. "Then how do we board that plane?" she asked.

"I've still got a few tricks up my sleeve," Stroud said. He took one hand off the wheel, reached into his tunic pocket, and handed Peter an envelope. "That contains a letter for the plane commander and another for the base operations officer at Dover—just in case you run into any problems. With a little luck, though, you won't need to use them. Sam Farrell's supposed to have somebody standing by to meet the plane."

"Luck's not exactly been on our side so far," Helen commented.

"Well, there's a first time for everything, Mrs. Carlson," Stroud said. He glanced at Peter. "Remember, Pete, you run into some officious bastard, you ask to see the ops officer. If he's still on your case after reading the letter, tell him your trip involves CORNICE. That should clear the way. And if anybody wants to know what you're doing, just tell 'em you 'work for the government.' "

This time she and Peter both grinned openly. That was the standard reply given by members of the CIA and other intelligence agencies when they were asked about their jobs.

They crossed the airfield perimeter, passed through the sentries, and drove out onto the hangar-lined tarmac.

Huge Air Force cargo jets—C-5s and C-17s painted a dark, dull gray—were parked along the flight line. People and vehicles moved among them, minnows next to whales. They passed several of the transport aircraft before Stroud found the right tail number.

"Wait here," the Special Forces officer instructed as he killed the engine and hopped out of the van. He was back in less than a minute, this time accompanied by a senior Air Force enlisted man. He waved them out.

"Chris and Katy Carlson, this is Master Sergeant Blue. He's the loadmaster for this aircraft—and your personal attendant for this flight," Stroud said.

Blue, a short, cheerful-looking man with a round face and a crooked nose, looked them over, then said, "Okay, Colonel, I guess you're right. These two don't look much like illegal aliens, after all." He shook hands, first with Peter and then with Helen. "Who you folks with?"

Helen smiled. "We work for the government, Master Sergeant."

"Right. And I'm the Queen of Sheba," Blue said, grinning back. He turned to Stroud and shrugged. "No harm in asking, right?"

The Air Force noncom waved them toward the C-17's open rear cargo ramp as he headed across the tarmac. "C'mon, folks, let's shake a leg! Engine starts in five minutes."

Helen looked at Stroud. "Colonel, I . . ." She faltered, unsure of exactly how to express her appreciation.

"You don't need to thank me," the Special Forces officer said. He turned toward Peter. "You take care of yourself . . . and Mrs. Carlson here, too."

Peter nodded somberly. "You can count on it, Mike."

"I will. Now get your ass aboard that plane, Colonel," Stroud said gruffly. He shook hands with Peter, hugged Helen, and then headed to the van without looking back.

By the time they caught up with the C-17's loadmaster, the short Air Force noncom was already halfway up the ramp. "This is a cargo-only flight," he explained. "There're no spare seats in the plane, but I know a spot where you can both bed down. It's comfortable and out of the way. Right now, only the pilot and I know you're riding with us today, and I'd kinda like to keep it that way."

"Understood, Master Sergeant," Peter said. "We'll stay low."

"Don't sweat it too much, Mr. Carlson." Blue grinned again. "Hell, I've got room to hide a Brownie troop on board this flying milk wagon."

The C-17's cavernous fuselage held row upon row of cases and crates strapped to cargo pallets. The cargo pallets themselves were strapped to the deck. Moving carefully, the three of them picked their way along an aisle on one side, until the loadmaster paused. He plugged in the headset he was wearing, took one last look aft, and reported, "Ramp is clear."

With a low whine, the rear door lifted off the tarmac and sealed—shutting off their view of the floodlit airfield and the rapidly brightening sky. Almost immediately, the jet's four engines spooled up, the sound deepening to a full-throated roar that rattled through the cargo compartment.

Blue showed them to a corner of the deck where some mats had been piled and then left, urging them to get some sleep. "By the time you wake up, we'll be landing at Dover," he predicted cheerfully, shouting to make himself heard over the engine noise.

Helen settled herself on one of the mats, oddly grateful for the deafening roar of the C-17's jet engines. Although the din might make sleep hard to come by, it would also make it difficult to talk. That was a plus. She still couldn't believe that the Bureau itself had a warrant out for their arrest.

Dover Air Force Base, Delaware

Colonel Peter Thorn woke up fast, immediately aware of a change in the pitch of the C-17's jet engines and the aircraft's altitude. They were descending. He looked across the pile of cargo mats they'd used as a makeshift camp bed. Helen was already awake. She blinked the sleep out of her eyes and tried a tentative smile.

Master Sergeant Blue appeared from the front of the plane. "Glad you folks got some sack time. We're almost there. We should be on the ground in maybe fifteen minutes or so."

"What's the drill once we touch down?" Thorn asked.

"Well, you can't take the crew bus, so you just wait for a clear spot and then get off this crate," Blue said. "Don't wait too long, though: The crews usually start unloading within fifteen to thirty minutes."

"Will do, Sergeant." Thorn nodded. He held out his hand again. "Listen, I really appreciate this. I just hope it won't get you in any trouble."

Blue shrugged. "Colonel Stroud's an okay guy—for a grunt. If he says what you're doing is important, that's good enough for me." Then the Air Force noncom grinned. "Besides, I got my twenty in already. What're they gonna do? Retire me so I can loaf around the house or go to work for United Airlines—and pull down twice the money?"

After wishing them good luck, Blue headed forward to strap in for the landing.

Thorn summoned up what he knew about Dover. He'd flown into and out of the base several times. It was a major transshipment point for military cargo going to Europe or being sent back from there. It contained the hangars, workshops, warehouse space, cargo-handling equipment, and personnel housing needed to maintain more than seventy transport aircraft. Over seven thousand people worked on the base full-time, and even in the age of a downsized U.S. military, Dover Air Force Base was huge.

He was counting on that. Once they were off the flight line, security should be much looser. Like all good plans, the essence of his was simplicity. Get away from the plane fast, get off the base faster, and then get back into civilian clothes. And if Sam Farrell's contact was there to meet them, leaving Dover should be a piece of cake.

The C-17 touched down, bumping heavily on the runway as it slowed and then swung off onto one of the taxiways to the apron.

Thorn turned as Helen touched his shoulder.

"Suppose they don't open the ramp right away?" she asked.

"I can open it if I have to," he assured her. "Or we slip forward to the cockpit and get out from there."

Thorn knew the layout of all U.S. military cargo aircraft intimately. Not only had he ridden them hundreds of times, but, as a Delta Force commander, he'd intensively studied their systems and blueprints—just in case he and his troops had needed to recapture a plane held by terrorists. Of course, he thought wryly, he'd never counted on using that knowledge to smuggle himself back into the United States as a fugitive.

The C-17 shuddered to a complete stop. Its engines spooled down—the sound fading from a dull roar to a high-pitched whine to silence. Almost immediately, the rear ramp began opening—flooding the cargo compartment with sunlight, fresh air, and a lot of outside noise. After so many hours spent in the plane's dimly lit interior, the sunshine was almost blinding.

With his eyes narrowed against the glare, Thorn led Helen further back—away from the open ramp. He could hear diesel engines outside, and voices. If the Dover ground crews were moving faster than scheduled to unload this plane, he and Helen were likely to find themselves in real hot water real fast. They pressed back between two cargo crates.

After five long minutes counted out on his watch, the voices died away.

Helen nodded toward the opening. "We go?"

"We go," Thorn agreed.

He led the way back toward the ramp, staying close to the fuselage and in the shadows. The vast stretch of concrete apron behind the transport was empty.

Helen frowned. "No sign of Sam Farrell's contact?"

Thorn shook his head, still scanning the opening. He could see fuel trucks and other vehicles moving across the taxiway, but they were still hundreds of meters off. If he and Helen were going, this was as good a chance as they were going to get. He shouldered the duffel bag Mike Stroud had given them at Ramstein.

Helen touched his sleeve. "Shouldn't we wait?"

"Too dicey," he said. "Maybe Sam couldn't get through to anybody. Maybe whoever he did find got cold feet after seeing that 'Wanted' order with our names plastered all over it."

Thorn led the way down the ramp and out onto the apron, trying to act as though stepping off a cargo-only C-17 were the most normal thing in all the world. Act natural, he thought. Most people zeroed in on strangers who seemed shifty or uneasy. But if you strolled right on by as though you had every right to be there, many people, including security guards, mistook that confidence for a legitimate purpose.

He moved around the side of the massive aircraft, squinted into the morning sun, and then nodded toward a long row of hangars already shimmering in the June heat. "There's a gate just beyond them. It's not the normal exit for arrivals, but we should be able to go through—"

"Morning, folks. You mind telling me where you're headed?" a voice asked from behind them.

Damn it. Thorn turned slowly.

A man in a light blue uniform shirt, darker blue pants, and a matching beret had come around the other side of the C-17.

His black boots were polished to the nines, mirrored sunglasses reflected the sun, and he wore a holstered pistol at his side. His name tag read "Thomas" and he wore sergeant's stripes on his sleeve.

Thorn nodded toward the distant line of hangars. "We're headed for the base, Sergeant."

"Well, sir, I'm sure you know that everyone's supposed to go through arrivals processing," the Air Force security policeman said flatly. He jerked a thumb over his shoulder in the opposite direction. "Which is that way."

He looked them up and down, and Thorn suddenly felt naked without any rank insignia or unit badge on his uniform. It was second nature for anyone in the military to scan a uniform for the rank of the wearer, and Sergeant Thomas was coming up dry.

"May I see some identification, please?" The noncom's tone was pleasant enough, but he wasn't smiling.

Thorn handed over his forged identification card, mentally crossing his fingers. White-faced, Helen did the same.

Sergeant Thomas studied them for a moment, then looked up. "Could I see your travel orders, too, Mr. Carlson?"

Double damn. Thorn knew there wasn't any point in lying. "We don't have any travel orders, Sergeant." Time to pull out Mike Stroud's promised get-out-of-jail-free card, he thought. He reached into his pocket. "I've got a letter here for the base operations officer that explains our presence."

He offered the folded piece of paper to the other man.

"You sure weren't headed for the operations office when I found you," Sergeant Thomas said dryly. He shook his head. "Nope. I think you two folks better come with me to the security office."

Triple damn.

Thorn eyed the Air Force noncom closely. Thomas had one hand resting on his sidearm, more to accent his authority than because he expected to use it. Still, he'd quietly taken two steps back, out of easy reach, and he'd positioned himself to face both of them.

Thorn tried again. "I suggest you read this letter."

"I'll let my boss read your paperwork," the Air Force policeman said. "My orders are clear, and I'm not getting my butt fried for letting you two walk off a plane and straight out a gate."

After a quick glance at Helen, Thorn shrugged, acting far more casual than he felt. "Fine, Sergeant. You want to go by the book, we'll go by the book."

The duty security officer was busy. He kept them waiting for thirty excruciating minutes before Sergeant Thomas even made his report. More minutes passed before Master Sergeant Blue and an irritated major wearing a flight suit with pilot's wings showed up.

Thorn saw Blue shoot him a sidewise glance—a glance he carefully ignored.

The C-17's pilot and loadmaster were ushered into the security office ahead of them. When they emerged ten minutes later, they didn't leave. Instead they plopped themselves down on chairs at the opposite end of the waiting room. The pilot's irritated expression had now matured into one of near-hatred. Blue looked resigned, like a man awaiting execution.

Sergeant Thomas came back out of the security officer's inner sanctum. "Mr. and Mrs. Carlson?" He held the door open for them. "You're up next."

Captain Forbes, the duty security officer, was a thin, strong-jawed man with thick glasses and a sour look. He didn't waste time with any courtesies. Instead, he crooked a finger. "Okay, pal. Let's see this mysterious letter."

Thorn handed it over without comment.

Forbes skimmed the letter fast, then took a more careful look. The corners of his mouth turned down. "Have you read this?"

"Yes, sir."

The Air Force captain ignored him. "It's supposedly signed by a Lieutenant Colonel Gibbs, the operations officer for the 352nd Special Operations Group at RAF Mildenhall, in the U.K. He says I'm to 'cooperate with your efforts to return to the U.S.' Now, I don't like this kind of vague, covert shit. Not at all. Not on my post and my watch. You mind telling me what the hell this is all about? Or whether or not Carlson is even your real name?"

Thorn shook his head. "I'm sorry, Captain. I can't discuss any of that."

"Naturally." Forbes tapped the letter for emphasis. "Look, anyone could have typed this damned thing up—even if it is on 352nd SOG stationery."

Thorn kept his face immobile with an effort. For all he knew, that was exactly what Stroud had done.

"So I'm going to hold you two while I check this thing out. And I want some fingerprints, to verify those ID cards of yours. This whole thing smells."

Whoa, boy, Thorn thought desperately. Our goose is almost inside that 350 degree oven. He saw Helen's shoulders slump. Well, Mike Stroud had given him one last card to play—and it was time to find out whether it was an ace, or just another joker.

He leaned closer to the security officer. "That would be a serious mistake, Captain Forbes. The whole point of this exercise is to avoid leaving a paper trail of our entry into the United States. And we can't be fingerprinted."

"Can't?" the other man challenged.

"Shouldn't," Thorn corrected. He stood up and closed the door, then turned back to Forbes. "This is a CORNICE matter."

The security officer shook his head, scowling. "That code word doesn't mean a damned thing to me."

"It does to your operations officer," Thorn said. "Ask him what it means. But I strongly suggest you avoid using it over an open phone line."

Forbes pondered that for a moment, then grunted. "Okay, goddamnit. I'll just do that." He swept the letter and their ID cards to one side of his desk and nodded toward the door. "Wait outside."

Once they were seated again, Helen leaned close enough to whisper in his ear. "Good grief, Peter! I never knew you were such a smooth-talking, thoroughgoing liar."

"Years of playing poker," he whispered back. "It's sure nice to know I didn't lose all that money for nothing."

Helen chuckled. "That's right. Build up my confidence and then tear it right back down . . ."

She fell silent.

More minutes passed, dragging by while Thorn worked hard to avoid staring back at the two C-17 crewmen. Getting caught was bad enough for the two of them. But this was snowballing fast into a fiasco that might drag a lot of other good people down with them. The only small mercy so far was the fact that the FBI arrest order must have been sent only to bases in Europe. If Forbes had been given a copy with their pictures on it, he and Helen would already be staring through the bars of the nearest cell.

The outside door banged open and a silver-haired Air Force colonel holding a walkie-talkie strode in. He swept the outer office with his eyes for an instant until his gaze landed on Thorn and Helen. Then he headed straight into Forbes' office.

Sergeant Thomas came out a couple of minutes later, still shaking his head in disbelief. He motioned them back inside.

Captain Forbes was now standing beside his desk, while the colonel sat perched casually on a corner. "My name's Callaghan, Mr. and Mrs. Carlson. I'm the operations officer here at Dover." He handed their ID cards and the letter back to Thorn. "I've explained the situation to Captain Forbes. I'm sure he now sees the error of his ways."

The duty security officer tried his best to look indignant without crossing the line into insubordination.

"One of my people was supposed to meet your plane—but you landed early," Callaghan explained. "Sorry about the mix-up."

"That's okay, Colonel," Thorn said with enormous relief, grateful they hadn't wound up in jail within minutes of arriving home.

Callaghan glanced sideways at Forbes and then turned back to them. "I've explained to the captain and Sergeant Thomas here that there will be no official record of this event. You weren't on that C-17. You've never been inside this office. This meeting never happened." He smiled thinly. "In fact, you don't even exist. Will that be satisfactory?"

"Perfectly, Colonel," Thorn said. He silently blessed Sam Farrell, Mike Stroud, and CORNICE—whatever deep-black covert operation that code word represented.

"Great." Callaghan swept his walkie-talkie off the security officer's desk and motioned them toward the door. "My car's just outside. I'll tag along to make sure you get off base without hitting any more snags. And then I'll have my duty driver take you into town. From there, you're on your own."

Once they were at the main gate, the colonel clambered out of the staff car and then leaned back inside. He handed

Thorn a sealed envelope. "A mutual friend sent me this fax last night."

"Thanks, Colonel. Thanks very much."

"Don't mention it," Callaghan said flatly. "And I mean, really *don't* mention it. I never met either of you, remember?"

Thorn nodded his understanding. If he and Helen were caught later, the Air Force colonel had one possible line of defense—that he'd simply helped government employees claiming they were involved in some secret operation code-named CORNICE. But if they were caught, it would be far, far better for Callaghan if they just "forgot" to tell the FBI how they'd returned to the U.S.

"Corporal Milliken here will take you where you want to go," the colonel said. He shut the door and slapped the car roof to signal his driver to move on.

The sentries waved them through the gate and outside onto Highway 113. Thorn sat back in the seat and tore open the envelope. He scanned the single sheet inside with intense interest. It was a list of economy-priced hotels and motels—all in the Washington, D.C., area, and all on a Metro line. Each had been assigned a different code name. He smiled broadly. Trust Sam Farrell to do his homework.

They pulled up to a major intersection.

"Where to, sir?" the driver asked.

Thorn handed the sheet to Helen. "What's the best way to get to Wilmington, Corporal?"

"You can hop a DART bus for about four bucks a head, sir. Should get you there in an hour and a half or so."

"That'll be fine," Thorn said. "Just drop us at the nearest bus stop, please."

Helen leaned closer. "Wilmington? We're taking Amtrak south then?" she asked quietly.

He nodded. The main New York–Washington rail line ran

straight through the northern Delaware city. "Yep. We're going cash-only from now on. No point in sending up flares."

"Good point," Helen said.

Although the FBI seemed to be focusing its search for them on Europe, it was a safe bet that the Bureau had the warrants necessary to trace all their credit card expenditures. If they rented a car, the odds were the agents looking for them would have the make, model, and license tag within an hour or so. The train would be slower and less comfortable, but it offered one priceless advantage—anonymity.

JUNE 17

Vienna, Virginia

Sam Farrell snapped the afternoon news off and spun around to grab the phone on his desk. "Farrell."

"Sam, it's Chris Carlson. My wife and I are in town for a conference, so I thought I'd look you up. Hope you don't mind."

Farrell breathed an inward sigh of relief. He'd been waiting for hours to hear from Peter Thorn—always aware that any one of the half-dozen links he'd so carefully forged could easily have come undone. His worries had intensified after Colonel Stroud had let him know about the FBI warrants out for Thorn and Helen.

"Damn, Chris," he said honestly. "It's sure good to hear your voice. Who're you two staying with?"

"The McIntyres."

Farrell pulled the coded list of hotels he prepared closer and ran his finger down it until he came to MCINTYRE. Peter and Helen had checked into the Madison Inn, a small bed-and-breakfast near the D.C. zoo. He nodded to himself. They'd made a good choice. That section of the city— Woodley Park—was quiet and almost entirely residential. Anyone conducting a search for them or trying to set up a surveillance net would stand out like a sore thumb.

"The McIntyres are nice people," Farrell said. He eyed the clock on his wall. It was a little after three in the afternoon. "You two free for dinner tonight?"

"Our social calendar is completely open, Sam," Thorn said dryly. "Come by at your convenience. Will Louisa be with you?"

"Not this time," Farrell said. "I'm an acting bachelor just now."

He'd put his wife, Louisa, on a plane to visit their son and daughter-in-law as soon as he'd realized how many rules and regulations he was going to have to break to get Peter and Helen home safely and not in handcuffs. While he doubted the military or the administration would be too eager to try a highly decorated retired general for obstruction of justice and aiding fugitives, he didn't see any point in making his wife an accessory to the crimes he'd committed.

"You take it easy now," Farrell warned. "It's real hot out there right now. Real hot. Sunstroke weather, if you ask me."

There was a pause while Thorn digested the renewed warning. "Understood, Sam," he said finally. "We'll lie up here in the shade until the heat dies down."

"Smart move." Farrell stood up. "I'm heading out the door now."

After hanging up, he went into the master bedroom and

pulled open the nightstand drawer closest to his side of the
bed. Inside lay a 9mm Beretta, a spare magazine, and a Milt
Sparks holster that fit inside the waistband of his pants. As a
former commander of all the U.S. military's counter-terrorist
units, he'd found it remarkably easy to obtain a special federal concealed weapons permit.

Sam Farrell strongly doubted he'd need the pistol, but
he'd listened too closely to Peter Thorn's accounts of the
nightmare ambushes at Pechenga and Wilhelmshaven to
take anything for granted. And more than three decades of
active Army service had taught him the wisdom of the old
Boy Scout motto—"Be Prepared." Hand-to-hand combat
might work out okay for Peter and Helen in a pinch, but he
preferred to be ready to meet trouble with three or four steel-
jacketed slugs.

Planning Cell, Caraco Complex, Chantilly, Virginia

(D MINUS 4)

Rolf Ulrich Reichardt listened intently, trying to ferret out
the hidden subtext from the welter of moronic American ba-
nalities and idioms. He turned to Jopp. "Rewind the tape."

The wiry sound specialist nodded and flipped another series of switches on his equipment.

Reichardt heard the conversation begin. Halfway through
he saw Ibrahim appear at the door. The Saudi prince spent
two or three hours each day at the complex now—monitoring each phase as the Operation came ever closer to fruition.

The German said nothing and kept listening, letting the voices play their childish dance of secret codes all over again. When the tape ended he pulled off the headphones.

"Well, Herr Reichardt, what is your report?" Ibrahim asked sharply. "Hashemi said you had news of our friend, General Farrell."

"Yes, Highness," Reichardt said. He offered the other man the headphones and signaled Jopp to recue the phone intercept. "We picked up this telephone call on the American's private line an hour or so ago."

Ibrahim heard it through himself in growing impatience. He looked up. "What of it? Farrell arranges dinner with this man Carlson and his wife? Of what possible significance is that?"

"That is what we are meant to think, Highness," Reichardt said calmly. He nodded at Jopp. "But then our clever friend here ran the conversation through his little black boxes—as a precaution."

"And?"

"Both men are lying," Reichardt answered.

"To each other?" Ibrahim sounded surprised.

The ex-Stasi officer shook his head. "To any potential eavesdroppers." He smiled, a hunter's grim smile. "General Farrell knows that the FBI wishes to arrest his two friends. Given that, he must suspect his telephones have been tapped by the authorities. These cheerful idiocies are obviously a rough, shorthand code to arrange a rendezvous."

"You believe this Carlson is actually Colonel Thorn? And that he and the woman Gray are now quartered in a safe house somewhere in this area?"

"Yes, Highness, that is what I believe," Reichardt said. Nothing else made sense. Somehow Farrell had smuggled his protégés back into the United States—evading the arrest order issued by the FBI.

"And their intentions?"

"I cannot predict precisely what they will do next," Reichardt admitted. "We can hope that your assurances to General Farrell will delay any further effort on their part. But prudence demands we assume they will again try to contact those with power in their own government—undoubtedly using Farrell as a go-between."

Ibrahim shook his head. "I find that possibility unacceptable, Herr Reichardt. There is an old proverb, 'News shouted loudly enough from the rooftops will not always fall on deaf ears.' "

The ex-Stasi officer nodded grimly. "True, Highness. And General Farrell's evident ability to smuggle these two back into the United States, right under the nose of the FBI, testifies both to his persistence and his residual power. Such a man is very dangerous."

He turned as Johann Brandt approached. "Well?"

"The American is definitely on his way to a covert rendezvous, sir," the tall, powerfully built man replied. "He left his house forty-five minutes ago and drove to the closest Metro station."

Reichardt read the faint hesitation in his subordinate's voice. "Harzer lost him there, didn't he?"

Brandt nodded reluctantly. "Yes, sir. Parking was difficult. By the time Max got to the platform, Farrell had already boarded a train. The American apparently timed it perfectly."

Unfortunate. The Metro system sprawled over two states and the entire District of Columbia. There were dozens of stations along its five interconnecting lines. Essentially, Farrell had now vanished into one of the world's largest haystacks. Reichardt risked a quick glance at Ibrahim.

The Saudi prince stared back at him dispassionately—an expression the German found somehow more worrying than even an open display of anger. "What now, Herr Reichardt? Do we simply admit defeat and pray to Allah that our enemies sit idly by until it is too late?"

"No, Highness," Reichardt said, thinking rapidly. The outline of a basic plan flowed into his consciousness with lightning speed. "Farrell will reemerge. He must—if he is to function as a go-between. More to the point, the general is still a law-abiding man—despite his recent defiance of the FBI. Given that basic fact, PEREGRINE should prove of great use in persuading Farrell to bring Colonel Thorn and his female associate within our reach."

The German smiled coldly. "After all, why not kill four birds with one stone—instead of just two?"

Ibrahim nodded in both understanding and approval. "Let it be so. And do it today. These people have already diverted too much of our time, energy, and resources."

The Madison Inn, Washington, D.C.

The Madison Inn had rooms spread across three adjoining Victorian town houses—all located on the same tree-lined cul-de-sac within blocks of the Woodley Park Zoo. The bed-and-breakfast was quiet, discreet, and reasonably priced. Peter Thorn and Helen Gray had managed to secure a third-story corner room with a good view of the whole street.

Sam Farrell took the staircase two steps at a time—pleased to notice that he wasn't winded when he reached the top landing. All those years of calisthenics were paying off—even in retirement.

Thorn opened the door at his first knock and ushered him inside with a strained smile and a quick, firm handshake.

Helen turned from the window where she'd obviously been keeping watch. She hurried over and hugged him tightly with a whispered "Thank you" in his ear.

Farrell took the chair they offered him and waited until they were both sitting down. He studied them carefully, noting the signs of surface fatigue and deep-seated worry. "You two look a little wrung-out. Something go wrong on the way from Ramstein?"

"Almost," Thorn said quietly. "I nearly walked us right into the Dover brig . . ."

Farrell listened while they filled him in on their narrow escape and the comparatively uneventful train trip down to Union Station. When they finished, he shook his head. "That was a little more nip-and-tuck than I'd planned. You were lucky, Pete."

"Yes, sir."

"But you're here and that's what counts."

"Does it?" Helen asked in a soft voice. "We're still wanted by our own people. And we're not any closer to nailing the bad guys we're chasing—not unless you've pulled a rabbit out of the hat in the last couple of days, Sam."

"No magic, I'm afraid," Farrell admitted. "But I haven't been sitting on my hands, either."

He briefed them on his trip to Fort Bragg and the EMPTY QUIVER alert he'd managed to trigger. Both Helen and Thorn smiled at that. But their faces fell when he broke the news that the FBI's first raid hadn't netted any hard evidence. And they grew longer still when he told them how Caraco's senior executives had used their political influence to shut the FBI probe down cold. He finished up with by recounting the meeting he'd had with Prince Ibrahim al Saud and Heinrich Wolf, his European security chief.

"What did you think of this Ibrahim character?" Thorn asked.

Farrell thought about that for a moment, looking for the best way to summarize his impressions of Caraco's chief executive. "He's formidable," he said at last. "I wouldn't want to bet against him in a fight."

"And this guy Wolf?"

Farrell frowned. "A nasty piece of work." He thought back to the meeting. "He was holding back—trying to make me think he was just Ibrahim's lapdog. But I'd lay odds that there's a lot more to Herr Wolf than appears on the surface."

"Have you heard anything from either of them since?" Helen asked.

"No." Farrell shrugged. "But that was less than twenty-four hours ago."

"True." She got up and walked over to the window, standing with her arms crossed while staring down at the street.

The silence dragged uncomfortably. Farrell felt the tension building in the room, and suddenly realized that both he and Thorn had turned to watch Helen.

At last she looked back at him. "Do you trust those two men, Sam? And I mean really trust them—the way you'd trust Peter or me?"

That was an easy question. "No. Not really." Farrell shrugged. "I don't like people who have so much political pull and use it to play God so easily."

"Careful, Sam," Thorn muttered. He grinned. "Some people might say you've been playing God a little bit these past few days yourself!"

Farrell chuckled. "Watch it, Colonel. You forget that I was a two-star general just last year. Divine powers are part of my retirement package."

For just an instant Helen looked as though she wanted to bang their two heads together. "When you boys are finished playing word games, I'd like to get back to the real world," she said.

"Sorry, Helen," Farrell heard Thorn say meekly.

He sneaked a glance at the younger man. Oh, brother, Farrell thought. A leader of men, a rough, tough combat soldier, and now Colonel Peter Thorn is outnumbered ten to one— by one woman. He smiled inwardly—knowing exactly how the other man felt. He'd fallen for Louisa the same way.

"Sam . . ."

Farrell snapped out of his reverie in a hurry. "Sorry, ma'am."

"That's better," Helen said, with the faint trace of a smile. Then her smile faded. "What I'm trying to get us to focus on is our next move."

Some of the happiness Farrell had felt for his two friends disappeared. He'd known this question was coming, but he'd been dreading it. Well, it was better to get everything out in the open. He sighed. "I'm not sure there is a next move. Not beyond finding a good lawyer for you and Pete, that is."

"What the hell do you mean by that, Sam?" Thorn asked, staring back at him.

"He means we've hit a dead-end, Peter," Helen said quietly. "When the Bureau came up dry in Galveston, the last little shred of credibility we had went up in smoke."

"Is that right, sir?" Thorn asked.

"Is what right, Colonel?" Farrell said. He felt himself bristling a bit at the younger man's tone of voice.

"That you think we sold you a bill of goods when we claimed somebody was trying to smuggle a nuclear weapon into this country?"

Farrell shook his head wearily. "I don't think you sold me a bill of goods, Pete. Look, you and Helen walked into something damned nasty aboard that Russian freighter in Pechenga—whether it was a heroin ring or a stolen atomic bomb. The problem is: You've really got no proof. Zero.

Zip. And I'm fresh out of Pentagon contacts we can prod into action on my unsupported word. Hell, I hear the White House is so mad at me that George Mayer may lose the JSOC post!"

Helen interceded. "So, what do you think we should do, Sam?"

"Let Ibrahim and this Wolf guy sort this mess out," Farrell argued. "I may not like them, but that doesn't mean I think they're incompetent. Caraco has a lot to lose if some of its employees get caught running a smuggling ring using company assets."

Thorn grimaced. "Jesus, Sam! I hate sitting on my ass doing nothing. And I really hate doing nothing while hoping that some corporate security boss does the work our own people should be doing!"

"So do I, Pete," Farrell said firmly. "You show me something else we can do—anything—and I'll be right in there with you. But until you can do that, I suggest you and Helen just lie low—real low—and wait."

Shafter-Minter Field, Kern County, California

(D MINUS 4)

The two planes touched down within five minutes of each other. Both were Jetstream Super 31 models—twin-engine turboprops with room for a crew of two and eighteen passengers. The first carried Caraco colors—white overall with a broad black stripe and the company's name superimposed in gold. The second plane was a rental from an air charter company.

One after the other, the two turboprops taxied smoothly past the ranks of small, single-engined private aircraft and larger crop dusting planes. Ground crewmen waved them to a stop outside the first of Caraco's two brand-new hangars. Others hurried forward to chock their wheels as soon as the propellers stopped turning.

The ferry crews, two men per aircraft, wasted no time deplaning. They expected quick payment and a quick return to their home base. They'd been hired for a one-way trip—not as part of a long-term contract.

As soon as the commercial pilots were safely off the airfield, the ground crews towed the two twin-engined turboprops into the nearest hangar. Then, under the watchful eyes of Reichardt's security force, mechanics and electronics technicians swarmed over the empty aircraft—tearing out seats and installing new control packages in the cockpits.

The Operation's final phase had begun.

CHAPTER SIXTEEN

REVELATIONS

JUNE 17

Washington, D.C.

Deputy Assistant Director Lawrence McDowell poured himself another generous-sized drink from the bourbon bottle he kept in his bottom desk drawer. Some of it splashed out and puddled on the surface of his desk, staining the pages of the latest faxes from his overseas field offices reporting their continued failure to arrest that bitch Helen Gray and her Army boyfriend. He ignored the mess. Gray and Thorn were irrelevant now. They were stuck in Europe.

What mattered was that Heinrich Wolf, that slimy, blackmailing bastard, had finally screwed up. The sainted J. Edgar had always told his underlings that every crook always made at least one mistake. That it was just a matter of looking hard enough and waiting long enough. Well, Wolf had made his—and just in time, too.

For nearly three weeks, McDowell had been quietly sniffing around—trying to get a handle on just who the hell Heinrich Wolf was. But every path he'd pursued had turned into a dead-end. Secure Investments, the company the German first claimed to represent, didn't exist—not even as a shell corporation. It was pure fiction. And none of the confidential files he'd asked the Berlin field office to pull on former Stasi agents had yielded any leads. Despite all his efforts, Wolf remained a faceless ghost—a shadowy, commanding presence heard only over the phone.

Until now.

McDowell raised his glass to Hoover's own ghost and swallowed the bourbon—reveling in the way it lit a smoky fire straight down his throat and straight up into his brain.

The pieces had finally started to fall into place yesterday—right after he learned that the Director had shut down the investigation into that Caraco-leased warehouse in Galveston. It hadn't taken him too much poking and prying to find out why.

McDowell had been impressed—very impressed. Not every corporation's top management had the kind of political clout needed to make both the White House and the FBI sit, roll over, and fetch. In his book, that made Caraco a power to be reckoned with—and a potential target for a little discreet brownnosing on his part. It was all a matter of doing your homework—of knowing exactly who to approach with an occasional background briefing on FBI operations that could affect Caraco's various enterprises.

So he'd ordered his staff to assemble a dossier on the company and its highest-ranking people.

The dossier sitting open on his desk.

McDowell smiled nastily.

There it was in black-and-white—Wolf, Heinrich, Chief of Security, European Division. That smug son of a bitch hadn't even bothered to use another cover identity when dealing with him. Well, that carelessness would cost the Stasi prick heavily. What would his new bosses say if they knew they had an ex-German secret policeman running heroin using Caraco as a cover?

McDowell knew that he wasn't out of the woods—not yet. But at least now he had some leverage. If Wolf threatened him with exposure and ruin again, he could turn the threat against him. And, if need be, he could always shop the German bastard to the FBI's counterintelligence section as part of a plea bargain.

He recapped the nearly empty bottle and slipped it back into the drawer. Have to remember to bring in a new one, he thought. The bourbon wasn't lasting as long as it once had.

The light on his phone flashed and he scooped it up. "McDowell."

"This is Wolf."

McDowell choked back a laugh. Speak of the devil . . . "Hello, Heinrich."

"I have an assignment for you."

McDowell shook his head. "Not sure I can help you, Heinrich." He picked the Caraco dossier off his desk and spun around in his chair to face his office window. "Fact is, I'm thinking about retiring . . ."

"From the FBI?" Wolf's voice hardened. "That would be a serious mistake, PEREGRINE. One with grave consequences."

The FBI agent shrugged. "I don't know about that, Heinrich. Seems there are a lot of opportunities out there in the private sector right now." He narrowed his eyes. "I could always apply at Caraco. Seems to me they might need a new security chief for their European companies real soon. What do you think about that, Herr Wolf?"

The German said nothing for several long seconds. Then he said slowly, "Are you attempting to renegotiate our arrangement, Mr. McDowell?"

"Yeah, I guess I am." McDowell turned back to his desk. "My terms are pretty simple: You leave me alone—permanently. In return, I keep my mouth shut about your little extracurricular activities. And everybody goes away happy."

"Your terms are unacceptable," Wolf said grimly. "You overestimate the strength of your position, PEREGRINE."

"Oh? How's that?" McDowell asked, feeling doubts creep into his mind for the first time since he'd pinpointed the German's current identity. This conversation wasn't going according to his plan.

"You may inconvenience me for a short while," Wolf explained. "You may even cost me some money. But I think you would find that a poor exchange for years of hard labor in one of your federal maximum-security prisons. I do not believe that your fellow FBI agents view traitors kindly. And, as you know, prison can be a dangerous place."

This time it was McDowell's turn to stay quiet. He chewed his lower lip in frustration. Wolf wasn't rolling over the way he'd expected.

"But I will offer you a compromise, PEREGRINE—as a token of my goodwill."

"What kind of a compromise?"

"If you successfully complete this one last assignment for me, I will cancel your remaining debt to my organization. We will be even, and you will be rid of me."

That sounded promising. Still holding the phone in one hand, McDowell fished the bottle back out of his desk with the other. "What do you want done?"

"Special Agent Gray and Colonel Thorn are in Washington, D.C.," Wolf said flatly.

"What?" The bourbon glass fell onto his carpeted floor and rolled under the desk. "Impossible!"

"Evidently not. Thorn and Gray are clearly quite . . . resourceful," the German said. "Too resourceful to be left at large."

"Well, what more do you expect me to do about them?" McDowell demanded. "Because of me, they're already subject to arrest on sight. I can pass the word they're hiding out somewhere around here to the local Bureau field office, but that's about it."

"No," Wolf said. "I insist on a permanent solution to the problem."

McDowell shivered involuntarily. He cleared his throat. "I see."

"Good," Wolf said. "Now, listen carefully. Your part is simple—but you must make no mistakes . . ."

McDowell heard him out in silence, desperately wishing he could take one more drink. The warm glow he'd been nursing all day had suddenly withered into a dull, pounding ache between his ears.

The Madison Inn, Near the Woodley Park Zoo

It was after sunset.

Peter Thorn lay flat on the bed with his hands folded behind his head. By turning his head, he could see Helen Gray sitting silently by the window. She was on watch—scanning the street below for any signs that the FBI or their mysterious enemies had finally tumbled to their presence back in the United States. Their room was in darkness—lit only by a soft yellow glow from the street lamps outside. Neither of them wanted to risk their night vision to brighter light.

Thorn frowned. Something had been nagging at him for days. Something about the trap they'd triggered near the Wilhelmshaven docks. He'd run the scenario backward and forward in his mind a hundred times, but he still couldn't see how the men who'd tried to ambush them had tagged them so quickly. The man who'd called himself Steinhof had come straight up to them—in the very first bar they'd visited.

That couldn't have been an accident.

And unless Thorn was willing to believe the impossible—that the people they were after had enough operatives to cover every waterfront dive in Wilhelmshaven—then Steinhof and his murder squad had spotted them earlier. But where? At the Port Authority?

He summoned up his memories of the office there. No, nobody had been within earshot when they'd asked their questions about *Baltic Venturer.* Could the bad guys have been alerted by the German clerk who'd helped them, Fräulein Geist or Geiss or someone like that? He shook his head, remembering the drab, rigid woman behind that counter. She hadn't struck him as somebody who would willingly involve herself in irregular intrigue.

No. Steinhof could have tracked them after they left the Port Authority or the customs office, but to do that he would have had to have known what they looked like—and roughly when they were likely to arrive in Wilhelmshaven.

Which left one disturbing possibility . . .

"We've got company, Peter," Helen said suddenly.

Thorn was off the bed and by her side in less than a second. "Where?"

"Under the second street lamp—this side."

He saw the car she'd spotted, a dark, four-door sedan that had just pulled up and parked—right beside a fire hydrant. He stiffened. "Shit."

The front passenger side door opened and Sam Farrell got out onto the sidewalk. Thorn let out a low whistle. "That's a relief. For a second there, I thought—"

"Not so fast, Peter. Look who brought him," Helen said tightly.

The sedan's driver came into full view under the street lamp. It was Larry McDowell.

Jesus, Thorn thought grimly. He turned to Helen. "Do we bug out?"

She sighed. "No point. There's another car further out—hanging a block or so back. And McDowell may be a moron—but he's not a complete moron. By now, he'll have units in position around the whole immediate area."

Thorn nodded. He watched Sam Farrell head for the front door to the inn, with McDowell right behind him. They were out of places to run.

The knock on their door came just a minute or so later. "Special Agent Gray. Colonel Thorn. This is Deputy Assistant Director McDowell."

Holding his temper in check, Thorn flipped the lights on, then opened the door and stepped back.

Sam Farrell came in first, shaking his head apologetically. "Pete, Helen, I'm sorry as hell about this, but he was waiting on my front steps when I got home . . ."

"You don't need to apologize to these two," McDowell said, pushing past the other man to stand in front of Thorn and Helen. "Colonel Thorn and Special Agent Gray should consider themselves very lucky to see me. The first people through that door could have been a SWAT team."

Helen glared at him. "If you're here to arrest us, just do it."

McDowell smiled smugly. "Now, Miss Gray. I suggest you watch your tone." He spread his empty hands. "I'm not here to arrest you."

Sure. Thorn looked narrowly at the senior FBI agent. "What's your game, McDowell?"

"No games, Colonel." The other man half turned toward Farrell. "Shut the door, please, General. I think we need some privacy."

Once the door was closed, McDowell turned back to Helen and Thorn. "It's simple, Colonel, so please try to pay attention. Despite what you might have thought, the Director and I haven't been sitting idly by these past few days. On the contrary, we've been very busy tracking down these illegal shipments you claim have been entering the United States."

"Then why close down the Galveston probe?" Helen demanded.

"Strategy, Special Agent Gray." McDowell shook his head. "I know that you're a competent tactician, but you clearly have only a limited comprehension of the big picture."

He quickly held up a hand to forestall Thorn's angry response. "Don't glare at me, Colonel. I'm merely pointing out the facts. The Galveston operation was a dry well—anyone who read the reports could see that. The place had been stripped clean. We knew we weren't going to find anything useful there.

"But the raid did generate a very revealing response from Caraco's senior management," McDowell continued. "And ever since, we've been very quietly investigating their personnel and several of their key American facilities."

"And you found something suspicious?" Helen asked.

"Yes and no," McDowell said. "We've certainly detected some odd activity at one of Caraco's sites—an industrial park complex out near Chantilly. We've got surveillance teams around the place right now."

Helen breathed out. "So the order for our arrest was—"

"A blind," McDowell confirmed. "We needed to get you out of Germany quickly and thought that might be the least conspicuous way to do it." He shrugged. "Evidently we underestimated your resources. And those of General Farrell."

"What do you want from us now?" Thorn asked sharply, still fighting his instinctive dislike for Helen's superior. The message the FBI agent was sending sounded good—almost too good to be true. Was this stuff about "all sins are forgiven" just a ruse to get them out of the inn quietly—without any unpleasant publicity?

"The Director would like both you and Special Agent Gray to come out and see if you recognize anybody. Some of the suspicious people we've observed prowling the grounds at this Chantilly complex recently flew in from Europe. We want to check the possibility that one or more of them might have been part of the team you say attacked you in Wilhelmshaven."

Thorn could see a look of hope suddenly emerging on Helen's face. She'd been trying to goad the FBI's higher-ups into gear ever since she'd sent McDowell that first fax urging him to investigate the Wilhelmshaven docks. And now it looked as though her efforts were finally making a difference.

He stood absolutely still.

Wilhelmshaven.

All the pieces of the puzzle that had been nagging at him abruptly fell into place. McDowell had known they were going to Wilhelmshaven. McDowell had known why they were going there. And that bastard had access to their service photos—the same photos he'd later faxed to the Berlin police.

It all fit. And it all added up to a very ugly picture of treachery, betrayal, and attempted murder. McDowell had set them up. Once. Twice, if you counted Berlin.

And he was about to do it again.

Without thinking, Thorn turned away and then whirled around again—sending a hard right cross smashing into McDowell's smug face.

The FBI agent's head rocked backward under the impact and then snapped forward—right into a left hook that caught him under the chin and threw him onto the floor, flat on his back.

"Peter!"

"What the hell are you doing, Colonel?" Farrell barked.

Thorn ignored them both. He moved closer to the man he'd knocked down. Still groggy, McDowell rolled over and pushed himself up on one knee. The FBI agent's hand fumbled under his jacket.

"Not so fast, you son of a bitch." Thorn's own hand flashed out and gripped McDowell's wrist. He yanked the other man's hand out into the open. The butt of a pistol came into view.

He squeezed.

McDowell squawked and let go. The pistol thudded onto the carpet.

Thorn released his wrist and scooped up the weapon in one smooth motion. It was a 9mm SIG-Sauer P228. He cocked it with his thumb and placed its muzzle squarely against McDowell's left temple.

The FBI agent froze. Sweat trickled down his forehead. Blood dripped from a cut on his lip.

"Nice weapon," Thorn said conversationally. He pressed harder, grinding the muzzle into McDowell's forehead. "I really hate to think of how messy it's going to get when I blow your brains out."

The other man's eyes widened. He whimpered.

"Pete," Farrell said softly. "Don't do it."

Thorn could see that his former commanding officer had his own pistol out now, and that it was pointing roughly in his direction. He shook his head. "I haven't gone loco, Sam. Not yet anyway."

"Convince me." Farrell's voice was strained.

"I'll let Deputy Assistant Director McDowell here do my convincing for me." Thorn caught a glimpse of Helen out of the corner of his eye. Still ashen-faced, she was working her way around to Farrell's blind side. Christ, they were all teetering on a knife edge. He cleared his throat. "Stay where you are, Helen."

She stopped moving.

Thorn turned his full attention back to McDowell. "Now then, let's have a little talk, okay? The rules are simple: I ask you questions and you answer them. If you don't answer, I blow your head off. If you lie to me, I blow your head off. If you tell me the truth, I let you live—at least for a little while longer."

He prodded the FBI agent's temple with the pistol. "Do you understand these rules, Mr. McDowell?"

Eyes still wide, the other man hurriedly bobbed his head up and down.

"Very good." Thorn smiled grimly, hiding the fact that he felt sick to his stomach. Torture was against every code of justice and moral law he'd ever been taught. And this came right to the very edge of torture—and maybe even slipped over the edge. Only the memory of seeing Helen apparently helpless and down on one knee on that blood-soaked street in Wilhelmshaven stiffened his resolve.

"First question," he said. "You're not taking us to meet with an FBI surveillance team, are you?"

McDowell licked his lips, wincing as his tongue ran across the gash Thorn's fist had torn. "Of course I am—"

"Wrong answer." Thorn tightened his finger on the trigger.

McDowell flinched. "Wait!"

Thorn eased up. "You want to try again?" Seeing the other man nod frantically, he asked, "Where were you taking us?"

The FBI agent hesitated, felt the pistol prod his temple again, and reluctantly admitted, "To a field outside Chantilly."

"And who's waiting for us there?"

McDowell's voice dropped off to a whisper. "A man named Wolf."

"Heinrich Wolf?" Farrell asked, clearly taken aback.

McDowell nodded abjectly.

Thorn looked down at the other man in disgust. "And what did Herr Wolf plan to do . . . in that field outside Chantilly?"

"Kill you," the FBI agent mumbled. He hung his head, utterly defeated now.

"Christ!" Farrell exploded. He slid the Beretta back into his holster. "Looks like I owe you a big apology, Pete."

Thorn shook his head. "None needed, Sam."

Helen stalked forward, drawing closer to the kneeling McDowell. Her lip curled in disdain. "Who's in that other car parked down the block? More of Wolf's men?"

"What other car?" McDowell said, plainly bewildered. "Farrell and I came alone. I swear it!"

She stared down at him. "You really are an idiot, aren't you? Didn't it ever occur to you that Wolf wants you dead, too? That once he'd finished us off, you'd have outlived your usefulness?"

Thorn watched the realization sink in on McDowell's sweating face. He caught the raw smell of alcohol under the sweat now. The FBI agent paled even further. He leaned forward again. "Now that we're all on the same page, Larry, let's take this from the top, shall we?"

Then, step by step, question by question, he dragged the whole sordid story out of the other man. How McDowell had sold his soul to the Stasi for a little hard cash years before. How Wolf had blackmailed him in Moscow—forcing him to feed the German information on the ongoing crash investigation. How he'd followed Wolf's instructions to blacken Helen's and Thorn's names with the FBI and other government agencies every chance he got. The one thing he didn't know was whether or not the German was the top dog in this criminal organization. He'd never had any contact with Prince Ibrahim al Saud.

When Thorn was through, he pulled the pistol back from the FBI agent's temple and decocked it. McDowell swayed and slumped forward onto his hands and knees, head down, panting as though he'd just stumbled over the finish line in a marathon.

Helen stared down at her former boss in cold contempt. "You fucking little weasel! I'm going to look forward to seeing you in prison for the rest of your life." She looked up at Thorn and Farrell. "What do we do now?"

"Take him to the FBI?" Farrell wondered.

Helen considered Farrell's suggestion, then shook her head no. "Somehow I doubt that Larry here will be quite as cooperative without a gun pressed to his head. Then it comes down to his word against ours . . . and he's stacked the deck there."

Farrell nodded slowly.

"There's only one thing we can do," Thorn said quietly. "Herr Wolf has gone to a lot of trouble to arrange a reception for us near Chantilly. Let's at least meet him halfway."

Mobile Surveillance Unit, Washington, D.C.

Max Harzer watched the four Americans emerge from the town house and climb into the FBI agent McDowell's dark blue Ford Taurus. With one hand, he lifted his cellular phone from the seat beside him and punched in Reichardt's number. The other hand turned the key in the ignition.

"Yes." It was Reichardt. There was no disguising that clipped, authoritative voice.

"This is Harzer, sir. They're on the way."

"All of them?" Reichardt asked.

"Yes, sir." Harzer watched the Americans drive past him, then put his own vehicle in gear. "The woman is driving."

He pulled out onto the street and turned after them.

"Very good, Harzer," Reichardt said. "But stay well back. There's no point in spooking the prey so close to the snare. Understood?"

"Yes, sir." The German reduced his speed slightly, careful to keep three or four other cars between his and the Americans' vehicle.

"Keep me informed."

The phone cut off. Harzer put it down on the seat again and concentrated on his driving. Ideally, he would have had a partner in the car to help keep the Americans in sight, but with the Operation so close to completion all of Reichardt's available manpower was fully committed.

He followed the Americans onto Connecticut Avenue heading south, trailed them around Dupont Circle, out onto New Hampshire Avenue, into Washington Circle, and then down 23rd Street. Harzer was four car lengths behind when McDowell's vehicle shot ahead through a yellow light that turned red before he could cross the intersection.

He dialed the phone again.

"Report."

"I've lost them, sir," Harzer said, quickly explaining what had happened.

"Was their action deliberate?" Reichardt asked.

The German thought back. Since arriving in America he'd noticed that most drivers seemed to view a yellow light the way a Spanish bull saw a red cape. He doubted that the woman Gray was any different. "No, sir. I don't believe so."

The light turned green again.

"And they were still headed for the Roosevelt Bridge?"

Harzer nodded into the phone. "Yes, sir. With no sign of any deviation. They should be almost on the bridge now."

"Then carry on, Harzer. You ought to pick them up again on Route 50. Reichardt out."

Off Route 50, Near Chantilly, Virginia

The grass field lay quiet under a dark, cloudless night sky. Crickets chirped ceaselessly in a whirring, rising and falling, rhythm. A light wind rustled through the trees surrounding the open, empty ground. Only a few survey stakes, a darkened construction trailer, and a newly graded dirt road indicated that the field would soon be the site of yet another office complex.

From his position in the treeline just to the north, Rolf Ulrich Reichardt looked down at the luminous dial of his watch again. Another ten minutes had gone by. He turned to Schaaf. "Anything?"

The taciturn ex-commando flipped down his night-vision goggles. He scanned the edge of the field where the new road cut through the bordering woods, and then shook his head. *"Nichts."*

Reichardt frowned. Schaaf had four men concealed in carefully chosen positions around the empty construction trailer. Each was armed with a silenced MP5 submachine gun. Once the four Americans arrived, the ambush team had orders to cut them all down as soon as McDowell led them toward the trailer. Thorn, Gray, Farrell, and the traitorous FBI agent would be dead before they even hit the ground.

Once they arrived . . .

His frown deepened into a scowl. They ought to have been here by now.

The cellular phone clipped to his belt vibrated softly. He snapped it open. "Reichardt."

"This is Harzer. I'm at the far end of the dirt road. But I don't see any sign of the Americans' car."

Unbelievable.

"Clear the area, Harzer. Return to the compound." Reichardt flipped the phone shut and spun toward Schaaf. "Something's gone wrong. Recall your men. We're getting out of here—now!"

He moved back deeper into the concealing woods while Schaaf loped across the open ground toward the construction trailer. An instinctive, unreasoning shiver ran swiftly down his spine. Thorn and Gray had obviously stumbled onto his plan to ambush them. But how? And, more to the point, what would they do now?

CHAPTER SEVENTEEN

THE ABYSS

JUNE 17

Outside the Caraco Complex, Chantilly, Virginia

Helen Gray lay flat in the tall grass beneath the spreading branches of a large oak tree. Sam Farrell lay right beside her, studying the main gate of the well-lit Caraco complex through the binoculars they'd appropriated from McDowell's car. They were a few feet back from the verge of the road and roughly fifty yards away from the perimeter fence surrounding the facility.

Peter Thorn was further behind them, deeper in the belt of trees—holding a gun to the still-cowed McDowell's head.

Helen stayed still as a convoy of three vehicles—two four-door sedans and a minivan—swept past them, slowed, and turned into the drive leading to the gate.

"Here we go!" Farrell said. "That's got to be them."

Helen nodded. The timing was about right—allowing a certain number of minutes for Wolf to realize they weren't going to walk blithely into his trap, and more minutes for the Caraco security chief and his men to regroup and drive back here.

One after another, the uniformed guards manning the gate cleared the three vehicles and waved them through. All of them turned left and pulled into a parking lot adjacent to one of the three buildings—the one with a forest of radio and microwave relay antennas on its roof.

"Well, well, well," Farrell murmured. "There that son of a bitch is—without those fake glasses, too."

He passed the binoculars to Helen. "Wolf just got out of the first car. Tall. Gray-haired. He's not carrying anything in his hands."

She adjusted the focus, zeroing in on the area Farrell had indicated. The angry-looking face of the man they knew as Heinrich Wolf jumped into view. She gritted her teeth. So this was the bastard who'd arranged the cold-blooded murder of so many people, including that of Alexei Koniev. In that instant, she knew that if she'd been looking through the scope of a high-powered rifle instead of a pair of binoculars, she'd have squeezed the trigger without hesitation.

Satisfied that she would recognize the German when she saw him again, Helen surveyed the others in the group. The rest were dressed in dark-colored clothing and carried black cases—the kind of cases used to carry weapons.

Moving as a group, the Caraco contingent filed into the building and disappeared from view.

Helen lowered the binoculars, tapped Farrell on the shoulder, and then slithered backward until she was out of sight from the road. The general followed her more slowly, making far more noise than she did despite his best efforts. She hid a smile. Sam Farrell was a very good friend and a brilliant strategist, but his tradecraft was a lot rustier than he'd ever admit.

They rejoined Peter near where they'd parked McDowell's Ford.

After filling him in on what they'd seen, Farrell asked the obvious question. "Okay, now that we know for sure Wolf's one of the bad guys, what's our next move? We still don't have enough to go to the FBI or the police."

"No, we don't," Helen reluctantly agreed.

Nothing they'd seen constituted significant evidence— not the kind that would get them safely through the front doors of the Hoover Building, or even come close to winning a judge's approval for a search warrant against the Caraco facility. That was why she'd argued they should bounce Wolf and his men at the ambush site—a plan both Farrell and Peter had vetoed. Both men pointed out that going up against an unknown number of armed enemies, on ground of their own choosing, and in the dark, could come close to counting as suicide. The clincher was the fact that they couldn't be absolutely sure the Caraco security chief had told McDowell the real location for the ambush. In a treacherous game where double crosses were the basic currency, they couldn't take anything on face value.

"Fine. We need more hard evidence. Then I suggest we take the steps needed to get it," Peter said abruptly.

"You have a plan, Pete . . . or just some noble intentions?" Farrell wondered.

"More a rough outline than a detailed blueprint," Peter admitted. He shrugged. "We know there's one guy who's got all the answers we need. So I say we wait for Mr. Wolf to leave his lair—and then we arrange a little chat."

"You proposing a kidnapping?" Farrell asked grimly.

"Call it a citizen's arrest," he said, grinning. He nodded

toward the assortment of gear they'd found in the Taurus's trunk and back seat. "Especially since Mr. McDowell here has so thoughtfully provided us with all the essentials."

McDowell opened his mouth to protest, then shut it abruptly when Peter jabbed him lightly with the pistol. He'd been told before to keep his trap shut unless they asked him a direct question.

Helen hated to rain on Peter's parade, but she had to ask the obvious question. "What makes you think Wolf is going to go anywhere?"

"Educated guesswork," he said. He ran quickly through his reasoning process. "Look, I don't think this guy Wolf is the head honcho of this operation. He's too involved in the detail work. Somebody else somewhere has to be pulling the strings—looking at the big picture. Now that we've slipped the leash, I think Wolf will go running to his master for new instructions. And I don't think he'll trust that kind of information to the phone. I think he'll go in person."

"To Ibrahim?" Farrell guessed.

"I think so."

"He's smart enough. And tough enough," Farrell said slowly. "But what I don't understand is why he'd run a smuggling operation of any kind—let alone one involving a Russian nuke! Caraco's a multibillion-dollar corporation, which means Ibrahim personally has to be worth at least a few hundred mil."

"Maybe the money's not enough," Peter said. "Or maybe money was never the real objective—just a means to an end. This end."

Helen jumped in. "We can leave finding the motive up to the U.S. attorney's office, Sam." She frowned. "I think Peter's right. From what you've told us, Caraco is practically Ibrahim's personal fiefdom. I doubt Wolf could run such a huge show without his knowledge—or consent."

"Yeah. That makes sense." Farrell turned back to Peter. "Which still leaves us with a problem. How do you propose divvying up the assignments for this little shindig you're planning?"

"I think that falls out pretty logically," Helen said, after a rapid glance at Peter. "You've got a cell phone, don't you?"

Farrell nodded. He patted his jacket pocket. "Last year's Christmas gift from Louisa. I don't like the damned thing, but she wants to keep tabs on me when I'm out of the house."

"So that plus McDowell's binoculars makes you the lookout," Peter said. "Between your Beretta and this"—he hefted the SIG P228 he was still pointing at the white-faced McDowell—"Helen and I shouldn't have much problem persuading Herr Wolf to listen to reason."

Seeing Farrell starting to look stubborn, Helen laid a hand on his arm. "Please, Sam. Let Peter and me do this. This was our fight first."

She left the other reason she wanted to leave the general behind as their watcher carefully unspoken. No matter how Peter tried to dress it up, what he'd proposed was actually a lot closer to kidnapping than to any recognized form of lawful arrest. If things went wrong, she wanted to build as big a firewall between Louisa Farrell's good-hearted husband and their actions as she possibly could.

Farrell looked down at the ground for several seconds before raising his eyes to meet theirs again. "All right, I'll stay put and keep watch." He handed over his pistol and nodded toward McDowell. "What about this little shit? Does he stay with me, or go with you?"

"He comes with us," Helen heard herself say tightly. She glared at her nemesis. "I want to be right there when Mr. McDowell meets his real employer face-to-face for the first time."

McDowell turned even paler.

JUNE 18

Just Off Route 50, Near Middleburg, Virginia

(D MINUS 3)

It was nearly one in the morning. Despite the hour, Reich-ardt sat rigidly upright in the front passenger seat of his Caraco-owned Chrysler LeBaron. He stared out at the black-ened landscape blurring past without seeing any of it—not the dark masses of trees stabbing up toward the star-speckled night sky, or the occasional, isolated flicker of light that marked a human habitation.

Ostensibly, Ibrahim had summoned him to Middleburg for a conference to discuss minor revisions to the Operation. In reality, Reichardt knew the Saudi prince wanted to vent his displeasure over his failure to trap and eliminate the four Americans—Thorn, Gray, Farrell, and McDowell—as promised. McDowell. The German felt his jaw tighten. The FBI traitor had obviously tipped his hand somehow.

Reichardt grimaced. He'd thought about eliminating Mc-Dowell earlier—but he'd needed the information given him by the American to keep track of Thorn and Gray. And now that had all gone wrong. Perhaps he'd made a mistake in al-lowing McDowell to live this long.

Johann Brandt, his closest aide and bodyguard, spun the wheel, turning onto the narrow, two-lane road that eventu-ally ran past Ibrahim al Saud's sprawling Virginia estate. The road wound up and down over a chain of gentle, rolling hills and then cut through a dense, dark stretch of forest.

"We're being followed, sir," Brandt said suddenly, with a quick glance at the rearview mirror.

Reichardt felt that shiver run down his spine again. Too many of his carefully laid plans had gone astray these past few days. He was beginning to lose faith in his own cunning and powers of calculation. "Are you sure?" he demanded.

Brandt nodded. "It's the same car. It turned off the highway after us. And now it's drawing closer."

Reichardt had noticed the headlights behind them gleaming in the sideview mirrors from time to time, but he'd discounted them. Many of the high-priced lawyers, lobbyists, and corporate executives who made their homes in this area were famed for working inhumanly late hours.

"How far are we from the estate?" he asked.

"Four or five miles."

Too far. Reichardt craned his head around, trying to catch a glimpse of the car that was following them. Nothing. Just the glare of the headlights. He narrowed his eyes against the dazzling light.

A new light blinked into existence—this one on top of the car pursuing them. Red and blue flashes strobed against the darkness, flickering against the tangled woods on either side of the road.

"The police?" Reichardt murmured, more to himself than to Brandt. Why? What had they done wrong?

"Should I evade them?" the other man asked, hunched forward over the steering wheel now.

Reichardt shook his head. They were on an isolated country road—far from the useful camouflage of the noise, chaos, and confusion of city streets. The chances of successfully evading a police pursuit were nil. And Ibrahim would not thank him for drawing so much unwelcome official attention so close to the Arab's own home.

Perhaps Brandt had been speeding, or had fallen afoul of some minor technicality in the state's arcane traffic laws. It didn't really matter. "Pull over, Johann," he instructed. "We shall play the poor lost German tourists, accept our ticket or warning with good grace, and then proceed."

Obedient as ever, Brandt braked gently and then brought the LeBaron to a full stop on the narrow shoulder. He tapped the button to roll down the driver's side window. Driven by a soft, whispering breeze, the cool night air rushed in—carrying with it the scent of pine and damp moss.

The police car pulled in behind them, its single roof-mounted light still flashing.

"Step out of the car! The driver first! And keep your hands where I can see them!" a commanding male voice barked.

Reichardt frowned. This wasn't the procedure for a routine traffic stop, was it?

He nodded briefly to Brandt, signaling the other man to obey. Perhaps the Virginia police were more cautious on such roads at night. Certainly, there wasn't any point in being spooked into foolish resistance to the authorities—not when Caraco's lawyers could smooth out any minor misunderstandings.

Brandt popped the door open, put one foot on the ground, and then froze as another voice yelled out, "It's a trap, Wolf! Run!"

They heard the sound of a muffled blow.

McDowell! The scales fell from Reichardt's eyes in one sickening instant. Thorn and that damned woman were coming for him! He snatched his leather briefcase off the floor and whirled toward Brandt. "Kill them!"

Thorn saw the LeBaron's driver throw himself headlong through the open door and roll frantically across the road—trying to get out of the light and into cover. Flame stabbed out of the pistol in the other man's hand as he fired while still rolling.

The Ford's windshield shattered. Fragments of safety glass cascaded across him.

Damn it. Thorn folded sideways—out of the line of fire. He grabbed for the passenger side door handle.

"Wolf dropped out the other side!" Helen warned him. "He's in the woods!" She already had the right rear passenger door open and Farrell's 9mm drawn.

"Got it." Thorn shoved the door open and rolled out onto the gravel-strewn shoulder—staying prone close to the car. "You take him. I'll take the driver!"

Another round slammed into the Ford, smashing through one of the side windows and out through the roof in a shower of torn metal and fiberglass. Helen dropped onto the ground right behind him—leaving a moaning McDowell slumped over in the back seat.

They had been too confident they had the FBI traitor under control, Thorn realized. Despite the risk involved if they'd been stopped by the police themselves, they ought to have tied McDowell up. Well, it'll serve the little bastard right if a stray bullet hits him, Thorn thought coldly.

With a quick nod, Helen sprinted into the trees—careful to stay low. Keeping the car between her and the unseen gunman, she angled off in the direction Wolf had taken and disappeared into the darkness and dense undergrowth.

Thorn yanked the SIG P228 out of the shoulder holster he'd appropriated from the FBI agent, spun around, and crawled rapidly toward the back of the Taurus.

A split second before he got there, another round ripped through the right rear tire, sprayed dirt and gravel in all directions as it hit the ground, and then ricocheted away into the forest. Thorn rolled away from the car—into the brush and tall grass bordering the road. Jesus. If he'd moved a little faster, his head would have been right in the line with that bullet.

Wolf's driver was good—maybe too good.

Thorn edged even further back and then belly-crawled to his left—snaking away from the two parked cars while staying parallel to the road. He stopped beside a small boulder that lay half buried amid the weeds. With his pistol out and braced in both hands, he studied the black, forbidding treeline on the other side—his ears cocked for the slightest sound, the first indication of any movement.

All sounds trailed away. Even McDowell's low, sobbing groans had faded to nothing.

Questions about the man he was facing raced through Thorn's mind as he lay absolutely still, trying to blend with the boulder and the shadows. Was Wolf's driver a former soldier used to fighting in wooded country? Or was he a former Stasi thug more at ease in an urban setting?

There was only one way to find out, he told himself. He felt through the grass for a good-sized rock, found one, and then lobbed it skyward with one quick overhand grenade toss. The rock sailed high, arcing toward the two lit-up cars. It bounced off the hood of the Ford and rolled off into the brush.

The gunman reacted immediately—firing twice in rapid succession. Both shots caromed off the car's engine block.

Strike one, Thorn thought grimly. Without hesitating further, he scrambled to his feet and raced across the road and into the woods beyond. He circled warily through the trees—listening intently and checking every footfall for the branch or twig that might trip him up, or snap and alert the man he was hunting.

Metal clinked on rock—close by.

Thorn froze in place. He was nearing the road again—within yards of the spot where he'd seen muzzle flashes stabbing out of the blackness. Wolf's driver hadn't changed position after firing—or at least not by much. Strike two.

He could almost sense the gunman's growing uneasiness now. Every small sound—every bird flitting from branch to branch, every small animal skittering through the brush, every stray breeze rustling through the leaves—must be gnawing away at the other man's resolution and confidence.

Moving slowly and with infinite patience, Thorn put his back against the trunk of the closest tree, a stunted scrub pine, and slid around it. His eyes were fully adjusted to the darkness now.

Bingo.

He could just barely make out the man-sized shape crouched behind a moss-covered boulder about five yards away. The gunman had found a good piece of cover—against someone firing from the other side of the road. A breeze stirred the trees above them, momentarily parting the leafy canopy that hid the night sky. Starlight gleamed off the barrel of the other man's pistol.

Thorn considered his options. If this were a combat situation, he could just put a couple of rounds into the gunman's back, make sure he was down for good, and move on after Wolf himself. But this case was a whole lot murkier. He and Helen were operating well outside the law. Shooting without warning would probably constitute murder. He shook his head—he couldn't just dry-gulch the guy, not under these circumstances. Anyway, they needed captives to question—not corpses.

Too bad.

Thorn took a fast, shallow breath, and then let it out. He took one step closer with the pistol braced in a two-handed shooting grip.

Now.

"Drop the gun or you're dead!" he barked.

For a split second, Thorn thought the other man would obey the order. He was wrong.

Instead, Wolf's man spun around, frantically trying to bring his own weapon to bear. Flame blossomed in the darkness. A bullet tore into the tree trunk just above Thorn's head.

Strike three.

Thorn squeezed the trigger three times—pushing the barrel back on line between each shot. Two rounds hit the gunman squarely in the chest. The third hit him in the head. The man slumped to the ground with one arm still draped across the boulder.

Half blinded and with his ears still ringing from the close-range gunfire, Thorn moved forward and dropped to one knee beside the man he'd shot. He felt for a pulse. Just a faint, spasmodic flutter . . . and then nothing.

He grimaced. "Shit!"

Suddenly Thorn felt the air stir as someone charged up behind him. Christ! He swung around with his right arm raised as a block. Too late.

Something heavy and hard glanced off his arm and smashed into his skull. Pain flared—white-hot and blindingly bright. Thorn slipped down into blackness.

The abrupt flurry of gunshots in the middle distance startled Reichardt. He'd been heading through the forest as fast as he could while trying to move silently. From time to time, he'd stopped—listening desperately for any sounds of pursuit. He'd heard none.

Were both Americans going after Brandt? It seemed almost too much to hope for. Johann Brandt was a man of somewhat limited imagination, but he was utterly loyal and fearless.

He stayed still a moment longer, waiting for more gunfire. Nothing.

Still panting in short, shallow gasps from his frantic dash out of the car, Reichardt took quick stock of his surroundings. He was deep in the woods—at least a hundred yards from the road. Briers he'd snagged during his initial, panicked flight had ripped holes in his wool slacks, torn his jacket, and even drawn blood from his hands. But he still had his pistol, his briefcase, and his cell phone.

The phone! He could summon help from Ibrahim's estate security force or even the local police.

Reichardt fumbled in his pockets. Where was it? He swore softly. The cell phone was gone. It must have fallen out onto the ground during his dash for safety. He tried drying the sweat from his palms on his jacket, knowing he would have to press on. If he could just outdistance his pursuers he could find a house and beg for help or flag down a passing car.

The German started moving again—still angling away from the road. For now he needed the concealment the woods offered more than the speed he could have attained on pavement.

Reichardt stumbled into a low-hanging branch, felt a sharp twig draw more blood from his cheek, and swore again angrily. This was not right. As a servant of the East German state and then as a freelance terrorist, he had been a master of men's lives for more than twenty years. He was always the hunter—never the hunted!

He pushed through more brush and then stopped dead in his tracks. He'd come to a sluggish stream wending its way downhill through the trees. The watercourse wasn't wide—almost narrow enough to jump, in fact. But the banks looked muddy and slippery. More to the point now, the forest canopy parted above the stream—allowing more light to fall on the weed-choked water.

Frowning, Reichardt turned to peer behind him again. He snarled. It was hopeless. It was as dark as a witch's heart under those trees. He could see nothing.

He plunged ahead, squelched through the soft ground,

and waded into the knee-high water. Ripples spread across the still surface.

"Freeze!"

Shocked by the shout from behind him, Reichardt felt sudden terror grip his heart. It was the woman, Gray. He exploded into motion—surging toward the opposite bank.

Blam.

The bullet caught him in the fleshy part of the left thigh and spun him halfway around. My God. He lurched forward. There was no pain. Not yet. That would come later. He gained firmer footing and stumbled forward, panting louder now.

Blam.

A second bullet hit him, this one in the right shoulder. His own pistol went flying off into the mud and tall grass. Reichardt moaned aloud. No!

Clutching his briefcase tightly to his chest, he limped out of the stream and into the sheltering darkness beyond. He'd gone a few yards when his wounded leg abruptly gave out—dumping him flat on his face in the undergrowth.

Reichardt heard someone else crashing through the woods nearby—on this side of the stream. It couldn't be that bitch who'd shot him. Could it be Brandt? His probing fingers found the torn and bleeding edges of the exit wound in his thigh and recoiled. It had to be Brandt. Please God, let it be Brandt!

Still holding the briefcase, he dragged himself toward the noise, crawling awkwardly on his stomach. "Johann! Johann!" he whispered harshly, hissing now as the first fiery tendrils of pain coursed through him. *"Hilf mir! Hilf mir!"*

His scrabbling fingers touched a shoe. A man's shoe. Reichardt looked up, smiling. His smile faded slowly.

Lawrence McDowell looked down at him. A puffy bruise covered half the senior FBI agent's cheek. He held a pistol—a 9mm SIG-Sauer.

Reichardt caught the acrid smell of burnt powder on the weapon. It had been fired recently. He grabbed at the cuff of the other man's pants, pointing back the way he'd come. "The woman Gray is there! You must kill her, PERE-GRINE! It is the only way you can be safe!"

McDowell smiled nastily. "I will kill her, Herr Wolf. After I finish my business with you." He raised the pistol. "I'm canceling my debt, you bastard. Permanently."

Reichardt saw the muzzle center on his forehead. In hor-ror, he saw McDowell's finger tighten on the trigger.

"Noooooo!"

Reichardt stopped screaming when the bullet tore through his brain and sent him straight to hell.

Helen Gray jumped lightly across the stream, skidded on the slippery ground, and quickly recovered her balance. She'd been tracking Wolf cautiously—aware that, like a wounded animal, even an injured man could still be danger-ous. Then she'd heard the voices coming from a thicket a few yards away. Had Wolf's driver evaded Peter and linked up with his employer? Her mind would not accept the other explanation.

Peter was alive. He had to be alive.

The high-pitched, womanish scream and the echoing gun-shot took her by surprise.

She lunged forward through the screening brush and froze—staring in shock at Larry McDowell, the gun in his hand, and the twisted, mangled corpse at his feet. Her old boss was still grinning nastily at the man he'd just murdered. Hein-rich Wolf, their only link to the smuggled shipment from Rus-sia, and their only hope of clearing their names, was dead.

"You shit, McDowell," Helen said softly. She swung her Beretta on line. "Drop the goddamned gun . . ."

McDowell looked up and seemed to see her for the first

time. An odd, almost maniacal glee danced in his eyes. He shook his head. "What are you going to do, Helen? Kill me? How are you going to explain that?"

"I'm not kidding, Larry," Helen said tightly. "Drop the gun. Now!"

McDowell laughed harshly. "Screw you, bitch!" He lifted the SIG-Sauer, pointing it toward her.

Blinded by a sudden wave of cold fury, Helen pulled the trigger. And again. And again. And again.

Slowly, still shaking, she eased up on the trigger, staring over the muzzle at the carnage her bullets had created. Her first shot had caught McDowell low—well below the stomach. Each successive 9mm round had climbed higher—ending in one that blew his face apart.

Helen sank to her hands and knees, retching uncontrollably. She felt ice-cold now, too cold ever to be warm again.

When she was done, she rose to her feet, still shivering. She slipped the Beretta back in her holster—succeeding on the second try—and fished out the cellular phone they'd taken off McDowell back at the bed-and-breakfast. In a daze, she punched in a number she'd memorized and then heard the phone connect.

"Farrell."

"Sam," Helen heard herself say weakly. "I need your help, Sam. Things have gone terribly wrong . . ."

CHAPTER EIGHTEEN

SHOCK WAVE

JUNE 18

Super 6 Motor Lodge, Near Falls Church, Virginia

Helen Gray blotted away some dried blood and dirt with a cotton ball soaked in iodine, finished taping down the gauze pad, and then stepped back to admire her handiwork. "How's it feel?"

"Ouch," Thorn said. He raised his bruised right arm, winced, and then gingerly touched the bandaged side of his head. "I'll live, I guess, but I have a feeling I'm not going to win any beauty contests this year."

"You've got that right, mister," Helen said—working very hard to keep the same light, cheerful tone.

She was still grappling with the emotional trauma of their

bloody early morning gun battle. Losing Heinrich Wolf, their only solid witness to the Caraco-run smuggling operation, was bad. Killing McDowell was worse. She was also uncomfortably aware that she'd carried out something very close to an execution on McDowell. Once she'd fired that first shot, she'd never even considered trying to take him alive.

But the biggest nightmare of all had been the sudden, blinding fear that Peter Thorn might be dead—torn forever out of her life. They'd faced death twice before in the past couple of weeks, but always together—never apart and alone.

After Helen had made that frantic phone call to Farrell, she'd held herself together just long enough to search Wolf's and McDowell's bodies for any possible evidence. Then, with tears staining her cheeks, she'd stumbled back through the pitch-black woods to where they'd left the two cars. And there she'd found Peter sitting by the side of the road with his injured head in his hands—blood-spattered, dazed, and furiously angry at himself, but alive.

McDowell had hit him over the head with a rock—clearly intending to kill him. Only the fact that he'd reacted fast enough to ward off some of the impact with his arm had saved his life. That and the fact that the traitorous FBI agent must have rushed off to chase down Wolf without making sure he was dead.

Still tearful, though with relief now and not sorrow, she'd managed to bundle Peter into the back seat of Wolf's Chrysler, pat down the body of the driver for any more evidence, and then head back to pick up Farrell outside Caraco's Chantilly complex. Pressed for time, she'd been forced to leave McDowell's bullet-riddled Ford parked out in the open on the shoulder.

Helen had hated to do that. The abandoned car would act as a beacon to the next passing patrol car—signaling that something very wrong had happened along that isolated stretch of road. More to the point, their fingerprints were all over the car, and even a cursory check of the government-issue plates would reveal it had been signed out to FBI Deputy Assistant Director Lawrence McDowell—now missing.

Not good, she thought grimly. Not good at all.

Helen checked her watch. It was after eleven in the morning. By now, there might very easily be an APB out for the three of them. And the charges against them could range from kidnapping to murder. Somehow, in the space of just a few days, she and Peter had managed to push the punishments they were facing from likely administrative reprimands to possible imprisonment, and now maybe even the death penalty.

She shook her head in dismay. It was best to focus on the immediate future. For the moment they were free and still in a position to try something—anything—to stop whatever Heinrich Wolf and his employer, Ibrahim, had planned.

The hours since their abortive attempt to capture Wolf had passed in a dizzying blur. After a quick cleanup in the rest room of a large, busy gas station, she, Peter, and Farrell had found an out-of-the way residential street and abandoned the Chrysler. With luck, it might be days before the neighbors compared notes and discovered it didn't belong to a visitor or anyone local.

Next, they'd phoned a cab and checked into this plain, clean, and relatively inexpensive motel. Close to the Beltway, the motor lodge mostly catered to truckers, traveling salesmen, and economy-minded vacationers touring the nation's capital. It offered privacy, easy access to the local road and highway network, and effective anonymity to anyone paying cash.

After a short rest, Farrell had left a couple of hours ago on a hurried shopping expedition.

Someone knocked on the door—softly but urgently.

Helen waved Peter down and checked the peephole. It was Sam Farrell.

He bustled in, set a large plastic bag down on the nearest bed, and displayed a set of rental car keys. "Okay! We're mobile again."

Helen read the tag. "A white Oldsmobile Ciera?" She tried hard to match his determinedly cheerful mood. "Not a brand-new, 007-type BMW? Hardly our style, Sam . . ."

Farrell grinned. "I know, I know—dull, boring. But there's a zillion of 'em out on the road. We'll blend right in with everyone else in the metro area.

"I also got this." He pulled a bulging manila envelope out of the shopping bag, opened the flap, and dumped several thick stacks of twenty-dollar bills onto the bed. "There's somewhere around five thousand dollars there. I cleaned out one of my savings accounts."

"Jesus, Sam," Peter said, looking down at the money. "Your wife will kill you when she finds out about this."

"Not with an IOU from you in hand," Farrell reminded him. "Louisa trusts you, Pete. It's her one big blind spot. Anyway, we need the money right now."

That was certainly true, Helen knew. Neither she nor Peter dared use their own credit or ATM cards, and their earlier travels had pretty well depleted their own cash reserves. And, unless the police or the FBI nailed them in the next few hours, they were sure to need money and lots of it.

She tapped the still-bulging shopping bag. "So, what's left, Sam?"

"This," Farrell said. He handed her a massive hardcover German-English/English-German dictionary.

"Perfect."

Helen led Peter and Farrell over to the small circular table where she'd sorted out the possessions she'd collected from the three dead men—Wolf, his driver, Brandt, and McDowell. She'd swept McDowell's into a separate bag for later disposal. What struck her about the other two men was the complete lack of commonplace personal items. Their wallets contained only some cash and one credit card apiece—both tied to a Caraco corporate account. There were no dry cleaning receipts, no shopping lists, no photos of their wives or kids.

Both Wolf and Brandt were "clean"—covert operations jargon meaning neither had carried anything that might contradict their cover identities.

Which left just two interesting items. Brandt had apparently been more than just a simple driver and bodyguard for his boss. He'd been carrying a fat, leather-bound appointment book. And Helen had found Heinrich Wolf's blood-soaked briefcase under his still-warm body.

Naturally, all the notations in both the appointment book and in the papers inside the briefcase were in German. Hence the hardcover monstrosity Sam Farrell had just handed her.

Farrell took one look at the small table and shook his head. "Two's company, three's a crowd—especially when you've only got one dictionary. You two take the first whack at this stuff. I'll take a gander at the TV and see if there's anything on about a shoot-out near Middleburg."

"Nothing on the local news yet?" Peter asked.

Farrell shrugged. "Not a peep. And that makes me kinda nervous."

Helen nodded silently. The Loudoun County sheriffs must have found McDowell's abandoned car by now—which probably meant the Bureau's higher-ups were stonewalling all inquiries from local law enforcement while they tried to sort out just what the hell was going on.

She laid the German-English dictionary in the middle of the table, sat down, and slid the appointment book across to Peter. Then she flipped open Wolf's briefcase. Aside from a few business cards, there were only two folded pieces of paper that struck her as significant.

The first was a list headed *"Flugzeug Piloten—Ankunfts-zeiten."* Which meant "Pilots—Arrival Times," according to her best guess and some rapid flipping through the dictionary. Today's date, *"18 Juni,"* appeared at the very top in crisp, neat Germanic handwriting. It was followed by a series of four airline names, flight numbers, and times—with the phrase *"nach Dulles"* circled to one side.

Several minutes on the phone with various airlines while Peter snagged the dictionary for his own rough translations elicited the information that Wolf had pilots arriving at Dulles on flights originating from Charleston, Los Angeles, Oklahoma City, and Seattle.

Helen didn't like even the vague picture she saw emerging. Caraco's operation involved aircraft in some fashion—and more than one plane, too. Had the pilots now arriving in the D.C. area been used to ferry Ibrahim's smuggled cargo into those four cities?

Oh, hell. Her blood ran cold. They'd been assuming they were chasing after one stolen nuclear weapon. What if there were more?

There was a second note on the same sheet, *"Drei zusaetz-lichen Wache von Deutschland nach JFK Flughafen."* Three cities—Los Angeles, Charleston, and Washington, D.C.—were listed below with an arrow pointing to each. More flipping to and fro in the dictionary supplied the information that Wolf had ordered three additional guards deployed from

Germany through JFK International in New York to un-named locations in each of those three cities.

And the word "additional" implied that he already had forces stationed at those locations. Wonderful. Just wonderful.

The second sheet didn't have a heading—just a set of what looked like five underlined place names with other words beneath them. She studied the first set:

> <u>Berkeley</u>
> *Adler*
> *Fuchs*
> *Katze*
> *Baeren*
> *Hase*

Eagle, Fox, Cat, Bear, and Hare. All were clearly code names of some kind, Helen decided. But code names for what? For people? For places? Stages in Wolf's operation? *"Katze"* had been crossed out and the German word for cow, *"Kuh,"* had been written in beside it—with a further notation, *"Wetter,"* or weather.

There were more animal code words beneath each of the other four underlined locations—five more under two, three under a third, and two under the last. A total of twenty then. With one more code word crossed out and another substituted—this one with the German words *"Eine Übung,"* or "an exercise," as an explanatory note.

Helen frowned. Without more than this, it was going to be impossible to decipher much about Ibrahim's real intentions. She showed the second sheet to Peter and Farrell. "Can either of you guys make heads or tails out of this stuff?"

The two men studied it for a few seconds.

Peter read the apparent place names out loud. "Berkeley. Godfrey. Page. Nampa. And Shafter-Minter." He raised an eyebrow. "Sounds like a bunch of small towns. Or suburbs, maybe."

He flipped open the appointment book Brandt had carried and showed them one page after another. "I think that bastard Wolf may have visited all of those places over the past couple of weeks. He's been flitting across the whole country on a Caraco corporate jet. See?" His finger stabbed each name as he read it out. "On June 11 he was in South Carolina. The next day, the twelfth, he was out in California—at this Shafter-Minter place."

Helen glanced ahead at the listing for June 13. Her eyes widened. "Look where he went next . . . Galveston."

Peter nodded. "Yeah. No wonder the FBI didn't find anything in that warehouse. The son of a bitch was a step ahead of us all the way."

"True. But we're still left in the goddamned dark about exactly what's going on here," Farrell pointed out. He shook his head. "Let me check out these towns or whatever they are at the local library. I'll see if I can dig anything up about them that would appeal to a nasty piece of work like Wolf."

"How are you planning to do that, Sam?" Helen asked. "Guide books? Atlases? It'll take you hours."

Still jotting the place names onto a piece of scrap paper, Farrell grinned back at her. "Helen, someday you and Pete are gonna have to spend less time learning how to kill people and more time dragging yourselves into the modern age." He waggled a finger. "All I need to do is find the nearest computer connected to the Internet, input this stuff, do a little word search, filter out the meaningless garbage, and bingo, I've got my data."

Middleburg, Virginia

(D MINUS 3)

Out of the corner of his eye, Prince Ibrahim al Saud saw his chief of security, Talal, appear at the door to his study. At a glance, the former Saudi paratroop captain stopped motionless and stood silently, waiting for permission to speak.

With a superficial calm he no longer felt inwardly, Ibrahim finished his prayers, carefully rolled up the prayer mat, and rose to his feet. It was ordinarily his custom to lead the five daily prayers of all the faithful in his household, but the press of events had forced him into these less fulfilling private observances. It was a pity, but he felt confident God would understand his need.

He crooked a finger at Talal.

The man stepped closer and stiffened to attention. "Highness."

Ibrahim crossed to his desk and sat down. "Yes, Captain."

"There is still no sign of Herr Reichardt, Highness. Or of the American, McDowell."

Ibrahim frowned. When Reichardt hadn't shown up on time for their scheduled meeting, he'd immediately dispatched Talal and a section of his security force to backtrack along the route the German would have taken. To his dismay, they'd found only an empty, abandoned car pockmarked with bullet holes—a car with U.S. government–issued license plates. A car that had been assigned to Reichardt's mole inside the FBI—Lawrence McDowell. Minutes later, his men had discovered the corpse of Johann Brandt just inside the forest. But both Reichardt and McDowell were gone. The German's corporate car had also vanished without a trace.

Determined not to draw any further official attention to his activities, Ibrahim had ordered Talal to bring both Brandt's body and the missing FBI man's Ford back to the estate—where they could be disposed of without awkward questions from the authorities.

It didn't require much imagination to piece together what must have happened. Somehow the two Americans, Thorn and that woman Gray, had turned the tables on Reichardt. Somehow the predator had become the prey.

Ibrahim scowled. He had cautioned the German before against overconfidence. Evidently, his warnings had fallen on deaf ears.

What troubled him most was the possibility that Thorn and Gray might have taken Reichardt alive. That would greatly complicate his plans. He didn't believe the ex-Stasi officer would break under questioning, but he could not be absolutely sure. For an instant, Ibrahim became disoriented—his mind casting up images of American agents appearing in force outside his gates, destroying the grand scheme he had worked so hard and spent so much to prepare.

Be still, he told himself. What will be, will be. So far the Americans show no signs that they are aware of their imminent peril. If Reichardt were alive and in Thorn and Gray's hands, he had not yet betrayed his master.

Of course, there were also the documents the other man would have carried on his person. The German was often circumspect, prone to wrapping even the most basic information in a concealing layer of code, but even vague references might provide the two Americans with more details about the Operation. And they already knew far too much.

Talal's quiet, deferential voice broke in on his thoughts. "Should I report the Chrysler stolen, Highness? Perhaps the American police could do some of this work for us?"

"No." Ibrahim shook his head forcefully. "We would need to explain the circumstances of the car's disappearance. For now we shall let sleeping dogs lie."

He sighed. "In any case, I am quite sure that Colonel Thorn is no longer anywhere near Herr Reichardt's vehicle. He could not have survived this long by behaving stupidly."

Ibrahim stood up suddenly. The hours were flying by. Whether Reichardt were alive or dead, the German's abrupt disappearance so close to the end had thrown sand into the Operation's once smoothly turning gears. There were decisions to be made—and now only he could make them.

"Captain Talal," he snapped.

"Highness!"

"Instruct the staff to continue packing. Then organize and equip a four-man squad of your best troops as an escort. I'm going to the Chantilly facility. You will accompany me. Understood?"

Talal nodded hurriedly.

Ibrahim would learn from Reichardt's mistakes. If Thorn and Gray wanted to come after him on the road to Chantilly, so be it. They would be met by overwhelming firepower.

Outside Leesburg, Virginia

A little more than thirty miles west and slightly north of Washington, Sam Farrell turned south off the highway onto a narrow, two-lane blacktop road. The area around them had once been predominantly rural—a stretch of green hills and fertile farmland. Now, though, the District was pushing its urban tentacles up Route 7, the old Leesburg Turnpike of Civil War fame. A few scattered farms still held out, but most had fallen prey to new housing developments and gleaming corporate buildings. Light industry lined both sides of the road now—and the scars of new construction in the green fields showed where still more houses and shopping malls would soon rise.

Colonel Peter Thorn leaned forward from the back seat, squinting as the early afternoon sun poured in from the west. His head still ached, despite Helen's soothing ministrations. "You mind telling me where you're taking us, Sam? Fun's fun, but we've been on the road for a while now."

Farrell raised his eyes to the rearview mirror. He smiled crookedly. "You just can't stand secrets, can you, Pete?"

"Not really," Thorn admitted.

Farrell turned their rented Ciera off the blacktop road and into a parking lot about half the size of that of any typical supermarket. He pointed toward the single asphalt runway just visible behind a pair of buildings. "Welcome to Godfrey Field, aka the Leesburg Municipal Airport."

"An airport?" Thorn heard Helen ask. He scanned the five long rows of private planes tied down just left of the parking lot. Most were small—single-engine two-, four-, and six-seaters.

"Yep. They're all airports," Farrell said. "From Berkeley, South Carolina, to Nampa, Idaho, to Page, Oklahoma, all the way to Shafter-Minter out in California. It took some work to narrow my search down to exactly what linked those names, but that's it—that's the common denominator."

"And they're all this size?" Thorn asked, eyeing a line of hangars beyond the airpark—three pairs paralleling the road. The path between the two nearest buildings, one a two-story FAA office, the other a small flight school, was the quickest way out onto the runway. No metal detectors. No boarding areas. No jetways. No security.

"On the nose, Pete," Farrell said. "All five are pint-size

municipal or regional airports—but all of them are reasonably close to larger urban centers: Los Angeles, Charleston, Boise, Oklahoma City, and D.C."

"My God," Helen said. She turned toward them. "There were five Su-24 engines in that last shipment from Kandalaksha."

Thorn saw it at almost the same moment. He felt cold despite the sticky heat rolling in through the car's open windows. "Then Caraco has five nukes."

"Five airfields. Five bombs. Five cities," Farrell concluded grimly. A bleak expression settled on his face, and, for the first time Thorn could remember, his former commander looked close to his real age.

"But why use aircraft?" Helen asked, clearly desperate to poke holes in their story. "Why not just put a bomb in a truck, drive it into the center of town, and hit the switch? That would be simpler and cheaper."

Thorn thought he knew why Wolf and his employer, Ibrahim al Saud, would want their nuclear weapons aloft. "They must be going for airbursts," he guessed—feeling even colder still. "Set a nuke off a few thousand feet up and you maximize its blast and heat. And casualties."

The silence stretched for more than a minute.

At last Thorn shook his head, and immediately wished that he hadn't. Smaller aches exploded into sharp-edged, stabbing pain. Ignore it, he told himself harshly, you haven't got time for weakness. The pain receded to a more manageable level.

He opened the Ciera's right rear door. "Okay, let's see if we're right. I say we take a closer look at those hangars."

First Farrell and then Helen nodded slowly. Like him, they preferred action to inaction—especially in the face of what might be coming.

The two closest hangars were large and modern. Red

signs on the sides indicated they were owned by Raytheon. The next two hangars in line were older—much older. Constructed of corrugated iron and covered with flaking paint, they hardly looked large enough to hold even a single-engine plane.

The third pair of hangars were as big as those belonging to Raytheon. But they were so far away across the field that it was hard to see much detail. Neither of the silver-gray structures had a corporate logo boldly emblazoned to identify their owners. Three sizable twin-engine aircraft, executive passenger planes, were parked on the tarmac in front of the hangars. Several men were visible—either working on the aircraft or lounging in the shade created by their wings. Despite the sweltering afternoon, the big sliding doors on both hangars were shut.

"That's what we're looking for," Farrell said. "Has to be."

Thorn nodded. The other man's snap assessment made sense. The two distant hangars were completely surrounded by a fence, with a guard shack by the gate. None of the other facilities at Godfrey had any security around them at all.

But they weren't going to be able to get any closer—at least not from here. The field was quiet, sleeping in the hazy June sunshine, and they were the only people in sight. There was no easy way to walk across the open space separating them from the hangars without being conspicuous.

Helen came to the same conclusion at the same moment. "No point in spooking them now." She pointed to a gravel-covered cutoff that ran past the twin hangars. "Let's see what's visible from that road."

The speed limit on the cutoff was forty-five miles per hour, but Farrell cruised by as slowly as he dared. A driveway led to the gate and guard shack, and a small white sign on the fence next to the gate read "Caraco Washington Region Air Maintenance. No Trespassing."

"I bet," Thorn muttered, after a quick glance at the guard shack and fence. The shack's windows were dark—tinted heavily enough to hide anyone inside from prying eyes. But coiled razor wire topped the chain-link fence and there were video cameras sited to sweep the entire perimeter.

A turnoff just past the airport led them back to the parking lot. This time they stayed in the car while mulling over what they'd observed.

Helen broke the renewed silence first. "Are you sure those planes out there are big enough to carry a nuclear bomb?"

Thorn nodded, remembering the OSIA briefing he'd received before flying out to take part in the crash investigation. Christ, that seemed like a lifetime ago. "Kandalaksha's special weapons magazine stored TN-1000s, and those things weigh in at about two thousand pounds."

He looked toward the parked twin-engine turboprops shimmering in the heat. "Any of those aircraft could haul a TN-1000 to altitude without even straining."

"And we know Caraco has the pilots," Farrell pointed out. "There're at least four coming from those sites in other states, plus at least one from this field."

Thorn thought about that. "Jesus, Sam. You think they could find five competent pilots who'd be willing to commit suicide like that? Anybody can drive a truck bomb, but how many wackos can pilot a plane?"

"The Japanese didn't have much trouble rounding up a few thousand kamikazes," Farrell pointed out.

"But that was during a global war and from a total 'death before dishonor' warrior culture," Thorn said. "I don't see that here. Ibrahim's a Saudi, but that bastard Wolf was German. And everybody we've tangled with outside of Pechenga has been German, or at least European."

"Maybe they're planning on setting the autopilot,

bundling on a chute, and hopping out before the blast," Helen suggested.

"Doesn't seem likely. If that was me, I'd want to bail out a long, long way from the detonation point." Thorn combed his mind for data. He wasn't a pilot, but he'd had friends who were, and his Delta Force training covered a host of different technologies. "Even on autopilot, you're gonna get some drift—and even a quarter mile would really throw your attack off."

"Not these days," Farrell cut in. He looked somber. "Link GPS into your autopilot, and you could put a bomb within a few meters of where you want it."

"Yeah," Thorn said slowly, running through the logic. Farrell was right. With signals from the GPS satellites as a navigation aid, none of the planes would wander off course. And GPS receivers were now widely available to the general public. He stiffened as the full implications of the available technology became clear. "Christ, you don't even need a pilot! Plug a computer into the autopilot, program in the required waypoints and altitude changes, and you've got an aircraft that can take off on its own—and then make its way straight to the target."

Helen's eyes opened wide. "You're talking about a poor man's cruise missile, Peter."

"I'm afraid so."

Farrell considered that. "Jury-rigged cruise missiles? Maybe." Then he shook his head. "Still a lot of things that could go wrong with that. You get some unexpectedly hairy weather, an engine problem, or maybe an air traffic control call that goes unanswered and you're going to start losing planes. And neither Ibrahim nor Wolf struck me as careless. If they are setting up to pop off five nukes somewhere in the U.S., they'll want some assurance that all five will detonate—on target."

"But they can work around that," Thorn said softly. "Install a communications link and maybe even a TV camera in every plane. That way a pilot sitting safe on the ground can run the thing by remote control if need be. Hell, he could even answer air traffic control challenges."

Farrell chewed that over and then nodded. "That'd be the way to do it all right. Pinpoint accuracy and no human element." His eyes narrowed as he looked out across the runway toward the Caraco hangars and the three turboprops parked outside. "Which do you think is the bomb-carrier here, Pete? Aircraft number one, number two, or number three?"

"Would you assign one pilot to every remote-controlled plane?" Helen asked suddenly, rummaging through Wolf's bloodstained briefcase.

Thorn thought about that for a moment and then shook his head. "Nope. There's really no need to. With the kind of gear they could assemble, one guy should be able to run two or three aircraft without even breathing hard. Plus, with the right radio and microwave links, you could orchestrate the whole strike from one secure, central location."

"So, why do they need five pilots?" she persisted.

Farrell shrugged. "Who knows? Redundancy, maybe."

Thorn stared at Helen more closely. Her fingers were curled around one of the pages they'd found in Wolf's belongings. "What's wrong?"

"Could they fit two more planes in those hangars over there?" she asked tightly, still looking down at the paper.

"Sure. No sweat." Thorn put his hand gently on her shoulder. "What're you thinking?"

She looked up and passed the piece of paper she'd been clutching to him. All the color had drained out of her face. "Caraco doesn't have just one nuke. They don't have just five. I think they've got twenty."

Twenty? Thorn took the printed page from her and studied it again. There were five separate animal code names listed under the heading for Godfrey Field. He'd looked at them before, but he hadn't made the connection. They'd all been focused on the identifiable place names first.

Christ. Five airfields with multiple codes under each one. Twenty code words in all. Twenty targets. Twenty bombs.

It made an ugly sort of sense. They knew Colonel General Serov had sold Ibrahim and his subordinates twenty used Su-24 engines—engines they'd used as a cover for the real cargo. They also knew that Caraco's chief executive had gone to a lot of trouble and expense to set up a secure pipeline to smuggle them into the U.S. So why would Ibrahim settle for reducing five American cities to smoking rubble if he could just as easily obtain the weapons needed to smash twenty?

"Pete?"

Setting his jaw against the knowledge that they were facing an almost unimaginable catastrophe, Thorn passed the page to Farrell. "She's right, Sam. No other scenario makes sense."

Farrell's shoulders slumped. Suddenly he looked like an old man—weary and worn out by years of stress and strain. "So any ideas on when Ibrahim's attack is set to go off?"

Thorn surprised himself by saying, "Yes, I think so."

The answer was there, right in front of his eyes. His subconscious must have been busy assimilating all the data they'd acquired and been fitting it into a coherent pattern. He opened the leather-bound day-timer they'd taken off the body of the late Johann Brandt. "Take a look at this. Notations for every day for the last couple of months. Airline trips from Europe to here and back. Snap visits to these airfields using a Caraco corporate jet. Conferences at Chantilly and Middleburg."

Both Helen and Farrell nodded. They'd paged through the appointment book, too.

"Then we come to June 19. Here's the first crucial notation: 'Primary departs. 1945 hours. Dulles.' "

"So who's this mysterious 'Primary'?" Farrell asked.

"Ibrahim would be my guess. He's the boss," Thorn said. "Our friend, the prince, evidently intends to be well out of the United States by tomorrow evening. Or at least that was the plan before we took out Herr Wolf."

He could see the light dawning in Helen's horrified eyes. "Go ahead, Peter," she said.

Thorn flipped to the next page. "Okay. Then we shift to June 20. 'Corporate jet transfers from Dulles to Godfrey Field at 1800 hours,' " he translated.

"Why do that?" Farrell asked. "Dulles can't be more than fifteen miles from here. Hell, that's less than a two-minute hop by jet!"

"Because these people know Dulles will be inaccessible after the twentieth," Helen said softly. "Either because it's inside the planned blast radius . . . or because the runways will be stacked high with rescue flights after a 150-kiloton bomb takes out D.C."

"Exactly." Thorn showed them the next page, the one for June 21. "This is the last notation in the whole book. '1300 hours. Depart from Godfrey.' There's absolutely nothing written after that—not one damned thing."

He snapped the day-timer shut. "My guess is that's the evac plane for the people coordinating the attack."

Thorn's headache came back with full force, but he pressed on—ignoring the feeling that red-hot pincers were tearing at his skull. "God help us, this bastard Ibrahim plans to detonate twenty nuclear weapons at targets scattered across this entire country. And he's going to do it sometime within the next forty-eight to seventy-two hours."

Planning Cell, Caraco Complex, Chantilly, Virginia

(H MINUS 65)

"Highness?"

Prince Ibrahim al Saud turned away from his contemplation of the latest intelligence reports. "Yes? What is it, Hashemi?"

His chief private secretary looked anxious. He offered a printout. "This just came over one of the news wires, Highness. I thought you would wish to see it immediately."

Ibrahim took it, rapidly skimming the important details.

> Loudoun County, VA—Murder victims discovered in woods near Middleburg. County sheriff's department confirms that a Boy Scout troop on a nature walk reported finding two unidentified corpses—both male, both Caucasian—earlier this afternoon. Crime scene teams have now cordoned off the area. Sources speaking on background claim both men were apparently shot to death at point-blank range. Preliminary descriptions follow. . . .

Ibrahim nodded to himself, studying the descriptions. He was sure that one of the dead men was Reichardt. The other must be McDowell.

Part of the veil of uncertainty Thorn and Gray had cast across his calculations lifted. The two American operatives undoubtedly had whatever documents the German and his aide had been carrying, but that was all. It would not be enough. Before they had died, Reichardt and McDowell had done their work well. The reputations of the American man and woman were hopelessly compromised. It was unlikely their superiors would listen to any of the wild stories they might try to tell.

Beware, a small voice prompted Ibrahim. Beware the sin of pride.

He nodded to himself. It would be best not to take any more chances. Let Richard Garrett handle this matter of murder. He paid the former Commerce Secretary large sums of money. And Garrett could be fed just enough information to make his protests credible. Let him take the lead in further blackening the names of Thorn and Gray in official Washington.

Ibrahim came out of his reverie to find Hashemi still standing close by, nervously watching him.

"Well? What more do you want?" Ibrahim snapped.

"I have assembled the primary operational staff as you instructed," Hashemi replied. "They are waiting for you in the conference room, Highness."

"Very well." Ibrahim noted the beads of sweat forming on his servant's forehead. "And what else troubles you?"

"Perhaps I should fly to Riyadh with the rest of the staff—as planned, Highness," Hashemi suggested quickly. "There is much to prepare—"

"Coward," Ibrahim said, icily cutting off the other man in mid-sentence. "You will remain here—with me. If you fail me, you will remain here permanently—without me. You understand me, Hashemi?"

His secretary nodded hurriedly, bowed, and backed away.

Ibrahim dismissed the matter from his mind. There would be time enough to deal with Hashemi's disloyalty once the Operation was complete. He strode through a nearby door and into the conference room Reichardt had used for planning meetings. Talal and two of his personal security guards followed closely at his back.

The men already crowding the room rose to their feet at his entrance.

Ibrahim wasted no time in pleasantries. These men prided themselves on their professionalism. Let them prove their competence now. "Reichardt and Brandt are dead—apparently at the hands of a pair of rogue American agents. Effective immediately, Captain Talal will take charge of security for this complex. We will go to maximum alert starting now."

He regarded Reichardt's chosen cadre carefully—studying the assembled planners, technicians, and security troops behind a bland expression that masked his true thoughts. How far could he really trust these men? he wondered. They were mercenaries—motivated almost purely by greed. Oh, he knew that Reichardt's Germans were all highly skilled and experts in their assigned fields. But he decided that he would still have welcomed the presence of a few Palestinians from the camps—fanatical, poorly educated, and rash perhaps, but utterly loyal, and absolutely willing to lay down their lives for the greater glory of God and their oppressed people.

He had opted for competence over faith. Perhaps that had been an error.

Ibrahim made a mental note to assign the troops Talal had brought to key points. If his mercenaries showed signs of wavering under pressure, they could always be kept at their posts by force—should that prove necessary.

He continued. "Herr Reichardt's demise does not affect any part of the Operation in any way. The countdown continues. I will assume personal command and remain here— until the planes are launched and we initiate our evacuation."

He paused for a brief moment. Not to allow them to ask questions. Just to give them a moment to absorb his instructions. "Very well. You have your orders. You know your assignments. Carry on."

As they filed out, Ibrahim signaled one of the few non-Europeans in the room, a young, stick-thin, Egyptian-born computer specialist. "Dr. Saleh?"

Saleh scurried over. "Highness?"

"I understand you have completed the attack simulation Herr Reichardt commissioned?"

The Egyptian nodded. "Yes, Highness."

"Show it to me," Ibrahim ordered. It was time for a final look at his master plan.

The computer expert led the way back into the crowded room used by the planning cell. With Ibrahim hovering behind him, he quickly booted up the computer at his desk. The large monitor glowed to life—revealing a digitized satellite display of the United States. It was as though a camera hovered in space several hundred miles above the surface of the earth.

The Egyptian's hands paused over the keyboard. "I am ready, Highness."

Ibrahim nodded. "Begin."

Saleh's hands danced over the keyboard, inputting instructions. A cursor flashed over the eastern seaboard, vanished, and then reappeared as the camera zoomed in. Washington, D.C., and its surrounding suburbs filled the screen.

The Egyptian pushed one final key, activating the computer simulation. "Initiating the attack sequence, Highness."

A thin white line appeared—heading out from Godfrey Field and moving southeast. The camera zoomed in even tighter—now focused tightly on the areas just north and south of the Potomac River. A blinking cross-hairs appeared, centered on the Pentagon. The white line merged with the cross-hairs.

"Detonation," Saleh said calmly.

A fireball appeared on the screen—a roiling cloud of flame that swallowed the Pentagon whole and blossomed out over the Potomac. A shock wave rippled outward, toppling buildings, smashing highway overpasses and bridges, shattering windows—biting deep into Washington, roaring over the Washington Monument, the Lincoln Memorial, the White House, and the Capitol. More graphic overlays appeared on the altered satellite image. Each showed the expected areas of maximum overpressure, heat, fire, wind, and radiation damage.

The screen froze, showing a sea of searing flame as a firestorm spread through the devastated area.

Ibrahim smiled at the screen, imagining the chaos this one weapon would cause. "And the results, Doctor?" he asked calmly.

The Egyptian tapped his chin thoughtfully. "Assuming an airburst height of three hundred meters . . . and taking into account only deaths and severe injuries from blast, heat, and radiation . . ."

"And the results?" Ibrahim asked again, this time in a firmer voice.

Saleh dropped back into reality from his abstract mathematical universe. "Two hundred thousand dead, Highness. With perhaps another two or three hundred thousand seriously injured. Including, of course, the vast majority of America's top political and military leadership."

Ibrahim nodded. Perfect.

"The detonation point for this bomb is unusually low in order to achieve maximum damage against the Pentagon, Highness," the computer specialist commented. "We could achieve even more significant civilian casualties with a higher altitude airburst. One more along the lines of the others—two thousand feet, for example."

"No." Ibrahim shook his head. His first target in Washington was America's military nerve center. Its total destruction was his top priority. Dead American civilians came second. They were a welcome dividend, however. This was not just a surgical strike. He wanted to twist the knife as he struck home.

He leaned closer to the screen. "Continue."

Saleh obeyed.

The monitor cycled through a succession of images—showing nuclear destruction spreading across another nineteen targets spread out across the length and breadth of the United States.

Langley and Fort Meade were vaporized next—taking with them the headquarters of the CIA and the National Security Agency. Then the heart of Fort Bragg—home of the 82nd Airborne Division, the Delta Force, and the JSOC—vanished in the blink of an eye. A fifth bomb destroyed the key areas of Fort Campbell—headquarters of the 101st Air Assault Division and the 160th Special Operations Aviation Regiment. A sixth destroyed the U.S. Central and Special Operations Commands at McDill Air Force Base, near Tampa. A seventh and eighth tore the guts out of the Ranger battalions, mechanized troops, and training units stationed at Georgia's Fort Stewart and Fort Benning.

More bombs detonated—vaporizing the central areas of the U.S. Marine Corps bases at Camps Pendleton and Lejeune. Other weapons slammed into the Air Force bases in Delaware, Idaho, New Mexico, Missouri, Texas, and Washington state—eliminating whole wings of C-5, C-141, and C-17 transports, KC-10 and KC-135 tankers, B-1B and B-2 strategic bombers, F-15 and F-16 fighters, and F-117 Stealth fighter-bombers.

Four more rained down across the vast naval bases at Norfolk and San Diego—the home ports for a large number of America's aircraft carriers and amphibious warships. Many of the ships would be at sea, but crucial support facilities and the personnel needed to man them would be wiped off the face of the earth.

When the dazzling images receded, Ibrahim turned slowly toward Saleh. "So what is your final assessment, Doctor?"

The specialist punched in one last key. His monitor displayed a series of numbers. "At a minimum, I would expect total American military casualties to run close to three hundred thousand dead and critically wounded. Equipment and aircraft losses will run from fifty to seventy percent for each unit we have targeted."

"And the 'collateral damage'?" Ibrahim asked, consciously using the sterile, inhuman jargon adopted by the West during its wars against Arab and Muslim nations.

The Egyptian brought up a new set of numbers. "Since so many of these bases are in or near major areas of habitation, I expect civilian casualties to be far higher—millions dead, with as many more seriously injured.

"Naturally, many of those injured by blast or fire will die in the following days," Saleh continued. "The detonation of even two or three weapons of this magnitude would saturate America's emergency medical services—especially its burn wards. After twenty bombs go off, a great number of those caught by the flames will simply die untreated."

Ibrahim breathed out, still staring at the numbers displayed on the screen. His thrust at America's heart would be even more effective than he'd dared to hope—God be praised.

Every Russian-made nuclear weapon he had purchased at such a dear price was an integral part of the grand design. By striking at U.S. intelligence agencies, he would prevent America from seeing any of its many enemies clearly. By emasculating its commando units and other rapid deployment forces, he would remove its ability to react swiftly to those challenging its parasitic interests—in the Middle East, in the Persian Gulf, in Asia, and all over the world. And by destroying its strategic airlift and amphibious forces, he would cripple America's power to intervene in strength in crises around the globe.

Ibrahim nodded solemnly. It would take the shocked and dazed survivors years to fully rebuild the elite ground forces and sophisticated aircraft and ships his chosen weapons would destroy in a single, devastating millisecond. And by then, it would be far, far too late. Other powers, including those loyal to Islam, and in solidarity with the oppressed Palestinian people, would rush to fill the void left as the United States curled inward on its bleeding wounds.

And the whole course of history—of the centuries-old struggle between the House of Islam and its enemies—would be altered forever. Nothing would ever be the same again.

CHAPTER NINETEEN

ARMS RACE

JUNE 19

**Outside the Caraco Complex,
Chantilly, Virginia**

(H MINUS 57)

The floodlights surrounding the Caraco complex were bright enough to turn night into day—even two hours past midnight.

Lying prone in the tall grass fifty meters away, Colonel Peter Thorn lowered the bulky Russian-made thermal imager they'd bought at a military surplus store several hours before. A quick check of the imager's small display confirmed his earlier supposition. The warehouse-sized building with the antenna-studded roof had to contain Ibrahim's command and control center. This many hours after the end of the normal workday, the other two buildings in the compound were both cool—near ambient temperature. But the third was still warm—with distinct hot spots near the main door and on the roof. There were people awake and hard at work in there.

Satisfied, he laid the thermal imager to one side and picked up a pair of binoculars—scanning slowly back and forth along the well-lit fence line. He fiddled with the focus on the binoculars and whistled softly. "They've got cameras covering every close approach to that perimeter. And I'd swear there are some power leads running up that fence."

Helen Gray turned her head toward him. "You think it's hot?"

"Not yet," he said. "But I bet they can throw a few thousand volts through it on command."

"Lovely. Just lovely," she muttered. "So we're looking at a complete security network—an electric fence, cameras, armed guards, and probably motion sensors, too."

Thorn nodded. "Nobody said this would be easy."

Sam Farrell spoke up. "As I recall, Pete, I said this would be impossible, crazy, illegal, and probably fatal."

Thorn grinned back at him, feeling somehow more cheerful than he had for weeks. The prospect of action, of actually striking back at a physical enemy, was acting as a tonic. "Geez, Sam! Somebody should really get you to stop mincing your words."

"Let's take what we have to the FBI and let them run with it!" Farrell argued heatedly. He glanced toward Helen. "Let the HRT handle any raid on this place. They've got the manpower, the gear . . . and the legal right!"

Helen shook her head. "What we have, Sam, is a lot of supposition and guesswork—some of it based on evidence we took off two dead men. Men who were killed in very suspicious circumstances."

Thorn nodded. They'd heard the first news reports on the bodies found near Middleburg while driving back from Leesburg. Nobody from the FBI was saying anything publicly yet, but they knew the Bureau had to be going crazy trying to figure out how its Deputy Assistant Director heading the International Relations Branch had wound up dead in the rural Virginia woods—right beside the corpse of Caraco's chief of European security.

Helen frowned. "If we walk into the Hoover Building with what we've got now, I guarantee you the first thing they'll do is handcuff us to the nearest solid object and start piling up charges. By the time we get anybody high-ranking enough to pay attention to our story—"

"Those nukes will be detonating left and right," Thorn finished for her.

Farrell still looked troubled. "I just don't like going off the reservation like this. Acting this far outside the law goes against the grain."

Hell, Thorn thought, it bothers me, too.

But he honestly couldn't see any other way through the tangle they were in. Not only didn't he believe official Washington could react fast enough to stop Ibrahim, he wasn't sure who they could really trust with their story. If Caraco had one mole inside the Hoover Building, why not two?

Even if McDowell had been the only traitor feeding information to Wolf and Ibrahim, Caraco's chief executive had already demonstrated the power he could exert over the capital's political establishment. What federal official with any brains or sense was going to take on the head of a multibillion-dollar corporation who also happened to be a member of the Saudi royal family with close ties to the White House? Especially on the unsupported testimony of a rogue FBI agent and a former Delta Force officer now slated for forcible retirement—both of whom were wanted on a variety of charges ranging from insubordination to kidnapping and murder?

Thorn snorted. That was an easy question. *No one.* Certainly not in time to make any difference.

He and Helen had also ruled out contacting the media. It would take the press too much time to get off its collective ass and start digging.

Besides, orchestrating a high-profile official or media investigation now would probably only spook Ibrahim into striking ahead of his planned schedule. The same argument ruled out going after the Godfrey Field hangars. The Saudi might not have all twenty bombs in place yet, but even one 150-kiloton nuke going off inside the U.S. would represent an unimaginable catastrophe. And it was highly likely that the Caraco chief had far more than one of his Russian-made weapons prepped and ready to go.

No, Thorn thought coldly, the only chance they had was to get inside that compound and find some way to stop Ibrahim from launching his attack themselves. He was realistic enough to know just how long the odds were against that outcome.

And so was Farrell.

But the retired general was also canny enough to run through their other alternatives and calculate the even longer odds that one of them might pay off.

Farrell stared back and forth from Thorn's face to Helen's, plainly looking for a sign, any sign, that he'd made some impression on them. Finally, he shook his head angrily. "Oh, shit, Pete. If I can't stop you two from trying to kill yourselves, I guess I might as well try to help you do this right. What's your plan? Hit the antennas on that roof and knock out their communications?"

"No, sir." Thorn shook his head. "We'd have to take down all their phone and data lines at the same time . . . and that's impossible. Destroying the antennas would only force Ibrahim to launch his planes on full autopilot. So maybe only eighteen or nineteen weapons hit their targets—instead of the full twenty. That's not much better."

"It sure as hell isn't," Farrell said. He chewed his lower lip. "You think you have to go all the way inside?"

Helen answered for him. "I'm afraid so." She sighed. "There's got to be a command center or a control center somewhere in that building. If we take that and hold it, we should be able to do something to stop Ibrahim."

Farrell snorted. "That's a hell of a lot of 'ifs,' 'somewheres,' and 'somethings,' Helen." He looked back at Thorn. "What makes you think taking out this son of a bitch's headquarters is going to matter? Those aircraft and weapons will still be out there—loaded and ready to roll."

"Timing," Thorn said quietly. "It all comes down to timing. Whether we go after Ibrahim personally or settle for holding the command center, we have to hit him before he releases the arming codes to his dispersal fields."

Like their American counterparts, Russian nuclear weapons could not be armed without the proper codes. Ibrahim must have obtained the necessary codes from somebody inside Russia's Twelfth Main Directorate—the military agency responsible for the manufacture, testing, servicing, and stockpiling of nuclear weapons for the Russian armed forces. But there was no reason for him to turn that information over to his subordinates until almost the very last minute. In fact, there were a great many reasons for him to hold those codes close to his chest as long as possible. Chief among them was the fact that it would prevent any of his people from going off half-cocked—or from absconding with one or more of the enormously valuable weapons. There were a great many dictatorships that would pay millions to get their hands on one usable nuclear bomb.

Farrell nodded slowly. "Okay, that makes sense." He glanced at the luminous dial on his watch. "It's after two A.M. now. You still confident about our estimate for Ibrahim's attack schedule, Pete?"

"Yes, sir," Thorn said flatly.

The three of them had hashed that out in more detail on the way back from Godfrey Field. The inside parameter for an attack was the planned transfer of the Caraco executive jet from Dulles to Godfrey—1800 hours on the twentieth. The outside parameter was 1300 hours on the twenty-first— the time the jet was scheduled to depart. That was still a big window, so they'd managed to narrow it down even further.

Ibrahim was unlikely to go for a night attack. Whether his targets were cities or military bases, they were always busier and more crowded in daylight. Since there were always more small private planes in the air after the sun rose, a daylight attack also gave his improvised cruise missiles a far better chance of making it all the way to their targets without being challenged. Given the three-hour time difference across the continental United States, the earliest Ibrahim would strike was somewhere around ten or eleven in the morning—East Coast time—on June 21.

"Which means you want to go in . . . when?" Farrell asked.

Thorn didn't hesitate. He'd been giving that a lot of thought. "Around one or two A.M. two days from now—on the twenty-first."

"That's cutting it kind of fine, Peter," Helen warned.

He nodded. "Yeah. But there's no way we can shave much off that. We need at least a day to find as much gear as we can. And it'll take us the better part of another day to prep and come up with a workable plan. The way I see it that takes us all the way up to late on the twentieth or very, very early on the twenty-first."

Farrell arched an eyebrow. "You actually want equipment

and time to prep?" He snorted. "Hell, Pete, I was sure you and Helen were going to try to do this armed with a couple of Swiss Army knives, a flashlight, and a baseball bat. You must be getting soft."

Thorn smiled wryly at his old boss. That was more like the Sam Farrell he knew. "We're also going to need another rental car. There's no way we can get all the gear we've got to buy in one pass. I'm afraid your credit cards are going to take another beating, Sam."

"At this point, money's the least of my problems," Farrell muttered.

"I still don't see how we're going to get through that perimeter fence without tripping every alarm they've got," Helen said quietly, staying focused on the matter at hand. "And if they see us coming, we're screwed."

"True. Getting through the fence is our first big problem." Thorn lifted the binoculars again. He studied the fence for a moment longer, then shifted his focus—intently studying the tall oak and pine trees that had been left standing outside the compound to preserve something of the area's once-rural feel. "So maybe we don't go *through* the fence . . ."

The White House

(H MINUS 47)

Richard Garrett tracked his chosen prey to a table in the White House mess.

He'd used his pass to get by the Secret Service guards at the main entrance. The White House pass, left over from his days in the administration and never revoked, was one of his prized possessions. His ability to hobnob at will with top executive branch officials had added hundreds of thousands of dollars to his annual income during his days as a lobbyist-for-hire. Now that he represented Caraco's interests full-time, it generated hundreds of thousands of dollars more in annual bonuses from Prince Ibrahim al Saud.

Garrett took the empty chair across from John Preston, the President's Chief of Staff. "John, you've got a problem. A big problem."

Caught off guard, Preston nearly choked on a mouthful of soup and hurriedly daubed at his mouth with a napkin. "Jesus, Dick, I'm eating my lunch here! Can't this wait until later in the day?"

"No, it can't."

Preston sighed. "I assume this is about the dead guy out in the woods. Hans Wolf or something like that?"

"*Heinrich* Wolf," Garrett corrected icily. "Who just happens to have been one of the top-ranking executives of the corporation I represent."

"Sorry." Preston set the crumpled cloth napkin to one side. "I suppose you know they've identified the other body as a top-ranking FBI administrator."

Garrett nodded. Ibrahim had briefed him on that development before asking him to go to the White House. He assumed the Saudi prince had sources inside the FBI or the Loudoun County sheriff's department.

"Then frankly, Dick, I'm not sure what more I can tell you," Preston said. He arched an eyebrow. "Fact is, I hear the FBI wants to find out just what on earth your man was doing with McDowell—before they both got shot, I mean."

Garrett nodded. "That's understandable. And I plan to talk to them." He leaned forward. "It's like this, John. Right after that Bureau fuck-up down in Galveston, I got a pretty strange call from a General Samuel B. Farrell."

"Farrell?" Preston looked vague. "Don't know him."

"Used to head the Joint Special Operations Command," Garrett explained. "He retired a year or so ago. Before your time."

Preston nodded. After a short stint as a Cabinet deputy secretary during the administration's first term, he'd gone home to Kentucky to tend the family business. He'd only surfaced as the new White House Chief of Staff after several of the other contenders tore each other to ribbons fighting over the job—mostly by leaking damaging revelations about their rivals to the press. His chief qualification for the post seemed to be that no one had thought enough of him to regard him as a serious contender.

Most Washington observers thought he'd be chewed up, spit out, and sent packing in short order.

Garrett suspected they were wrong. He'd known Preston and his family for a long time. He'd also seen the other man ride out the President's frequent temper tantrums unfazed. Never underestimate the staying power of a good punching bag, he thought.

"Anyway," the Caraco lobbyist continued, "this retired general came to us with a really bizarre claim . . ." He rapidly sketched Farrell's allegations that Caraco employees were involved in a deadly smuggling ring.

When he was through, Preston commented, "That sounds exactly like the story that got the FBI all hot and bothered down in Galveston."

"It *is* the same damned story," Garrett growled. "That's why Prince Ibrahim asked Wolf to find out who was spoon-feeding the general this crap. Turns out it was a couple of real loony-toon types—a Colonel Thorn and an FBI agent named Gray. You ever heard of them?"

This time Preston nodded slowly. "I've seen a few pieces of paper cross my desk lately," he admitted cautiously.

"Like a pair of FBI-issued arrest warrants?"

The chief of staff smiled thinly. "You do know a lot of things, Dick."

Garrett smiled right back. "That's why people pay me so well, John."

"So what does this have to do with your man Wolf and this FBI guy, McDowell?" Preston asked.

"McDowell was Special Agent Helen Gray's superior officer," Garrett said flatly. "We believe that Herr Wolf contacted him about Farrell, Thorn, and Gray—and arranged to meet him. And then something must have gone wrong."

"Something?"

Garrett nodded. "Thorn and Gray, to be precise. We believe they murdered both Heinrich Wolf and Deputy Assistant Director McDowell—probably as part of some crazed, psychotic attempt to foil this nonexistent smuggling conspiracy they've dreamed up."

Preston shook his head. "That's a real stretch, Dick. I've read the reports on Thorn and Gray. The FBI is sure they're still on the run somewhere in Germany."

"Then the Bureau has its collective head up its collective ass." Garrett scowled. "Unless you can think of some other pair of trained killers with a grudge against both Caraco and the FBI, I suggest you instruct Director Leiter to get off his own rear end and start looking for those two closer to home."

Preston looked back levelly at him. "I'm guessing there's an 'or else' attached to that sentence."

Garrett spread his hands. "This is a very serious matter, John. And Prince Ibrahim is not pleased by the slapdash way it's been handled so far. You tell the FBI they've got just forty-eight hours to nail Thorn and Gray, or we're going public with our suspicions. I really don't think the Director wants the kind of bad press we can generate with a story

bout a deranged Army colonel and his FBI girlfriend run-
ing wild inside the U.S."

Preston winced. "I'll talk to Leiter. If Thorn and Gray are
ack home, we'll find them."

"You've got forty-eight hours," Garrett reminded him, al-
eady getting up to go. "After that all hell's going to break
oose."

Planning Cell, Caraco Complex,
Chantilly, Virginia

(H MINUS 40)

Prince Ibrahim al Saud stared down at the blank screen on
Reichardt's laptop computer. He looked up. "What does this
mean?"

Saleh, his computer wizard, swallowed hard. "The German protected his files with an unusually sophisticated security program, Highness. I was able to penetrate one
level—but an auto-destruct sequence was triggered on the
second—"

"And now the files are gone," Ibrahim interrupted.

"Yes, Highness." The Egyptian cleared his throat. "There
are methods for recovering data in such instances. With
enough time, I could—"

Ibrahim glared at him. "Get out."

Saleh fled.

Ibrahim stared down at the maddening little machine. For
a split second he had the urge to toss it against the nearest

wall. The urge receded. Saleh was right. Something might yet be recovered.

But not in time.

The computer had included all of Reichardt's information on the two American agents who had caused them so much trouble—including the FBI and U.S. Army dossiers and photographs the German had obtained from the traitor McDowell. All hard copies had already been destroyed as part of the ex-Stasi officer's strict security regimen.

The system Reichardt had established was admirably efficient—if typically rigid. As little as possible about the Operation was committed to paper. For those few documents deemed essential, shredders were placed at strategic locations throughout the complex. The waste was collected twice a day and burned.

Ibrahim approved of the German's security system—in theory. In practice, it was proving far less satisfactory.

Since Reichardt had been in charge of hunting down the two Americans—Thorn and Gray—he alone had kept permanent records on them. And now all those records were gone—wiped into some form of electronic gibberish. Which meant he would have to rely on the FBI to hunt them down for him. Unless, of course, the Americans came to him . . .

"Captain Talal," Ibrahim snapped.

The former Saudi officer moved closer. "Highness?"

"Issue another alert to all the airfields. Warn them that the two Americans, and possibly this General Farrell, may make some further attempt to disrupt the Operation. They may attempt to destroy some of our aircraft or to gather additional evidence. Include the descriptions I gave you earlier in your alert message."

Ibrahim had racked his brains for those descriptions. Farrell's had been the easiest of all. They'd actually met. But

he'd only seen photos of the other two briefly—and only
black-and-white photos at that.

"Yes, Highness."

"I also want security tightened here." Ibrahim closed
Reichardt's laptop with one hand—shutting off the meaningless, blinking C:\ prompt that seemed to mock him.

He looked up and began snapping out his orders. "Deploy
a patrol around this building—beginning at sunset. And I
want our guard force strengthened. Most of Reichardt's people have East German military or secret police training.
Issue them with sidearms for use in an emergency."

"Should I electrify the fence, Highness?" Talal asked.

"Not yet." Ibrahim smiled mirthlessly. "I might find that
difficult to explain to our American employees in the rest of
the complex. The fence can wait for another day."

To clear the compound of all nonessential personnel on
the Operation's crucial final day, the Saudi prince had
arranged a series of motivational seminars at one of Washington's finer hotels. All the region's legitimate Caraco employees were expected to attend. Call it a special kind of
severance package, he thought coldly.

When Talal had gone, he turned his gaze back on Reichardt's computer. Who could say how much potentially damaging information was still hidden deep in its recesses? Certainly
the German had known far too much about Ibrahim himself,
the terrorist organizations he funded, and his methods. Ibrahim
made a note to take the machine with him when they evacu-
ated this facility. He would keep it safely in his grasp until
Saleh or some other expert pried all its secrets loose.

He turned away and stalked through a gray, unmarked fire
door into the room just beyond the planning cell.

The lights in the Operation's control center were kept
dim—to avoid any interfering glare on the multiple television and computer monitors that were placed strategically

around the room. Two rows of four aircraft control consoles occupied most of the space, but communications equipment took up one entire wall, and metal workbenches filled nearly all of another. The benches were littered with tools, electronic components, and circuit diagrams.

Ibrahim noticed that the screens on one of the control consoles were dark. He frowned and moved up behind the two technicians who were crouched peering into an open panel in the back. They were speaking softly to each other in German—probably debating some technical point.

"What is going on here?" he asked sharply. "Why wasn't I notified of this equipment malfunction?"

Startled, both men spun around and then hurriedly straightened up.

"I'm sorry, sir, but this just happened. A video board failed," the senior technician answered quickly. "We've identified the problem and we expect to have the unit back up in a few minutes at most."

"This equipment is all new, sir," the younger man added. Even the control center's dim lights gleamed off the German's smooth-shaven head. A small gold loop piercing his left eyebrow waggled when he spoke. "The components are still burning in. These 'infant mortality' cases are quite common at this stage. But we'll sort them out."

Ibrahim kept his temper under control. With Reichardt dead, he had to take up the reins—and that included tolerating grubby, dirty-fingered mechanics like these.

"The technical details do not interest me, gentlemen," he ground out angrily. "The fact that a piece of equipment failed does. I expect to be informed instantly of such an event in the future. Is that clear?"

Both technicians nodded rapidly.

"Very well, then. Finish your repairs."

Ibrahim turned away, focusing his attention on one of the working aircraft control consoles. It was built around two monitors—one a television, the other a color computer display. The television screen was blank. So was the computer monitor. In use, the TV would show the pictures taken by one of the cameras his crews had mounted on each attack plane. The computer screen would display the position, altitude, speed, fuel status, and other relevant flight data of up to four separate aircraft.

Ibrahim ran his eyes over the rest of the console. A custom-designed electronics panel augmented a standard computer keyboard. The panel held UHF radio controls, jacks where headsets could be plugged in, basic flight instruments, and a series of selector switches. A joystick, black cable coiled around it, perched on top of the console.

He nodded, satisfied by what he saw. These consoles were for use only in an unforeseen emergency. Barring that, his aircraft would fly to their targets entirely on their own—using the preset flight plans loaded into each autopilot. Once they were airborne, nothing could stop him from plunging the United States into a cleansing nuclear fire.

JUNE 20

Super 6 Motor Lodge, Near Falls Church, Virginia

(H MINUS 22)

Helen Gray finished laying out the first wave of their newly purchased equipment and stood back to look it over. The gear completely covered one of the room's two queen-size beds. Acquiring it had taken several trips and a sizable chunk of their cash reserves.

The big-ticket items they'd picked up had come from one of northern Virginia's police supply stores. To get them, she'd had to show her FBI credentials and fill out a form—but that piece of paper should take several days to make its way far enough up the official ladder to set off alarms. She was sure the store owner had been surprised when she'd plunked down close to three thousand dollars in cash, but nobody questioned the FBI too closely.

Helen moved closer to the bed and hefted the heavy tactical assault body armor she'd bought. These bulky Kevlar vests had been among the most critical pieces of gear on their wish list. No matter how she and Peter got inside the Caraco compound, they were going to be heavily outnumbered. Armor tough enough to shake off pistol and light rifle rounds might give them at least a fighting chance to last long enough to do some good.

She put the assault vests back down and moved on to unwrap the radios she'd purchased at the same store. They were police-issue, two-way "vox," or voice-activated, sets. Each weighed about a pound or so and came with a headset. She installed the batteries and then adjusted all three radios to a common frequency.

A military surplus store had supplied the web gear and rucksacks they would need to carry everything they were taking in with them. The same place had also sold them a tube of black camouflage grease paint.

The packs of firecrackers next to the web gear had come courtesy of one of the Fourth of July fireworks booths already springing up on what seemed like every open street corner.

Helen put the firecrackers down as the door swung open and Peter Thorn came in, weighed down by shopping bags.

"Success," he announced. "I put a couple of hundred miles on the car, and I had to run through two hardware stores, an autobody shop, a gun store, a chemical supply house, a Radio Shack, and a building supplies place—but I got everything."

"Any trouble?"

Peter shook his head. "Nope. I only had to show my handy-dandy Chris Carlson armed forces ID two times. Once at the chemical supply place and the second time when I picked up the Primacord and detonators from the building supply store."

"Nobody asked what you wanted those for?" Helen asked.

"Sure," Peter said. "I told 'em I wanted to clear some stumps off a piece of property I'd just bought. No muss, no fuss."

"*And* you paid cash?" she finished for him.

Peter grinned. "Yeah. And I paid cash." He set one bag carefully apart from the others and in a corner of the room. "That one's got the nitric acid in it."

Helen nodded.

He started unloading the rest of his purchases, building a pile on the other bed: plastic pipe sections and caps, glue, duct tape, a sack of nails, black powder, a container of the putty auto body shops used to repair dents, and other ingredients.

When Peter was done, he started sorting them into the order in which he would need them. He picked up the auto body putty and frowned. "There's going to be one hell of a stink when I start mixing this stuff up. Let's hope the bathroom exhaust fan can handle it."

Helen nodded. The resiny putty, the black powder, and a few other common household chemicals could be combined to make a low-grade equivalent of C4 plastic explosive. But it was a dangerous process—one that required precise measurement and timing. It was also a process that was notoriously hard on the olfactory nerves.

She caught the pair of tiny digital cooking timers he tossed her and laid them beside the firecrackers and some small lengths of tungsten filament. "Houston, we have liftoff," she murmured to herself.

Peter disappeared into the bathroom with the bulk of his purchases.

Helen was just finishing her preparations when Sam Farrell returned from his own various expeditions. His arms were full, and she had to go back to the car and help him carry in the rest of his plunder.

Farrell had drawn the best part of the shopping list—at least as far as she was concerned. He'd bought the extra weapons and ammunition they would need for the assault. While he'd joked about "pulling rank" to get the job, the plain truth was that neither of them could have done it. To buy firearms you needed to show a driver's license and other forms of ID. Their phony armed forces badges wouldn't have cut it. There was also the fact that some of the more expensive purchases could only be made by credit card.

Swiftly, efficiently, with the expertise of people trained to use them, Helen and Farrell unwrapped and examined three Winchester 1300 Defender pump-action, 12-gauge shotguns. The general had also picked up bandoliers, speedloaders, and two hundred rounds of shotgun ammunition—plus more ammo for his Beretta and McDowell's SIG-Sauer P228.

The shotgun ammo came in five-round boxes. Most of it

was triple-ought, three-inch magnum loads holding nine pellets the size of pistol bullets, but there were also several boxes of solid slugs and sabot.

The solid slugs were just that—one lead round filling the entire shotgun shell. They were terribly inaccurate when fired from an unrifled barrel, but they made very good "door-breakers."

The Winchester sabot rounds were more exotic. Each shell carried a smaller, finned projectile. Using them allowed a shotgun to be fired accurately at a distant target—and with enough punch to go through a steel door.

They'd almost finished when Peter emerged from the bathroom in a cloud of noxious vapor.

Farrell coughed. "Any problems?"

"Aside from my stinging eyes?" Peter shook his head. "The stuff's curing now in the tub." He took in the arrayed weapons with a satisfied smile—a smile that grew even broader when he saw the aluminum suitcase Farrell had set beside the bed. A small, embossed plate above the handle read "Mossberg."

"I'll be damned, Sam, you actually found one," he said.

"Had to, didn't I?" Farrell countered. "This whole thing would have been off otherwise."

Peter nodded. "True."

"I called eight places before I found one in stock, and even then I had to drive all the way out to Annapolis to get it," Farrell said with some satisfaction.

"A gun store in Annapolis?" Helen asked.

"A boating store." Farrell released the catches on the front and opened the case. A Mossberg 590 shotgun nestled inside, securely seated against dark gray foam. The stainless steel barrel had a Day-Glo orange plastic cylinder attached. The case also contained two boxes of special ammunition, three bright orange packages marked "Spectra line, 360-

pound test," two large, line-carrying plastic heads designed to float on water, and two arrow-shaped heads intended to carry a line longer distances.

"Say hello to the Mossberg line launcher conversion kit," he said. "I paid extra to have them throw in the shotgun."

Peter stared down at the Day-Glo orange cylinder. "Black electrical tape," he said. "We've got to wrap that thing in tape."

Farrell nodded. He plucked a grappling hook out of another bag. "I also picked this up at a sporting goods store."

"Perfect."

"There's just one problem, Pete. Somehow you've got to fit this," Farrell said as he tapped the grappling hook, "onto this." He held up one of the narrow, arrow-shaped distance heads.

Peter's boyish grin crept back onto his face. "Not a problem, Sam." He rummaged around in the pile of equipment he'd bought. He turned around. "Welcome to Thorn Construction, Incorporated."

Helen and Farrell both stared at the small welding torch and goggles in his hand.

"Jesus, Pete," Farrell said finally. "Louisa's going to be so glad I gave you all our savings. That'll sure come in handy around the kitchen."

Helen hid a smile.

"French toast in one point five seconds," Peter said matter-of-factly. He put the welding torch down. "Any luck on the night-vision gear?"

"Yeah," Farrell said, still shaking his head. He pulled two large boxes out of another bag. "I found these in the first sporting goods store I went in. And every store after that. Apparently almost everyone has this model in stock."

Helen flipped open one of the boxes and lifted out a clumsy-looking assembly that seemed like something out of a Rube Goldberg nightmare. Two eyepieces were connected to a rectangular case and then fed into a single long lens. There were two straps to hold the whole assembly in place. One strap went around the wearer's head while the other ran across the wearer's chin. A heavy battery case in the back offered some counterbalance. Wires connected every component. It would have been comical if she hadn't known how useful something like this could be. She looked up. "Russian-made?"

Farrell nodded. "They're second-generation light intensifiers, but they're not surplus. They're brand-new, with a one-year warranty."

"How much?" she asked.

"Seven hundred each." Farrell shrugged. "One of the places had some Western-made imagers. They were nicer, lighter, and clearer, but they were also twenty-five hundred bucks a pop. My Visa card has overdraft protection, but that kind of tag would have given it vapor lock."

Helen nodded her understanding. Counting the credit card bills that would eventually come due, they'd already spent more than ten thousand dollars of Farrell's money. Obtaining additional funds would require cashing in some of his investments—and that would take time they didn't have.

"You want to check them out now?" Peter asked.

"Let's do it." She adjusted the straps, slipped the Russian-made night-vision gear over her head, and clicked the battery switch.

Farrell killed the lights.

Helen fumbled for the focus knob, adjusting the intensifiers for a wide field of view. The familiar pale green image was grainier than that produced by the more sophisticated gear she'd trained with, but it was serviceable.

The intensifiers amplified every bit of reflected light in the hotel room—showing detail that would have been shadowed even in normal illumination. She swung toward the window and the gain-control feature cut in. The sunlight showing through a crack in the drapes would have been blinding if it hadn't been automatically stepped down by the device.

Helen turned her head rapidly—first one way and then the other. The Russian-made intensifiers were heavier than the American-designed, third-generation AN PVS-7Bs she'd trained with. She adjusted the field of view, narrowing the angle and providing greater magnification.

At last, satisfied, she slipped them off.

Farrell flipped the lights back on.

Helen stared at the gear piled high on both beds. Their equipment wasn't as compact or as modern as that supplied to the HRT or the Delta Force—but it should work.

Their real problem wasn't an equipment shortage—it was the lack of information.

She frowned. Good intelligence was the key to victory. That was how both the HRT and Delta trained. Comprehensive research could eliminate uncertainties. Meticulous planning could compensate for inferior numbers. And exhaustive rehearsal could let a team hit its objective and escape without a scratch.

But what did she and Peter have?

Nothing. No building blueprints. No accurate assessment of the enemy's strength or security arrangements. Not even any sure way to stop Ibrahim's plan from unfolding.

Christ, Helen thought, we're trusting almost entirely to luck. She fought down the first strands of despair. She had Peter. And Peter had her. And that would have to be good enough.

Berkeley County Airport, Outside Charleston, South Carolina

(H MINUS 12)

Dieter Krauss took one last look at the clear, star-studded sky and went back inside the hangar. He mopped at his forehead and neck with a handkerchief. Even this close to midnight, the Southern heat and humidity were almost unbearable.

"Everything is in order?" his senior technician asked.

Krauss nodded abruptly. The warning from Chantilly hadn't caught him completely off guard. He'd posted half his security detail in concealed positions overlooking the fence around their three hangars. He would be ready if the American agents who had his employer in such a panic tried to infiltrate the field.

He ran his eyes over the two twin-engine turboprops parked wingtip to wingtip inside this hangar. "The weapons are loaded?"

The senior technician nodded. "They are, sir."

"And the evacuation plane?"

"Standing by, Herr Krauss. We can be airborne five minutes after the last strike aircraft reaches altitude."

Krauss nodded. The plan called for them to fly straight out into the Atlantic. Once the bombs went off, their aircraft would make an "emergency divert" landing in the Bahamas, refuel, and continue south. Once they arrived in Mexico, he and his team would receive their final payments and disperse. The units stationed at other fields would be flying to other destinations in either Mexico or Canada. All were confident that no one would track them—not in the almost unimaginable chaos that would follow the simultaneous detonation of twenty nuclear weapons.

"Herr Krauss!"

The German looked toward the door to his office—a small room in the corner of the hangar. One of his subordinates stood in the door frame, waving him over.

"What is it?" he shouted.

"A signal from Chantilly, sir."

Krauss crossed the hangar in seconds and tore the fax out of his machine.

WARNING ORDER

From: Operations Control
To: All Stations

Message — The Operation proceeds as planned. Arming codes and target coordinates will follow as per schedule. Stand by.

Krauss nodded to himself. As a final security measure, Reichardt had decreed that none of the teams readying the strike aircraft would be given the arming codes or their target coordinates until an hour before the first planes took off. Once Chantilly released the data, it would take only minutes for his technicians to input each set into the appropriate aircraft.

He read the message over again. It was straightforward and to the point. Perhaps this Arab who had replaced Reichardt would do after all.

The Operation was in its final hours—and now nothing could stop it.

CHAPTER TWENTY

DEAD RUN

JUNE 21

Outside the Caraco Complex, Chantilly, Virginia

(H MINUS 9)

His face and forehead blackened with camouflage grease paint, Colonel Peter Thorn led the way through a thin patch of forest toward the perimeter fence of Caraco's Chantilly office complex. They were coming in from the back side— away from the road—cutting through ground left wild as a buffer between the corporation's Washington-area facility and the buildings belonging to its nearest neighbor—a prominent consumer electronics firm.

Fifty meters or so from the fence, he glanced over his shoulder.

Helen Gray followed silently in his wake. Only her eyes gleamed in a face daubed with the same black camouflage paint. Like him, she was heavily laden with weapons and a bulging rucksack containing her share of their hurriedly improvised assault equipment.

He started moving again. Crickets chirped nearby and then fell silent—momentarily hushed by the whispering passage of their feet through the grass and underbrush. An owl hooted mournfully somewhere off in the distance.

A few meters from the cleared area surrounding the fence, Thorn stopped at the foot of a towering oak tree and looked up through the tangle of broad, gnarled branches and leaves. Then he turned toward the brightly lit Caraco compound—measuring angles and distances by eye.

He nodded to Helen.

"Delta Two to Delta Three. Delta One beginning ascent." Her hushed voice ghosted through his headset, reporting their position and status to Farrell. The retired general was hidden among the trees on the other side of the compound—keeping an eye on the main gate.

Thorn flipped up his night-vision gear. This close to the edge of the compound he had enough light—and he needed the depth perception denied by the Russian-made light intensifier's single lens.

Moving rapidly, he unslung his Winchester shotgun and rucksack, clipped a hacksaw onto his web gear, and then tugged on a pair of close-fitting, heavy leather work gloves. Knee pads and shin protectors completed the outfit. He was set.

"Peter," Helen whispered in his ear.

Thorn turned. "What?"

"If you even think of whistling 'I'm a lumberjack, and I'm okay,' this whole mission's off," she warned.

He grinned, then swung back, grabbed one of the large, thick branches just above his head, and levered himself up and into the oak. He climbed higher, moving from one limb to another—but always staying close to the trunk and well inside the concealing canopy of leaves.

Thorn stopped about halfway up. Going higher was impractical. The boughs were clustered closer together—barring easy passage. They were also narrower and less likely to support his weight. He looked down. He was roughly twenty-five feet off the ground. Good enough.

Slowly he edged further out from the tree trunk, gingerly testing each step to make sure the limb he was standing on could take his weight without snapping. To transfer some of the load, he wrapped his left hand tight around a higher branch and pulled himself partway up.

Two steps. Three steps. The bough swayed suddenly, creaking as it sagged toward the ground. Thorn froze. Far enough, he thought—inching backward ever so slightly.

He was facing the Caraco compound—about ten meters from the fence. Beyond the fence, a cleared strip of close-cropped grass soon gave way to a half-filled parking lot. The square, antenna-topped building they believed contained Ibrahim's command and control center rose just beyond that—roughly sixty meters in from the fence. Leaves and the slender twigs branching off from other boughs obscured much of his view.

Time to make a nice, discreet hole, Thorn thought.

Still balancing himself with his left hand, he carefully unclipped the hacksaw from his web gear. He paused and whispered, "Delta Two, am I clear?"

Helen's equally quiet reply crackled through the headset. "Wait one. Two-man patrol coming down the fence now."

Thorn stood motionless, every sense straining. There. He heard them now—the clink of metal on metal, the muffled sound of boots tromping across grass, a quick mutter in guttural German. From his vantage point he caught one quick glimpse of the guards as they passed by, checking the fence for any signs of tampering.

One side of his mouth quirked upward. Both men in that patrol were carrying what looked an awful lot like H&K MP5 submachine guns slung over their shoulders. They were also wearing body armor. These guys sure as hell weren't the usual corporate rent-a-cops working for minimum wage and the chance to wear a fancy uniform.

"You're clear, Delta One," Helen said. "They've turned the corner and are moving away. We should have another fifteen minutes before they make the next circuit."

Without waiting any further, Thorn started in—sawing rapidly away at the tree limbs that blocked his view of the headquarters building. Leaves and slender pieces of branch spun away into the shadows below. He was taking a calculated risk—betting that none of the debris would drift far enough to land within view of the TV cameras monitoring the fence.

More narrow boughs felt the hacksaw's sharp-edged bite and spiraled away toward the ground below. When he'd cleared a rough two- by three-foot oval in the foliage, he stopped cutting and clipped the saw back onto his web gear.

Thorn reversed course, climbing down by the same route he'd taken coming up. He crouched on the lowest and largest branch and leaned outward. "I'm set. You ready?"

In answer, she reached up and handed him the Mossberg 590 shotgun they'd converted into a line launcher. He slung it carefully over his shoulder, feeling the points of the grappling hook he'd welded on dig into his back.

Thorn looked back up toward the top of the tree, calculating how long it would take him to get there and get set. He glanced down at Helen, held up three fingers, and saw her repeat the signal.

Her voice came over the radio again, issuing instructions to Sam Farrell. "Delta Three, this is Two. Set your timer for three minutes on my mark."

Thorn saw the second hand sweep through the number twelve on his faintly luminous watch face.

"Mark."

"Got it," Farrell's laconic voice replied. "Timer set. I'm backing off."

Climbing back to his chosen perch was a little more difficult this time—mostly because he had to avoid snagging the Mossberg or any of its attachments. Once in the right spot, he settled carefully into position—straddling a thick bough with both legs, his back firmly planted against the oak tree's trunk.

Thorn pulled the converted shotgun off his shoulder and carefully sighted down the length of the barrel. His eyes narrowed. A tiny droplet of sweat rolled down his forehead. He shook it off impatiently.

He didn't need anyone else to tell him how crazy this was—in every detail. The Mossberg line launcher kit was designed to fire precisely shaped flotation or distance heads. With the completely unaerodynamic, six-pronged grappling hook attached, its maximum range and the trajectory would both be wildly imprecise—at a time when precision was at an absolute premium.

If he fired just a fraction of an inch too far up or down, or left or right, the grappling hook and the line it carried would slam through the tangle of the surrounding foliage and veer completely off course. If his shot fell short or the grapple failed to bite on target, a couple hundred feet of super-strong line was going to fall right over the perimeter fence—triggering every alarm system in the compound.

And millions of people would die when Ibrahim's strike aircraft reached their chosen targets unmolested and undetected.

Plus, he couldn't be absolutely sure just *how* his improvised attachment would affect the shotgun's aim. There hadn't been either the time or opportunity to test the jury-rigged system. Besides, he thought wryly, where the hell would you go to practice firing off a grappling hook and eight hundred feet of tightly wound line?

Noise should also have been a factor. Nobody could build a silencer for a 12-gauge shotgun. But at least they had a way to deal with that.

Thorn's hands steadied. He and Helen had gone over the plan a dozen or more times. And this was the only way that offered them even the ghost of a chance to get far enough inside Ibrahim's heavily guarded compound to make a difference. Well, he thought calmly, if you only had one roll of the dice, you rolled the dice and prayed that you didn't crap out.

The second hand on his watch swept past the number twelve for the third time since Helen's signal.

Now.

Two hundred meters away, on the other side of the compound, a digital timer blinked from 00:00:01 to 00:00:00. An improvised circuit closed, sending electric current through a short length of tungsten filament. The filament heated rapidly—glowing white-hot. That, in turn, ignited a fireworks squib. Flame hissed through the gunpowder-filled tube and lit the closest fuse of one of the more than two dozen firecrackers daisy-chained together to a piece of cardboard.

The firecrackers began detonating off one after the

other—each small explosion echoing loudly through the trees.

Pop-pop-pop-pop . . .

Thorn pulled the trigger. The Mossberg kicked back in his arms as it fired—propelling the grappling hook straight through the ragged hole he'd hacked in the tree's leafy canopy and up into the night sky. Trailing behind the hook, the Spectra line unwound with dizzying speed from the spool and through the smoking barrel—whining shrilly as it payed out.

He held his breath, waiting.

The grappling hook arced down out of the darkness and disappeared somewhere in the forest of radio and microwave antennas on top of the building seventy meters away.

Security Command Post

With Talal close at his heels, Prince Ibrahim al Saud took the steps up from the basement two at a time. He hurried across the open area that filled most of the building's first floor—ignoring the sleeping figures huddled on cots in the middle of the open space. Since they'd only arrived three days ago, the eight pilots he needed to remotely control his planes hadn't required more elaborate living quarters. They were being paid more than enough for their part in the Operation to justify temporary discomfort and a certain lack of privacy.

By rights he should have been asleep himself. But sleep had proved impossibly elusive. The growing excitement as he watched the carefully hidden dream of nearly a lifetime drawing ever closer to reality had kept him awake and pacing through both the planning cell and the aircraft control center.

He went through the door into a room just off the building's main entrance. Banks of small monitors covered one whole wall—showing the grainy, black-and-white images continuously transmitted by the video surveillance cameras posted around the perimeter fence. Several computers in another part of the room displayed the data gathered by the motion sensors scattered across the compound.

Ibrahim ran his eyes quickly over the camera views—seeing nothing out of the ordinary. He spun toward Hans-Jurgen Schaaf, the former East German commando Reichardt had designated as second-in-command of the headquarters security detail. "Well? You summoned me. What for?"

"Two minutes ago, the outer patrol reported a series of sharp reports—possibly gunshots—coming from the woods to the west."

"Gunshots?" Ibrahim repeated. His lips tightened.

Schaaf shrugged. "Possibly gunshots." He nodded toward the calendar. "But it might also be schoolboys playing pranks with firecrackers."

Ibrahim nodded. That was true. They were close to the American national holiday, the Fourth of July. And the newspapers were already full of stories about fires set by carelessly handled fireworks. For an instant, he wished again that he could have found some way to set the attack for July 4th—but too many of the military units, intelligence specialists, and political leaders he'd selected as his prime targets would have been gone for the holiday when his strike aircraft arrived.

"What do your sensors show?" he asked.

"Nothing. No movement," Schaaf answered.

Ibrahim pondered that. "Very well. But let's not take any chances. Activate the fence."

The German nodded and began entering the keyboard commands that would send lethal amounts of electricity sleeting through the perimeter fence.

Ibrahim turned to Talal. "Dispatch a four-man team to sweep the woods on that side. Equip them with night-vision gear and automatic weapons. If they encounter unarmed civilians or uniformed police, they are to avoid contact and return here. If they come across either Colonel Thorn or that woman of his—they will shoot to kill. Clear?"

The former Saudi paratrooper nodded. "Yes, Highness."

For another instant, Ibrahim pondered the wisdom of the orders he'd just issued. Taking into account the four security guards he'd brought from the Middleburg estate and counting themselves, Talal and Schaaf had fourteen men at their disposal—but only half were normally awake at any one time. So he was deploying over half his ready-alert force to chase down what might be only a few drunken American teenagers out on a spree after an all-night party. Was that a foolish waste of his manpower?

Then he shook his head. It was better to act than to sit passively—especially with so little time remaining.

Outside the Caraco Complex

Thorn finished securing the line around the oak tree's massive trunk and then tugged on it again with all his might. It didn't give an inch. The line stretched away into the darkness—a taut, almost invisible strand heading straight for the top of the headquarters building.

He nodded to himself. Almost as soon as the sound of the firecrackers Farrell had triggered died away, he'd slowly reeled in the grappling hook until it made firm contact with one of the antenna support structures.

Moving quickly but still carefully, he worked his way back down and dropped lightly onto the ground beside Helen.

"Success?" she asked quietly.

"We're in business," Thorn replied—taking back the Winchester shotgun and rucksack she offered him. He laid the Mossberg down in the tall grass and then levered himself back into the oak tree. Thirty seconds later, he was back at his perch.

Helen climbed up after him, stopping on a branch just a few feet below.

He shrugged off the rucksack, secured the unloaded shotgun to it, and then ran a length of the strong, lightweight nylon rope coiled at his waist through an eyelet on the rucksack. At a hand signal, Helen passed her pack up to him and he rapidly rigged it the same way. Then he tied both rucksacks to a nearby branch. She would finish prepping them once he was on his way.

Which had to be soon.

Thorn made sure his gloves were snug, checked his web gear to make sure all the pockets and pouches were sealed, and then looked over his shoulder at the line leading off into the darkness. Now all he had to do was shinny uphill along seventy-plus meters of ultra-thin Spectra line—all without making too much noise or dropping anything.

Sure.

He took a deep breath and nodded to Helen.

Her terse report to Farrell sounded through his headset. "Delta Three, this is Two. We're going in."

Thorn took hold of the line with both hands, gripped it

tightly, swung himself up, locked his legs around it, and set off—moving hand over hand up the long slope.

Helen Gray watched him go. The nylon rope he'd tied to their rucksacks dangled behind him as it payed out from the coil at his waist.

At last, Peter's voice came through her own headset. "Delta Two, this is One. In position."

That was her cue.

Helen pulled herself up onto the gnarled branch he'd set off from, reclaimed the rucksacks, fastened them together, and then clipped the whole assembly to the taut Spectra line. "Haul away," she said quietly.

The rope attached to the rucksacks tightened, slowly at first, and then faster as Peter began pulling it in. They started moving upslope—trundling toward the distant rooftop of Ibrahim's headquarters building.

Helen stood watching, knowing full well it would be her turn to make the arduous ascent next. She flexed the fingers of her own gloves and started working on her breathing.

"Two, this is One. Come ahead."

Helen gripped the line and started climbing—using the same hand-over-hand technique as Peter.

The first few meters were relatively easy. That was an illusion.

Soon Helen could feel the Spectra line trying to slice through her gloves. Her shoulder, neck, arm, and wrist muscles all quivered under the constant strain needed to maintain her grip on the thin cable. It was like dangling from piano wire.

Ignore the pain, she told herself sternly, remembering the rigors of her training. Ignore it. Keep moving. Don't stop.

She kept moving.

Helen was almost halfway across when Farrell's frantic voice shattered her single-minded concentration. "Two, this is Three! You've got an enemy patrol right below you! Two men just came out of the building and joined the rovers. Total is four men armed with SMGs and night-vision gear."

God. If any of those bastards so much as looked up at the night sky, he couldn't possibly miss seeing her dangling just thirty feet or so above them. Her back tensed as she imagined the agony of a quick burst of 9mm Parabellum submachine rounds slamming into her.

Worse yet, she couldn't even look down to see the men who might kill her in the next few seconds. Hell, she couldn't even stop moving. Not on a line like this. If she lost her momentum, she'd never be able to regain it.

Helen heard the sound of boots ringing on pavement. Her hands started to slip.

No, damn it!

With absolute determination, she shoved all her fear and doubt to the back of her mind. Everything in the universe narrowed to a single point—the short length of line always just a little ahead of her steadily moving hands. Slowly, painfully, she kept going—climbing hand over hand along the cable, drawing nearer and nearer to the roof and relative safety.

"Thank God," she heard Farrell say softly. "They're heading away—moving toward the main gate."

Ibrahim is sending men out to check the noise made by our distraction device, Helen realized suddenly. He's dispersing his troops. Incredibly, despite the pain, despite her fatigue, and despite her fear, she could feel herself almost smiling.

"You made it, Helen," Peter whispered, laying a gentle hand on her shoulder.

She looked to the side with a start—aware only then that

she'd cleared the edge of the roof. She unlocked her legs, let herself swing away from the line, and willed her weary, aching hands to let go.

They were at their first objective.

Peter already had the rucksacks open with the equipment they would need straight away laid out.

First came their body armor. Both quickly donned the heavy Kevlar vests. They would have been far too bulky and awkward to wear during their climb up to the roof, but now they were headed deep into enemy territory. As she struggled into hers, Helen wished for what felt like the millionth time that the manufacturers could get it through their heads to take some aspects of female anatomy into account.

Next came the two Winchester shotguns. Peter handed her one. "You've got triple-ought. Mine's loaded with sabot."

Helen nodded. She looked around the roof without being able to pick out much detail. They were above the level of the compound lights and it was much darker here. She flipped the night-vision gear down over her eyes and waited while they adjusted to the flat, green-tinted view.

Farrell reported in from his concealed position outside the compound. "Delta Two, this is Three. Patrol has left the main gate and entered the west woods."

"Understood, Three," she said. "Moving toward entry now."

She checked the magazine in her Beretta and looked up at Peter. He had his own light intensifiers on. "You find a door?"

"Yeah." He gestured toward the southern edge of the roof. "Over there by that big air-conditioning unit."

Helen slung the Winchester over one shoulder and the rucksack over the other. "Let's get this done, Peter."

She followed him through the cluttered array of satellite dishes, radio antennas, and microwave relay towers. They'd called it a forest, and that was an accurate term, she decided—stepping over a massive power cable that lay snaked across the roof like a giant, exposed tree root.

The door down was metal and set into a raised section of the roof at a forty-five-degree angle. There was no exterior handle. Helen looked it over carefully, noting the thick metal bolt holding the door in place. "You want speed or subtlety?"

Peter smiled. "Just for once, let's change our MO. I vote for subtlety."

"Agreed." She went down on one knee and fished through her rucksack for a small plastic bottle. The cap went into one of her web gear's pouches. She replaced it with an angled plastic tube that ended in a tapered nozzle. "Stand clear."

Gingerly, Helen tilted the bottle over the bolt, laying down a thin line of nitric acid across the metal. She pulled back fast as a cloud of bitter, poisonous smoke sizzled off the bubbling metal. When the smoke dispersed, she could see where the acid had eaten deeply into the bolt. A second application finished the job.

Peter knelt beside her holding a slender metal ruler he'd picked up at a drafting store and a powerful magnet from a hardware store. After swiftly rubbing the magnet over the ruler, he cautiously slid the now-magnetized ruler through the door frame. Using it as a probe, he felt around the frame for pressure plates or other sensors that might trip an alarm.

He stopped halfway along the bottom sill. "Got one," he said. "There's a raised spot where they've installed a pressure pad."

Helen watched as he put the magnet back on one end of the ruler, and then squeezed out a dollop of Krazy Glue under the door frame. The glue would help hold the ruler in place against the pad—ensuring that the alarm wouldn't trip when they opened the door.

A screwdriver sufficed to lever the door up and away from the melted bolt—revealing a darkened set of stairs leading down.

Peter started moving, but stopped when Helen stuck her arm out in front of him.

"Not so fast," she said, showing him the second squeeze bottle she'd packed along in her rucksack. This one was filled with white chalk dust. "Subtlety, remember?"

He grinned sheepishly and hung his head in mock shame. "Sorry."

"Uh-huh." Helen squirted a cloud of chalk dust into the doorway. A laser beam appeared right across the middle of the opening—glowing red through the swirling white fog.

Peter whistled softly under his breath. "Jesus Christ. A pressure plate *and* a laser sensor! These bastards aren't screwing around!"

Helen nodded slowly. Now that they knew it was there, it wouldn't be difficult for them to wriggle under the laser beam—even in body armor. But who knew how many more alarms or booby traps the bad guys had rigged throughout the building they were about to enter?

She watched as Peter slid under the beam and then followed suit.

The stairs from the roof ended in a closed steel fire door.

Peter unholstered his 9mm SIG-Sauer and stood ready while she tried the handle. It was unlocked. She pushed down gently, unlatching the door, and pulled out her own pistol. The shotgun slung over her shoulder was a two-handed weapon and too unwieldy for what she had in mind.

The fingers on his left hand flashed out a count. One. Two. Three. Go.

Crouching low while Peter covered her from above, Helen pulled the door open a crack. Dim light spilled into the darkened stairway. She flipped the eyepieces of her night-vision gear back up and poked her head through the opening—rapidly scanning the area beyond. She was facing north now.

The fire door opened up into a hallway that ran east before dead-ending to her left and then turned north not far to the right. There was no one in sight.

A faint, familiar smell hung in the air—the odor of too many people crowded into too tight a space without adequate personal hygiene. She sniffed. It was an aroma she associated with college dorms.

She slipped out into the hall and took up a firing stance, covering Peter as he glided out behind her.

He nodded toward an identical fire door adjacent to the one they'd just come through and mouthed, "Stairs down."

Helen nodded. They'd have to clear this floor first. Without knowing anything about the building layout, they couldn't risk leaving any door unopened or any room unchecked. Doing anything else was just asking to be bushwhacked from behind.

At Peter's signal, she moved slowly down the hall to the right, with her Beretta out and ready to fire. He followed her, periodically checking behind them.

Helen turned the corner. The hallway stretched north and then turned back east. There were doors on either side.

She drew nearer to the first door. A three-by-five card taped to the outside of the door displayed what looked like two names, "Eberhardt," and "Priess." These must be living quarters. She arched an eyebrow at Peter and nodded toward the door.

He nodded back.

She tested the knob. It turned easily and quietly. The door

swung open under gentle pressure—just far enough to show the foot of a cot. She pushed the door open a bit further and then moved inside—angling right to clear the entrance for Peter.

Once they were both in, he closed the door behind them.

From her position on the floor, Helen scanned the room. The light spilling under the door bottom provided ample illumination for her intensifiers.

Two holstered pistols hung from a single chair placed between two cots. Each cot was occupied by a soundly sleeping man. Perfect. She smiled coldly. Why fight fair when you didn't have to fight at all?

Taking care of the two men took just a couple of minutes. The procedure was simple: Whack each sleeping man over the head to stun him. Shove a piece of old cloth into his mouth and wrap several lengths of duct tape around the man's face to hold the ready-made gag in place. Then tightly bind the wide-eyed, thoroughly frightened, and still groggy German's wrists and ankles with cable ties. Easy and effective—the best combination. Helen snagged their weapons and shoved them into her rucksack. Even though these clowns weren't going anywhere anytime soon, she wasn't going to make the mistake of leaving usable weapons behind.

Two down, an unknown number to go, Helen thought as they left the bedroom and edged back out into the hall.

She softly recounted their progress to Farrell and listened as he made his own report. "That patrol seems to be still mucking around in the woods. I'll keep you posted if I see them heading back your way."

They kept working their way from room to room—moving carefully and cautiously, consciously fighting the urge to hurry. Stealth was their best ally now—not speed. The next two bedrooms were empty, though both showed signs of recent occupancy.

By now Helen had a pretty good mental picture of how this floor was laid out. Living quarters ran in a giant U along the outer walls—at least five rooms laid out to house two men each. The inner loop of the U contained a rest room, a small kitchen, and a conference room that obviously served as both a lounge and an eating area.

They found and disposed of two more sleepers in the fourth bedroom. Body armor and web gear hanging from hooks above the cots made it clear that these guys were guards—not technicians.

The fifth and final bedroom was unoccupied, and the only two other rooms on the floor were both dedicated to machinery and equipment storage.

Helen closed the storage room door behind her and looked at Peter. He was down on one knee with his pistol out—covering the stairwell leading down. "Ready?" she asked.

"Yeah," he said, starting to rise.

And then the fire door to the stairs swung wide open.

Startled, Thorn raised his weapon.

A young, thin man wearing overalls stepped out into the hallway. He carried a steaming mug in one hand. His other hand was still holding the fire door open.

Time stood still.

No weapon, Thorn realized suddenly. He's not carrying a weapon. Years of training warred against the instinct to kill, and his training won. You did not shoot unarmed civilians. Especially not when you were already acting outside the law. They'd have to take this guy alive. His finger relaxed on the trigger.

The young technician saw them at the same moment. His eyes widened.

Time kicked back into gear.

The mug went one way in a spray of scalding brown liquid. The technician went the other—whirling round and throwing himself down the stairs. *"Alarm! Alarm!"*

Shit.

Thorn raced toward the stairwell. He took the stairs down at breakneck speed, skidded onto a landing, rebounded off the wall, turned—and threw himself flat as a high-velocity round fired from below tore low over his head. The bullet gouged concrete chards out of the stairwell wall and then tumbled away.

He stuck the SIG over the edge of the landing and squeezed the trigger twice—firing blindly down the stairs. He yanked the weapon back without bothering to see if he'd hit anything.

The gunman below switched to full automatic and sprayed bullets back—ripping at the forward edge of the landing. Ricochets whirred everywhere—slamming into the walls, the ceiling, and the stairs. One smashed into his body armor hard enough to leave a bruise.

Thorn rolled away, frantically wiping the powdered concrete dust out of his eyes. Jesus! There was no way he was going to get down those stairs alive—not against that kind of firepower.

He spun around and threw himself back up the stairs almost as fast as he'd gone down them—clutching his left side where the stray round had hit him.

Helen grabbed him and pulled him through the door as a new burst of firing broke out below them. More submachine gun bullets lashed the stairwell wall and whirred away overhead. She patted him down frantically. "Are you all right?"

Still trying to catch his breath, he nodded.

"Thank God," she said and then fired her own pistol down the stairs.

Thorn went prone beside her, and squeezed off another round—still firing blind. The aim now was to discourage the people below from trying to rush the stairs.

Another three-round burst of submachine gun fire spattered bullets across the pockmarked concrete.

"Any ideas?" Helen asked dryly, half shouting to be heard over the rising crescendo of gunfire.

Options raced fast through Thorn's mind. He discarded most of them just as rapidly. Right now he and Helen were locked in a stalemate. They couldn't get down the stairs. And the bad guys couldn't get up.

Ultimately, though, a stalemate worked against the two of them. The bad guys had more men, more weapons, and more ammunition. More to the point, time was on Ibrahim's side. The longer the gun battle went on, the more time he would have to launch his weapons of mass destruction.

Strike Control Center

Ibrahim grabbed Talal's shoulder and spun him around. "What do you mean there are intruders in the building?" he demanded. "How many? Who are they?"

Still holding the phone, the other man shrugged. "It is impossible to say, Highness. One of the off-duty technicians spotted two strangers with weapons on the top floor. He escaped them and raised the alarm. Fortunately two of our men were close enough to seal off the stairwell."

His mind still reeling from the sudden bad news, Ibrahim

snapped. "An enemy force still holds the roof and the upper floor?"

Talal nodded. "True, Highness. But we hold everything else. The control center is secure."

Ibrahim forced himself to calm down. It would not do to show fear in front of his inferiors—especially not in front of Reichardt's German hirelings. Besides Talal, the room held one of his Saudi security guards, an electronics technician, and one of the computer techs. The others—including his pilots—were all supposed to be in their quarters on the floors above, resting up before being summoned to their duty stations for the coming attack.

"Has the patrol we dispatched to search the woods reported in yet?" he asked finally.

"Yes, Highness. A moment ago. Schaaf says they've found nothing so far."

Ibrahim pondered that. If the American government had somehow learned of his plans and launched this commando raid, then why hadn't they also attacked the men he'd deployed outside the secure perimeter? Leaving them unmolested didn't make sense. His fingers drummed rapidly on one of the control consoles. "This technician says he saw *two* intruders? *Only* two?"

Talal nodded.

It must be the two Americans—Thorn and Gray. It had to be them. He couldn't imagine how they had bypassed all his alarm systems, but there was no other reasonable explanation. Somehow they'd evaded the FBI, and now they had the audacity to attack him directly.

He shook his head. Two lone wolves against his guard force and all the armed technicians. It was madness.

"Order Schaaf to recall the patrol!" Ibrahim ordered.

"Highness."

"And I want the pilots and other control center personnel to report for duty—now!"

Ibrahim watched Talal turn back to the phone to relay his instructions. He would let the professionals deal with Thorn and Gray, while he and the rest of the experts he needed to launch the strike waited safely here below.

Second Floor

Thorn fired down the stairwell again, ejected the SIG's spent magazine, and slammed in a new one. He put his mouth close to Helen's ear. "I need your package."

She nodded, rolled away from the door, and quickly sorted through her rucksack. She pulled out a plastic-wrapped parcel and offered it to him. "Opting for brute force?"

He took it and then shook his head. "Not quite. Here's the plan . . ." He hurriedly sketched out his idea and then sent another three 9mm rounds winging down the stairwell.

"Not bad," Helen said, wriggling back into position. "It might even work."

Thorn grinned at her and then started to crawl back down the hallway, lugging his rucksack behind him. "Keep the bastards pinned down for me!"

"No sweat."

He crawled backward until he was out of the line of fire, scrambled to his feet, and sprinted down the hall toward the door to the conference room. He threw open the door and darted inside.

Tables and chairs dotted the carpeted room. A water cooler and coffeepot sat in one corner.

Thorn scanned the layout quickly—checking for obvious structural supports. If he did this wrong, he could bring down the whole floor. Satisfied that he had the right spot, he tossed a table and two folding chairs out of his way and knelt down. He unwrapped the package Helen had given him—revealing a half-pound brick of homemade plastic explosive.

More gunfire erupted back near the stairwell—the higher-pitched stutter of enemy submachine guns mixed with the slower, steadier bark of Helen's Beretta.

Moving as fast as possible, Thorn tore the brick into two roughly equal lumps, and then did the same with the second half-pound brick of plastic explosive he retrieved from his own rucksack.

He eyed the lumps carefully. Close enough, he decided. He slapped the lumps down on the floor—outlining the four corners of an approximately three-by-three box—and then connected them with Primacord and detonators. Satisfied, he rocked back on his heels and checked his watch. Sixty seconds had gone by.

One more detail to attend to, Thorn thought to himself, without which his rigged charges would make a nice loud bang, blow the hell out of the room, set a few fires—and do little else but scorch and shred the carpet. He hauled a large, plastic leaf bag out of the rucksack and moved toward the water cooler and coffeepot. One after the other, he sloshed the contents of both into the leaf bag and then tied it off.

Thirty seconds more gone.

He dragged the liquid-filled bag over on top of the plastic explosives. It would tamp the explosion—directing most of the blast downward. The water should also help suppress any fires he started.

"Delta Two, this is One. I'm set," Thorn radioed.

"On my way," Helen said.

He grabbed the rucksack, slung it over his back, lit the end of the Primacord, and raced out into the hallway—slamming the conference room door shut behind him.

Peter's signal galvanized Helen into action. She thrust her pistol back into its holster and took one of the plastic-tube pipe bombs he'd manufactured out of her rucksack. It contained almost half a pound of explosive. A length of fuse poked out of the cap on the end.

She lit the fuse.

One thousand one. One thousand two . . .

Helen lobbed the pipe bomb down the stairwell. It bounced once on the landing, then rolled down the second flight of stairs—and out of her line of sight.

Move! Move! Move! She scrambled upright, kicked the fire door shut, and sprinted down the hall.

One thousand four. Now!

Helen rocketed around the corner at a full run and threw herself prone.

Thorn looked up and saw Helen skidding toward him.

One floor below, the pipe bomb exploded—sending the nails they'd buried inside the plastic explosive sleeting outward through a deadly arc.

WHAMMM.

The steel fire door banged open—blown almost off its hinges by the blast. His ears rang . . .

And then the breaching charge he'd rigged detonated.

WHUMMPPP.

This time the whole floor bucked up and down as the shock wave rippled through it. The door to the conference room flew out into the corridor and smashed into the opposite wall.

"Here we go!" Thorn yelled, extending a hand to help Helen to her feet. "You ready?"

She nodded tightly. "Yes!"

He whirled around and rushed back into the smoke-filled conference room. The chairs and tables that had once filled the room were piled in a jumble of broken, twisted wreckage in the corner. There was nothing left of the water-filled bag he'd used to tamp down the charge. In fact, the only thing left in that spot was a scorched patch on the floor.

Thorn took a running leap and landed squarely on that charred, smoking section.

First Floor

Dieter Schmidt, a onetime meteorological officer in the East German Air Force, threaded his way through the knot of groggy, cursing pilots fumbling for their gear and boots amid a tangle of overturned cots and spilled duffel bags. The sudden commando raid had caught them all by surprise.

He clutched a handful of charts, thanking God that Ibrahim wanted his key personnel down below—out of harm's way. The only trouble was that the stairs down to safety were right next to the stairs leading up to the floor above. And he could see two security guards crouched there—spraying the stairwell with rounds from their submachine guns.

Schmidt swallowed hard—trying to steel himself to make the dash past that opening. This was supposed to have been easy money, he reminded himself bitterly. Run a few weather predictions, keep them updated, and then collect a hundred thousand marks to stash in that rather meager pension fund of his . . .

A white cylinder bounced down the stairs and rolled out onto the floor.

Some animal instinct prompted the meteorology officer to dive for cover.

WHAMMM.

A bright white flash strobed through the room—lighting every darkened corner for a single, dazzling, deadly instant. Pieces of shrapnel shrieked outward from the explosion—tearing into everything in their path.

Half deafened by the blast, Schmidt raised his head cautiously. The two guards were gone—blown into bloody rags by the full force of the explosion. Half the pilots around him were also down—stunned and bleeding. He saw one man staring in horror at a nail protruding out of the back of his open hand.

You should have ducked, the meteorologist thought smugly.

WHUMMPPP.

Schmidt buried his head in his hand and then lifted it again. What the devil? He was soaked. Where in God's name had all this water come from?

The meteorologist stared up at the ceiling in shock—just in time to see a large piece of it break away and come hurtling straight down on top of him.

Thorn hit the floor hard and rolled away—ignoring the pain stabbing through his ankles and legs. His pistol broke loose and skittered across the floor. The fall had been further than he'd anticipated—more like fifteen feet instead of ten. He was damned lucky he hadn't sprained an ankle—or broken his neck.

Like the poor dumb son of a bitch he'd landed on.

The dead man's eyes were open wide in stunned horror—

staring sightlessly up through a pair of crushed, wire-frame glasses. His head lay cocked at a sickening angle.

Helen dropped through the opening, landed on the smoking pile of debris, and rolled in the other direction.

Thorn swore silently. He and Helen were smack-dab in the middle of a hornet's nest. They'd come out right in the center of a huge open space—not an isolated, enclosed room as he'd hoped. And there were people all around them. Most appeared to be armed.

Sooner or later these bastards were going to realize their enemies had jumped right into their midst. And when they did, all hell was going to break loose. Like right about now . . .

It was too late to retrieve his pistol. He yanked the Winchester shotgun off his shoulder, flicked off the safety, and pumped the fore-end—chambering a 12-gauge round.

One of the men closest to him heard the sound and swung around. *"Mein—"*

Thorn saw the pistol in his hand and pulled the trigger—riding the recoil back and automatically pumping another shell into the Winchester's chamber.

The sabot round he'd fired blew a big hole clear through the German's chest and blasted out his back in an impossibly large spray of blood and pulverized bone. The dead man flew backward and landed in a splayed heap beside an overturned cot.

Helen's Beretta barked three times—knocking down another man, this one carrying a submachine gun.

The rest scattered—diving for cover behind cots or wriggling frantically away across the floor toward some of the doors that opened up into this one vast room. Panicked shouts in German and what sounded like Arabic echoed across the space.

A pistol round slammed into Thorn's back and glanced off the Kevlar vest. A red-hot wave of pain washed through him. Christ. He spun around and saw a figure crouched behind one of the cots.

He fired. Pieces of bedding, metal frame, and flesh exploded away from where the sabot round struck home.

Thorn pumped the Winchester again and scanned their surroundings rapidly—frantically searching for a way out of this killing zone. They were too damned exposed here.

He turned toward the south wall—toward the staircase Helen had tossed her pipe bomb down. There. Another fire door stood right beside the stairs leading up. He'd bet good money there was another staircase behind that closed door—and that those stairs led down.

Lying prone on the floor beside one of the men she'd just shot, Helen Gray spotted movement near the far wall. A man carrying a submachine gun had just come out of the room closest to the main entrance. He looked tough and totally unafraid.

Not good.

She fired twice. Both rounds hit her target squarely in the chest. Incredibly, the other man stayed up and fired back with the submachine gun—calmly walking three-round bursts through the chaos in the middle of the room.

She flattened herself as bullets whipcracked past just inches to the right—tearing huge strips of linoleum from the floor. Body armor! That son of a bitch had body armor on, too.

Without hesitating, Helen raised the muzzle of her Beretta slightly, altering the view over her front and rear sights. She squeezed the trigger.

A neat, red-rimmed hole appeared in the other man's forehead and he went down.

Strike Control Center

Ibrahim could hear the sounds of gunfire now—the stutter of submachine guns, shotgun blasts, and the crack of pistols. He shook his head in disbelief. The battle was moving closer. How could this be?

He whirled toward Talal. "What's happening up there? Where are my pilots? I want an accurate report!"

The former paratroop officer spread his hands helplessly. "I can't give you one, Highness. I've lost contact with Schaaf. He left the security office to lead the defense—and immediately dropped off the com nct."

Ibrahim swore sharply. Incompetents! He was surrounded by fools and incompetents. First Reichardt had failed him. And now Reichardt's chosen deputy.

He stabbed a finger into Talal's chest. "Get up there and take command!" He nodded toward the only security guard still in the control center. "Take that man with you!"

Talal stared at him. "But Highness, you will be unprotected!"

Ibrahim glared at him. "Do your job right, Captain. Then I won't need any protection!"

Talal stiffened. "Yes, Highness." He snatched up his submachine gun and headed for the door that led to the planning cell.

Ibrahim didn't bother watching him go. Instead, he swung around on the two German technicians who were left. He pointed to the 9mm pistols they wore. "You know how to use those weapons?"

They nodded hurriedly.

"Good. Then guard the door. Move!"

The technicians scurried into position.

Ibrahim turned back to contemplate the secure phones that linked him with the five strike airfields. His eyes narrowed. Should he transmit the arming codes and target coordinates now—and order an immediate launch?

Such an order would utterly disrupt the final stage of his carefully planned timetable. It would certainly throw the ground crews and security troops at those airfields into confusion. He frowned. Some were paid mercenaries like those who were failing him here. They were sure to panic when they heard his command center was under attack. A few might even abandon their posts without launching their aircraft.

And even if all the planes left the ground, Ibrahim knew the damage their bombs caused would be dramatically reduced—perhaps even halved. Too many key American personnel would be at home asleep—and outside the target areas. His hired planners had run through several night attack scenarios when drafting the Operation. None had yielded the kinds of results he desired.

No, he thought furiously. He would *not* be panicked into wasting so much of the destructive power he had spent so much effort, time, and money to obtain.

Besides, once the four heavily armed men he'd so foolishly deployed outside the compound returned, the two Americans would find the odds tipping even more heavily against them. Thorn and Gray were only human. They could be killed.

First Floor

Thorn dropped another pistol-armed man taking potshots at them—swinging away to look for new targets before the man he'd shot even hit the floor. The sudden movement sent fire streaking down his side. Might have a broken rib there, he thought clinically.

"Pete!" Farrell's voice sounded through his headset. "You've got company coming! That patrol's on its way back—at the double! They're heading for the gate."

Damn.

Thorn scanned the room around them. He and Helen were each covering different sectors—moving from position to position whenever they fired. Several more of their enemies were down—either torn in half by his shotgun rounds or hit by one or more of Helen's 9mm bullets. Others had thrown their weapons away and were either lying doggo amid the clutter or fleeing out the building's main entrance.

He let them go. There wasn't any percentage in shooting unarmed men in the back—especially when they were abandoning the fight. Running away was exactly the kind of behavior he wanted to encourage.

But he and Helen were still taking fire from a couple of different locations. Throw four more guards wearing Kevlar and carrying automatic weapons into this battle, and you've got two very dead people, Thorn realized. Two very dead people who are us.

"Can you delay them?" he asked desperately.

"I'll try," Farrell said matter-of-factly.

Thorn heard the sudden boom of a shotgun blast over the radio as Farrell opened up.

From his concealed position in the trees across the road from the Caraco compound, Sam Farrell saw the man he'd shot crumple to the pavement. Not even Kevlar body armor could stop a sabot round fired from less than forty meters away.

After a split second's stunned amazement, the other three guards threw themselves flat and opened up—flailing away at the trees and brush on full automatic.

Pieces of torn bark and leaves rained down on Farrell. Shit, he thought, I am getting too damned old for this crap. He wriggled back behind the thick trunk of one of the trees and reloaded.

Helen Gray heard the desperate radio exchange between Peter and Farrell. The building entrance was in her sector. Which made stopping this new threat her responsibility.

She fired the Beretta two more times. Both shots slammed into the wall—right beside the man she'd been aiming at. With a startled yell, he threw his own pistol away and scuttled for the big double doors leading out.

Fair enough.

Helen tugged the empty magazine out of her own weapon and reached for another. Nothing. She'd used up the ammo she'd stuffed in her ready-use pouch. There were more rounds in her rucksack, but it would take far too long to get them out.

She switched to the shotgun, pumped it, and rose to one knee. "I'm going for the doors, Peter," she warned.

Without waiting for a response, she rose to her feet and moved forward, dodging around the tangle of cots, gear, and bodies.

A gunman appeared in one of the open doorways on the far wall.

Still running, Helen fired from the hip. Nine pistol-size pellets blasted out of the barrel and spread through a narrow arc. Two hit her target in the chest and two more tore his face apart.

Another man popped up to her right and fired twice. The

first bullet snapped past her face. The second caught her in the side.

Momentarily stunned by the fiery impact, she stumbled and fell—still holding her shotgun. Another 9mm round spanged into the floor by her face and whirred away.

Helen spun on her side, fired, pumped the action, and then fired again.

An eerie, echoing, bubbling scream told her she'd hit the shooter.

Wincing, she levered herself upright and started for the main doors again. This time nobody tried to stop her.

On the other side of the vast room, the fire door to the stairs going down started to open.

Thorn caught a fleeting glimpse of two men, both wearing body armor, in the doorway. He fired quickly and swore as the sabot round tore a small, jagged hole through the wall a foot away from the door. He'd missed.

The steel door slammed shut.

Thorn scrambled to his feet. He had to take these new enemies now. Before they recovered the initiative.

He pumped another round into the chamber and ran toward the stairwell—firing on the move. Once. A finger-sized puncture appeared in the steel door. Twice. Another sabot round struck home—ripping a second hole at waist height near the handle.

Thorn pulled the trigger again. Nothing. He'd used the whole seven-round magazine. Christ, he thought, no time to reload. Now what the hell do I do?

He reached the fire door and jerked it open.

One of the two men he'd spotted lay faceup on the top landing in a spreading pool of blood. The second, a tough, middle-aged Arab, was very much alive.

The Arab brought the submachine gun he was holding on line—ready to fire at point-blank range.

And Thorn swung the Winchester up through a vicious two-handed arc—slamming it into the other man's face with enough force to shatter bone.

Screaming and clutching at the red, pulped ruin that had once been his face, the Arab dropped his weapon and toppled backward down the stairs.

Helen cautiously pushed open one pair of double doors with the barrel of her shotgun. Nothing. No reaction.

She kicked open the door and slid through into a hallway closed off by another set of double doors—these leading outside into the compound. Blood trails on the linoleum showed that some of the wounded had fled this way. A guard room stood empty to her right.

Naturally, she thought coldly. The guards were all inside—and dead or dying. Except for the men she was after now.

Helen moved on down the hall, pushed through the second set of doors, and came out onto the sidewalk fronting the half-filled parking lot.

Submachine gun fire rattled in the distance—drawing closer. A single, echoing shotgun blast answered.

"Delta Three, this is Two. How're you doing?" she asked.

"They're pulling back through the gate, Helen," Farrell replied, breathing heavily. "I can't stop them."

Helen spotted the retreating patrol. Two were half dragging a third man, while a fourth provided covering fire. They would be in among the parked cars and vans in just a few seconds.

Too bad for them.

She knelt, laid her shotgun aside, and rifled through her rucksack. Her fingers closed on the cylindrical plastic surface of a pipe bomb. Her lighter came out of one of her assault vest's breast pockets.

The retreating guards were sixty meters away. Fifty-five. Fifty.

Helen lit the fuse, stood up, and hurled the pipe bomb toward the enemy patrol. It spun end over end through the air, fell a little short, bounced once, and rolled under a minivan just meters away from them.

Perfect.

She snatched up her shotgun and rucksack in one hand, yanked open the closest door, and threw herself prone into the hallway.

WHAMMM.

The pipe bomb detonated directly under the van's gasoline tank. A fireball tipped with nails and torn pieces of metal and plastic roared outward—consuming everyone and everything in its path.

"Jesus," Farrell said simply over the radio.

Helen looked back over her shoulder at the inferno raging outside the building. That ought to get a few official pulses finally pumping, she thought calmly.

She stiffened as Peter's voice came over the circuit. "I'm at the top of the stairs to the basement. I may need some help with this."

Helen sprinted toward the inner set of double doors, slinging the rucksack over her shoulder. She started reloading the shotgun as she ran. "Give me thirty seconds, Peter!"

Strike Control Center

The sound of gunfire faded away on the floor above. At last, Ibrahim thought.

He signaled one of the technicians. "Find out what's happening!"

The technician, an older man, swallowed hard. He hustled out the door leading to the planning cell. And then stopped dead. "Sir!"

Ibrahim hurried over. "What is it, man?"

The gray-haired computer specialist lifted a shaking hand, pointing toward the stairs leading up.

Ibrahim froze. Talal lay dead on the steps. His mangled face was covered in blood.

Impossible. Absolutely impossible.

The sudden realization that he was on the verge of losing everything flooded through Ibrahim's stunned mind. He grabbed the shaking computer technician, pulled him through the door, and brutally shoved him toward one of the control consoles. "Activate that console! Now!"

Then he whirled toward the other man—the younger one with a shaved head and a gold loop through his eyebrow. "Seal that door! Shoot anyone who comes through it! Understand?"

The young man nodded convulsively, his face ash-gray.

May Allah protect me, Ibrahim thought bitterly. All would not be lost. He could yet inflict a massive death blow to his great enemy.

He moved to the secure phone linking him to Godfrey Field. "This is Control One. Get me Deckert! Now!"

Peter Thorn led the way down the stairs, with Helen coming right behind him.

He turned the corner. The Arab he'd clubbed lay crumpled at the foot of the steps. A few more feet brought him out into a large room crowded with empty desks.

He stopped in sudden confusion. Was this it? Had they

been wrong about the whole setup? Where the hell was Ibrahim's control center?

"Peter," Helen hissed—pointing her shotgun at a gray, unmarked door in the far corner.

Thorn nodded.

He moved closer. Helen drifted off to the side so that they approached the door from different angles.

Thorn put his back against the wall, leaned over, and gently tested the handle. It was locked. Well, well, what a surprise, he thought grimly.

At a hand signal, Helen moved into position—ready to cover him.

He raised his shotgun, now loaded with solid slugs, and fired twice—smashing the hinges, first the top and then the bottom.

Helen spun out, savagely kicked the door in, and spun back into cover.

From inside the room a pistol cracked twice—sending steel-jacketed rounds screaming through the opening.

The stupid bastard's firing high, Thorn thought. He dropped to one knee and then threw himself flat in the doorway with his shotgun angled up. A figure loomed in his sights—a young man, obviously terrified, but still holding a weapon.

Bad move.

Thorn pulled the trigger.

The slug caught the other man in the stomach and threw him back against some kind of equipment console. Eyes already glazing over in death, he slid to the floor, smearing blood across the console, and toppled sideways.

Helen flowed in through the doorway, yelling, "Hands up! Get your hands up!"

A second man, this one older, hurriedly tossed his pistol to the side and stuck his hands in the air.

Thorn scrambled upright and joined Helen inside.

"Eight. Four. Alpha. Two . . ." someone said, speaking rapidly, but precisely.

He swung toward the voice and saw a tall, slender, handsome man with dark hair and dark eyes speaking intently into a telephone. Ibrahim. That had to be Prince Ibrahim al Saud—the man responsible for all this carnage. Rage flared inside him.

Thorn aimed the shotgun at the Saudi. "Drop the phone!"

Ibrahim smiled thinly and shook his head. "Delta. Tango. Five . . ."

Helen fired. She was less than three meters away, and the pellets from her triple-ought shotgun shell were still tightly grouped when they hit—blowing Ibrahim's right hand, the hand still holding the telephone, off just below the wrist.

The Saudi prince stood motionless, staring in horror at the blood pumping out of his shattered right arm.

Thorn grabbed the older man they'd taken prisoner and tossed him toward Ibrahim. "Use your belt! Put a tourniquet on him!"

"Oh, my God," Helen said in horror.

Her shocked voice stopped Thorn in his tracks. He turned toward her.

She pointed at the several computer consoles that filled the room. One of them was live. It showed a digitally generated map of the surrounding region.

And a white dot blinked rapidly as it moved across the screen—heading inexorably toward Washington, D.C. One of the strike planes was airborne and closing on its target—with an armed 150-kiloton nuclear warhead aboard.

CHAPTER TWENTY-ONE
DETONATION

JUNE 21
Strike Control Center, Chantilly, Virginia

Colonel Peter Thorn stared at the blinking dot in shock. Godfrey Field was barely thirty nautical miles from Washington, and the aircraft they'd seen based there had a cruising speed of two-hundred-plus knots. Which meant they had maybe six or seven minutes before the equivalent of one hundred and fifty thousand tons of high explosive detonated right over the nation's capital.

Several seconds trickled past—each an imagined lifetime of sorrow and regret. His shoulders slumped. "Oh, Christ."

Helen turned toward him. "We have to do something, Peter!"

Do what? What more *could* they do? Despite all the risks

they'd taken, despite everything, they were too late. Ibrahim had managed to get one of his nuclear-armed planes off the ground. And now the aircraft was following its preset flight plan—drawing ever closer to its programmed target.

He focused on the computer display. A single line below the digital map of the Washington metro area read: F1, FLIGHT CONTROL MENU.

Thorn grabbed the nearest chair, set his shotgun down, and sat down in front of the computer keyboard. He punched the F1 function key.

A new cursor popped on-screen, replacing the notation about a flight control menu: AIRCRAFT ID?:

Swell.

Thorn whirled toward the older man they'd taken prisoner with the Saudi prince. The man had just finished rigging his belt around Ibrahim's maimed right arm as a temporary tourniquet. "You speak English?"

The balding, gray-haired man looked up from Ibrahim's slumped, unconscious figure. The wounded man had fainted halfway through the effort to save his life. He hesitated. *"Was? Ich verstehen Sie nicht."*

Something in their prisoner's eyes told Thorn he was lying. He stood up and kicked the chair backward. "Bullshit," he said softly.

The German flinched.

Thorn stalked up to the other man, grabbed hold of him by the shirt, and yanked him upright. "I said, do you speak English?"

Their prisoner stayed mute, his eyes wide in fear.

It was time for more active measures, Thorn decided coldly. He scooped his shotgun back and casually, almost negligently, aimed it toward the other man's head. "I'm going to ask you that question one more time. If you lie to me . . ."

He chambered a round.

The German bit his lip, trembling even harder now. "But you cannot do this! You cannot torture me. It is against American law!"

Thorn leaned closer. He pressed the shotgun right against the other man's temple. "That plane is carrying a nuclear weapon. What makes you think I care about the law right now?" His finger tightened on the trigger.

"*Mein Gott.*" The German swallowed hard. "I . . . I will help you. Do not shoot me . . . *bitte* . . . please!"

Helen patted him down, fished a wallet out of his pocket, and showed Thorn a tourist visa issued to one Klaus Engel.

He grabbed the German and dragged him back to the live console. The blinking aircraft indicator was now roughly halfway between the towns of Leesburg and Herndon, Virginia—which meant they probably had somewhat less than five minutes remaining. He pointed to the question asking for the aircraft identification. "What's the ID number for that plane?"

Engel shook his head frantically. "I do not know, I swear it! I merely built and programmed the machine. I was not part of the planning cell!"

Thorn lifted the shotgun again.

"They are not numbers. They are code names," the other man said, stumbling over the words in his haste to get them out. "But I do not know these names!"

Code names? Thorn glanced at Helen. "Do you still have that list we took off Wolf?"

"Yes." She fished it out of one of her pockets and handed it over.

He scanned down the list until he found the five animal code names listed under Godfrey: Lion, Tiger, Leopard, Jaguar, and Cheetah, all in German. He looked up at Helen. "What do you think?"

"Try Lion," she said flatly. "It's the first on the list and the king of the beasts."

Thorn nodded. That was logical. Except for Ibrahim and a few others, most of those involved in this conspiracy were German. Putting their primary target at the top of a list and attaching the name of the top of the animal kingdom to it would appeal to them.

He sat down at the keyboard and typed in L,O,W,E.

A new line appeared on the display: ID INCORRECT. AIRCRAFT ID?:

Damn it.

Helen leaned over his shoulder. "Peter, there's no umlaut symbol on this keyboard!"

Of course. Thorn tried again, typing in L, O, E, W, E, this time.

New data appeared below the digitized map on the computer display—showing information on airspeed, altitude, the plane's attitude, heading, and degree of bank, throttle settings, and fuel remaining. At the same time, the video monitor just to the left of the computer screen flickered to life—showing a black-and-white image of lighted suburban streets passing slowly astern.

Thorn scanned the numbers quickly, trying to make sense of them. From what he could tell, the strike aircraft was currently flying southeast at two hundred thirty knots—at an altitude of two thousand feet.

Two sets of coordinates—latitude and longitude—stayed constant. A third decreased constantly. As he watched, it flickered from 25.4 to 25.3. He turned toward Engel and stabbed a finger at the screen. "Are these what I think they are?"

The German computer tech nodded nervously. "That is the detonation point. And the range to the target."

Something about those coordinates looked familiar to

Thorn. Then it clicked. This aircraft was headed straight for the Pentagon—which would put most of Washington inside the bomb's blast and shock radius. He glared hard at Engel. "All right, how do I give this plane a new set of coordinates?"

"You cannot."

This time Helen ground her weapon into the technician's cheek. "Try again!"

"Please. It is true." Sweat rolled down the German's face. "You cannot change the aim point once the aircraft is aloft. Herr Reichardt insisted on that as a security precaution!"

Reichardt? Who the hell was he? Thorn filed the name away for future reference. He focused on the task at hand. "Are you telling me that goddamned plane is totally locked on autopilot?"

"No, no!" Engel insisted. "You can control the aircraft manually."

"How?"

The technician plucked a joystick off the top of the console and held it up. "Using this . . . and the keyboard."

"Set it up. Now!" Thorn growled. Ibrahim's bomb-laden plane would be over the Pentagon in roughly four minutes.

Engel leaned over his shoulder, hastily plugged the joystick into a port near the display, and began entering commands on the keyboard.

"Peter?" Helen said quietly.

He looked at her. "Yeah?"

"Can you fly that plane from here?"

Thorn shrugged. "I don't really have a choice, do I?"

They were out of other options. Rounding up one of Ibrahim's surviving pilots and getting him to cooperate would take too long. For a brief instant, he wished he'd spent more time playing around with the computer flight simulators that were so popular nowadays. For now, the computer tech would have to do.

"The system is ready," Engel announced, taking his hands off the keyboard. He quickly pointed out the keys that would activate various aircraft controls. "Those are your throttle settings, your rudder controls, and . . ."

Thorn listened intently, forcing himself to memorize each key. He could feel his heart rate accelerating. When the German finished, he nodded abruptly. The aircraft indicator was now over Reston—and the distance to target changed to 16.1. "Is there anything else I should know?" he asked.

The computer tech nodded. "You must keep the aircraft at least two nautical miles away from the detonation point. Once it flies inside that circle, the bomb is armed—and it will detonate if the range begins to open again. Also, you must not let the aircraft drop below three hundred meters—a thousand of your feet—or climb above five thousand meters. Once it reaches either altitude, a barometric fuse will detonate the weapon. Herr Reichardt's and Prince Ibrahim's instructions were very explicit."

"How truly wonderful," Helen commented acidly.

Thorn thought a moment. "If we can't dive, we'll have to get this sucker to climb. Even fifteen thousand feet above the ground is better than nothing."

Helen frowned. "With a 150-kiloton bomb on board, Peter? That's still not high enough."

"It's a start," he replied.

"Yeah."

"This will relay any air traffic control communication you receive," the German computer tech said, offering a radio headset plugged into a control panel next to the keyboard.

Thorn yanked the earphones he was wearing off, and

slipped the new headset on. Then he tapped the keys controlling the throttle settings for both engines—pushing them
to one hundred percent power. Then he took a deep breath.
"Here we go."

He tugged the joystick to the right.

Strike Aircraft Lion, Over Virginia

Two thousand feet above the densely populated suburban
landscape, the twin-engine Jetstream 31 turboprop abruptly
rolled to the right—almost standing on its wingtip. It lost altitude rapidly.

Inside, a tiny instrument linked to a constant barometric
pressure reading prepared itself for the last act of its short
life.

Strike Control Center

Helen Gray saw the video picture suddenly shift as the aircraft practically turned onto its side. The altitude reading
spun down—falling from two thousand to seventeen hundred and then sixteen hundred feet in seconds. She held her
breath.

Peter quickly pulled the joystick back to the left. Slowly,
the image showed the aircraft rolling back to level flight. Its
altitude stabilized around fourteen hundred feet.

The computer technician's face turned a ghastly shade of
white. "Careful! The controls are sensitive. And they are not

integrated. To turn safely, you must use the rudder control key *and* the joystick!"

Helen could see the sweat on Peter's forehead now. He stared intently at the screen. She kept quiet.

His hand holding the joystick slowly relaxed, while the other hovered over the computer keyboard. The range to target now read 10.9.

Farrell's laconic voice broke over their headsets. "Delta One and Two, this is Three. I've got my weapon on ten-plus bad guys out here. Some of them are pretty badly shot up. And a Fairfax County police unit just pulled up outside the main gate. Any suggestions on what I should tell them?"

"Try to stall them," Helen said tersely. "We're a little busy in here, Sam."

"So I've heard," Farrell replied. "You let me know when to duck and cover, okay?"

Helen suddenly realized the retired general must have heard almost everything going on inside the control center over the voice-activated radio circuit. She swallowed. "I'll let you know, Sam. Scout's honor."

"Okay," Farrell said. "I'll keep you posted."

Peter glanced over his shoulder and flashed her a quick, worried grin. "Second time lucky, right?"

Helen nodded seriously. They weren't going to get a third chance. "Right."

His hands started moving, this time gently tugging the joystick right while simultaneously tapping the key controlling the aircraft's rudder.

Strike Aircraft Lion, Over Arlington, Virginia

The twin-engine plane banked slowly, gradually changing its heading from southeast to almost due south. Once on that new course, it rolled back to level flight, pitched up slightly, and began climbing.

Control Center

Thorn felt his pulse slow a bit as the strike aircraft's altitude started increasing—rising steadily from fourteen hundred feet. He glanced at the range to target. It read 6.8. The number changed—to 6.9.

He breathed out.

An irritated voice suddenly squawked through his radio headset. "Unknown aircraft climbing through two thousand on heading one seven seven, this is Washington Center ARTCC. Who are you? And what the hell do you think you're doing? Be advised you are straying close to restricted air space."

Thorn hit the mike switch. "Washington ARTCC, this is Colonel Peter Thorn, United States Army. The twin-engine plane you're monitoring is a remotely piloted aircraft carrying an armed 150-kiloton nuclear warhead. I repeat, this nuclear warhead is armed."

"What?" the air traffic controller said sharply. "Jesus Christ, if this is some kind of joke—"

Thorn cut him off. "This is no joke. I repeat, that plane is carrying a live nuclear weapon. I've got control over it for now—but I suggest you give me a safe heading that will take this thing away from the District and any other inhabited area."

The radio went dead.

He watched the altitude number creeping up through three thousand feet and then glanced up at the digital map. The robot plane was now over Alexandria. The TV monitor showed an array of brighter city lights and the winding, black trace he knew must be the Potomac River.

The Washington Center air traffic controller came back on line. "Okay, Colonel. We're going to assume you're telling the truth . . ."

"Good move," Thorn said sharply, still watching the screen.

"We're clearing a corridor that should take your plane out to sea a safe distance. What's your fuel status?"

Thorn checked the numbers and read them off.

"Okay. You should have plenty of range left. Here's what I want you to do. Maintaining your air speed and your current rate of climb, come left to new heading one two zero. That'll take you out over southeastern Maryland to Chesapeake Bay. I'll relay further instructions as needed."

"Understood." Thorn complied, carefully moving both the joystick and the rudder control. "I also suggest you alert both the FBI and the DOD about this situation."

"Don't you worry about that, Colonel," the traffic controller said. "The shit's already hitting the fan all over Washington. For your sake, I really hope this isn't some cock-and-bull story to get attention."

"Considering that I'm not a trained pilot, and that there is a real nuke aboard that plane, you'd be a lot better off hoping I'm full of crap," Thorn snapped back. He adjusted the controls again. "Coming left to one two zero. Let's get this crate out over the Atlantic as fast as possible."

Strike Aircraft Lion, Over Maryland

New bits of data flowed through the onboard computer inside the Jetstream 31. Range to target: Increasing. Heading: Steady. Time elapsed since original projected detonation: three hundred seconds.

The data triggered a new subroutine—one added by Dr. Saleh, Ibrahim's computer expert, after Reichardt's German specialists finished the basic programming.

A readout attached to the TN-1000 suddenly blinked to life. It read 00:15:00.

Control Center

Thorn saw a new set of numbers flicker into existence in the lower right-hand corner of his monitor: 00:14:59. 00:14:58. 00:14:57.

His heart seemed to stop. "Oh, hell."

Helen leaned closer, her own face pale. "What is it, Peter?"

"The bastards must have put in another backup arming trigger," Thorn said quietly. "I think that bomb is going to detonate in less than fifteen minutes. And there's nothing I can do to stop it."

Engel, the German technician, stared at the damning numbers on the screen in shock. "It is impossible. I did not write such a subroutine."

The other man was probably telling the truth, Thorn decided. From what they'd seen so far, Ibrahim and Wolf had both liked to exercise complete control. He'd bet that few, if any, of their subordinates had ever known all the pieces of the puzzle. Not that it made much difference now, he realized coldly.

The hard truth was that fourteen-plus minutes didn't leave him enough time to get the plane safely out over the ocean. He ran the numbers hastily through his mind. He could fly that aircraft roughly fifty or sixty nautical miles further down-range before the nuke went off. On its present course that would put the new detonation point somewhere over thinly populated Dorchester County, Maryland. That was better than having the bomb explode right over Washington—but there were still half a dozen or more small towns inside the probable blast radius. And that meant civilian casualties could number in the thousands.

Thorn keyed the radio mike. "Washington ARTCC. We have a new problem here."

"Go ahead, Colonel."

Thorn quickly laid out the situation they were facing.

There was a moment's silence before a stunned voice came back over the circuit. "Oh, God."

Thorn saw the detonation countdown on his screen blink through 00:13:00. His hand tightened on the joystick. "Look, I need some help here. Right now!"

"I'm patching you through to the Pentagon Crisis Operations Center," the anxious air controller said hurriedly. "Wait one."

Thirty seconds passed before another voice, this one older and calmer, sounded in his headset. "Colonel Thorn? This is Brigadier General Dodson. Let me make sure I've got this straight: We're looking at the detonation of a 150-kiloton Soviet-era warhead in roughly twelve minutes, right?"

"Yes, sir." Thorn could see streetlights glowing against the dark earth below. The aircraft was over Washington's fast-growing southeastern Maryland suburbs now.

"Then here are the parameters we're facing," Dodson continued. "Assuming optimum burst height, we can expect the following . . ."

Thorn listened to the general's grim statistics in silence. They paralleled his own rough mental calculations. Lethal radiation exposure up to one and a half miles from the detonation point. A shock wave strong enough to tear most houses apart out to four and a half miles, and to shatter glass nine miles away. And a thermal pulse hot enough to cause second- and third-degree burns to anyone caught outdoors over an area eleven miles in diameter.

He grimaced. The optimum burst height for a warhead of this size was around two thousand feet. Pushing the aircraft up to nearly fifteen thousand would help reduce the damage when the bomb went off—but it was still going to be ugly. Very ugly.

Thorn waited until the general finished giving him the bad news. "So, then what do you suggest, sir?"

"We can't have this damned thing going off over land," the other man stated firmly.

"Agreed."

"Then we're down to just one option, Colonel," Dodson said. "You'll have to fly it south over Chesapeake Bay."

Thorn nodded to himself. Then he stopped suddenly, remembering the maps he'd studied of the Washington area. "Sir, that means the bomb's going to detonate—"

"Six miles away from the Pax River Naval Air Warfare Center," the general finished. "I know, Colonel. But we're getting a warning through to them right now. We couldn't possibly alert any civilians anywhere else in time. So we're just going to have to ride this one out."

"Jesus," Thorn said softly.

"I don't like it either, Colonel," Dodson agreed. "But it's the best we can do. So you just concentrate on keeping that

plane in the air long enough to give us a chance to put th
alert out to everyone we can."

"Yes, sir." Thorn refocused his attention on the controls i
front of him. The detonation countdown flickered throug
00:09:00.

Crisis Operations Center, Pentagon

Brigadier General Andrew Jackson Dodson, U.S. Air Forc
tore his gaze away from the clock. They had a little less tha
six minutes left. He swung around toward the short, baldin
Navy captain at his right. "What's the word from Pax Rive
Frank?"

"The sirens just went off, sir. I've got the duty officer o
the phone now. He understands the situation. Everybody'
heading for the shelters."

"What about their equipment?" Dodson asked. Pax Rive
was the U.S. Navy's premier test center for new aircraft.

"We're going to lose some planes, sir," the Navy captai
admitted. "It's not a combat base. The hangars aren't hard
ened."

"Understood." Dodson nodded. That was going to hur
But it was still better to lose hardware—even expensiv
hardware—than lives.

The Air Force general turned toward one of his other of
ficers, a Marine lieutenant colonel. "What about civilian ai
traffic, Jim? Anything inbound?"

"No, sir," the Marine answered. "Washington ARTCC i
rerouting everything well north or south. Not that there'
much in the air right now."

"What about shipping traffic?" the general asked. Th

Chesapeake Bay intercoastal waterway was one of the busiest shipping lanes in the U.S.

"I've checked with both Baltimore and Norfolk. There's nothing in the danger zone."

Dodson nodded again. Thank God for small favors, he thought. This early in the morning there wasn't much stirring along the eastern seaboard.

"General," another aide said suddenly, motioning to the secure phone in his hand. "The White House is on the line. They want to know if they should evacuate the President."

"Negative. There's no time." Dodson frowned. Somebody over at the White House wasn't thinking straight. He checked the clock again. Four minutes left. They'd barely have been able to get a chopper airborne before the bomb went off.

"Shit," the Marine lieutenant colonel said suddenly.

Dodson swung around. "What?"

"We just got a call from Norfolk, sir. There's a *Spruance*-class destroyer en route to Baltimore for a goodwill visit— DD-987, *O'Bannon*."

The general swore suddenly. "Where is she exactly?" He followed the Marine officer's pointing finger to a large digital map of the Chesapeake Bay region and paled. "Christ almighty . . . get a flash warning off to her! Now!"

Aboard USS *O'Bannon,* in Chesapeake Bay

The long, gray, graceful silhouette of the destroyer *O'Bannon* slid quietly through the waters of the Chesapeake Bay—moving north at a steady twelve knots. To the west, lights marked the location of the Patuxent River Naval Air

Warfare Center. Smaller lights glimmered on the easter
shore—marking waterfront homes belonging to wealth
Washingtonians or locals.

Lieutenant Mike Rydell, U.S. Navy, *O'Bannon*'s watc
officer, felt his jaw drop open. He stared at the signal rating
"We just got what?"

"A flash nuclear strike warning, Lieutenant! They say it'
no drill!"

Rydell grabbed the message from the rating—scannin
the coordinates shown and comparing them with the bridg
plot. Oh, hell. The Navy ran periodic exercises on how to re
spond to a nuclear attack, but he'd never expected to ever d
it for real—not in a million years. He froze for an instan
but only for an instant, and then reacted.

Rydell tossed the message to one side and whirle
around—already snapping out orders. "Captain to th
bridge!" He swung toward the helmsman. "All ahead flank
Left full rudder! All lookouts inside! Sound General Quar
ters! Now!"

Caught by surprise themselves, the rest of the bridge crev
stared back at him for a split second—their horrified face
ghost-white even under the red lamps used to preserve nigh
vision. Then they exploded into action.

Klaxons howling, the destroyer heeled sharply to port
throwing a higher bow wake as four eighty-thousand
horsepower gas turbines kicked her up toward full speed.

Control Center

Thorn nudged the controls slightly, altering course to bring
the aircraft onto a heading of one five five degrees. The

bomb-laden turboprop should be right in the middle of the channel now. And almost directly over those poor bastards aboard that destroyer. His hands tightened again.

My God, he wondered desperately, isn't there someplace else I can send this damned thing? He forced the thought away. There wasn't anywhere else.

He glanced at the digital readout winding down in the corner of his display. "Ops Center, this is Thorn. Thirty seconds."

Dodson's strained voice came over his headset. "Understood, Colonel. Give me a running count, please."

Thorn felt Helen's tense hand on his shoulder. She squeezed slightly. He cleared his throat. "Twenty-five. Twenty. Fifteen. Ten.

"Nine. Eight. Seven. Six. Five. Four . . ." His pulse hammered in his own ears. "Three. Two. One."

The screen blanked abruptly—wiped clean of all data. Static replaced the picture on the video monitor.

Thorn swallowed hard. "Detonation."

Outside the Control Center

Surrounded by a crowd of stunned prisoners and Fairfax County police, Sam Farrell stared southeast.

A roiling fireball flashed above the horizon, turning darkness into a flickering, deadly, man-made day for several seconds. Slowly the fireball faded from white to orange to a final dull, bloody red.

At last, even that vanished—leaving the stars and the night sky untouched.

Over Chesapeake Bay

Fifteen thousand feet over the still, placid waters of the Chesapeake Bay, the Jetstream 31 turboprop ceased to exist—blown first into its constituent atoms and then stripped down even further into a muddled sea of subatomic particles.

In its place, a sudden pinpoint of boiling energy burst into existence—a fireball spearing through the night sky ten thousand times hotter than the surface of the sun. Gamma rays sleeted outward—smashing into and ionizing the surrounding air molecules. Chemical reactions formed a dense layer of smog tens of meters deep around the small, still-expanding fireball.

X rays raced outward ahead of the plasma core, heating everything in their path to tens of millions of degrees.

Two hundred microseconds after detonation, a shock wave formed at the surface of the fireball—roaring away from the explosion at one hundred times the speed of sound.

USS *O'Bannon*

Four miles from the base of the mushroom cloud, the shock wave was still moving at nearly the speed of sound when it slammed into *O'Bannon*'s stern. Caught in its powerful, howling grip, the destroyer bucked forward—buried under a wall of water thrown skyward. Railings, radar, and radio antennas all tore loose and vanished.

The ship disappeared from view inside a maelstrom of spray and flying debris.

Control Center

Thorn sat numbly, staring at the static on his screens and listening to the crackling hiss over his headset. There were nearly four hundred men aboard that destroyer. Men who might already be dead—fried by heat or radiation, crushed by impact, or trapped in a ship already heading for the bottom.

Helen stood at his side, her hand still on his shoulder.

A voice sounded in his headset. "This is Dodson."

Thorn sat upright. "Go ahead, sir."

"We've reestablished contact with Pax River, Colonel," the general said "They've taken a hell of a lot of damage—planes thrown around, instruments smashed, but nobody was hurt. They all made it into cover in time."

"What about *O'Bannon*?" Thorn asked softly.

Dodson hesitated, then replied: "There's no word, yet, I'm afraid. We're still trying to make radio contact."

Thorn stiffened—feeling as though he'd been punched in the stomach. "I see."

"Look, son, you did everything you could. Nobody could have done more," Dodson said.

Thorn shook his head. "I wish I could believe that, General." He lowered his head, staring blankly.

Helen knelt beside him. There were tears in her eyes. "Oh, Peter . . ."

Thorn's head snapped bolt upright. There were cheers coming through his headphones!

"Thorn, this is Dodson!" the general said suddenly. "Pax River just called in. They've established contact with *O'Bannon* by signal lamp. Her radio antennas were smashed, but she's still afloat! Pax River says she's battered, she's lost most of her topside gear, and she's scorched as hell, but she's steaming in under her own power!"

"What about casualties?" Thorn heard himself ask, still not daring to believe the destroyer had survived the blast.

"They have wounded—mostly impact trauma cases—but no fatalities," Dodson answered. "Whoever was on watch put her stern to the blast point and ran like hell! She made it just far enough away to ride out the shock wave!"

Slowly, with shaking hands, Thorn pulled off the headset and turned toward Helen.

She looked up at him with shining eyes full of joy and wonder. "You did it, Peter. You did it."

"No," he said, pulling her closer. "We did it."

CHAPTER TWENTY-TWO

END GAME

JUNE 21

Strike Control Center, Chantilly, Virginia

Fifteen minutes after the fireball faded out of the night sky, Helen Gray still knelt at Peter's side—holding him tight as his hand lovingly stroked her hair.

She turned her head as a tall, dapper man came into the control center, pushing through the several Fairfax County sheriff's officers who were now studying the tightly packed array of computer hardware in stunned amazement. Ibrahim al Saud was gone—hauled away under arrest with the other wounded terrorists shortly after the police entered the bullet-riddled headquarters building. So far, her FBI credentials had kept them from being arrested themselves.

Despite the early hour, the newcomer's gray suit was perfectly pressed and his black loafers perfectly shined. She'd known him for more than five years. FBI Special Agent Paul Sandquist stopped in front of her, took in the scene silently for a minute, and then shook his head in amazement. "Jesus Christ, Helen. How the hell do you manage to stick your neck out so far every single time? You know I have orders from the Director himself to arrest you and Colonel Thorn on sight?"

Helen nodded. "Yep." She calmly let go of Peter, stood up, and held out her wrists. "Okay, Paul. You want to handcuff us and take us to your fearless leader?"

Sandquist smiled wryly. "Somehow I don't think we're going to need the handcuffs, Special Agent Gray."

Helen felt Peter Thorn's warm hand slip into hers and smiled back. "No, somehow I didn't think we would either. But let's get going. Colonel Thorn and I have a few things to discuss with Director Leiter."

Godfrey Field, Near Leesburg, Virginia

FBI Hostage Rescue Team section leader Felipe DeGarza stepped outside the Caraco hangar and immediately took the full brunt of the late morning sun. Sweat trickled out from under his assault helmet. Black coveralls, black boots, and heavy Kevlar body armor didn't make the most comfortable outfit under the circumstances, he decided. But it was a hell of a lot safer when bullets went flying around. Better hot and sweaty than cold and dead.

Or so his old boss, Special Agent Helen Gray, had always said. For DeGarza that made it gospel.

"Director Leiter is on the line, Felipe," Special Agent Tim Brett said.

DeGarza handed the H&K MP5 submachine gun he'd been cradling to his second-in-command and took the secure cell phone Brett offered him. "This is DeGarza. The airfield is secure."

"Thank God," Leiter said. "Any trouble?"

The HRT section leader shook his head, watching a line of dazed prisoners streaming out of the hangar under the watchful eyes of his own troopers and the local SWAT team. "None, sir. We caught them with their pants down. Apparently they weren't slated to get their first plane off until well after sunrise. Their leader—some German guy—was still trying to get through to Chantilly when we blew the door open."

"And the bombs?" Leiter asked. "The bombs are still there?"

"Oh, yeah," DeGarza replied. He turned back toward the hangar. "Besides one Caraco corporate jet, I've got four twin-engine aircraft here—and all four of them are carrying devices that look a hell of a lot like the pictures of those TN-1000s you faxed us."

"Don't touch those weapons," Leiter ordered. "Leave that to the experts. There's an Army EOD team on its way to your location now. The commander's name is Lieutenant-Colonel Greg Lyle. He's their best man. You let him check them over first, clear?"

"Absolutely, sir," DeGarza said, unfazed by Leiter's apparent lack of trust in his common sense. Only an idiot would want to screw around with weapons packing a one-hundred-and-fifty-thousand-ton punch—especially when nobody knew whether or not these terrorists had booby-trapped them.

Which left him with one burning question. "Is there any word yet from the other dispersal fields, sir?"

"So far, so good," Leiter replied. "We've hit them all now. Took a couple of minor casualties in a firefight at Page and at Shafter-Minter, but nothing serious. A few of the bastards apparently got spooked early and ran when they couldn't make contact with Ibrahim—but we know where they're headed. They won't get far. And we've recovered nineteen bombs. According to Special Agent Gray and Colonel Thorn, that's all they had left."

All they had left, DeGarza thought in disbelief. He sure hoped Leiter knew just how lucky the Bureau had been— and how much it owed to Helen Gray.

JULY 5

Vienna, Virginia

Colonel Peter Thorn gingerly poked his head into Farrell's book-lined office. "Hope I'm not interrupting anything, Sam."

Farrell looked up from the yellow legal pad he'd been furiously scribbling on. He tossed the pad onto his desk and stood up to shake Thorn's hand. "Not at all, Pete! But I'm surprised Louisa didn't let me know you were here."

Thorn grinned sheepishly. "I don't think she saw me come in. I waited till I saw her go out into your garden and slipped in the back way."

Farrell wagged a finger at him. "No more cloak-and-dagger stuff in my house, Colonel. I'm retired for good this time."

"Yes, sir."

The general waved him toward a chair and sat down himself. "I don't see why you're acting so skittish around my wife, Pete," Farrell continued, smiling. "You know you're one of her favorites."

Thorn shook his head. "That's hard to believe—since we both know I dragged you into the middle of one hell of a mess—not to mention the ten thousand bucks of your money we spent. And Louisa's been around the Army long enough to know how long it'll take the green eyeshade boys to cough up any reimbursement—if ever!"

Farrell shrugged. "Who knows? I may just write that ten thousand off as research on a book I might write someday. And maybe I'll even bill the FBI for the time I spent answering their questions."

Thorn grinned. Sam, Helen, and he had been held in FBI "protective" custody for nearly two days while the Bureau, the Pentagon, and the CIA all ran them through extensive and exhausting debriefing sessions. At first, it was clear that the government would really have preferred to keep the whole screwed-up affair hushed up. But there was no way the administration could clamp a lid on a major firefight out in suburban Virginia and half a dozen heavy-duty HRT and SWAT raids around the country. Not to mention a nuclear explosion right over Chesapeake Bay.

Thorn frowned. He looked out the window at Farrell's big, green, peaceful backyard.

They'd been lucky. Very lucky. Because it was an airburst, the blast hadn't created a lot of fallout. Plus, the prevailing winds had pretty rapidly pushed what radiation there was well out into the Atlantic. Still, the police and National Guard units had been forced to temporarily evacuate several thousand people from the Virginia portion of the Delmarva peninsula—mostly as a precaution. Fortunately, the Defense and Energy Departments decontamination teams surveying the area were reporting only very minor levels of background radiation.

Anyway, what started out as a trickle of news leaks had rapidly turned into a flood.

The first stories had focused on the horrifying news that someone had somehow smuggled a large number of stolen Russian nuclear weapons into the U.S. itself. That had generated a whole week's worth of mile-high headlines and hour-long TV news specials. Now the other shoes were starting to drop—one right after another.

There were questions about Caraco's involvement in domestic American politics, questions about Ibrahim's close ties to the administration, and questions about the roles senior officials had played in trying to shut down investigations into Caraco's secret arms smuggling.

So far he had dodged the press, but he was just about out of excuses and running room. Especially now that Congress was getting its act in gear. Both the House and the Senate were talking loudly about forming special committees to investigate the administration's recent conduct. One of the people they were zeroing in on was Richard Garrett—Ibrahim's former chief lobbyist. There were also stories that the IRS was focusing its attention on the ex–Commerce Secretary—pursuing evidence that he'd avoided paying taxes on large unreported bonuses paid by the Saudi prince.

Perhaps even more intriguing, Thorn had heard of new developments from his contacts in the intelligence community—developments that were starting to shed some light on Ibrahim al Saud's motives for trying to destroy the United States as a world power. Investigators combing through his estate in Middleburg and through his private files in Caraco's various headquarters kept stumbling across intriguing proof that Ibrahim had been a major player in world terrorism—maybe even *the* major player. There were dozens of highly complex bank transactions that led to virtually every terrorist cell operating against the United States.

Farrell whistled when Thorn told him that. "Now there's a golden opportunity to do some good, Pete!"

Thorn nodded. "Our guys are going to have a field day ripping out the financial roots that armed and paid people like Reichardt."

"Reichardt?" Farrell asked.

"An ex-Stasi officer. Aka the late Heinrich Wolf," Thorn said with grim satisfaction.

Facing charges that included terrorism and conspiracy to commit mass murder, the dead Stasi officer's underlings had been only too happy to come clean in the hopes of receiving a life prison sentence instead of death by lethal injection.

He looked up to find Sam Farrell eyeing him closely.

"So, what are *your* plans these days?" the general asked.

Thorn detected the long arm of Louisa Farrell in that question. The general's wife had always taken too pronounced an interest in his private life. He decided to play dumb. "Oh, the debriefers are still keeping me pretty busy. I've run backward and forward over everything we learned so many times that I'm dreaming about it now."

Farrell snorted. "I mean, what are you and Helen up to? You see much of her these days?"

Thorn hesitated, then shrugged nonchalantly. "Not as much as I'd like. She's pretty hot stuff where the FBI is concerned. They're parading her in front of every news organization and congressional staffer they can find—touting her as the agent who almost single-handedly put an end to one of the greatest national security threats this country has ever faced."

Farrell nodded. "Smart move on the Director's part. I assume she's off the hook for McDowell's death, then?"

"Hell, she may even get a medal for it," Thorn said, smiling broadly. "The Bureau's higher-ups are practically kissing her feet. After all, she got rid of the highest-ranking traitor the FBI's ever found in its own ranks. McDowell alive and

going to trial for treason would have been acutely embar
rassing. McDowell dead is a story that will soon blow
over—especially with all the other stuff that's swirling
around out there right now."

"Uh-huh." Farrell folded his hands together over his
stomach and rocked back in his chair. "Pretty slick, Pete.
But it won't wash."

Damn. Thorn kept his face immobile. "What won't wash?"

"Trying to lure me off the subject." Farrell leaned forward. "Which is, what's going on between you and Helen
personally?"

Thorn hurriedly checked his watch. "Sorry, gotta run,
Sam. I'm late for another skull session over at Langley."

"Pete!" Farrell said in mock desperation. "You've got to
give me something. Helen's not talking to Louisa either.
And if I don't get some news out of you, I'm liable to be eating Burger King tonight instead of that fat juicy steak I've
been promised!"

Thorn relented slightly. Farrell did have a right to know
part of what was going on. "Okay, Sam. The truth is that
Helen and I have both scheduled some leave together in a
couple of weeks. We've got some serious things to discuss."

JULY 21

In the Rocky Mountains, Colorado

Peter Thorn turned and helped Helen up over an outcropping
of rock and onto a wide, open ledge. He waited until she'd

shrugged off her backpack before asking, "Well, what do you think?"

She turned to face the view and caught her breath. "My God, Peter. It's beautiful. Absolutely stunning."

Thorn nodded. They were several thousand feet up the side of a mountain—high on an isolated spur overlooking a green, forest-covered valley. "My dad and I used to climb up here when I was just a kid."

Oddly enough, mentioning his father didn't hurt as much as it once would have. His dad's death had hit him hard three years before—especially since his mother had abandoned them both when he was just a teenager. When his father had finally lost his battle against cancer, Thorn had been left all alone in the world—until he met Helen.

She smiled at him. "So this is a special place?"

"A very special place," Thorn confirmed.

He saw her take a deep breath.

Now. The time is now, Thorn told himself. All the doubts that had always lingered somewhere far in the back of his mind withered and vanished—replace by a rock-solid certainty. He slipped his hand into his pocket, brought out a small case, and dropped to one knee.

Helen looked down at him, her eyes open wide in surprise and wonder. "Peter? What on earth are you doing?"

"I'm proposing," he said simply, opening the case to show her the diamond ring inside. "Will you marry me, Helen?"

"But what about the Army . . ." she started to say.

Thorn shook his head. They'd gone over this ground a dozen times before. Helen had often worried that they would be torn apart by the demands of their respective careers. But now he had an answer for that. "I'm leaving the Army. I signed the papers last week. As of December 1, I plan to hang up my uniform for good."

"Oh, Peter," she whispered. "You love being a soldier."

Thorn nodded simply. "Yes, I do." Then he took her hand. "But I love you more, Helen. I love you with all my heart and soul. And I want to spend the rest of my life with you—wherever you go, and whatever you do."

He meant every word, he realized suddenly. He knew he would miss the Army—the camaraderie, the pride, the traditions, all the emotions bound up in the time-honored phrase "Duty, Honor, Country" that had been drummed into him first as a boy and then as a young man. But the turmoil and heartache of the last few weeks had forced him to confront a deeper and even more basic truth: Helen was more important to him than anything and anyone else in the world. And he was prepared to sacrifice everything to win her heart and to stand by her side.

Still kneeling beneath a cloudless blue sky, Thorn looked up into her bright, tear-filled eyes, waiting for the answer that would change his life forever.

AUGUST 20

World News Round-up

"Dateline—Riyadh, Saudi Arabia:

"Ibrahim al Saud, once a scion of this desert kingdom's vast ruling family, was put to death this afternoon. He was beheaded in a public square outside the Saudi Ministry of Justice—after a trial that reportedly lasted twenty-five minutes.

"The execution came as a surprise to many observers here

who had not even known that Ibrahim had been secretly returned to Saudi Arabia—apparently as part of high-level bargaining between the American and Saudi governments.

"Before his public execution, Ibrahim was stripped of all princely honors and titles, and his remaining assets were declared forfeit to the Saudi crown. However, financial experts doubt those assets will yield any significant sum. Caraco's stock price has plummeted ever since the corporation's involvement in illegal nuclear arms smuggling became public knowledge. And its share price fell another fifteen percent yesterday on rumors that several governments plan to strip Caraco of its right to do business within their borders.

"In other related developments, the Russian government today reiterated its demand that all nineteen of the TN-1000 tactical nuclear weapons currently in U.S. hands be returned immediately. At a press conference in Moscow, Kremlin spokesman Anatoly Perotkin claimed, 'These weapons are stolen state property. Therefore, we call on the American government to hand them back promptly and without any special conditions.'

"The U.S. State Department had no immediate comment . . ."

SEPTEMBER 4

Joint House and Senate Committee Hearing

The first full session of the special congressional committee investigating the administration's conduct during what had become known as "The June Bomb Plot" drew an overflow crowd. Staffers, journalists, and curious members of the general public occupied practically every square inch of the large committee room and much of the nearby hall space—all eagerly awaiting the testimony many believed would blow the lid off a massive case of private and political corruption. Several members of the administration, the White House Chief of Staff and the Attorney General among them, were already gone—driven out of office in disgrace following revelations of their witting and unwitting involvement in Ibrahim's machinations.

". . . I swear to tell the truth, the whole truth, and nothing but the truth, so help me God." Helen finished the oath, lowered her right hand, and sat down beside Peter Thorn—resplendent in the dress uniform he was still entitled to wear.

He smiled at her, squeezed her hand under the table, and then forced a suitably solemn expression as the committee chairman began asking his opening question.

"Now, Deputy Assistant Director Gray, I understand—"

Helen leaned forward abruptly. "Excuse me, Mr. Chairman, I feel compelled to correct the record." The television camera lights gleamed on a diamond ring and gold band on her left hand. "Actually, it's Deputy Assistant Director Thorn now."

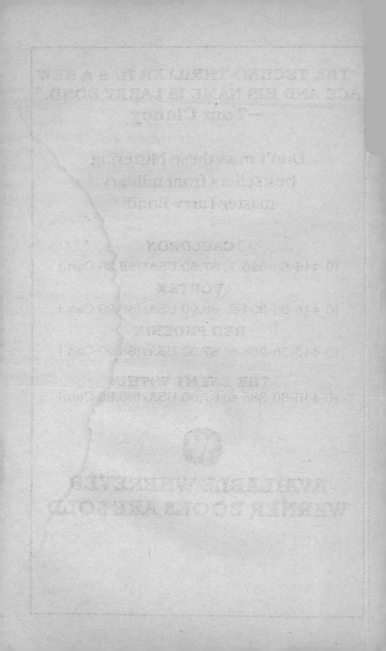